THE QUEEN'S BLADE

THE BROKEN BLADE
BOOK ONE

EVELYN WARD

Cover design by Igor Andrich

Editing by Marilyn Haynes at MH Editorial Services

www.mheditorialservices.com

CONTENT WARNING

Thank you for choosing to spend a few hours with us. Before you begin, be warned that this book contains strong adult content, including graphic sex scenes, violence, murder, and a veritable *fuck ton* of swearing. It also contains references to domestic abuse and drug use.

This series will include queer romance and on-page sex (MF, MM and FF), as well as polyamory (why choose). If you prefer your books without those elements, then you should stop now. Go on, I mean it. Put the book away.

This is a story of blood and sex and rage. If that interests you, then welcome. We're so happy you decided to join us here in the dark.

This book is dedicated to every woman who ever thought
'Wouldn't it be so nice
To burn it all to the ground?'

PROLOGUE

When the War of the Fallen tore through our realm three hundred years ago, it left a broken world in its wake. Demons, Vampires, Shifters, and Witches all turned on one another, each claiming supremacy over the others, and by the time the Witches had emerged bloody and victorious, the other Factions had been driven near to extinction.

When they crowned the First Witch Queen—her hands still wet with blood from the battlefields—the world was but a fraction of what it once had been. Our realm, splintered and broken, yearned to be united under a single ruler. The Witches may have won and put one of their own on the throne, but even they had suffered. Those Factions who had lost, those we now call the Fallen to reflect their fall from the Goddess's grace, were even worse off. Among the Vampires, only the strongest families had survived the slaughter, and the remaining Shifters had retreated into hiding out of fear. Entire species of their Faction were gone, lost to the violence—there would be no more Dragon Shifters, no more Hydra. *Surely,* those remaining thought when they retreated to the edges of the world, *this new Queen would hunt them all down one by one, would rid her new realm of all but the Witches, and punish the other Factions who had defied her.*

But the First Queen had no such plans. She had seen enough death for a thousand lifetimes and destroying the remaining Fallen would bring about nothing but more suffering to the Witches. She looked around at this newly fractured world and knew it displeased the Goddess. Though she is capable of fathomless destruction, the Goddess is also Mother to all things, equal parts destroyer, and creator. She would want peace, the First Queen reasoned. She would want the realm united once more.

And so, the Eternal City was born—a place for all beings of the realm to live and work in peace, under the common rule of the Witch Queen.

The jewel of the Eternal City was the palace itself, set at the highest point of the city. Visible from miles around, it stood as a beacon of hope for Witches everywhere, and a warning to the Factions who had Fallen. At the base of her palace, the First Queen built four temples—one for each of the four natural elements—to honor the gifts the Goddess had given to her and her daughters. Priestesses were appointed to lead them, and thus the four covens were born: Earth, Air, Fire, and Water.

There would be no temple for the fifth element, of course. No Priestesses, no coven. The Goddess had blessed the First Queen with all four pure elements in equal measures, but the power over the fifth element, the power of Blood, was a wicked thing, and it would find no worship in the Eternal City.

At the palace's back, the Queen built a different sort of temple, dedicated not to the Goddess, but to war. She erected two massive arenas to house her army: Solare and Lunairea. They towered above the palace proper, lest anyone forget the power the Witches held, the power that had allowed their armies to break the other three Factions and emerge victorious.

And beneath the palace and the temples, beyond the twin rivers that flanked the jewel of the Eternal City where she dwelt, the First Queen sectioned off portions of the city for all her subjects, regardless of Faction, and invited the Fallen to return.

And over time, they did.

The Demons came first, opportunists that they are. They had no problem kneeling before the new regime. After all, no Demon truly cares what side they're on, so long as it is the winning side.

The Shifters came next, though their return took longer, and their story was much sadder. They came in waves, from all corners of the realm. First to arrive were the prey Shifters, their leaders coming to pay homage to the new Queen. They were used to being subjugated by stronger forces, having learned their place in the world at the oftentimes cruel hands of their carnivore brethren. Then, bit by bit, over the course of the following years, the predators made their return. The Wolves, the Bears, the birds of prey, even the Cat Shifters—though pride made their return last, of course. One by one, their leaders bent the knee to the First Queen, and she welcomed them to their new homes.

Finally, only the Vampires remained. In the wake of the War of the Fallen, the patriarch of the strongest remaining Vampire family had crowned himself a King and declared that no Vampire would ever kneel before a Witch and claim fealty.

Still, even he eventually returned to the city with what few of his kind remained, though many years later. And though he did not kneel, it is said that he did bow and offer his counsel, which the First Queen accepted. She allowed him into the city, as her subject, and did not demand he relinquish his fool's crown.

And thus, the Eternal City was built—with a place for all Factions. It took time for peace to settle fully, of course. But over time, the denizens of the city learned to live with one another, and while the Factions themselves did not entirely trust each other, at least they managed not to kill each other. Not frequently, anyway, and when such things did inevitably arise, the Queen's justice was swift and merciless. When squabbles broke out among the Factions, the Queen dispatched her Blades to eliminate the guilty. They were four specters of death, terrifying as any storybook monster, and no one survived a visit from the Queen's Blades.

Over time, the wounds in the realm turned to scars, and even the scars faded. The Shifter population swelled once more, and though there would never again be Dragons, so many of their kind remained thanks in part to the compassion of the First Queen herself. The Queen's youngest daughter eventually inherited her throne, and her daughter not long thereafter. The lineage of the First Queen continued, and though their magic seemed to lessen, with time, they continued to carry each of the four pure elements—a sign from the Goddess herself that the line was destined to rule. For nearly three hundred years, the Eternal City thrived, and the realm knew peace.

But this isn't a story about peace, or how the realm was united after the War of the Fallen. This isn't a story about the past.

This is the story of how the Eternal City fell.

PART ONE

CHAPTER I

The Solare training camps smelled of heat, sweat, and violence. To Fey, it smelled like home. She leaned her head further out the open window, savoring the scent of it. The sharp tang of body odor, the metallic bite of blood, scents as familiar to her as her own body. The gossamer fabric of her mask was thin enough that it did little to filter the smell of violence, and the scents from the soldiers training below were oddly comforting.

This had been her first home, after all. Her first *real* home. Much of the tall circular building that surrounded the Solare training yard was abandoned now, the dormitory-style rooms empty and gathering dust and spiders. This entire wing was abandoned, but Fey's old room was still here, tucked away just a few stories above where she and her sisters now waited.

A shame to let such a great building be so empty, Fey thought. A shame a realm in peace had so little use for an army.

"They're going to see you," Lilith warned. She sat away from the window, hidden from those training below, dressed in the same uniform as Fey. The uniforms of the Queen's Blades had changed very little in the last three hundred years—designed with thickened leather patches across the chest and legs, and thin pliable suede at the joints to allow for

7

quick, easy movement. A matching mask covered the bottom of Lilith's face, and a dark cowl kept her raven black hair hidden so that only her sharp dark eyes were visible. A whetstone sat balanced on her thigh and as she spoke, she sharpened her blade against it.

It was a habit of Lilith's, sharpening her knives whenever they were idle for too long. Not a *nervous* habit, not really. Fey doubted Lilith had the capacity to be nervous. Angry, yes. Horny, frequently. But nervous? *Never.*

Fey snorted in response, making no effort to conceal herself as she gazed down at the chaos below. The sounds of the soldiers fighting hummed like music in her ears. Her muscles craved to join them, to fight.

"Then let them see me," she answered.

The scrape of Lilith's blade against the whetstone stopped, and Lilith sighed, annoyed.

"Joy, can you convince our sister to step away from the window?"

Leaning against the dirt and grime-coated wall, her eyes closed, Joy seemed lost in thought. Dust moats swirled, circling her, catching the light and dancing intricately close to her skin as they moved through the air around her. Even without thought or intention, Joy's power came out like this, the very air around her in constant motion and bending to her will. Fey had never known an Air primary as strong as Joy—it was as though the world itself swayed to the rhythm of her breath.

"You should know by now that I can't convince our sister to do anything, and neither can you," Joy answered, not bothering to open her eyes.

To an outsider, it would be impossible to tell the three of them apart. Joy's blonde wavy hair was hidden under her cowl, her face covered. Only the shade of their skin and the color of their eyes set the three of them apart. Joy's bright blue and full of laughter. Lilith's dark and brooding. And Fey's emerald green and flecked with brown.

With their names and even their abilities hidden from most in the realm, the Queen's Blades were faceless killers. The masks served not only to protect their identities but also made them more specter than Witch. They were a nightmare brought to life, something whispered to children to make them behave.

Go to sleep, or the Queen's Blades will find you.
Be good, or the Queen's Blades will get you.
Follow the edicts of the Goddess, or the Queen's Blades will hunt you.
Will hurt you.
Will kill you.

In their masks and their black leather uniforms, their arms covered in identical sigils, they were a match set. Three perfect assassins, virtually indistinguishable from one another.

Three, when there should have been four.

Fey took another deep breath, filling her lungs with the smell of the training yard. Joy opened a single eye to watch her.

"You miss it here, don't you?" she asked. No judgment, no scorn, just simple observation and curiosity.

"Sometimes," Fey answered truthfully. There were no lies between them, not now, not ever. "When I was here, I felt…" She struggled to put the feelings into words. "I felt like I was finally home. Accepted."

Joy's mask twitched slightly, and Fey knew she was smiling. Joy had a kind smile, one she gave to the world often and without artifice.

"Didn't you like it here?" Fey asked.

"No," Joy answered, without hesitation. "I didn't, not like you. It was…" Joy made a face, wrinkling her nose. "It was *empty*. Barren. There's no kindness here, no pleasure. Just…" She shrugged. "Just violence and pain."

Lilith snorted. "Sister, you kill for a living. All you know is violence and pain."

"It's different," Joy insisted. "What we do serves a purpose. It's necessary for the realm. But here? The infighting, the scrabbling for top marks. It was all so… empty. Pointless."

Fey could understand that, at least. The training grounds were full of raw power and emotion. Anger, pain, frustration. It was a brutal place. For Joy, who found pleasure and happiness in everything around her, who reached for the good in the world like a plant reaching for the sun, it would have been a dark place indeed.

By the time Fey had enlisted in the army, Joy was already a Blade, and their paths had never crossed during her time at Solare. None of their paths had crossed before they had become Blades. Before they became sisters.

"What about you? What did you think of your time here?" Fey asked Lilith.

Lilith paused to assess her knife's edge, twisting the blade in her hand to catch the light. Then, satisfied, she slipped it back into the sheath on her thigh and pulled its twin from the identical sheath on her other leg to begin the process all over again.

"What does it matter? Liked it, hated it, it's in the past." The blade purred against the whetstone while she worked. "I am a Queen's Blade. Who I was before? That person is dead and gone. This is what I am now, and that's all that matters."

Joy rolled her eyes in Lilith's direction and pushed herself from the wall. Her shoulder bumped against Fey's as she joined her at the window.

"Can you see him down there?" she asked eagerly.

Fey sighed. "Not yet."

There were whispers among the Queen's Guard that Dameon would be inspecting the soldiers in Solare today. While it was part of his duties as the Queen's right hand and something he deigned to do every few months, this visit would be different. On this visit, he would be looking for a new Witch to join their ranks.

A new sister to be inducted into the Queen's Blades.

Joy's eyes danced across the training yard, bouncing between groups, and stopped. "There." She pointed, extending her hand out the window.

The training yard was divided into groups. Soldiers of different skills and different elements, clustered together under the watchful eyes of the Queen's generals. Though the vast majority of those below were Witches, there were groups of men scattered among them. They may lack power over any of the elements, but force was force, and the Queen rarely turned away a willing soldier, regardless of sex.

But Joy was pointing to a small group, a handful of Witches training in hand-to-hand combat. They were paired together, slowly practicing their motions, as a familiar figure moved among them, assessing.

Even at this distance, his features barely visible, Fey recognized

Dameon, their handler. He had once been one of the Queen's most highly ranked generals, though he spent little time here in the training yard with the soldiers these days. No, his job was more specialized. For the last ten years, Dameon had been the face of the Queen's Guard, her right-hand general—and their trainer. When he spoke, he spoke with the voice of the Crown itself, and he was the one who pointed the Queen's Blades in the direction her justice was required.

He was the one who sent them to kill.

Fey liked Dameon as much as she liked any man. She respected him, at least, despite the rumors of how he had advanced so quickly through the ranks. Since his promotion to the Queen's personal guard years ago, it had been whispered behind his back that he bore an uncanny resemblance to the young Princess Amalia, the Queen's heir, and good money said he was the girl's father. There were a great number among the aristocrats who believed Queen Edelin had him promoted to the role to keep him close to her bedchamber. But he was a good general, a good soldier, and a great trainer. He kept the four of them in impeccable shape, kept them bloodthirsty and ready.

No, Fey corrected herself, swallowing the pain the thought conjured. *Not four, not anymore.*

If Dameon were here, that meant they wouldn't be three for long. They would be complete once again.

Fey watched the group of Witches he instructed closely. One of them could be their next sister.

Moving from some unheard command, the Witches stopped their training, separating from their pairs to form a circle. Fey watched as Dameon motioned for two of the Witches to enter the ring. Immediately, they both took up fighting stances, circling one another, looking for an opening.

"Can you see any of them? How do they look?" Lilith asked, glancing up from her sharpening.

They were too far away to make out much of the fight, but Fey knew the moves like it was a dance she'd performed a hundred times. The fight was quick and messy. Unimpressive, to say the least. Fey only snorted, and behind her, Lilith laughed darkly.

The winner declared, two more moved forward to begin their fight.

Fey and Joy watched them together, leaning against the windowsill, not needing to speak.

It was the fourth fight that finally caught their interest. It was fast, even faster than the first, and when a dark-skinned Witch with auburn hair was pinned to the ground it should have signified the end of the match. But she refused to yield. She fought and bucked against her partner, who looked briefly at Dameon for help. That was all the opening the Witch needed to strike. She freed a hand, gathering a fistful of sandy earth and throwing it in her opponent's face. The victor reared back, hands going to her eyes, and the auburn-haired Witch grabbed her by the neck and slammed their heads together.

Fey barked a surprised laugh, and next to her, Joy squealed in delight. The victor went down hard, and even from up here, three floors above the training grounds, they could hear her scream with indignation and pain.

Dameon was shouting, but the Witch refused to stop. She tackled the victor, fighting like a crazed animal as the girl shouted for help.

Lilith appeared next to them in the window to watch, her dark eyes sparkling.

"That's the one," she said, as below them Dameon fought to restrain the auburn-haired Witch. Fought and nearly failed.

"Oh yes," agreed Fey. "She's the one, alright."

"So," Joy clapped her hands together excitedly. "Who wants to go meet our new sister?"

FEY WENT, of course.

Somehow, these problems always landed on her shoulders.

She waited outside the grand arched entrance to Solare, leaning her back against the cool stone building. The afternoon sun hung heavy in the sky above her, and the small lip of shade she sheltered in was quickly fading.

A bell tolled from the palace, announcing the midday hour, and the sounds of fighting and training within the arena faded as soldiers dispersed for lunch, flowing from Solare, and out into the afternoon sun.

Fey was quickly spotted, and soon a crowd gathered around her, with soldiers openly staring as they left the training yards. Though only her eyes were visible through the mask, her blood-red hair pulled back and covered by her cowl, there was no mistaking what she was. No mistaking the sigils that covered her arms and the dark tattoo of the Queen's Blade that marked the inside of her left forearm.

She was the best of them, the highest rank of soldier under the Crown.

She was a monster.

Fey suspected for many of them, this was their first time seeing one of the Queen's Blades in the flesh. Was it any wonder they stopped and stared? If they were lucky, this would be the only time they ever saw her. If they were unlucky, she would be the last thing they ever saw.

Most of the Witches bowed their heads reverently as they passed, but a few—mostly the men—paused long enough to bow more formally, bending long and low at the waist. She ignored them, not bothering to spare any of them a passing glance. She simply waited, silent and cold as the stone against her back.

Her sisters had gone back to the palace—Lilith to prepare for her assignation, and Joy to get in a bout of training. That just left her alone, waiting for Dameon.

Fey forced down the frustration rising in her chest. There was an emptiness inside her, a piece that was missing. And Dameon—Dameon was dragging his feet. He was failing in his duty, failing to keep them whole.

It had always been this way, ever since the beginning. The Queen's Blades were a group of four Witches—powerful, cunning, and deadly. There had always been four, and for three hundred years when a Blade fell, another was picked to take her place.

But now?

It had been just over a month since Alice's death—since the four of them were reduced to three.

Alice had been the oldest but was still only thirty-five when she was murdered. The Queen's Blades don't live long happy lives. They don't get a happily ever after and don't get their names recorded in the history books. They don't even get proper funerals.

No one had known that better than Alice. She had seen other sisters rise and fall, seen too much blood and death in her brief life.

Hell, Fey thought, they all had.

Alice had been careful, always so careful. Guarded, but never with her sisters. She was their pillar of strength, their leader, and their friend.

And now she was gone. Her absence was a constant physical pain in Fey's chest.

Dameon spotted her immediately the moment he left the training yard. He was handsome, middle-aged but still well within his prime, with brown hair that had only the barest hint of silver peppering his temples. Handsome even with the scar that split his face, running down his face in a diagonal slash—the remnants of a fight with a Bear Shifter from his time as a foot soldier, Fey had heard.

"What's her name?" Fey asked immediately, ignoring the surrounding crowd and pushing away from the wall to approach him.

Dameon sighed. "Good to see you too, Fey," he said, his voice quiet enough that none of the spectators could overhear.

It didn't matter that she was in full uniform, didn't matter that she looked nearly identical to her sisters. Dameon knew each of them, knew their stance, knew their postures.

"Her name, Dameon."

"Why yes, Fey, it is a lovely day out, so nice of you to notice. How am I, you ask? Fucking terrific, thanks for asking. Just in the middle of doing my Goddess-damned job." He paused, watching her, and the scar across his face twitched as he clenched his teeth together tightly. "You're not supposed to be here, Fey. You and your sisters aren't involved in this."

"You're picking my next sister. How can we not be involved?"

"Because that's not how this works, and you know it." His voice held a sharp bite. "I pick the candidates for the Queen's Blades. I hand deliver them to the three of you for their trials when I'm ready. That's my job, not yours."

Fey snorted a laugh. "Don't pull rank with me, Dameon. You won't like how it ends."

It wasn't an idle threat, and he knew it. While Dameon was their handler and their trainer, he was no Blade. He wasn't even a Witch. And no one, save for the Queen herself, outranked the Blades. A spark of anger flashed in Dameon's eyes, but he smothered it quickly enough Fey could almost convince herself she'd imagined it. He sighed, running a hand through his hair.

"You still shouldn't be here. Do you know what sort of rumors it sparks when a Blade is seen in the open like this? Do you know how frightened some of those soldiers are?"

Fey chuckled. She glanced at the few groups still standing around the Solare entrance, gaping at her. "Frightened? They seemed more awestruck than frightened."

"You and your sisters are to keep to the palace when you're not on assignation. You know this. Fuck the Goddess, Fey, what were you thinking?"

"It's not my job to care about frightening your soldiers," Fey snapped back. "The Crown doesn't employ me to consider people's *feelings*."

Dameon laughed. "You're starting to sound like Lilith, you know that?"

"What's her name?" Fey repeated.

For a moment, she wondered if he'd play dumb. If he'd pretend not to know who she meant. But Dameon, bossy and pigheaded though he may be, wasn't stupid.

"Willow. Her name is Willow," he answered with a resigned grunt. "Come on, walk with me. You need to get back to the palace. You're expected at the Queen's side tonight."

They walked together across the palace yard. The remaining soldiers parted around them, giving them ample space.

"What's her element?"

"Fire and Earth," Dameon answered. "I've had my eye on her for a while now, for that alone. There's less than a handful of soldiers who command two elements left." He scratched at the stubble on his jaw. "She reminds me of you, you know."

Beneath the mask, Fey's lips curled in a smile. Fire and Earth would give her the exact opposite elemental powers as Fey. "Why?" she asked.

"Stubborn. Fierce. Never taps out, even when she should. You saw it, I assume? Her sparring partner had her dead to rights in the first few seconds, but she just wouldn't give up."

"I saw," Fey answered.

"And your sisters?"

Her smile grew. "They saw too."

"It's not always a good thing, Fey. She doesn't know when to quit, doesn't know when she's lost."

"She didn't lose," Fey said, and Dameon cocked his head toward her, frowning. "She didn't lose," Fey repeated.

"Her opponent had her on the ground in under a minute. That's a loss."

"In Solare, maybe. But for a Blade?" Fey shook her head. "You don't lose until you're dead, Dameon. There's no fighting dirty, there are no rules to break, no decorum. She wouldn't give up, even when she was beaten. That's not a loss to me, that's a win. That's what we need. That's what the realm needs."

When Dameon said nothing, she continued. "You should bring her to us for her trials. She's the one, Dameon. No one else we saw today even came close."

When he didn't answer, her patience snapped. She stopped, forcing him to stop alongside her. "It's been a month, Dameon. We're tired of waiting for you to make your move. A *month*. We're not..." She searched for the words, searched for a way to convey the emptiness left inside them. "We're not *whole* with only three."

Dameon clenched his jaw but nodded.

"Fine. Consider it done," he conceded. "I'll bring her to you within the week for her trial. But if she fails, Fey..."

"She won't," Fey answered.

She couldn't.

"Go on—" Dameon nodded toward the path leading toward the palace entrance. The white marble doors stood open, flanked by a pair of the Queen's guards. "You're needed at the party tonight."

"You're not coming?"

Dameon smirked. "Blessed be the Goddess, no. I have other business to attend to tonight." He motioned toward Lunairea, the massive crescent-shaped building on the palace's other side that housed the generals' quarters. "I have a meeting with the generals."

He motioned her toward the palace and turned to leave, but Fey stood rooted to the ground, studying him. She chewed the inside of her cheek, a question pounding against her chest.

"Do you ever miss her?" she asked, finally, and before the words had fully left her mouth, she saw Dameon stiffen, his shoulders tense. Alice's name hung between them, unspoken.

He kept his back to her. His voice was dark when he answered. "Miss who, Your Grace?"

His answer was a warning.

We don't speak of the dead.

Fey took the hint. She left him without another word and went to find her remaining sisters.

CHAPTER 2

As a Queen's Blade, Fey had performed countless unsavory tasks. She had known her share of violence and gore while working for the Crown and had dismembered and beheaded more enemies of the throne than she cared to count. She'd buried bodies, burned bodies, and even dissolved a body in lye (though only once, and she swore to never do it again. It had taken days, and it was immensely easier to dispose of a corpse than a body's worth of *goo*).

During her work for the Crown, she had bled, cried, and vomited. Some nights she'd even done all three.

But nights like tonight were perhaps her least favorite of all the unsavory tasks required of her.

"*Happy birthday*, Princess," the man kneeling on the dais crooned in an unctuous voice. He set a delicately wrapped present on the already massive pile beside Princess Amalia's throne, beaming a saccharine smile up at the realm's heir and her mother.

Fey fought the urge to squirm. She hated this, hated the groveling and the posturing. Hated standing in one spot, unable to move, for hours on end.

If either the Queen or Princess felt the same, seated in their matching thrones on the dais, they certainly didn't show it.

Princess Amalia smiled at the man as he fussed with placing his present. A dull, rather brainless smile, but a smile, nonetheless. Fey only vaguely recognized him. He was someone important enough to warrant an invitation to the Princess's birthday celebration, clearly. He was a duke, maybe? Or the brother of a duke? But Fey lacked Lilith's seemingly endless fount of knowledge about the comings and goings of the royal court and couldn't place him. Joy would know, of course, but Joy stood at the Queen's other shoulder, still and quiet as a statue, and the two of them were not to move, not to speak, during the celebration.

The Queen gave the duke—or possibly a duke's brother—a nod of appreciation. At her side, the little Princess mirrored the gesture, saying in her soft lilting voice, "Thank you, Lord Cameron. Your generosity is much appreciated. You have my leave to enjoy the party."

A Lord? Oh, I was way off, Fey thought with a sigh.

After their trip to the training yards this morning, she'd barely made it back in time for Princess Amalia's party. It was a meaningless show of strength to require the Blades to attend, and Fey wished she'd had an assignation like Lilith just as an excuse to miss this. But, alas, she hadn't had an assignation from Dameon all week, so she was stuck here tonight, standing with Joy behind the Queen's throne. Twin specters, silent and deadly.

Silent, deadly, and very bored specters.

The party itself filled the expansive throne room, spilling out into the hallways beyond. Tables lined the white marble walls, full of food, sweets, and games. Princess Amalia's peers were gathered in all corners, voices shrill with excitement as they enjoyed the festivities and food. Their guardians, after paying due homage to their Queen and presenting their gifts to the Princess, watched on with wry amusement, gossiping among themselves and picking at the expansive spread of food around them.

It seemed cruel that the Princess was stuck here on the dais, receiving their well wishes and their gifts but unable to join in her own party. Fey couldn't recall the last time she'd seen the Princess play with someone her age. Wasn't sure she ever had.

Another Lord approached the dais, and Fey was pleased to find she recognized this one. Lord Cyanean—or Lord Cinnamon, as Joy teasingly called the ruddy-faced, red-haired man. Joy's eyes flicked sideways to hers for the briefest moment, and Fey knew they were sharing the same memory. Beneath her mask, she grinned.

It would be another few hours of this before they would be dismissed. Joy, at least, never seemed to mind guard duty—playing the role of an object, propped up behind the Queen like a piece of art—but Fey found it mindlessly dull. And Lilith, somehow, always managed to find ways out of it.

Traitor, Fey thought.

The line of well-wishers and present bearers continued their procession to the throne, showing no signs of slowing. It had already been hours, and guests were still arriving and joining the line. Boredom gnawed on Fey's attention, and she found herself watching the Queen and her heir if only for something to occupy herself.

Princess Amalia did look a little like Dameon, Fey thought, chewing her lip. In a certain light, her brown hair was a near enough match to his, and her skin had a more golden cast than her mother's. But if she was anything like her mother, that brown hair wouldn't last much longer. Queen Edelin's hair had begun to fade and lighten in her late teens, and by her mid-twenties, her hair was a perfect snow white. Now, in her early forties, it struck a contrast with her lightly lined skin, giving her the ethereal appearance of a woman both aged, and unageing, young and old all at once. The hair was a throwback to some of the oldest and strongest Queens, Lilith had told her once. Proof that she could trace her ancestry back as a direct line to the First Witch Queen.

Queen Edelin was beautiful and intimidating, and the combination of her regal air, white hair, and dark eyes reminded Fey of an ermine in its winter coat. Princess Amalia could be an ermine, too, one day. But she was young, and she still had the brown cast of an ermine in the summer. She was a soft, fragile thing, completely lacking the hard steel of her mother. It was hard to imagine she would be Queen one day, gentle as she was.

The procession continued, and momentarily lost in her thoughts, Fey didn't notice the danger in the room until he reached the dais and spoke.

"Thirteen years old," said a cold, dignified voice. Fey tensed, instincts flaring to life. Next to her, standing at the Queen's other side, she felt Joy do the same. "What a magical year, Princess. I wish you the joy of it."

Salvatore deSanguine spoke with a lilting accent from a time long before Witches ruled the realm. Three hundred years ago, after the War of the Fallen had left him the strongest remaining patriarch of the great Vampire families, he had declared himself a king, or so the stories said. As far as Fey knew, he still called himself that, and only a man as stubborn and arrogant as the Vampire King would be foolish enough to attend a royal event while wearing a crown.

It was a simple thing—a thin band of iron resting on his silver-gray hair—but the meaning was clear. Salvatore deSanguine still considered himself the Fallen King, even now, so many generations later.

And he saw fit to rub it in the royal family's face at every opportunity.

Salvatore didn't kneel before the Queen, but he did hand Princess Amalia a box wrapped in gold paper, ignoring the pile of presents at her side. Amalia reached her hand out to take it without thinking, blind to any danger.

The air in the throne room stilled and went quiet as Fey drew her blade. It made a sharp metallic noise as she unsheathed it, and the sound cut through the din of the party, silencing the merriment. Joy hadn't drawn her blades, not yet, but she took a step forward toward the Vampire King, her hands resting on the hilts.

Salvatore glanced up at them, surprised, and seeing Fey's blade in her hand, he *smiled*. If the Queen were an ermine, Salvatore was a shark. His hair was silver to her white, and while he was unmistakably handsome in the hard-lined way of most Vampires, everything about him screamed danger.

The Queen's gaze drifted from the box in his hand, which he still held out for the Princess, to Fey's blade, before she casually shook her head. The blade disappeared back into its sheath without a sound, and Fey stepped back to position, returning to her statue-like state.

"Go ahead," the Queen ordered her daughter, nodding to the present Salvatore offered.

With hands shaking only slightly, the Princess took the box from him.

"It's a necklace," Salvatore said. But he wasn't addressing the Princess or even the Queen. He spoke to Fey, and she nearly raised her hand to make sure her mask was still fastened. He *looked* at her, as though he could see straight through the mask to her face. "You may open it if you wish to check?"

"That won't be necessary," the Queen said, dismissing him with a wave of her hand. But Salvatore didn't leave. His cold silvery eyes looked slowly from Fey, taking her in as though memorizing every part of her, then to Joy, and then finally to the Queen.

"Aren't there normally four of them?" he asked, his voice casual. And hungry. He smiled as he spoke, wide enough to show his set of fangs, sharp and lethal. He was a predator circling, looking for any weakness, any avenue of attack.

"Of course," the Queen said. Nothing in her voice or demeanor gave anything away. "They are on assignment this evening. Keeping the peace of the realm."

"Naturally," Salvatore replied. His smile widened, and Fey's fingers itched to draw her blade again. "Enjoy your special day, Princess," he said, inclining his head to Amalia. And then he was gone, joining the rest of the party as though he were just another guest. The line moved forward, and the Queen's twin sister Cassandra replaced him. Fey breathed out slowly, forcing her shoulders to relax, watching the Vampire until he disappeared in the crowd, heading toward the exit.

"Niece," Cassandra crooned, placing her gift on the pile. Though twins, Queen Edelin and her sister Cassandra were near opposites, in both appearance and power. If Edelin was made of snow and ice, Cassandra was made of coal. Her hair was raven black, and she stood nearly four inches taller than her sister.

The real difference, though, and the reason Edelin sat on the throne while Cassandra knelt, lay in their gifts. Edelin could command all four pure elements—holding mastery over Earth, Air, Fire, and Water. Cassandra held power over only two, and even in them, her gifts were weak. The royal line followed strength, and only those blessed with all four elements held the right to rule. If not for that one thing, that one difference between them, Cassandra would have been Queen.

When it became clear which twin would inherit the throne, Cassandra renounced her claim—choosing instead the life of a White Priestess, a life of helping young witches through their Awakening, the ritual that revealed their elemental gifts.

If Amalia hadn't shown the same powers as her mother, the same gift of all four elements, she wouldn't be seated here to receive presents either, Fey knew. It had been a relief three years ago when the Princess had gone through her Awakening. And though it was rumored that her strength for Earth was barely more than a pulse of power, it had been enough.

The Queen thanked and dismissed her sister in the same bored way she had spoken to all the others, and the next Lord or Lady or Duke or Goddess-knew-what approached to kneel.

The evening continued in this way until it bled into night. Fey stood still and silent, counting the seconds into minutes into hours. Eventually, the seemingly endless line of those paying homage to the Princess died down, and not long after, the party faded. Just as the guests grew tired and the children became decidedly bored with the games around them, the Queen stood.

"We thank you for your kind words and your gifts," she stated. She neither shouted nor whispered, simply speaking with the confidence of someone who knew every single person in the room would stop to listen. And, of course, they did, taking in each word she spoke as though it were scripture. "But the hour has grown late, and we wish to retire."

And with that, they were dismissed. Guests filed out the door, some bowing a final time to either the Queen or the Princess. Fey and Joy stayed until the last guest had left, and the servants slipped into the throne room to start their cleaning. Two of the Princess's attendants began to remove her presents, one by one, carting them away.

Finally, it was over.

THE ROYAL PALACE is not a small building, by any means. Still, guests and visitors were only ever given access to the center of the building, where the throne room and various ballrooms and entertaining chambers were housed. Most knew little of what lay beyond those rooms, and few had reason to suspect they saw only a quarter of the actual building. Fewer, still, were allowed access to the Western Wing, where the Queen kept her private entertaining parlors and rooms for special guests and friends. Dameon had a room reserved here, Fey knew, though he used it rarely, if ever. He preferred the bedchambers next to the Queen's suite, in the Northern Wing. He was, after all, head of her guard and spent much of his time in the company of her and the Princess.

The smallest and most secretive wing was the Eastern Wing, the entrance hidden in such a way that it would be nearly impossible for a visitor to stumble upon it by accident. Even if they tried, the hallways that led there were always teeming with members of the Queen's Guard, carefully monitoring the comings and goings of the palace.

No one entered the Eastern Wing accidentally. And no one, save for the Queen and Dameon, entered the four bedchambers tucked away there.

The Eastern Wing was home to the Queen's Blades, and it was a secret very few in the realm knew about. Built beneath ground level, there was no reason to suspect it existed at all.

The four bedchambers shared a common living space and a small kitchenette, but each room had an *ensuite* complete with a shower and bath. There was a training gym filled with equipment and healing elixirs, and various rooms, large and small, to do with as they wished. Fey had yet to claim one as her own, preferring to split her time between her bedchamber and the training gym.

It was late evening by the time Joy and Fey made their way from the main palace floors to the Eastern Wing and back to their rooms, and Fey was ready for a long shower and bed.

Joy didn't waste a single moment, unclasping her mask and cowl the moment the door shut behind them, shaking her blonde hair out and letting it fall over her shoulders.

"Hello, my darling, did you miss me?" She beamed at the small lump of fur curled in the armchair. Merle made no effort to move, but his ears piqued at the sound of Joy's voice, and a soft purr gradually filled the room, the only sign he had heard.

No one was sure where the cat had come from, or how he had managed to make his way into the Eastern Wing. But Alice had given him a piece of chicken when she'd found him hiding in their kitchen, cowering in a corner, and since then he'd refused to leave. Why would he, after all, when Joy kept him fat and pampered and loved?

"Took you two long enough," Lilith remarked. She leaned against the kitchen island, a bowl of instant noodles in one hand, her long dark hair wrapped in a towel and piled on her head. "How was the party?"

Fey snorted. Whatever assignation had kept Lilith from joining them hadn't taken her long if she had already finished and managed to shower and change into her loungewear.

"The Vampire King made an appearance," Joy answered. She crouched next to Merle's armchair, scratching him beneath his furry black chin. Merle stretched lazily and rolled onto his back to better appreciate her attention.

"You're kidding." Lilith's smirk widened.

"She's not." Fey unclasped her mask and began the process of removing her weapons when Lilith interrupted her.

"Uh, uh, uh, not so fast there," Lilith nodded her head toward an envelope on the counter next to her. "Dameon dropped that off for you earlier."

Fey swore when she saw the black envelope sitting there. A black envelope meant an assignation, and while Fey had been itching for one all week, tonight she was tired, and all she wanted to do was go to bed.

"He couldn't have dropped it off *before* the party?"

Lilith smirked. "Guess not. Sorry, sweetie, but your night isn't over yet."

"I can take it tonight if you want, sister," Joy offered, but Fey shook her head.

"It's my name on the outside, it's my assignation."

She plucked the envelope from the table. The paper was thick and heavy, sealed with the Queen's sigil in golden wax. Fey slid her long nail under the wax seal, breaking it open, and pulled the sheet of paper inside of it out to read.

It was a single name and an address, written in black, and Fey bit back a snarl of frustration. Black meant observe, don't kill, and don't engage. A fact-finding mission—usually Joy's specialty. If the name had been written in red, well... that was a different matter altogether. Names written in red were nothing but walking corpses—people who had already signed their death warrant, but just didn't know it yet.

Fey would have preferred a quick assassination to this, but when she read the name, she paused, blinking in surprise.

"Oh Lord Cinnamon," Fey said, shaking her head with a smirk. "What have you gotten yourself into?"

CHAPTER 3

The address on her assignation was one Fey recognized, though she made a point of avoiding it. The Eternal Crown bar was a favorite among the Queen's generals and the lower nobility, thanks to its proximity to the palace itself. The interior had even been designed to mimic the aesthetics of the throne room—white marble, gold trim, and dark red accents. But the gold trim was painted on and noticeably flaking off from wear, and the red privacy curtains were thin, threadbare material and nothing like the thick, luxurious velvet found throughout the palace.

Most of the patrons of The Eternal Crown bar were unlikely to have ever set foot inside the throne room, and thus unlikely to notice what a mockery this place was.

Everything about the bar rubbed Fey the wrong way. The drinks were overpriced and underpoured, and the pretentious decorations were a far cry from the palace interior they sought to copy. It was a poor man's facsimile of luxury.

Fey didn't wear her Blade's uniform, not for this assignment. This was a simple fact-finding mission, with Fey serving as little more than an unbiased eavesdropper. She would be better served blending in. So, she made do with a pair of light linen pants and a long-sleeved shirt that clung to her curves and muscles. The sleeves covered her sigils and Blade's mark, but even still she engaged the spell that kept them hidden, that fooled an observer into seeing only pale, unmarred skin. Fey wore her red hair down and reluctantly let Joy apply just the faintest hint of makeup to her face.

To the patrons of The Eternal Crown, she looked like an unassuming recruit, eager to soak up the atmosphere in a popular bar sure to be crawling with potential suitors. She looked like she belonged.

Lord Alexander Cyanean was already there when she arrived, nestled in a corner table near the bar with a group of lesser nobility. She recognized a few of them from the Princess's party, but most were of such low consequence they wouldn't have merited an invite.

Fey positioned herself at the bar, close enough to overhear their conversation but hidden from their sight by the garish red privacy curtains hung with little rhyme or reason around the place. She ordered a seltzer from the bartender and waited.

There is an art to this sort of assignation, and it requires patience and focus. Of the three of them, Joy was best suited for this sort of work. Not only could she blend into any situation, moving flawlessly between different personalities she had cultivated for just this sort of thing, but she had an aura about her that made her easy to trust.

Joy didn't need to interrogate her assignations—they spilled their secrets to her willingly. And when she'd pulled every scrap of information she needed from them, when they served their purpose, she happily helped them spill their blood as well.

But Joy worked best in a close, one-on-one environment, where she could develop that trust and convince them to open up to her. This assignation was different. A name and an address, a public space, meant someone had tipped Dameon off. It meant this was a trap, and all that was required of Fey was to sit and observe. Watch, listen, and report back to Dameon what she heard.

Lord Cyanean and his friends were just as boring as she feared. They spoke of trade, travels, and trivialities, and it was a trial to pay close attention to their conversation, especially after such a long day. But if Lord Cyanean had been accused of something untoward, if it was known he would be here in this bar tonight, it was likely one of the patrons drinking with him had been the one to report him to the Crown. They would be looking to lead the conversation, to set a trap for Alexander Cyanean to walk right into.

Fey sipped her drink and waited.

The men talked and gossiped, and Fey was starting her second drink by the time they said anything of consequence. After ordering another round, and pouring drinks for all at the table, someone said loudly, "To the Queen!"

The sound of glasses clinking, and comradery.

"To the Princess!" said another voice. And this time the murmuring was subdued, less enthusiastic.

"I heard deSanguine made an appearance tonight," someone said.

A few of the men chuckled.

"Oh, you know how the Fallen King is," another voice answered. "He can't help but to make a scene. The Queen nearly set her Blades on him, from what I could see."

"I'm shocked she didn't."

"DeSanguine is harmless. He's too frightened of the Queen to make too much of a nuisance of himself. He'll never make a move while Edelin sits on the throne."

Murmurs of assent and agreement followed. And then, after a brief pause, a dark voice.

"And what will happen when Edelin no longer sits on the throne?"

Fey paused her drink at her lips. A few of the men murmured.

"Cluck your tongues and shake your heads all you want, but Edelin will step down from the throne, eventually."

"And Princess Amalia—"

"Amalia is no Princess of mine."

That was Lord Cyanean's voice. Now, it was getting interesting.

The bartender set a drink in front of her, momentarily pulling Fey's attention away from the conversation.

"I didn't order this," Fey said, staring at the drink.

"Vodka soda. From the gentleman," he grunted in response. He nodded toward someone at the other end of the bar, but Fey didn't bother to look. She thanked him, picked up the drink, and pointedly set it as far away from her on the bar top as possible.

"Come now, Alex," someone at Lord Cyanean's table was saying, but he was interrupted.

"The girl has the mere shadow of her mother's strength," Cyanean said, speaking over the other man. "My connections in the palace say she's not even a true heir..."

Murmurs, some angry. Some intrigued. All dangerous, traitorous.

"He's right. I've heard she can't move Earth," someone said, their voice quiet and frightened. "And in the others? Well... the Princess barely has the power to command three elements."

A man appeared at Fey's shoulder, tapping the bar in front of her. He stood over her, encroaching on her space, his presence demanding attention.

Well, well, well. This must be Mr. Vodka Soda.

"Hey," the man said. He was blond and thick-shouldered, and to Fey he looked indistinguishable from every other soldier in the bar. Handsome, but with the undeserved swagger of someone used to getting what they want. "I saw you over here all alone and thought you could use some company."

"Fuck off," Fey answered, taking a sip of her drink.

He laughed. "It's okay, I get it. The tough girl act. You're a recruit, right?" When Fey didn't answer, didn't even acknowledge the question, he kept going. "I figured since I haven't seen you here before."

He sat, uninvited, at the bar next to her, but Fey wasn't paying him any attention. Cyanean was still talking, and she tuned out the soldier to listen.

"What do you think the other Factions are going to do, when a Queen without all four powers takes over? When the line blessed by the Goddess herself finally breaks?"

"Come on, Alex, power isn't the same as it was 300 years ago. Witches aren't as strong as they used to be. Maybe it's unreasonable to expect the line of the First Queen to be as strong as it once was, huh?"

Murmurs of agreement.

Murmurs of dissent.

"Do you have a sigil yet?"

Fey blinked. Vodka soda was still talking—hadn't stopped talking, she realized.

"I do," He answered himself, rolling up his sleeve and showing off the raised scar of a tattoo on his inner wrist. Fey recognized it immediately—the sigil for strength.

She did have the same sigil, on her wrist. Had four others, as well, tattooed up and down her arms. Only Dameon and the other Queen's Blades were gifted so many and were allowed to hold so much power. Dameon, the Blades, and the Queen herself.

"I'm going to be a general," Vodka-soda was saying, leaning towards her conspiratorially. "You don't get your first sigil until you get promoted out of the lower ranks. But, hey, I know it's tough when you're first starting, so don't stress, okay? I can help you out, you know, show you the ropes. I can be good for you, so good. If you're good to me." His hand hovered over her knee, as though trying to decide if he was going to touch her.

"I said fuck off," Fey repeated, tuning him out and focusing on her assignation. He was like an annoying insect buzzing around her.

"The Queen could always have another heir," someone at the table was saying.

"At her age?" A cruel laugh. "No, that well is tapped. We got two potential heirs, and if the rumors are true, neither was Goddess blessed with all four elements. "

Two heirs?

"How do you think the realm will take it when Amalia is crowned?" Cyanean was saying. "Even if they hide it, even if they keep everyone convinced she can control all four elements, do you think her children will carry all four? The royal line holds the crown because they are Goddess blessed. How do you think the Fallen will react to a Queen who can't claim that blessing?"

"You're beautiful, you know," Vodka-soda said, his face close enough to hers that she could feel the heat from his alcohol-heavy breath on her cheek. "Your hair... I've never seen such a dark red before."

He reached his hand up to touch her, and Fey's temper snapped. She snatched his hand out of the air, squeezing his fingers painfully.

"Don't fucking touch me," she snapped, releasing his hand as quickly as she'd grabbed it. He hissed in pain and anger, but Fey was straining to hear the rest, straining to make out the other at the table. Could she recognize them later? Put a face and a name to the voices?

Vodka-soda's face was twisted in rage, all that helpful sardonic pleasantry gone in an instant. "Look, I was just trying to be nice," he snarled. He cradled his hand against his chest. "I'm offering to help you, okay? And don't act so fucking innocent, you know what you're doing, coming to a bar and peacocking like this. You're practically begging for someone to come chat you up, but you don't have to be such a bitch about—"

He didn't have time to finish that thought before Fey grabbed him by the back of the head and slammed his face against the edge of the bar. He screamed, his hands muffling the sound as blood slipped from his mouth and through his fingers.

But Fey was already gone, slipping out the bar door and into the streets. She had all the information Dameon would need to label Lord Cyanean a traitor to the Crown.

And the next time Lord Cyanean's name would be delivered to her in a black envelope, she knew it would be written in red.

CHAPTER 4

She was in a dream.

Fey knew and recognized this simple fact, but it didn't change anything. She could do nothing but watch the events as they unfolded around her. Do nothing as she found herself lost in a memory, her body going through the steps just as it had all those years ago.

She was ten, and this was her Awakening.

The steps to the temple seemed to stretch forever as she made her way up them. Step by step, inching closer to her destiny. Around her, other Witches were gathered—her peers, all of them girls, all of them coming here on their tenth birthday to be tested.

The village where she'd been raised in the sixth octant had been large enough to have its own White Temple, but just barely. If it hadn't, Fey and her mother may have had to travel to another octant, or even to the Eternal City itself, where the lines would have been longer, the crowd of waiting girls larger.

Distantly, Fey knew the other Witches were here for the same thing, but in the way of dreams, she also knew she didn't need to wait for any of them. She climbed the steps, making her way past all of them, their faces blurred and shapeless as they turned and watched her ascent.

She was shaking from the effort by the time she made it to the top, and all at once, the scene changed. She was inside the temple now, standing before the Priestess. And Fey was afraid.

She'd spent so much of her childhood in fear. Fear of her father, and his drunken anger. Fear for her mother, for the caged indifference in which she lived her life. Standing here under the scrutinizing glare of the ancient, wrinkled Priestess, she felt that fear again.

The White Priestesses were members of no single coven, serving instead as representatives of all four covens equally. They existed to guide Witches through the Awakening of their powers, to read the clues left by the Goddess herself to judge what elemental gift each Witch received.

Fey had knelt before the White Priestess, like she'd been taught to do, her eyes on the wood grain of the floor.

Then, just like now, the Priestess took Fey's chin in her hand, wrenching her face up and staring into her eyes for a long, terrifying moment before releasing her. She took Fey's hand, tracing the lines of her palms and clicking her tongue.

Her grip had been hard, and Fey fought the urge to rub away the memory of the old woman's touch from her skin.

The Priestess wasn't done. She retreated further into the temple, grabbing a handful of beads and stones and something that looked suspiciously like bones. She chanted softly to herself, casting them upon the altar, and watching where they fell. Suspicious. Displeased.

Fey didn't like the Priestess, didn't like her angry stares, didn't like the way her eyes darkened with each test she performed. The woman was old and wrinkled, like an apple left to rot in the sun, and Fey didn't like that either. She hadn't liked being touched by this ungentle woman, who clicked her tongue in disapproval but didn't speak. She had wanted to leave.

But Fey did all that had been expected of her. She wanted to be good. So when the old woman had poured water in her hair, she hadn't flinched. When she had waved the incense smoke in Fey's face, Fey hadn't coughed. The Priestess spoke only to herself, under her breath, taking her time as she brought Fey through each of the tests and rituals until she said just one word.

"Drink," the Priestess said to her now, just as she had back then, thrusting a cup of gray liquid into Fey's hands.

And Fey drank, though the elixir tasted of rot and soil, and made her choke. She drank, and when the woman refilled the cup, she drank again.

But when the woman filled the cup a third time, something sparked in Fey's mind.

No, a voice far away from her said in the dream. Her own voice, years older, somewhere different. Safe in a bed, miles and years away from this moment.

No, the voice said, *this isn't how it happened.*

She couldn't finish the third cup. It tasted of rot and earth still, but also ash, and it was thick in her throat. She gagged on the taste of it but, determined, she drank, and drank, and drank.

This cup was endless, and Fey drank that awful concoction for what felt like hours, gagging and choking, as the old Priestess watched her, clicking her tongue, antipathy etched in every line of her face.

No, the voice in her head repeated. *This isn't right. This isn't how it happened.*

Finally, the old woman took the cup from her, though some still remained at the bottom, a testament to her failure. The front of Fey's ceremonial white robe, the robe of those not yet Awakened, was covered in elixir, and Fey's saliva and tears.

The Priestess shoved her toward an altar, and the dream returned to the past, as Fey recognized the items there.

A bowl of oil.

A bowl of sand.

A single clod of dirt.

And a bowl of water.

"Water," the Priestess had demanded, pointing to the bowl.

Fey raised her hand, focusing her power.

Years ago, when she had been to the temple on her tenth birthday, she had needed to wait only a moment before the elements reacted. The water, her primary elemental power, roiled and moved under her command. The Priestess had only nodded and demanded she switch to

Air. And a moment later, the sand from the bowl twisted and rose in a spiral of wind.

Water primary, Air secondary, the Priestess had declared, draping a blue sash around her neck—marking her as a member of the Water Coven. And Fey had been shepherded out of the temple before the words could even sink in.

But... again, the dream changed, and what *had* happened was not what *did* happen.

Fey focused her power, as she had back then, but the water remained motionless. She focused harder, sweat beading on her skin.

She reached for her power, willing it to rise to her command, as she had a million times since. But where that power dwelt, where that pulse of water usually pooled under the surface, there was nothing.

Gone.

It was all gone.

She was crying in the dream now, and the old Priestess was shaking her head in disgust.

Nothing. No power, no strength, she was useless. Broken.

Fey screamed as hands grabbed her, pulling her away from the altar. She screamed and pleaded.

This was *wrong*, she knew it was wrong. Something burned in her, power burned in her, and she *knew it*. She had to show them, had to do something. She couldn't go back home like this, couldn't go back to being a helpless child. She couldn't.

But it was too late, and she screamed and thrashed to no avail, as the hands pulled her out the door.

And shoved her down the temple stairs.

Fey awoke with a shuddering gasp, her hand coming up to cover her mouth and stifle a scream. She was coated in sweat, drenched in it, despite the cold chill of her room. Her sheets pooled around her, as wet with sweat as her skin.

Heart hammering in her chest, Fey sat up and swung her legs over the edge of her bed, taking deep shuddering breaths.

A dream. It was just a dream.

Shaking with something that could have been fear, Fey reached inside for her power.

Her skin hummed in answer, and she felt it. The pulse of power as Water filled her, energy flowing just under her skin, filling her entire body.

The sound Fey made in relief could have been a laugh, a sob, or some combination of the two. She called Air next, and a different sort of power filled her veins. A softer power, a whisper beneath her skin. The air in the room swirled in response, dancing around her, cooling the sweat on her skin.

Just a dream.

A soft knock on her door announced her sister's arrival a fraction of a second before she entered.

"Fey?" Joy called, poking her head inside the room. "Are you okay?"

Fey tried to nod, tried to say something, *anything*, in response, but all that came out of her mouth was a strangled sound. She was crying.

Joy crept into the room, closing the door silently behind her. She crawled onto the bed behind Fey, wrapping her in a tight hug.

"Shhhh," Joy murmured against her neck. Her hands rubbed soft, comforting circles over Fey's shoulders and down her back. "It's okay. Whatever it is, it's okay. We've got you. You're safe. Deep breaths, Fey. Breathe with me, little sister."

Fey struggled to draw an even breath, leaning back against Joy as she breathed in, her breaths wet and ragged. She tried to match her sister's even, slow breathing.

It took longer than Fey would have liked, but eventually, her sobs lessened, and Joy's soothing worked. She took deep, even breaths, willing the fear to subside.

"I'm okay," she told Joy, finally. "I'm okay. It was a dream, that's all. Just a dream."

Wasn't it?

Joy's hands slowed their soothing path over Fey's back and stilled. She leaned over Fey's shoulder, cocking her head to look her in the face.

"A dream?" Joy repeated, Fey's fears reflected in her bright blue eyes. "And you're sure it wasn't something more?"

Sometimes a dream is just a dream—a random assortment of thoughts and images cobbled together into a nonsensical story while you slept. Sometimes they reveal the things that we struggle with during our day-to-day lives, the myriad problems and anxieties we encounter throughout our waking moments laid bare before us. And sometimes they mean something *more*. A warning. A message from the Goddess herself.

Fey shook her head, swallowing. "No," she insisted. "It *was* just a dream. A regular dream." She laughed humorlessly, looking down at her hands and remembering that horrible emptiness where her power should have been. "A nightmare."

Joy watched her as though she still wasn't sure. But finally, she nodded, accepting the statement.

They stayed entwined like that a while longer, Joy holding her in a gentle embrace while the dream faded into a bad memory.

"Do you want me to stay?" Joy asked softly.

"No," Fey answered. She took Joy's hand and squeezed it gently. "I'm okay. Truly."

Joy smiled in return and planted a kiss on Fey's tear-streaked cheek.

"You sure?" She asked, her eyes twinkling. "We wouldn't have to sleep, you know." She teased in a breathy voice.

It had been an offer Joy had made for Alice years ago. An offer Alice had taken her up on, night after night. An offer Fey wasn't at all surprised by.

She smiled. To Joy, who saw love in everything around her, joining Fey in bed would be as natural as breathing. There would be no shame in it, no strings attached. Just a night of comfort. Love.

It was tempting after the night she'd had. Oh, so tempting to forget it all and invite Joy to share her bed, if only for the night. But Fey shook her head. "I'm sure," she said. And meant it. "Now get out of here. Let me rest."

"Fine," Joy huffed, hopping from the bed and wriggling her hips as she left. "But the offer stands if you change your mind." She winked at Fey over her shoulder, before opening the door and slipping out into the hallway.

After Joy left, Fey pulled her sweat-soaked sheets from the bed and grabbed herself a spare blanket from her closet.

Wrapping herself in the blanket, she lay back in bed and waited for sleep to calm her.

It was a long, long wait.

CHAPTER 5

People are remarkably predictable when they know they are going to die. Fey had killed enough of them to know firsthand that almost everyone reacts to their impending death in the same few ways.

It starts with bargaining. Bargaining is a type of denial, Fey reasoned, of refusing to accept the inevitable, even when it's standing in front of you, masked and deadly. Once the split second of shock wears off, and her victim realizes who—and what—is standing before them, most of her assignations launch straight into bargaining.

Fey had been offered gold. Sex. Power. She had been told that they could give her anything and everything if only she would spare their lives. They could give her things beyond her wildest dreams, her darkest wishes.

And when bargaining inevitably fails, they cry. Sometimes, they run, and very, very rarely they try to fight.

It's always more fun when they fight.

But the rarest cases are when someone simply *accepts* their fate.

Fey could count on one hand the number of assignations who had done so. Who had seen her, blades in her hands, and truly understood what was happening, that there was no way out, and... just accepted the inevitability of it. She respected them for it, respected them for being brave enough to accept death with their eyes wide open.

True to his word, Dameon brought Willow to them within the week, and when Willow saw the three of them, unmasked and waiting, their sigils and Blade's marks unhidden, Fey saw that awareness hit her. Saw the moment Willow realized she was going to die. And when Fey saw her accept that fate, and face her death head on, she loved her a little for it.

"Do you know who we are?" Lilith asked when Dameon brought the young Witch to their chambers. A black eye had formed from her fight, swelling blossoming under her eyes, turning her dark skin purple, but Fey recognized the tightly curled auburn hair that spilled messily from the bun at the base of her neck. Recognized the fierce glare in her wide brown eyes.

She had the heart of a Blade.

Willow was young. Eighteen, maybe nineteen. Short and curved, but she was strong. Well-defined muscles bulged under her brown skin. Something about the way she had fought in Solare made Fey think of a wolverine, and seeing Willow standing there now, her muscles tense and ready to fight, the resemblance only grew.

Willow swallowed under their gaze. She looked at each of them, taking in their matching tattoos and the sigils on their arms. "Yes," she answered. "You're the Queen's Blades."

Fey nodded. "And do you know why you're here?" she asked.

They already knew the answer. Dameon would have approached Willow with the same offer he'd made to Fey all those years ago—a chance to be a Blade, a member of the strongest Witches in the realm. A chance to prove you're worthy.

But if you fail...

Death.

The offer came with an escape. Any Witch could tell him no and continue their life as though the offer were never made. But to say yes meant giving up everything—your past, your family, your friends. Regardless of whether you were inducted into the Blades, you would cease to exist in the outside world. You would be a ghost.

Most Witches who joined the Queen's army had no family to speak of, anyway. In all the years the Blades had existed, no Witch had ever turned down the offer.

But many—far too many—had failed the trials.

Three tasks were required. Mental, elemental, and physical. It was up to the current Blades how the tasks were performed, up to them whether a potential recruit passed or failed.

"I do," Willow said, her head held high. Fire blazed in her eyes.

Lilith smiled wickedly at her. "Follow me, then."

LILITH'S TRIAL WAS FIRST.

The room she chose was a small library, tucked away in the Eastern Wing. It held some of her favorite books—historical records from the aftermath of the War of the Fallen, and ancestry records of every Queen who had ever ruled. Fey knew Lilith could name them all, and could name each of their children, heir or not. It was an obsession of hers.

Lilith's other obsession was power.

"Fire and Earth," Lilith mused. She paced the bookshelf in front of her, fingertips tracing the spines until she found the one that she was searching for. Plucking the book from the shelf, she flipped it open and thumbed through the pages.

"One of the first four Blades had those powers, you know," Lilith said, her fingers trailing down a page.

From her seat by the desk, Willow's head lifted with interest. The history of the Witches, the history of their realm, was a closely guarded secret. Few knew anything about the first Blades or even the First Queen.

"Really?" Willow asked.

"Mmhm," Lilith answered. "Ah, here it is. Celeste. She was the First Queen's steadfast companion throughout the War of the Fallen. They were raised together, friends since childhood. A Fire primary, Earth secondary, just like you." Satisfied, Lilith snapped the book closed. "A strong combination. She could command metal; did you know that?"

Willow blinked, shaking her head, eyes wide in amazement.

"See, that's the true power of our elements, isn't it? It's not a single gift, but what you can do when you combine them. Together, your powers are more than just two parts of a whole. They can do something grander. Something bigger."

Standing at the edge of the room with Joy, Fey fought not to roll her eyes. She'd heard this all from Lilith before. Lilith was obsessed with the power that having control over two elements gave to Witches.

Obsessed, Fey knew, because she had command over only one. *Fire*.

"That's the real gift of having more than one power," Lilith told her. "It's not that you have control over an extra element. It's that you can combine those powers into something new."

Lilith grabbed a jar from the seemingly random assortment of trinkets and bobbles on the bookshelf and placed it on the desk. It was full of bits of metal—old pieces of jewelry, rusted screws. A hodgepodge of metal bits and shavings.

"Move them," Lilith commanded.

The metal shavings in the jar were rusted and dirty. Plenty of Earth for Willow to work with. She glanced at Lilith suspiciously, then turned her concentration to the jar before her.

Power pulsed in the room, and the metal debris shifted. Bits of jewelry clanked against the glass as they wiggled in the jar. They were like insects, batting their wings against the glass to get out.

"Good." Lilith nodded, appreciatively. "Now, form them into a ball."

Willow frowned, furrowing her brow in confusion.

"What do you mean?"

"Earth and Fire," Lilith said simply, like she was speaking to a child. "You just showed me you can move the earth around the metal. You have command over Fire too, don't you? So... burn it all and move them together to form a ball."

A pause. And again, that pulse of power. Again, the metal shifted. But try as Willow might, the pieces in the jar remained just that—pieces. Bits of metal stubbornly separated into fractions. The metal moved and shifted, but didn't melt together to form anything.

Fey could see Willow's jaw clenching as she focused that power. But the metal remained in the jar, unchanged.

"I can't," Willow said, finally, a hint of a growl in her voice. "I can feel it, but… I've never drawn Earth and Fire together, they're not…" She struggled with the words. "They're so different. It's like trying to breathe and swallow water at the same time. I can't call on them both at once like that. I can only do one at a time."

Lilith nodded, as though she had expected this. Leaning over the desk, she reached into a drawer to pull out a gold chain—the links pristine, untouched by time or rust.

"This is solid gold," Lilith told Willow. She held the chain out for her, letting the metal flow out of her hand and into Willow's palm. "Feel it. Get to know the metal. Gold is soft—soft enough you could scratch it with your fingernails if you tried."

Willow held the chain, running it between her fingers. She scratched it. Smelled it. For a moment, Fey thought she might even put it to the tip of her tongue and taste it.

"Feel the metal, Willow. Get a sense of it. Now, melt the metal and form the chain into a ball."

Willow frowned down at the gold in her hand, and there was no pulse of power this time. She sighed, shaking her head.

"I told you, I can't," she said, handing the chain back to Lilith. She hadn't even tried.

Lilith smiled at her. Smiled as she took the chain, and smiled as she walked behind Willow.

Smiled, even as she wrapped the gold chain around Willow's neck from behind and tightened it around her throat.

No one could interfere with the trials, but it wasn't an easy thing to watch. The chain bit into Willow's neck, straining against the skin, as Lilith lifted her from her chair with it. Willow fought her, of course, her hands coming to the chain at her neck, scratching at where it dug into her skin, scratching at Lilith's hands, at her skin. She struggled to speak, to scream, but Lilith only pulled the chain tighter.

"You have a choice here, Willow," Lilith said, voice strained as she fought to hold the struggling Witch still. "You can feel the metal. Feel it, feel every link in the chain, and command it to *break*. Or…" Lilith paused, tightening her grip for emphasis. "Or you could die. Choose fast. You only have a few minutes. Less, if your neck snaps."

The chair fell as Willow thrashed. If she'd had breath, she would have snarled, would have spat like a cat.

No, Fey thought with a smile, *not like a cat. Like a wolverine.*

But she didn't. She had no breath, no air to hiss with. Her fingernails scraped on her skin, fighting for purchase, fighting to get between her skin and the chain. But it was too tight. There was no give to allow her access.

Her face was turning red, her eyes bulging.

Such a waste, Fey thought sadly, watching Willow as her struggle began to slow. Hands now slapping ineffectually at Lilith's. Dameon wouldn't ever let her forget this, either, if the Witch they'd been so certain of couldn't even make it through the first trial...

Willow's hand slapped at Lilith's one last time, softly, barely enough to make any noise, before going limp, her arm falling by her side.

The surge of power that fired through the room was enough to shake the books as the chain glowed white hot under Lilith's grip. Glowed and *snapped*.

Lilith swore, dropping the metal to the ground and stepping away, her hands red and coming up in welts from where the molten metal had burned her. The gold hit the ground as a liquid, a thick stream of metal that almost immediately cooled and solidified on the carpet.

Willow was on her hands and knees, coughing and gasping for breath, one hand still clutching her neck where the metal had bitten in. She hadn't been burnt, Fey noticed with an appreciation. The heat of the metal hadn't left a single mark on her skin. But she'd have some impressive bruises around her neck from the chain.

"You would have killed me," Willow gasped from where she knelt. Her voice was angry, shocked. She stared over her shoulder at Lilith, eyes blazing with fire. "You would have just killed me."

"Yes," agreed Joy, with a smile. "But she didn't."

"Fuck the Goddess, that *hurts*," snarled Lilith, clasping her hands, ignoring Willow's glare entirely. "Joy, where's the damn elixir?"

"Serves you right, you fucking psycho," Willow gasped, still struggling to draw breath. Then she laughed, almost deliriously. She stared at the puddles of gold around her and whispered. "Holy shit. I did it. I melted it."

Joy pulled a small Med Witch bottle from her pocket, taking her time uncorking it, before pouring the concoction into Lilith's hands. Lilith unleashed a stream of creative swearing as the elixir coated her hands, soothing the burns, and licking away the pain.

"Fuck, that hurts," she whimpered.

Rubbing the elixir into her hands, coating the burns and blisters there until they receded, Lilith reached over and took the jar of metal debris. She twisted it open, pouring the contents onto the carpet in front of Willow.

"Make it into a ball," she demanded again.

Willow snarled, face contorting in anger at the command.

But she reached out to scoop up a handful of metal, and it purred and glowed under her touch. It pulsed with a warm glow and melted. Willow held the molten metal in her palm and closed her fist around it. When she opened it again, a perfect sphere of metal sat there.

Lilith smiled, red lips twisting up in a near sneer.

"See, little sister? You could do it, after all. You just needed the right incentive."

Willow's only answer was a growl.

JOY'S TRIAL WAS NEXT.

Mental.

This was where Joy truly excelled. While she may have been the most skilled Air Witch in history, her best strength was in her ability to look inside people and see them for who they really were.

Joy took them to her mediation suite—a large circular room, empty save for the hundreds of candles that lined the walls and a variety of cushions covering the floor.

"Sit," Joy instructed Willow, motioning to a cushion in the center of the room. When Willow did so, taking her time to settle into a comfortable seated position, Joy waved her fingers and one by one the candles around them lit, bursting to life with a flick of her Fire.

Joy took her time, walking around the edge of the room, lighting incense, and humming to herself. Smoke drifted through the air around them, thin tendrils that carried strong, heady scents.

Even with the candlelight, the room was dark and far too warm. Fey wrinkled her nose and leaned against the rounded wall. Next to her, Lilith did the same.

"Close your eyes," Joy instructed. From her seat in the center of the room, Willow closed her eyes, a hint of a smile tweaking her mouth.

This was not what she had expected. And this? Compared to Lilith's test, this would be easy, the little Witch thought.

Fey fought the urge to laugh.

Joy paced in a slow, lazy circle around the room. She moved with a cat-like grace, unhurried and exuding calm. Her aura was gentle and soothing.

"Don't worry, little one. I won't attack you, like my sister. I just want to look inside your mind. I just want to know you. Breathe in, little Witch, and feel the air around you."

Willow took a deep breath in. Incense curled around her, tendrils flowing into her nostrils.

"Breathe out and breathe out all of your troubles. All of your woes."

It went on like this for a while. Joy moved silently around the room, circling Willow like a cat, and Willow sinking deeper and deeper into a trance. The heat of the room was overpowering, the smell of the incense cloying and thick. Fey fought the urge to yawn, fought to keep her own eyes from closing. The room wanted to pull her down, pull her onto the cushions, and lull her to sleep.

"Can you hear me, little sister?" Joy asked.

"Yes," Willow responded, voice heavy. Relaxed.

"Good. Breathe in. Hold your breath with me. Three.... Two... One... release."

Willow exhaled.

"What was your name, again, little Witch?"

"Willow."

Joy smiled. Smiled and paced. "A strong name for a strong Witch. Tell me... why are you here, Willow?"

"I want to be a Queen's Blade."

"Why?"

Willow shifted slightly, uncomfortable.

"Find stillness," Joy instructed. "Breathe in with me. Hold. Three, two, one. Exhale. Good. Tell me...why do you want to be a Blade?"

"I want to be strong."

"Are you not strong already?"

A pause. Then, in barely a whisper, "Not enough."

Joy nodded, more to herself than Willow. The air grew heavier and warmer. Candles flickered and went out. The smoke from her incense followed Joy's path around the room, trailing behind her as she circled.

"What scares you, Willow?" Joy asked suddenly.

"Spiders," Willow answered immediately. Fey fought the smile that tugged at her lips. Oh yes, she liked this little Witch. This clever, disobedient Witch.

"Spiders," Joy rolled the word in her mouth, tasting it. Considering it. "No," she said, finally. "I think not. Not spiders."

"It's their legs," Willow explained. "They have no right to so many legs."

Lilith's harsh laugh was cut off by Fey's swift elbow to her ribs.

"It's not fair, is it?" Willow continued, opening her eyes a fraction and turning toward where Lilith and Fey stood. "Snakes don't have any at all."

"Breathe," Joy reminded her, trailing her fingers over Willow's shoulder as she passed. Willow recentered herself and took a deep breath.

"I think you're lying to us, little Witch," Joy said.

She paced around Willow in slow, steady circles. Calm, considering.

"You wrap yourself in jokes to protect yourself," Joy said, her voice suddenly heavy with sadness. Pain. "But you're scared. And your jokes won't protect you here. Not from me. You want to be strong. Not just *strong*, you need to be the strongest. The best of the very best. Why? What scares you so much you would risk it all for strength? What scares you even more than death?"

Willow's lips twitched but she didn't answer. The smoke curled in tighter and tighter circles around her, circling her like a storm.

Joy took a deep breath in and stopped pacing.

"They left you, didn't they?" she said, suddenly, and Willow's breath faltered.

"Breathe," Joy commanded. "Inhale. One, two, three. Hold. Exhale."

When Willow's breathing had resumed a measured pace, Joy continued.

"And you were young, weren't you? So young." There was a deep sadness in her voice. Fey thought she might be crying. "Not even Awakened yet, were you? Not even a real Witch. They didn't even bother to wait to see what you would become."

Willow said nothing.

"Just a child and your family left you. Left you to be raised by strangers, left you to die. Why did they do that, little Witch? Why would they leave you?"

"I don't know," Willow answered. Her voice sounded strangled.

"What did you do to make them leave you? To make them abandon you?"

The room heated.

"I didn't do anything," Willow said through clenched teeth. Her eyes were still shut, tightly.

Joy was shaking her head. "Oh no, you don't believe that. Don't lie to me. You say that, but you don't mean it. And if you don't believe it, why should we? You must have done something. Why would they leave you if it wasn't your fault?"

Willow's breathing wasn't calm anymore. It hitched and grew erratic.

"Maybe you were too much for them. Asking so many questions, making too many of your little jokes, wanting so *much* from them. Is that it? Were you just too much? Or maybe they just didn't like you. Maybe no one likes you."

The air heated. Some of the candles Joy had extinguished relit with a spark.

"Maybe you weren't strong enough, hm? Maybe you were nothing but a weak little girl, always in the way, always just a *little too much* for everyone to handle. That's why, isn't it? That's why they had to leave you."

"It wasn't my fault," Willow snarled. Joy shrugged, though Willow couldn't see it.

"It doesn't matter, I suppose." Her voice was harsh as she circled. "It doesn't matter what you did to make them abandon you. They left you, and you were so young. So vulnerable."

Fey could feel sweat dripping down her back. It was insufferable, being stuck in this room, the heat of it, the smoke. It was all too much. The very air felt like fire, and it thrummed around her, coating her skin with oppressive violence.

"How did it feel, Willow? To know you were all alone? To know that no one would help you, no one would protect you?"

The ground shook, and the air crackled with power. Willow didn't answer, didn't make a sound.

"You're alone. You are nothing. And they will hurt you, Willow," Joy was saying, her voice growing pitched. "They will come, they will find you, and they will hurt you." Willow's breathing was erratic and unfocused, her chest heaving, but Joy showed no signs of stopping, no signs of giving up. "Who will protect you? Such an unlovable thing? Such a powerless thing? Who will save you when they come?"

The air was smothering. Lilith inhaled deeply, tilting her head back. Like called to like, and as Willow's power grew, Fey knew Lilith and Joy could feel it calling to them. Fire calling to Fire.

Fey was alone in not feeling it.

To her, all she felt was the clawing heat against her skin, the overwhelming blanket of smoke around them. Her stomach roiled, and for a moment she thought she might faint.

Joy stopped before Willow and crouched, their faces near to touching.

"Who will save you when they come, little Witch? Who will stop them when they hurt you?"

The heat in the room thrummed. It was a near-physical thing, licking at Fey's skin.

"You're *alone*, Willow." Joy's voice was low and cruel. Her lip curled in a sneer as she stared at the Witch before her. "Who will save you now?"

Willow's eyes snapped open, and the flames from the candles

around the room arched, their tips reaching the ceiling, vanishing the dark in the room as they burst with light.

"I don't need anyone to save me," Willow snarled, meeting Joy's eyes. Her power filled the room, suffocating, intoxicating. She bared her teeth, eyes narrowed and dangerous. "I can save myself."

Power pulsed between them as Joy stared into Willow's eyes.

Then she smiled.

"Good," Joy said.

And just like that, the air lifted, the blanket of heat disappearing, vanishing under Joy's command. Cool air whispered against Fey's skin, washing away the heat, the smoke, the fear. It soothed where the heat had antagonized her flesh, Joy's gentle, seemingly endless font of power touching them all, comforting them all.

Joy took Willow's face in her hands, beaming at her, no trace of her anger or cruelty left. Only love, pure and unconditional love. "I believe you, little sister," she said, before planting a kiss on Willow's lips.

***

AND THEN IT was Fey's turn.

"This is your final test," Fey told Willow, leading her into the training room.

She stopped right over the threshold, taking a deep breath in, filling her lungs with the smell of the gym. With the obvious exception of her bedroom, this was Fey's favorite place in the entire palace. This was where she spent most of her time.

Willow blinked in the bright lights of the training gym, the atmosphere a stark contrast to the dark candlelit room where Joy had tested her.

"The rules are simple," Fey continued. She walked across the padded floor and grabbed a folded chair and an hourglass from the equipment closet.

Willow watched, wary, as Fey stalked back toward her, setting up the chair and placing the hourglass down on the metal seat.

"You have one hour. One hour to draw blood. That's it."

Willow eyed the hourglass skeptically. "That's it?" she asked.

Fey nodded. "No rules, no tapping out. You have one hour to make me bleed." Fey smiled, then—a cruel twisted smile that saw Willow's brown skin pale. "Or fail."

Lilith and Joy climbed onto a pair of benches at the side of the room to watch.

Years ago, this had been Alice's trial. She had been the one standing here, before Fey, giving her the rules. She had been the one to determine if Fey would live or die.

But Fey wouldn't think about that, not now. Instead, she plucked the heavy wooden hourglass from the chair and turned it over to start the countdown.

"Begin."

CHAPTER 6

"**A**gain."

Fey braced herself for the hit, arms raised to shield her face, feet planted in a defensive stance.

Willow was already dripping sweat, and it gave her skin an ethereal shimmer under the artificial lights of the training room. Fey knew she was pushing the younger Witch too hard, but this was the only way to be sure she could be one of them and make it as their fourth.

Lilith and Joy watched from the benches, their faces betraying nothing. Fey remembered that same masked indifference from her induction into the Queen's Blades. She hadn't appreciated back then just how hard it must have been for Joy to sit there, still as a statue, and watch.

"*Again*," Fey hissed, and this time Willow complied, gnashing her teeth together and shifting her stance to deliver a solid punch aimed at Fey's right cheek. Fey blocked it easily with her forearms, and Willow snarled in frustration.

"*Again!*"

Grain by grain, the sand slipped from the top of the hourglass until barely a few minutes remained. Willow was exhausted, shaking, and barely able to stand, but she kept it up, kept trying to get even one good hit in. Pride might be the only thing keeping her on her feet at this point, but if pride could keep you going when nothing else did, then it could be a powerful weapon in a fight.

Willow had heart. She could fight. And she could wield her power better than any of the other recruits Fey had sparred with before. But that wasn't enough to be a Blade.

To be a Blade, you had to be merciless.

You had to be a killer.

Willow's next punch didn't even land, her fatigue getting the best of her and slowing her down. Fey saw the swing coming a mile away and only had to move a fraction of an inch to avoid it.

"Come on, you worthless little Witch, is that all you've got?"

Willow's face twisted with rage, but Fey only laughed, a harsh mocking sound.

"Tick Tock, little Witch," she taunted. "Time's almost up."

That did it. Fey saw the panic hit Willow as she twisted to check the hourglass. Sure enough, the last few bits of sand were filtering toward the bottom.

A minute left, maybe less.

Fey moved like a snake, striking out hard. She had spent the hour on her back feet, letting Willow tire herself out trying to land one good punch. But they were out of time. Her fist cracked against Willow's jaw, and the Witch fell to the ground with a scream that was equal parts pain and rage.

"Tick Tock," Fey repeated. "You better think fast if you want to live."

Fury filled Willow's face as she stared up at the Witch above her. The last grains of sand slid down the hourglass curve, racing toward the bottom.

Willow moved faster than Fey expected, throwing herself from the ground and toward...

No, not toward Fey. Toward the hourglass.

With a snarl, the young Witch snatched the hourglass from the chair before the final grains could fall and slammed it hard against the metal seat. Glass shattered, wood splintered, and Fey barely had a moment to react before Willow made her move.

Fey didn't have time to dodge the next swing, barely even had time to register the surge of energy as Willow instinctually called Earth, pulling the sand toward her and wiping it toward Fey's face. Swearing, Fey tried to cover her eyes, but the ground shifted beneath her, jostling her off balance, and—

Bam.

When Willow's fist connected with Fey's jaw, it connected with far more power than she held in her well-toned muscles; it connected with the force of the Earth pushing her, the combined force of her power and her rage hitting Fey like a brick.

Pain exploded in Fey's face, and she hit the training mat before she had even realized that she was falling. Through a haze of white-hot agony, Fey curled onto her side and groaned, spitting blood onto the padded floor. The red was sickeningly bright and shiny against the puke green of the exercise mat.

All at once that surge of power dissipated, and through the ringing in her ears, Fey heard Willow gasp. Just like that, her rage, her power, was gone in an instant as she realized what she'd done.

"Oh, fuck!" Willow dropped to her knees next to Fey. Her face was pale. "Fuck, I am so sorry, I didn't mean to—"

Fey held up a single hand to silence her, propping herself up on an elbow and spitting out another glob of blood onto the floor. She probed her mouth with the tip of her tongue, ignoring the new flood of pain the movement generated. Willow hadn't managed to knock out any teeth, thank the Goddess, but when Fey's tongue prodded the split in her bottom lip, she hissed.

"Now that?" Fey told her, each word sending a jolt of pain through her jaw. "That was a fucking *punch*, little sister."

Willow's eyes widened, and on the other side of the training room, Joy squealed, leaping to her feet and bounding forward to scoop Willow into her arms for a hug. Lilith approached more slowly, a smile blooming with slow deliberate care on her face.

"We knew you could do it, little sister!" Joy squealed, her arms crushing little Willow to her chest. "I knew you had it in you!"

"I... I did it?" Willow asked, her voice slightly strained from the strength of Joy's embrace. "Do you... do you mean it?"

"Welcome to the family," Fey confirmed, shifting up to her knees.

Smiling split her bottom lip open even further, and she could feel blood starting to drip down onto her chin, but Fey couldn't stop the grin from spreading across her face. For the first time in over a month, she felt close to being complete again. One of four.

"That was clever," Lilith said, a trace of pride sparkling in her dark hooded eyes. "Using the sand like that. Very clever."

"Fey used the chair," Joy told her excitedly, still squeezing Willow tight to her chest. "Barely even waited for the hourglass to start timing before she picked it up and bashed Alice right in her face with it. It was *brilliant*."

"I really am sorry," Willow squeaked, staring down at Fey.

"Don't be," Fey reassured her, slowly coming to her feet. The training room tilted dangerously in her vision for a few seconds, but she managed to stay standing. Fey touched her jaw tenderly with the tip of her fingers and immediately regretted it when a blast of pain shot through her. *Great... the little wolverine might have fractured it.* "Trust me, little sister, Lilith has done much worse to me, before."

Lilith laughed. "And I'll do worse to you again."

"We need warriors who will *act* on that instinct," Fey added. "We need warriors who can harness their power in unexpected ways. You did exactly what you needed to do, exactly what the Crown will need you to do when on an assignation."

Joy squealed again, and Willow giggled helplessly against her, caught up in her boundless enthusiasm. Joy was infectious. When she smiled, the whole world felt it and smiled alongside her.

Fey left them to their celebrating and made her way to the healing station in the corner of the room, where a large basin of clear filtered water waited next to their stock of healing elixirs. As the only Water Primary, it should have been Fey's job to prepare their elixirs. But Dameon knew too well to ask that of her. Healing didn't come as naturally to Fey as it did to the others in the Water Coven, and whoever he outsourced their elixir-making to did one hell of a job. Why mess with a good thing?

Pulling a cork from one of the bottles, Fey upended the entire elixir into the basin, watching as it swirled and danced, giving the water an opalescent sheen. She whispered a quick activation spell to strengthen the potency, one of the few Healing spells she had little trouble with. Fey felt her power purr to life as she drew on the water's surface. She loved that feeling, the promise of power as Water's energy filled her.

Fey was an anomaly. Before her induction, there had only ever been one Water Witch in the Queen's Blades. She had been one of the original Four, the founders of their order appointed by the First Queen herself. And even she had been a healer.

Young Witches are taught that each of the four elemental powers gifted to us by the Goddess are powerful in their own right, and no one power is greater than any of the others. Fey knew it for a lie, of course, and had recognized it as such the moment she'd had her Awakening ceremony. The elements are not equal. Of all the powers gifted to us, Fire is the strongest. In the old days before the war, a powerful Fire Primary could bring entire cities to their knees.

In the last two hundred years every member of the Queen's Guard had the gift of Fire, as either their Primary or Secondary Power. It was the element of battle, the element of death.

Water was the element of healing. Of love.

Not the way Fey used it, of course.

Fey scooped a handful of healing drought from the basin and placed it gingerly on her cheek. It was cold, near freezing, and the sudden sensation made her to suck in air through her teeth. She could feel her bones shifting back into alignment, feel the bruising under her skin stop spreading and start to recede. Her jaw clicked, and the pain disappeared completely, leaving nothing but a dull icy chill where the ache had been. Fey dipped her fingers back into the basin and ran the elixir over her bottom lip, shivering as the skin re-knit itself. It would be tender for a bit—healing elixirs were never perfect on open wounds—but she knew it should be fully healed in the next day or so if she left it alone.

Behind Fey, Joy was busy telling Willow all about what was going to happen next, her words running together with excitement. There would be a ceremony, Willow's official induction, by the Queen herself. And, of course, before that there would be a final test—an official assignation, given to her by Dameon on behalf of the Crown. One last obstacle to prove her mettle.

Fey looked back over her shoulder to smile at them.

The test wouldn't be a problem. She could tell already that Willow was the one. Not just a potential member of the Queen's Blades, but another sister. This was the family she had needed when she was a little girl, growing up in that hell. This was the family all of them needed. And little Willow, fierce and determined, bringing Fey to the floor with a combination of pride and rage, fit right into their hearts. Fey loved her already.

Willow would become one of them and she would be good, Fey knew.

No, not good—Willow would be *great*.

But she could never replace Alice.

IT HAD BROKEN something inside of them, the night Alice died. The night someone had planted enough explosives in her safe house apartment to nearly take down the building.

Alice was working alone on an assignation in the week leading up to her death. Dameon had hinted to them it had something to do with devil dust, an out-of-fashion party drug that was suddenly seeing a revival in the club scene. The Crown wanted it handled, wanted it gone, and that was their job, after all. No matter what the problem was—or more often, *who* the problem was—the Queen's Blades handled it. Quickly and efficiently.

And when the four of them finished a job, no one found the bodies unless they wanted them to be found.

Lilith, Joy, and Fey had been working together to take down a rogue Lesser Demon on the outskirts of the city, one that had already left two young Witches dead. Alice told them she could handle her assignation on her own, without their help. Fey believed her, of course. They had always believed her.

And they kept believing her right up until her apartment in their safe house exploded and she was wiped from the face of the earth in one horrible moment of fire and pain.

Dameon had been the one to break the news to them, but in truth, they'd known the moment it happened. The four of them were linked, so close that each of the remaining three had felt her sudden absence like the loss of a limb. Fey knew she'd remember that moment until the day she'd die—the tightness in her chest, and the sudden feeling like something had been ripped out of her, leaving a hollow void where there had once been light. She'd heard Joy's scream and felt the loss and devastation coming off her like a wave. And they'd known. Known Alice was gone.

Alice wasn't even supposed to be at her apartment that night. When they're on the job it is protocol to return to the palace, to their connected rooms. There's safety in numbers, in staying hidden and together. That was protocol, and Alice was a stickler for protocol.

But she hadn't come back to the palace that night. She'd gone to one of their shared safe houses in the city, her favorite little apartment, the one with the veranda and all her plants. The one they all thought of as *hers*. Alice had broken protocol, and in doing so she'd gotten herself killed.

She left behind nothing, no clues about her investigation, no evidence to point them toward her murderer. Just a gaping hole in their chests where she'd once been. A hole Fey wasn't sure could ever really be filled.

CHAPTER 7

The Last Drop was not where Fey had envisioned spending the rest of her evening.

And as far as night clubs went, it didn't have a lot going for it. Sure, the music was great, the atmosphere dark and dripping with sex...

But why in all hell had Joy picked a *Fallen* nightclub?

Fey sighed, drumming her fingertips on the table, watching a bull-horned Demon chatting up a wide-eyed Doe Shifter two tables over. She should have put up more of a fight when Joy had insisted that the three of them go out to celebrate with Willow. But Willow had been so thrilled with the idea of going out in the Eternal City, of spending time with them all, and getting to know her new sisters. And Joy? Well... how can you say no to those big puppy dog eyes of hers when she had her mind set on something?

You couldn't. The world would stop spinning the day she said no to Joy when she got that look in her eyes.

But now with the excitement of Willow's trials and progress behind them, and her muscles starting to grow heavy from a full day of training, Fey couldn't help but feel like she'd rather be back in their rooms luxuriating in a hot bath. Hell, she thought, she'd take a lukewarm shower over this place. Usually, Fey was all for the nightlife of the city, happy to dance and drink the night away with her sisters at her side, stumbling back to their rooms at dawn exhausted and still a little drunk. With their sigils hidden and their masks, their gear, back at home, it was one of the few times they were all allowed out to be themselves. But today she just couldn't get into the spirit of it.

It didn't help that this wasn't one of their usual clubs. Fey had never even *heard* of this club before tonight. It was in the Fallen section of the city, on the outskirts of the Shifter district, and the clientele reflected that. Looking around at all the Shifters, Demons, and even a few Vampires filling up the dance floor, Fey would have bet a full gold mark that they were the only Witches there tonight.

The heavy bass of the club's music beat in time with the growing pulse of her headache as Fey watched Joy and Willow sashay their way through the crowd to their booth, both Witches looking perfectly in their element here. Joy's golden blonde hair spilled over her bare tan shoulders as she moved seductively across the dance floor. Her turquoise dress clung to her like a second skin, and more than a few men turned to watch her as the crowd parted to make room for her.

Next to her, Willow looked almost modest in comparison. She wore her hair down, the highlights in her natural curls catching the flashing lights of the dance floor. She'd picked a corset top and tight black jeans to wear tonight—by far the most clothing out of all of them.

Compared to what Lilith was wearing tonight, Willow looked positively pious.

Fey had raided Joy's closet, and though she was just a tad curvier than Joy, her clothes usually fit just fine. Tonight, she wore the twin to Joy's turquoise dress, in ivory white, though Fey's curves pulled the hem a little higher on her thighs and showed a bit more cleavage. The color made her red hair pop, and from the way men in the club were looking at her, she knew she could have her pick from the crowd tonight.

Joy deposited their drinks on the table and pushed one in front of Fey. "Where's Lilith?" she asked, yelling to be heard over the music.

Fey smiled and motioned across the neon lighting of the dance floor and toward the bathrooms, where she'd seen Lilith disappear a few minutes previously. It had taken Lilith less than a minute to find and capture the hottest male in the club—a Lion Shifter by the look of him. By the time they'd headed off together, her hands were already fumbling with his fly and his had been making their way down the front of her dress.

"Oh!" Joy's eyebrows shot up to her hairline. Willow giggled, and Fey grinned and winked at her.

They never begrudged their sister for her casual hookups, and Fey certainly never judged her for it. In fact, Fey envied her. Lilith always returned from these nameless boys with a smile on her face and a look of deep satisfaction.

Whereas Fey... well... Fey never felt anything after a one-night stand but a deep desire to take a hot shower.

Lilith lived and breathed sex, and it invoked something in her Fey never understood. In Fey's experience, men knew so little about the female body it was a shock they managed to put their dick in the right hole. She'd had her fill of fumbling, slobbery encounters in the last few years—Lilith was welcome to all of them, as far as she was concerned.

Fey took a sip of her drink while Joy and Willow shimmied into the booth, pausing at the taste. She held the seltzer in her mouth, registering Joy's eyes on her as she swallowed. Fey's smile never slipped as she set the glass down, grinning at Willow like nothing was out of the ordinary.

"Hello, my loves," Lilith purred, strutting up to the table. Whoever the Shifter was, he must have done a damn good job based on the wobble in her step and the satisfied glaze in her eyes. Lilith grabbed the unclaimed glass from the table and downed her vodka in a single gulp.

"Dance with me, little sister," she cooed at Willow. Willow grinned and hopped out of the booth, not needing to be told twice. Before they turned to the dance floor Lilith cocked an eyebrow at Joy and Fey, an invitation to join them.

"I want to finish my drink first!" Joy said, beaming, and Fey just shook her head with a smile. Lilith nodded, and Fey watched the crowd split around her and Willow as they joined the dance floor.

"So," Fey said casually, toying with the tiny plastic straw in her drink. "Do you want to tell me why you and I are drinking seltzer tonight?"

Joy's smile faded for a moment as she chewed her lip. Fey should have noticed right away, should have smelled the difference in the drinks when Joy had set them down—two vodka sodas, two seltzers, looking almost identical.

"This is where she came," Joy said, finally. "This is where Alice was the night she died."

The words were such a shock Fey nearly choked on her drink. Her hand shook as she set her glass back down on the table. "How do you know?" she asked.

"Security cameras," Joy answered, voice barely above a whisper. Her smile was back like they were just two friends chatting it up, but it was a mask. Joy was rattled, and it had been a long time since Fey had seen her rattled. "I spent hours combing through footage from all around the city. Alice was here the night she died, and then she left and didn't go anywhere else but to the safe house."

Fey schooled her face to match Joy's, smiling at men as they walked by their booth. It wasn't hard. She'd perfected this exact smile over the years—just enough to look seductive, but not enough to look welcoming, not enough to convince any of them to approach. It was a smile that said *you can look, but you can't touch.*

"Why didn't you tell us?" Fey asked. She tried to keep the anger from coloring her voice. Tried, and failed.

Joy's smile didn't waiver for so much as a second when she answered. "I'm telling you now, aren't I?"

Fey let the information sink in. This was good, she decided, even as her heart broke all over again. This was a lead; this was one step closer to finding her killer, to finding out what had happened.

Fey never drank during an assignation. Trust Joy to think of that. Joy was a tactile genius, after all, always thinking at least two steps ahead of everyone else. Fey needed every brain cell at full capacity, and something about alcohol messed with her connection with Water—not a lot, but just enough that it could be a problem.

And a risk, even a small one like that, could be the difference between living and dying in their line of work.

Joy wanted her alert, wanted Fey at her best. And she was trusting her with this tonight.

"Alright," Fey sighed. "We're here. You have my support. What do we do now?"

Water, Water, gives us life.
Heals our ills, and calms our strife.
Fire, Fire, born to fight.
Brings us pain, and rage and light
Earth, Earth, sure and calm.
Stubborn often, but rarely wrong.
Air, Air, fast and quick.
Smart and clever, full of wit.

THE CHORUS from a children's nursery rhyme bounced through Fey's head as Joy outlined her plan. Joy was, without a doubt, the smartest Witch she'd ever met.

"This place has cameras everywhere," Joy explained. Her eyes darted quickly to a few stationed around the nightclub, a subtle look that Fey followed. She was right—Fey could see at least a few of them. They weren't even hidden. "The owner must have a voyeurism kink, I think—there isn't a single corner in this place that's not being watched. But I can't access it since it's all on a closed system."

"'Closed system' meaning?"

"Meaning the cameras are recording but not connected to the internet or any outside source. Everything must be saved and managed here, locally. Which is good news and bad news. The bad news is I can't get the footage using my usual ways. No hacking, no breaking in remotely and getting the files we need that way."

"And the good news?"

Joy had beamed at her. "The good news is you're going to steal it for us."

And that's how they ended up here, standing in a dark corner past the bathrooms on the second floor of the nightclub. The VIP area was a few feet away, guarded by a massive Shifter who was built like a brick wall of muscle and body odor.

They were far enough from the action on the dance floor that the music was dulled to a tolerable level. The smell of desperation and cheap liquor that permeated the lower floor was barely perceptible up here. It was a relief, honestly, and Fey found herself thinking she could learn to like this place if she could manage to get a table behind the VIP rope.

"I was here a few nights ago staking out the place, and the owner's office is down the hallway on the left," Joy said, pressing an object into Fey's hand. "Get in, find a computer, and slip this into the USB port. I programmed this one myself. It should download everything I need in a matter of minutes."

Air, air, Fast and quick. Smart and clever, full of wit. Fey laughed softly, to herself. "Joy, you never cease to amaze me."

Joy smiled brightly back at her, blue eyes sparkling. "I know."

The mountain of a security guard beside the VIP rope hadn't seen them yet. Joy eyed him, chewing her lip in concentration.

"Ready?" Joy asked. Fey nodded next to her, and Joy took a deep breath.

The calm, confident assassin Fey knew disappeared in an instant and appeared nothing at all like the hysterical Witch who stumbled forward toward the bouncer.

"Oh, thank the Goddess," Joy gasped, her voice strangled with fear and panic. Fey pushed herself against the wall, further into the shadows, struggling to remain unnoticed.

"You have to help, they're fighting!" Tears pooled in Joy's eyes as she closed the distance between them and reached for the Shifter, all but collapsing against his arm.

"What do you mean? Who's fighting?" he asked in a gruff voice, but she was already pulling him away from the rope, already leading him further into the club. And, like men always do, he followed her, letting her pull him along by his sleeve.

"There's no time, *they're going to kill each other!*" she sobbed. "*Please! You have to stop them!*"

Fey had to hand it to her, watching Joy lead the confused Shifter away, Joy could have been an actress.

She probably wouldn't have enjoyed it nearly as much, though.

The moment they were out of sight Fey ducked under the velvet rope separating the VIP from the ordinary patrons below. She rolled her eyes as she slipped past, heading for the hallway Joy had indicated.

Velvet rope, she thought to herself. *What a fucking pretentious cliché.*

In the hallway, the music from below was almost imperceptible. It was still dark back here, and Fey used it to her advantage, keeping to the shadows stretching down the hallway to stay hidden until she reached the owner's office.

She tried the door.

Locked. Of course. Not a surprise, but also not a problem, especially for her. Fey had mastered unlocking sigils when she was fourteen.

Fey placed her finger on the wood of the door and drew the complex symbol against the grain. She was rewarded by the audible *click* of the deadbolt retreating as the door unlocked. Sparing one more glance down the hallway to make sure she hadn't been seen, Fey opened the door just a crack and slipped inside, shutting the door behind her.

The office inside was unoccupied, just as Joy promised, but for a brief moment, Fey assumed she must have had the wrong room. She sure as hell hadn't expected the manager to have an office like this.

It was... cozy.

The entire room was furnished in solid wood, from the heavy desk that dominated the middle of the space, to the bookcases lining the walls. Full bookcases, Fey noticed with appreciation. What she wouldn't give to spend a few hours here, picking out a nice book, lounging in the huge oak and velvet armchair near the desk, sipping something hot and sweet...

But Fey didn't have a few hours, so she pushed the fantasy out of her head. Joy couldn't guarantee how long the office would be empty, and she needed to get to work.

There was a laptop open on the desk and no other computer in sight, so Fey figured it was their best shot. She moved around the desk, making sure to keep the door in her line of sight, and fumbled with Joy's thumb drive before connecting it to the laptop. It emitted a pleasant electronic hum as it went to work.

The giant oak desk was covered in sheets of paper, some haphazardly separated into stacks, and Fey flipped through a few curiously, looking for... something. If Alice had been here in this club, if her investigation led her to this place, there had to be something here explaining why, some piece of evidence to help them figure out what had happened to her.

A cursory glance through the pages scattered on the desk didn't reveal anything interesting, and the thumb drive continued to hum, so she tried opening one of the desk drawers instead.

Jackpot.

The top drawer opened without so much as an unlocking sigil, and Fey found herself looking down at a row of carefully organized manila folders. She picked through them at random, pulling out a few to read what lay inside. It was mostly invoices and receipts, exactly the sort of boring documentation you'd expect from managing a club.

Fey sighed, frustrated.

She didn't know what she had expected. A folder marked "Here's what happened to Alice Kelly"? Still, the disappointment left a sour taste in her mouth.

Joy's drive gave one final hum and went silent. Perfect, Fey thought. She returned the file she was flipping through—some sort of expense report for liquor—to the drawer and was just about to reach for Joy's thumb drive when a voice growled from behind her.

"Just what the *fuck* do you think you're doing in my office?"

Fey squealed and twisted around to find herself trapped between the desk and a Vampire.

And just her luck—he looked angry enough to rip her limb from limb.

CHAPTER 8
ALASTAIR

This day just keeps getting better and better, Alastair thought bitterly, watching as the Demon tied to a chair in front of him broke down sobbing.

"I don't know what the fuck you're talking about, I swear it," he blubbered. The collar of the Demon's cheap silk shirt was wet with tears and snot. "Please, I promise I didn't do anything. You've got the wrong guy, I swear!"

Pathetic.

Lesser Demons were always like this, all bluster and slick words, but underneath the cocky attitude, they had no fucking backbone. They played the part of tough, powerful little shits, but the moment you threatened to cut off just *one ear*, suddenly here comes the waterworks.

Boo-fucking-hoo.

Alastair dug the blade across the Demon's jaw a little harder, drawing a line of blood, and he was rewarded with a fresh sob from his captive. This was almost too easy.

"I think you do know what I'm talking about," Alastair told him calmly. He applied a little more pressure to the knife, dragging the blade up and under the Demon's earlobe, but not pressing hard enough to do any real damage. Not yet anyway. "See, I can smell a lie from a mile away, and guess what? You're lying to me right now. You fucking reek of it."

The Demon tried to say something else, but his sobs were so loud and so disgustingly wet that Alastair couldn't understand a single word. The guy could barely breathe through the crying, and as Alastair watched, a glob of snot fell from the tip of the Demon's nose and onto the front of his shirt, leaving a long string of slime hanging in its wake.

Disgusted, Alastair straightened, taking the knife from the Demon's face and moving far enough back to ensure he was out of slobbering distance. He didn't care much about getting blood on his suit, but with all the stuff dripping out of this guy right now, he'd just as soon avoid getting too much of this asshole's fluids on himself.

Two hours ago, this know-nothing Fallen was drinking up a huge tab in Alastair's club and enjoying his night. Two hours ago, he was having fun, laughing and dancing, picking up chicks. Two hours ago, he made the fatal mistake of trying to sell drugs under Alastair's fucking roof.

Other Vamps sometimes asked him why he employed a full staff of Wolf Shifters to tend the bar and run his security, why he didn't stack the club with Vampires, and his answer was always the same: A Wolf can smell drugs better than a Vamp ever could. Alastair would let a lot of shit fly in his club, but drugs were something he wouldn't tolerate. This is why he kept the Shifters under his employ paid well enough to keep them loyal. A good paycheck ensured his employees came to him the second they sensed any of that shit in his club.

And that's exactly what happened tonight.

"Here's what we're going to do, you little shit," Alastair said to the Fallen, speaking a little louder than necessary so he could be heard over the sound of the Demon's crying. "You're going to tell my friend Ferus here every single person you sold to tonight. And then you're going to tell him exactly who gave you the drugs, and who made you think even for one fucking second it was okay to bring this shit into my territory."

The Demon was shaking his head, saying something that just came out as wet mewing. Alastair ignored it. He was done with this asshole, anyway.

Alastair motioned for Ferus, who leaned against the wall, and the

Wolf gave a solid grunt and straightened. Ferus was huge, six foot seven, and nothing but muscle. Alastair had never seen his Wolf form, but even his human form was feral enough to scare the piss out of most hardcore patrons.

When Alastair's favorite bartender had smelled drugs on this piece of shit Demon two hours ago, he'd immediately sent word to Ferus, who'd brought the dealer back here. They'd found enough baggies full of devil dust on him to know he was a fucking dealer, but that's not what was pissing Alastair off so much.

This was the second small-time dealer that had been caught in his club in as many weeks. The second low-life Lesser Demon who thought he could pull this shit under his nose. The second round of baggies all marked with the same symbol. All from the same supplier.

"I want to know who you're selling this shit for." Alastair waved the baggy underneath Mr. Sobs-a-Lot's nose, making sure he got a good long look at the symbol printed there. "And after you've told Ferus everything you know, then you and I can have a good long chat about whether you're going to walk out of here alive."

Alastair's knife was wet, a combination of blood and tears, and he wiped the blade clean on a dry patch of the Demon's shirt. The way he flinched away from the knife made Alastair smile coldly.

He wasn't going to kill him, of course. Not really. Alastair wasn't *unreasonable*, after all.

Just really fucking pissed off.

"Find out everything he knows. I want a name, even if you have to carve it out of him," Alastair hissed at Ferus, handing him the knife, handle first. He said it loud enough for the Demon to hear. Ferus nodded, taking the blade, and palming it with another grunt. It was for show. Alastair knew from experience that Ferus would have the guy talking in five minutes flat, without getting even a drop of blood on that blade.

That's why Alastair hired him.

And if Ferus couldn't get it out of him, well...

Alastair had plenty of other tricks up his sleeve to get the answers he wanted.

Alastair turned and left, shutting the stockroom door behind him and leaving Ferus to work his magic. No one would hear the mother-fucker scream, not over the club music blaring throughout the place tonight.

With a groan, Alastair leaned back against the door. He reached up, brushing his black hair back and out of his face. A headache was starting to form behind his eyes, and the flashing lights and constant noise from his club weren't helping.

"You get a name yet?"

He opened his eyes to see Jasper standing in front of him, a glass of whiskey in his outstretched hand and a lazy crooked grin on his face. Alastair gave him a nod of thanks and took the drink from him. He swallowed the entire thing in a single go.

Jasper was the bartender who had smelled the guy tonight, and even though he'd only been working with Alastair for a few years, he was quickly becoming his favorite employee. He had a sixth sense for when Alastair needed a drink, and the Goddess knew that was the sort of talent he needed to keep around.

Not to mention the fucker was handsome enough to keep women coming back time and time again, wearing less and less clothing, trying to catch Jasper's eye.

A few of the males, too.

Alastair handed him back the empty glass. "No, not yet. But Ferus will get it out of him." He tried rolling his shoulders, hoping to work out some of the tension in them. No such luck. "Thanks for the heads up about him. And for the drink."

Jasper just nodded. A Wolf of few words.

"If anyone comes looking for me, tell them I'll be in my office, okay?"

Alastair left before Jasper answered, pushing his way from behind the bar, into the crowd and past the VIP rope on the second floor. A few women eyed him hungrily from the dance floor, but he wasn't in the mood for company tonight, not with the shit he was dealing with. The club was bouncing tonight, and even though it was early, he could tell they were already near capacity. The bouncers at the door would be turning people away tonight, which was fine by him. A full club meant money in his pocket.

The music was quieter up on the second floor, and as Alastair moved into the back hallways, his headache was finally feeling manageable. Or maybe it was the shot of whiskey finally working its way through his system. Who could know for sure?

He needed a shower to wash the stench of that Demon's terror off himself, but it would have to wait. He had a few hours of work left to do while he waited for Ferus to deliver that name, so he figured he might as well get started and—

Alastair froze mid-step, directly outside his office door, and his nostrils flared as he smelled an intruder.

What the fuck was a Witch doing in his office?

It was unmistakable, that scent of power from the other side of the door. Alastair clenched his teeth together to keep from snarling, rage growing inside of him. As if he wasn't already in a foul fucking mood. She wasn't even being subtle. Alastair couldn't just smell her, he could *hear her* inside his office, shuffling papers around.

Fucking little thief.

Well. If she can sneak into his office, two can play that game. She wouldn't even fathom the tricks he had up his sleeve.

So many in our world believe power is finite. That's why it's becoming less with each generation—as we grow in numbers, as we overpopulate, that power is stretched thinner and thinner leaving less of it to go around. They say that's why the oldest of our kind are the strongest, and why some of our gifts are fading.

But Alastair never believed that shit. Even before he realized his strength rivaled that of the oldest Vamps, he hadn't believed it. Power wasn't fading from the world, far from it. It was just consolidating. And he had enough of that power flowing through his veins to know that beyond a shadow of a doubt.

Alastair put his hand against the door to his office and smiled. After all, these were the same idiots who believed there weren't any Vampires capable of immaterialization left.

Focusing on the sensation of the wood of his office door against his palm, Alastair took a deep breath and let himself slip out of existence. It was easy once you got the hang of it. One moment you were here, and the next, *poof* you were nothing but a thin shadow.

The old-world Vampires called it Shadow Walking, and as far as he knew, Alastair was the only one left who could do it. It was his little secret, even from his family.

Especially from his family.

The feeling of wood beneath his palm vanished as he slipped into the immaterial world and passed through the wall. He couldn't hold this form for long, but it sure was handy in a pinch.

Like when you want to sneak up on a thief, Alastair thought, slipping through the wall and into his office. He moved around behind her, placing himself between her and the window before he took another breath and brought himself back into the material world.

Everything looked different when he Shadow Walked. Colors were bleached, everything muted and faded, and the world around him bled together into nearly indistinguishable shades of gray like his eyes couldn't perceive the lights and colors correctly. As he started to solidify, the world solidified around him, colors and textures returning to their rightful place.

And there was the fucking Witch herself, going through his shit, completely oblivious to the danger that just materialized behind her.

Even with the growing rage inside him, he had to admit she was gorgeous, at least from the back. He took a moment to soak in the image of her, leaning over the desk. Long red hair ran down her back in silky waves, a perfect shade to complement her pale skin. She wore a white dress, just a touch too tight, and when she bent over to rifle through his desk drawer, it slipped obscenely high up her legs until he could see just a hint of the bottom curve of her ass.

"Just what the *fuck* do you think you're doing in my office?" Alastair growled, and the scent of fear that wafted from her when she whipped around was intoxicating.

CHAPTER 9

*F*uck.

How the fuck did he get in without me seeing him?

The Vamp standing in front of her wasn't at all what Fey pictured when she'd envisioned the owner of this club. For one, he was young, though with Vamps you could never really tell their true age, not well anyway. And secondly, he was jaw-droppingly gorgeous.

Easy there, Fey.

His ink-black suit looked obscenely expensive and was a perfect color match to the shade of his hair. Tall, well-muscled, and dangerous-looking, he would have been exactly Fey's type if he didn't look like he was about to murder her.

Okay, Fey, relax. Remember your training.

The first rule of fighting a Vamp is you never do it unless it's your only option. They're faster and stronger than Demons, and even Shifters can't hold a candle to them in a fight. Fey tried to calm her pounding heart and held her hands out in front of herself, palms first, in the least threatening stance she could muster. When he didn't immediately rip her throat out with his teeth, she took it as a good sign.

"I'm so sorry," Fey told him, her voice husky and breathless. There is an art to appearing non-threatening. She had never really mastered it, not the way Joy had, but Fey was doing everything she could to channel Joy's feminine power to appear nonthreatening as she silently prayed to the Goddess to help her pull it off. "I was looking for the washroom, and I must have gotten turned around." Fey flashed him the ditsiest smile she could manage. "This place is just, like, such a maze, you know?"

One look in his eyes told her he wasn't buying it for a second.

Fuck.

His nostrils flared.

"You're lying," he said, his voice full of cold rage. He took a step toward her.

Shit. Hands still raised, Fey tried to take a step back but found the desk pressing against the small of her back, blocking her retreat. *Double shit.* "I'm not lying, I swear. I had no idea this was your office, and I'm so sorry—"

He was on her before she could blink, moving faster than she could register to stand over her. The sudden appearance of him towering above her cut her off mid-word.

In the training yards, they teach Witches that the single deadliest thing about Vampires wasn't their strength or even their bloodlust. It was their speed, something no Witch could counter without being prepared.

Fey had never faced a Vamp one-on-one before, and she sure as hell didn't feel prepared for it tonight.

The Vamp reached up between them and took Fey's face in his hand, his fingers digging painfully into her cheeks.

"I can smell that you're lying," he hissed. His eyes burned into Fey's and his gaze was piercing. She felt like she was being swallowed by the golden ring of his irises.

Huh, well, that's something they didn't bother to teach us at training. Good to know.

"Get the fuck away from me," Fey warned him, dropping the ditzy drunk girl act. She registered a brief flicker of surprise in his face at the sound of her real voice. At the surety of the threat in it.

But he didn't move. He squeezed his fingers tighter, and Fey felt the split in her bottom lip reopen. The Vamp's nostrils flared, and his eyes immediately left hers, darting down to where a single drop of blood began to blossom from the tear in her skin. The anger in his amber eyes turned to hunger as he watched the drop slide down onto her chin.

That was the opening Fey needed.

"I warned you, you know."

With her hands against his chest, Fey summoned Air, feeling the power rush through her and out her palms, flinging him off her and straight into the back wall of his office. His pained grunt brought her a small shiver of satisfaction, but Fey didn't bother waiting to see him hit. She was already leaping over the desk, running for the door.

Fey's fingers just barely grazed the doorknob when he slammed into her, knocking her off balance and sending her careening against the wall. He pinned her there, pushing her front against the wood while his hands struggled to find her wrists.

Fucking Vampire speed. Fey fought against him, knowing she couldn't let him immobilize her hands.

He managed to catch one of her wrists, squeezing it in his grip and twisting her arm behind her back. The moment he managed it, though, Fey brought her heel down with her entire weight on the top of his foot. The Vamp roared in pain, and she managed to twist far enough to send another gust of air against his shoulder, throwing him off balance and giving her enough leeway that she tried reaching for the door again.

"*Stop!*" he growled, and her body went instantly rigid against his, every muscle tensing. Fey tried to move, tried to fight, tried to do anything, but her body ignored her.

No, no, no.

"Did you just use *persuasion* on me?" Fey snarled between her clenched teeth, forcing the words out. Her muscles were slowly relaxing, back under her control, but when she tried to struggle, tried to fight back, and shrug him off, they refused to listen. She was helpless. The Vamp took the opportunity to wrap his arms around her, pinning her hands against her chest where they were useless against him.

Fucking vamp, Fey thought, filling with rage and power.

Very few Vampires still had the power of persuasion—the ability to force others to act against their will. It was an old talent, one nearly diluted out of their power set. Still, Dameon had trained them for it. Just in case.

Fey squeezed her eyes shut and focused, bringing her awareness to her body. At first, all she could feel was him, the hard muscles of his body pressed against her back, the strength of his arms pinning her against him. He smelled like whiskey and wood smoke, and the combination momentarily distracted her.

He felt... good pressed against her, like this.

The moment she thought it, her nerves flared to life, and she became aware of every point of contact between them, every place his body touched hers. It was an effort not to sink deeper against him, deeper into that smell, into the heat of him.

Focus!

Water.

Fey summoned her power, visualizing it as she gathered her strength inside herself. Water rushed through her, washing away his commands. She imagined his words as a sheen of oil, pooling in her, and she washed them away bit by bit until there was nothing left.

"Why were you in my office?" the Vamp growled, and his persuasion roared the command through her mind. Her tongue moved of its own accord to answer him, but Fey clenched her teeth together and let her power wash the words away. He could use all the dirty tricks he wanted, but she sure as fuck wasn't going to tell him anything.

His arms tightened around her when she didn't answer, and Fey couldn't help but smile at the victory.

"Go fuck yourself," she purred at him over her shoulder.

With a growl, he turned her away from the door and threw her back into the room, pushing her against the desk. Fey let out a gasp in shock, pinned between his body and the wood.

He released her arms, bringing one hand down to hold her in place by her hip, while the other swept her hair over her shoulder and off her neck.

"My people used to have a way of dealing with thieves," he threatened. The heat of his breath against the back of her neck made her shiver. With him pressed flush against her back, she could feel every hard muscle of him, and her body responded with a flood of heat under her skin. His hips were keeping her pinned in place, making the lip of the desk press below her hips. Press against her in a way that wasn't entirely unpleasant.

Fuck.

He brought his hand up and curled it into her hair, grabbing a fistful and using it to wrench her head backward. Fey gasped in shock, completely immobilized against him.

"If a thief was caught in the act, they used to pay the price in blood," he growled. His lips brushed against the skin behind her ear, and each word sent a violent shiver across her too-sensitive skin. She felt a heat rising in her and tried not to think about the last time she'd had a man this close to her. Tried not to pay attention to where the desk pressed against her, tried not to imagine what he would feel like inside of her.

Her tongue ran across her bottom lip, and she tasted blood from where he'd split her lip open.

Fey felt it, then. A razor-sharp whisper against her neck as his fangs drifted over her skin. It was a bluff, and they both knew it. Nonconsensual feeding was outlawed, and the Crown took the penalty seriously. By feeding on a Witch without her consent, he would be signing his death warrant.

A bluff, Fey tried to convince herself. He wouldn't dare do it.

His fangs slid across her skin again and Fey couldn't stop herself from letting out a whimper. Her skin was on fire, her pulse quick and panicked.

"Is that what you want?" he asked her. His voice was full of barely contained rage, and suddenly Fey wasn't so sure he was bluffing after all. Her mouth went dry with terror. He might do it, he might bite her right here and now, and pinned between him and his desk, there wasn't a single thing she could do about it. *"Is that what you want?"*

Fey felt his persuasion wash over her, and she could do nothing as she heard her treacherous voice answer him.

"Yes!" she gasped.

The Vamp went instantly still behind her, and at that moment, Fey wasn't sure which one of them was more shocked by her answer. She hadn't been expecting him to use persuasion, hadn't been ready to wash his words away before she could answer.

And she sure as fuck hadn't been expecting to say *that*.

Fey clenched her mouth shut, embarrassment replacing the desire that had been building in her body. Heat rushed to her cheeks, and she prayed to the Goddess he would just let her go. Or maybe the ground could open beneath her and swallow her up. Maybe she could just drop dead. Anything to get her out of this humiliation.

She couldn't even feel him breathe anymore; he was so still behind her. But something in his stance had changed, and when he pressed her forward against the desk again, she felt something hard against her back that she hadn't noticed there before.

"I didn't mean that," Fey said. His hand shifted against her hip, gripping her harder, and she whimpered. He still held her hair in his fist. When he pulled her head back again, he brought his face to her cheek.

"Oh, I think you did, little Witchling."

His lips were torture, a soft caress against her skin. Fey trembled against him like a bird, feeling the heat return to her blood.

"And do you want to know why I think that?" he asked.

Fey couldn't answer. She couldn't think, couldn't breathe.

She felt him take a deep breath, inhaling her scent, his nose against the space between her ear and her neck. "You smell like scx, Witchling," he purred into her ear, and a moan escaped her throat before she could stop herself.

This time it wasn't his fangs she felt against her neck, it was his lips. The barest touch as he whispered against her skin. "Tell me, Witchling —are you wet right now?"

"No." she snapped.

His laugh was a taunt. "Lying, again."

His hand moved from her hip and onto her stomach, pressing hard against her abdomen and moving lower. Every movement of his fingers as they snaked down her body felt like a threat.

"I think you are. I think when I reach my fingers down there, I'll find you dripping wet and ready for me."

He moved his hips back, peeling her away from the desk just enough to slide his hand down the front of her dress a little more. Fey knew he was right.

Without him pinning her against the desk, she had more freedom of movement, and she used that freedom to grind herself back against him. She found his cock hard against her ass, and he hissed through his teeth as she moved against it.

"I don't think I'm the only one who got a little turned on," Fey taunted, craning her head so she could look back at him with a mocking smile. "So why don't you let me go, and we'll call it even?"

He growled, and Fey briefly wondered why she would be stupid enough to make him angry again when he suddenly spun her around to face him, the desk now against the small of her back.

His fist still clutched her hair, angling her head up so she was forced to look him in the eyes. His stare was full of anger and lust, and Fey wasn't sure which one terrified her more.

Fey brought the tip of her tongue out once more, poking at the wound on her bottom lip and wetting the drying blood she found there, her eyes never leaving his.

The noise he made was nothing short of animalistic as his lips crashed against hers. Every thought in her brain abandoned her as he bit down on her bottom lip, drawing a fresh burst of pain and blood to the surface. He took her bottom lip between his and sucked greedily before kissing her.

He kissed her like it was a battle, and Fey could taste her blood on his tongue. She found she didn't care. She didn't care that he was a Vampire, didn't care that her lips would be bruised tomorrow. Fey didn't care that her sisters were waiting for her. Joy was probably beside herself with worry. She didn't care about anything but what his lips and tongue were doing.

Letting go of her hair, his hands moved to her ass, lifting her onto the desk without breaking the kiss. He pushed her legs open to bring himself closer, pressing himself flush against her body. His hands moved up her thighs, shoving her dress to her hips.

Fey moaned against his mouth, pulling him closer by his shirt. His thumbs were a searing heat on the inside of each of her thighs. He started to move them in slow, luxurious circles against her skin, and Fey thought she'd go mad if he ever stopped.

She *wanted*. More than she'd ever wanted anything in her life. The heat of him was driving her insane.

He broke the kiss then, moving back just a fraction to look her in the eyes as his right hand moved higher up her leg. The hunger was still there, burning in his golden eyes, and so was that cold rage, but both were nothing compared to the lust she saw in his stare as he looked down at her.

"You're going to tell me what you were doing here in my office," he told her. His right thumb moved up to the top of her thigh, brushing over her panties. Her back arched involuntarily as he touched her.

"Fuck you."

His fingers traced her slit through the fabric, and Fey moaned, grinding herself against them and squeezing her eyes shut. He was right —she was wet for him, already soaking through her panties. He hissed as he felt it too, and he pulled her even closer to him, crushing her against him.

His left hand reached up to grip her hair again, and he pulled her head back.

"Look at me," he demanded. Goddess help her, she did. Fey opened her eyes and stared at him. His amber eyes glittered menacingly, and his black hair was messy from their fight.

His thumb teased her through the fabric.

"You're going to tell me what you were doing in my office," he repeated. His eyes bored into hers, his hips moving in time with his thumb.

The light touch of his finger was driving her mad. Fey could feel herself already building to a release, but he was wrong. She wanted this, wanted this sensation to never end, but nothing would make her give up her sisters.

He must have seen the defiance in her eyes because he bared his teeth in a snarl, flashing those sharp and deadly fangs at her, and moved his thumb faster. Fey groaned, fisting her hands into the fabric of his suit jacket.

"You're going to tell me what you were doing in my office, and then you're going to beg me to fuck you." His thumb pressed harder, and her breath hitched. "And I will make you beg me for it, Witchling."

Fey stared into his eyes and knew she was close to shattering. She wondered if he was right. Wondered if she would beg him for it. She opened her mouth to say something, her thoughts lost to the sensation of him –

A hard knock against the door burst through the moment, and Fey jumped with an involuntary gasp.

"Sir?" a gruff voice called from the other side of the office door. "Sir, we need you out here."

"Fuck off Ferus!" the Vamp snarled, his eyes never leaving Fey's as he answered, his touch never stopping. He was looking at her like she was the only thing that mattered in the world right now. Like he wanted this even more than she did.

"I'm sorry, sir, but I can't do that," the voice called back.

Even with the interruption, Fey was climbing closer to her peak, whimpering as the pressure between her legs built. He must have realized it too, because he bared his teeth in a snarl.

"Ferus, I swear to the Goddess if you don't fuck off right now, I will rip your arms off, and I will fucking enjoy it."

Her hips bucked and moved as his hand tightened in her hair, before lowering his head to lick the blood dripping down her lip. Oh Goddess, this was heaven.

"Ignore that Wolf fucker," he purred into her skin, lips soft against her own. "Ignore everything but me, Witchling. Everything but this."

His touch was fire, and she lost herself in it. Then the voice came again.

"I understand that, sir. But you should know that I have a name. And he's here right now."

That did it.

The Vamp froze, and those delightful circles against her skin stopped.

"*Fuck!*" he barked, involuntarily tightening his grip on her hair. The bouncer at his door must have taken that as some sign of assent. Fey heard heavy footsteps move a few steps away and stop at the end of the hallway.

Fey gasped as the Vamp released her hair and wrapped his hand around her throat. The finger between her legs pressed down against her clit and her back arched painfully.

"I have to take care of something," he said, restrained violence coloring his voice. "But I'm not done with you, Witchling." His hand moved away from between her legs, and she whimpered at its sudden absence.

He brought his hand to her face and pressed his thumb against her lips—the same thumb that had been teasing her. Fey could taste herself as he pressed it to her lips like a kiss.

Her tongue snaked out between her lips, and she licked the tip of his thumb, earning a groan of surprise from him.

"*Stay here*," he commanded, and this time when the persuasion washed over her, it felt like a caress. Fey whimpered, closing her lips around the tip of his thumb to suck on it in response.

"I want you ready and wet for me when I get back. *Do you understand?*"

"*Yes*," Fey purred, the persuasion answering in her voice.

His other hand tightened around her throat. "*Yes, what?*" he asked, and her body shook with the command in his voice.

"*Yes, Sir,*" Fey heard her voice respond.

He sucked in air through his teeth at her answer and ground his body against her one more time. Fey closed her eyes, lost in the sensation of him pressed against her core.

"I meant what I said, Witchling. I'm going to enjoy making you beg for me."

She shuddered in his embrace, and then, just like that, he was gone. The weight of his body against her, that deliciously thick feel of him against her thigh, was gone. The office door shut with an audible click and only then did she open her eyes.

It took a minute for her breathing to calm and her pulse to drop back to normal. Longer still for her thoughts to return. Somewhere nearby a clock ticked by the seconds, as piece by piece she returned to her body.

Fey let her power slowly build inside of her, washing against her thoughts in a gentle lapping rhythm. The heat from his touch cooled, and the throbbing between her legs dulled to a quiet hum.

Over and over, she let Water run over her mind until she was Fey again.

Fey stood, shocked by the way her legs wobbled and almost bucked underneath her. She tugged her dress back into place, shivering as her thighs clenched together.

Her hand reached up to touch her neck where he'd pressed his fangs, and desire flooded back into her body so hard her knees almost buckled. Fey almost considered finishing herself off, then and there on his desk, but she had no idea when the bastard might return. No. She needed to leave while she still had the chance.

She was soaked, more aroused than she'd ever been in her life. The fabric between her legs was uncomfortably wet, and she shimmied her panties down her legs and stepped out of them. Fey wondered vaguely what to do with them before deciding to toss them on his desk.

Fuck you and fuck your persuasion, Fey thought, her lips twisting into a smile.

Feeling smug in her decision to leave that little gift for him, she slipped Joy's thumb drive out of his computer and palmed it. She'd head to the nearest safe house and send Joy a text from there to let her know she was safe.

His office window wasn't locked and thank the Goddess the drop to the ground was close enough that she only needed a little gust of air to slow her fall. Fey wasn't sure how much more strength she had left in her after all of that, and she didn't trust herself with anything more complicated than a simple spell.

As she walked through the city, Fey kept running her tongue over the split in her lower lip and thinking about him.

CHAPTER 10
ALASTAIR

"You're fired," Alastair informed Ferus, straightening his shirt and buttoning his jacket. But there was no heat to the words, and Ferus ignored him, looking away pointedly as Alastair adjusted himself in his pants. His cock was so hard it ached.

Fuck the Goddess, he was a wreck. His skin was on fire from where he'd touched her. It had been so fucking hard to leave her there, on the verge of breaking for him. Five more minutes, that's all he would have needed, and she'd have been ready to give him anything. He'd make up for it when he returned. He'd have her screaming his name by the time the night was over.

Alastair took a deep breath to calm himself.

But, until then, he had work to do.

"You've got a name for me?" Alastair asked, knowing Ferus did.

"Yes, sir, but you're not going to like who it is," Ferus told him.

Alastair just stared, waiting. Ferus sighed.

"The dealer is your cousin, Santiago."

Alastair ground his teeth together. Ferus was right—he didn't like the answer.

As a general rule, Alastair avoided his family at all costs. Excluding his younger brother, there wasn't a single member he could stand to be in the same room with for more than a handful of minutes.

Santiago was no exception.

The younger vampire had situated himself in a VIP booth, and he occupied it like a king keeping court. He was a slippery scavenger of a thing, Alastair thought, more rat than Vampire.

Santiago's eyes lit up when he saw Alastair approaching, and he raised a glass of cheap liquor in greeting.

"Cousin!" he called cheerfully, and the conversation at the booth stilled as his makeshift court turned to watch. "Join us! I just ordered a bottle for the table! To what do we owe the pleasure of your company?"

A necklace glittered at Santiago's neck, and his shirt shifted just enough to give Alastair a look at the pendant hanging there.

At the symbol on it. One he immediately recognized.

"Grab him," Alastair told Ferus, and as one he and four other Shifters moved forward.

"Wait, what is—"

"Out," Alastair snarled at the other patrons at Santiago's booth. They didn't need to be told twice, some nearly climbing over the others to get out of the way.

Santiago moved deeper into the booth, protesting, but Ferus grabbed him by the leg and yanked him unceremoniously out and onto the ground.

"Alley," Alastair snarled as the Shifters grabbed his cousin, ignoring his shouting and struggling.

They had to drag him through the entire club to get there, but that was part of the lesson. A reminder to the patrons, lest they forget who they were fucking with.

This was his club. And if Alastair wanted to drag someone kicking and screaming across the dance floor, he fucking would.

Santiago didn't pause in his protesting, not until Ferus flung him out the club door into the alley, where he landed hard against the concrete.

"What the *fuck,* cousin!" Santiago snarled, coming to his feet, his chest puffed out. The lame attempt to appear intimidating was lost on Alastair, who looked at Santiago like he was something he'd found at the bottom of his shoe. Santiago barely came up to Alastair's shoulders, and in power level, the two weren't even on the same planet. He was as intimidating to Alastair as a gnat.

"You're banned from the premises. Come here again, and I will personally rip your throat out."

"You have no right, I haven't done—"

"I have *every right,*" Alastair snarled. He took a step closer to his cousin and was pleased when the younger Vamp flinched and stepped backward away from him. "You forget who you're speaking to, *cousin.*"

Santiago held his hands up, shifting tactics. "Hey, man, sorry, I didn't mean any disrespect. Let's talk about this, I'm sure this is just a misunderstanding, okay? I know we can come to some sort of—"

Alastair was on him in a moment, and Santiago's head cracked against the alley wall where Alastair had thrown him, before slumping to the ground.

"You came to my club," Alastair said, his voice low and dangerous. "You brought this shit"—he pulled a baggie from his suit pocket and shook it in Santiago's face—"into *my territory.* Did you think I wouldn't find out?"

Santiago groaned on the ground.

"And you know what gets me, *cousin*? Not that you would do it under my nose, but that you were stupid enough to mark the bags with the same symbol as that stupid fucking necklace you wear."

Santiago started to protest again, but Alastair was done with him.

"If I see you here again," he repeated, turning back to enter his club, "I will kill you, cousin. That's not a threat, it's a promise."

As the club door shut behind him, Alastair called out mockingly over his shoulder.

"Send father my regards."

JASPER HAD another whiskey ready for him when Alastair entered the club. Whatever disturbance Santiago's trip through the club had caused was already forgotten, and the dance floor pulsed with bodies and lust. Memory was a fickle thing in a place like this, where pleasure reigned, and a bit of fear could just be fuel to the fire.

"I'm going to my office," Alastair told Ferus, handing Jasper the now empty whiskey glass. "And I swear to the Goddess herself if you disturb me for anything—and I fucking mean it, Ferus, even if the fucking building is on fire—I will drag you out of this club just like him, and I will leave you broken in that fucking alley."

Ferus's lips twitched with what could have been a smile.

"Fuck you," Alastair said. "Fuck you and fuck that twinkle in your eye, Ferus."

"Yes, sir," Ferus said, and Alastair left with a snarl.

He should have felt something after throwing his cousin out on his miserable ass. Not guilt, fuck no, but *something*. Relief? Accomplishment? If Santiago had been the one supplying devil dust to those low-level dealers in his club, then the problem he'd been struggling with over the last few weeks was solved.

But he didn't feel accomplished, and he sure as hell didn't feel relieved. He had an itch under his skin that he needed to scratch.

It took all his willpower not to run back to his office. To walk, perhaps faster than usual, from the bottom floor back up to the VIP area.

His heart beat faster and faster as he approached the door, already responding to the trace of her scent that lingered in the hallway. But there was no need to rush, he assured himself—not now. They had all night, after all, and he intended to make every second count. If he could get her that worked up after only a few minutes, what could he do in an hour? What could he do in a night?

He stifled a groan at the thought.

He needed this, needed the relief that awaited him in his office. He'd been rough with her, maybe too rough, but he'd make up for it now. Witches were the closest Faction to the Goddess, so they said, and by the end of the night, he'd have her praying to him instead. It had been a long, long time since he'd been this worked up, and he intended to make sure she'd never forget this night. Make sure she couldn't walk the next morning.

He was already hard by the time he opened the door.

"Hello, Witchling," he called, his voice husky. "Where were we?"

He blinked. The room was empty.

She was gone.

CHAPTER II

Lord Cinnamon was a crier.

"Please," he sobbed, his face red and splotched with color as he looked up at her. "Please, you don't have to do this."

Fey's bored sigh warmed the fabric of her mask.

Just as she had expected, when Lord Alexander Cyanean's name had appeared in a black envelope in their quarters again, it had been written in red.

The Crown wouldn't tolerate treason. *Couldn't* tolerate it. And anyone who dared to imply that the Queen was lying about her heir's abilities was destined for death.

"I know I don't have to do it," Fey told him. "But it's what I'm good at."

Her blade didn't make a sound as it cut through his neck, spraying the wall of his poorly furnished home in blood. Fey stood over him, watching him fall to the ground, clutching at the hole in his throat.

Inside, she felt numb.

It had been easy enough to find him after Dameon had delivered the assignation. Easy enough to follow him home from The Eternal Crown and slip unnoticed into his townhouse. Too easy when what Fey needed was a distraction from the storm inside her head.

Four days. It had been four full days since she'd given Joy back her thumb drive, and four long, torturous days of them scouring through the data Fey had managed to steal.

After she'd left the club and let Joy know she was okay, Fey had returned to her room at the palace. She'd managed to have a long, much-needed shower, and spent a good hour alone with her vibrator before her sisters had finally returned from their celebrations.

At first, Joy had been thrilled with the wealth of data her drive had managed to collect. She was right—the owner had a camera in every corner of that damn club, and there wasn't a single place unmonitored aside from his office. If Alice had been there, they'd be able to find what she had been doing, and who she might have met with.

But the video feeds weren't organized in any way that made sense, and it wasn't long before Joy's enthusiasm waned. They had terabytes of video feed, none of it in chronological order, and none of it labeled in any way to help them figure out which videos corresponded to what dates and times. The file names were nonsense, just strings of nonlinear numbers, none of them seemingly related to anything Joy could understand.

"It's almost like an encryption," Joy had explained after her first day with the drive. She'd spent the entire day hunched over her computer and only stopped when her eyes hurt too much to continue. "These numbers mean something to someone, but without some sort of code to figure it out, I'm just going through these videos blind. It might take me weeks to find anything like this, and even then…" She trailed off, sounding hopeless.

Weeks. They didn't have weeks. They'd already wasted enough time, and every extra day they spent on this made Fey feel as though Alice's murderer was slipping further and further out of their grasp. This was the only lead they had, and if they didn't figure out something fast, it might be too late.

Alexander Cyanean gave one final gurgle, one last death rattle deep in his damaged throat, and died at Fey's feet.

Satisfied, Fey tried to look on the bright side, tried to look past the dead man bleeding on her boots, tried to look past the roadblocks to solving Alice's murder.

Tomorrow was another day, after all.
Tomorrow was Willow's official induction to the blades.
Tomorrow they would officially have a new sister.

CHAPTER 12

The list of things that Fey truly hated was blessedly short.

She had hated her father, of course. She hated sewing, having tried for years to learn when she was training in the Queen's army and having nothing to show for it but pinpricks all over her fingers and hands. She hated the smell of lavender, which her mother had insisted was good for relaxation, but did nothing for Fey but make her gag.

And she hated meeting with the Head Priestesses of the four covens.

Fey stood outside the door, trying to calm her rage enough to enter without being openly hostile to the four women waiting inside.

"You okay?" Joy asked. Her sisters were waiting for her, watching her.

"No," Fey answered with a snarl, and Lilith chuckled darkly.

It was one of the few palace events they would attend unmasked, and Fey pined for the anonymity of her uniform. Pined for the mask to hide her from the Priestesses inside.

Deep breaths, Fey. She squared her shoulders. *You can do this.*

"Ok. I'm ready."

"Try not to kill anyone, okay?" Joy whispered as she put her hand on the door handle. Fey smiled, and they filed inside.

When a new Blade is introduced, it's a tradition that the heads of the four covens are informed before the official initiation by the Queen. It was a formality, and the High Priestesses had no real power to either accept or reject a candidate, but it was a matter of politics and tradition.

Two more things Fey hated—politics and tradition.

The High Priestesses were seated when Fey and her sisters entered the entertaining room, clustered together in high-backed chairs and sipping tea. The attendants had been dismissed earlier, none having the sort of access that would allow them to see the Queen's Blades unveiled.

Joy, Lilith, and Fey bowed deeply to the High Priestesses. Fey avoided looking at any of them directly, and one in particular.

She'd only met Sana a few times but loathed being in the same room as the Water Coven High Priestess. Sana was everything Fey wasn't, everything a Water Witch should be. Quiet, gentle. She was a healer and, of course, an expert in elixir craft.

Fey felt her judgment like a physical weight whenever they were together.

But Sana smiled at them in a seemingly warm welcome, setting her teacup down gently when they entered. She wore full Priestess Robes in the soft blue of the Water Coven. Next to her, the head of the Air Coven, Linh, looked at the clock pointedly and tsked. She was the oldest of the High Priestesses by several decades, and every year her patience for events outside her temple grew shorter.

"Sorry to keep you all waiting," Joy said politely, inclining her head. "We were unavoidably detained."

They hadn't been detained by anything, of course. They were simply late. Later still, since Fey had needed time to collect herself in the hallway. But Joy was a skillful and charming liar, and even Fey would have believed her if she hadn't known the truth.

The Priestesses nodded appropriately. Fey could feel Sana's gaze but refused to look at or acknowledge her.

"I understand we have a new Blade joining the ranks?" Leandra asked. The Fire Priestess sat proud as a Queen in her seat.

"Another Fire Witch, no doubt," Linh complained loudly.

Fey clenched her teeth together, but Joy's smile never faltered.

"A Fire Witch, yes," Joy conceded. "But Willow is also an Earth Witch."

The Earth Coven Priestess Claudia looked up with interest. It had been quite a while since an Earth Witch had been a Blade.

It was a trophy to them to have their covens represented in this. Though their identities were supposed to be secret, the powers they held always seemed to leak out, and Fey was sure that leak started here, with these women. There were bragging rights to be had when a Blade could wield their coven's element.

"Earth primary?" Claudia asked, hopefully.

Joy shook her head. "Willow is a Fire primary. Earth is her secondary power."

Linh snorted. "See? Another Fire Witch."

"My Priestess," Joy responded, emphasizing the word *my*. "Are you not pleased with my work on the Blades? Have I not brought honor to the Air Coven?"

Linh waved her comment away. "You're fine, child." Fey's jaw was pressed together so tight she worried she might chip a tooth. "I'm only pointing out the obvious. The Fire Coven has always been overrepresented among the Blades. And, again, you bring us another Fire Witch. Why not another Air, eh? Or even Water, hm?" Linh gestured at Fey.

The look Fey gave her could have killed, but Linh paid it no attention.

"And why should my Witches be punished for our strength?" Leandra smirked. "Fire is power. Aggression. Does it not make sense that the Blades should wield the strongest element?"

"I think Fey's presence on the Blades disproves the very notion that Fire alone is the element of aggression, Leandra," Sana responded, her voice soft but somehow rising above the hum of discussion. She was looking straight at Fey—had been since they'd entered the room. Fey refused to meet her eyes.

"Exactly!" Linh pointed at Fey triumphantly. "A Water Witch, just as deadly as a Fire Witch, eh? Why not bring us another? Bring me an Earth Witch, a full Earth Witch, just as bloodthirsty as this one. Now *that's* a Blade I want to see!"

Leandra argued, and as the Priestesses spoke over one another, Fey wanted nothing more than to turn and walk out of the room. She even considered it briefly before Lilith spoke up.

"You all seem to be under the impression that your opinion here matters."

The Priestesses stopped and turned as one to look at her. Joy, too, snapped her gaze to Lilith, eyes narrowing.

Lilith met their stares, the very picture of calm. "It doesn't," she told them with a haughty shrug. "You have no say in who becomes a Blade and who doesn't. We are *telling you* that Willow will be inducted this afternoon. We are not *asking*."

Linh's mouth opened and closed in outrage. No one spoke to the High Priestesses like this. Not even the Queen. Her mouth gaped like a fish as her mind struggled to put her indignation into words. "Now see here, you disrespectful little—"

"You serve at the pleasure of the Queen," Lilith snapped, speaking over her. There was steel in her voice, harder than anything in Linh's. The Priestess stopped. Stared.

"We," Lilith continued, gesturing at Joy and Fey at her side. "We serve at the pleasure of the Queen. And today the Queen herself will induct whoever the fuck we say she will into our sisterhood. If you have a problem with that, I suggest you take it up with her. But never forget that you *serve at her pleasure*."

Everyone gaped at Lilith as she continued.

"And if the day comes when she no longer claims the pleasure of your service—" Lilith shrugged, but her eyes were glittering dangerously. "Well, then you might find yourself learning exactly what the Queen's Blades are capable of."

And with that, gasps of outrage rising behind her, Lilith turned and walked out of the room.

Fey barked a laugh, shocked, while Joy made a quick apology for their sister before bowing hastily and pulling Fey from the room. The door behind them closed with a sharp, painfully loud crack.

"You're fucking insane," Joy shouted after Lilith's back in the hallway, hurrying after her. "That wasn't necessary, Lilith, and you know it."

Lilith shrugged, stopping to let them catch up. "What's insane is that they think they can talk to us like that. If I wanted to be criticized by a sex-starved old crone, I would have stayed at home with my mother."

Joy opened her mouth to continue her berating, but whatever she was going to say was interrupted by a soft cough behind them.

A hand caught Fey's elbow, and she turned.

Sana stood there. The very last person Fey wanted to see.

"Fey," she said softly. "Could I have a word?"

Great.

Fey had managed to avoid Sana successfully since her induction to the Blades. She was the youngest of the High Priestesses, having just taken over from the last head of the Water Coven shortly after Fey came to the Eternal City.

Fey inclined her head. "Of course," she said, and she gestured to Lilith and Joy to continue. "I'll be there in a few minutes."

"It's good to see you, Fey," Sana said as Fey's sisters disappeared down the hall.

She always sounded so... *sincere.* But Fey knew she was lying. Sana didn't think it was *good* to see her.

Fey made Sana *uncomfortable.* She wasn't what a water Witch should be—she wasn't a healer, wasn't interested in the calm, soft energy Witches of her coven should exude. She didn't use her power the way it was intended, and Sana knew. To Sana, Fey must be the ultimate form of blasphemy.

A Witch who used her power over Water to kill.

"I haven't seen you at the Temple, recently."

"I've never been," Fey said honestly with a shrug. She hadn't been to any temple, not since her Awakening.

Sana blinked in surprise. "Oh. Oh, well, you must come sometime. We would love to have you join us."

"I don't think that's a good idea," Fey answered. She felt uncomfortable standing here, talking to the High Priestess. Her skin felt too tight, too awkward around her body.

When Sana cocked her head in question, Fey sighed loudly.

"Do you want your temple to see me, Sana?" Fey held her arms out, the raised scar tissue of her sigils covering her arms and fully visible. "Do you want them to see an example of how their power could be used? Not to heal, but to hurt? You don't like the way I use my gift. Do you want me to inspire anyone else?"

Sana was shaking her head. "What you do with your powers is between you and the Goddess, Fey. I hold no judgment."

Liar.

Fey sighed. "I'm sorry, but it's a bad idea and you know it. I'm not a healer. I'm not the sort of Witch you want in your coven, okay?"

"Please just consider it," Sana insisted. "You're welcome to join us whenever you please. No matter what you think, Fey, I would love to have you there."

"Fine," Fey said. "I'll consider it."

She wouldn't, and they both knew it. But before Sana could say anything more, Fey had already turned and walked away.

CHAPTER 13

They barely had time to process the disastrous meeting with the High Priestesses before it was time to prepare for Willow's induction.

More tradition, and more posturing, but at least this ceremony was something to look forward to. Fey refused to bring any negative energy to Willow's special day, and she took an extra ten minutes in her shower to go through her breathing exercises, calming her irritation and bad mood, and grounding herself.

By the time she was showered and dressed in her fighting leathers and mask, she felt like a new Witch. She took in her appearance in the full-length mirror. A killer stood before her, nothing of her face visible but her eyes. Fey smiled at her reflection, and the monster in the mirror didn't smile back.

She was ready.

To some, the rite of induction must seem like a cruel thing. But cruelty doesn't necessarily negate the beauty of something. Is a lioness any less beautiful for being deadly?

They entered as a group. Dameon, in front, and Willow behind him. She wore her uniform, freshly commissioned for her, but her hair and face were uncovered.

Lilith, Fey, and Joy entered behind them, a triplet of dark shadows.

The Queen sat on her throne. Four identical high-backed chairs had been brought for the Priestesses, and Fey was only moderately surprised to see they were all full. She had thought Lilith's outburst may have cost them Linh's support, at the very least. But there she was, present, though perhaps not as thrilled as she could have been.

"Who do you bring to my throne room?" Queen Edelin asked, her voice strong enough that it filled the entire room.

It was tradition, this song and dance. A ritual of sorts. A play they all knew by heart.

"A recruit, to the Queen's Blades, Your Grace," Dameon answered.

"And who claims her?"

"I do, Your Grace," said Leandra.

"As do I, Your Grace," echoed Claudia.

"A Witch of Fire and Earth," the Queen mused. "And has she passed her trial?"

Has she made her first kill, was the real question. The day after their celebration at the club, Dameon had given Willow an envelope with her first assignation. The name, photo, and known locations of her first kill. She could get no help from her sisters, not for this first time. They were forbidden to know the details, forbidden to offer any aid at all. In this, Willow had to act alone to prove her worth.

"She has, Your Grace," Dameon answered. Willow preened with pride behind him.

Queen Edelin's eyes traveled from Dameon to Fey and her sisters.

"And you, my Blades? Do you accept this Witch?"

"We do, Your Grace," Fey answered for them. "We would be proud to call her sister."

The Queen nodded, as though considering all the evidence before her. Then she stood.

"Kneel before me, Blade." Queen Edelin commanded.

Willow approached the dais and knelt. The Queen descended the steps but did not approach Willow, not at first. She went instead to the items an attendant had placed at the base of the dais, off to the side.

She picked an item from the pile. A metal plate, fashioned to form the image of a dagger.

The mark of the Queen's Blade.

The plate had a long handle rising from its back, and the Queen grasped it. She dipped the plate in a bowl of dark black ink.

"Earth," she said as she dipped it. The ink coated the metal, and the inside of Fey's arm, her Blade's mark, twitched in response.

"Fire," The Queen continued. She touched the metal image reverently, and it burst into flames.

When the Queen approached Willow where she knelt at the base of the dais, the air was full of tension. Sana, seated among the High Priestesses, looked away. She couldn't watch.

But Fey could.

"Your arm, Blade." Queen Edelin commanded.

Willow thrust her left arm out, holding the soft inner skin of her forearm out like a sacrifice.

"Air," the Queen intoned, and as she pressed the brand to Willow's arm, the flesh steamed.

Willow didn't scream when the metal was held to her arm. Fey hadn't either, and there was a measure of pride to it. To be able to accept that much pain silently.

When the Queen pulled the brand from Willow's skin, the mark it left was dark and raised. A perfect match for the scars on Fey, Joy, and Lilith.

A ripple of pain shot through her mark, and Fey struggled to not react. At her side, Joy and Lilith stiffened, as a shadow of Willow's pain seared through their marks and thundered through their bodies.

This was their secret. A secret hidden even from the Queen herself.

Through their marks, all pain was shared. Love, fear, hatred, and every emotion they felt tied the four of them together, braiding their lives together into one.

The four of them were more than sisters. They were parts of the same whole.

Queen Edelin put the branding iron down and lifted a pitcher above Willow's arm.

"Water," she said, pouring the salted water over the mark.

This time, Willow did scream.

***

"You did great, little one," Joy purred in Willow's ear as they helped her down the hall.

After the ceremony, Willow had managed to stand without aid. Stand, and bow, to her Queen and the four Priestesses, drawing her blades and holding them straight out from her sides in the traditional bow of their order. She'd even managed to make it out into the hallway, out of sight of all but her sisters, before collapsing.

"Lilith fainted," Joy told her. "Before the metal even touched her, I think."

"Fuck you, no I didn't," Lilith snapped, but the words held no real venom. Willow *had* done great, and Fey could feel Lilith's pride humming through their mark. Willow gave them both a shaky smile, leaning her weight against Joy and Fey as they escorted her back to the Eastern Wing.

"Is it over, now?" Willow asked.

"One last thing," Fey told her. "You need to get your final sigils. Then we'll get you to bed and you can rest."

Five, in total. Healing, strength, speed, power, and perception. The ritual wasn't nearly as painful, but it was tradition to do it all at once.

"Will... will it always feel like this?" Willow asked. "I mean... will I always feel you all through it?"

She looked down at her mark as she said it.

"Yes," Joy told her. "But it gets easier. You'll learn to tune us out, for the most part."

Willow shook her head. "I don't think I want to. I... like feeling you all. It feels..." She swallowed. "It feels like you're all a part of me now."

Fey stooped down to place a quick kiss on Willow's cheek. "We are, little sister. You're one of us now. And you never have to be alone again."

Willow's answering smile was a ray of sunshine, and for the first time since that night Alice had been taken from them, since they'd felt her ripped away through that same mark, Fey felt whole.

LILITH GAVE WILLOW HER SIGILS, just as she had done for Fey.

It required Fire, and though Joy had the power to tattoo them as well, Lilith had been made for it. She even kept her nails long, the points sharpened, to hide the metal blades she glued to the underside of both index fingers.

They wouldn't do much in a fight, her finger blades, but they were very handy for this.

Tapping the metal tip against the bowl of ink, Lilith called a small lick of Fire, letting the flames coat down her fingers and over the blade.

"This is going to hurt," Lilith told Willow, without preamble. From her seat in the common room armchair, Willow stiffened. Merle watched from a distance, tail twitching in irritation that his favorite spot had been usurped. "Not as much as the brand, mind you. But enough."

Placing a hand on Willow's forearm, Lilith held her steady as she brought the hot metal to her skin.

"We'll start with strength," Lilith said. Her finger descended and Willow screamed.

Fey felt her arm twitch in pain and rubbed at it absently.

"We start with strength because it'll make the rest easier," Joy explained as Lilith burned the intricate sigil into Willow's flesh. She stopped frequently to dip her finger back into the bowl of ink. "She'll do healing next, and after that, they'll all feel easy,"

Willow nodded, swallowing. After her initial scream, Willow clenched her teeth together and refused to make another noise.

"It's okay, you know," Fey told her. "You can scream if you need to. It's just us, now. And there's no judgment here."

But Willow shook her head quickly side to side.

"You're lucky," Lilith said, face drawn slightly in concentration as she worked. "Only Dameon has as many sigils as we do. It makes us practically invincible."

"Dameon and the Queen," Joy corrected.

"The Queen?" Willow gasped. "She... fucking hell, Lilith, *ow*... She has sigils?"

Joy rolled her eyes. "Oh yes. She has *ten*. Double each of the sigils we do."

"How does she... keep them hidden?" Willow asked through clenched teeth. Lilith paused to dip her finger again, and Willow let out a shaky breath.

"Same way we do," Fey shrugged.

She held her arm out for Willow to see, twisting it in the light to show off her sigils and dark Blade's mark. Then, running a finger down her arm, Fey whispered the incantation to hide, the words flowing from her lips with ease and practice.

The skin on her arm wavered, like a heat wave, and the scars and sigils on her arms vanished. Like they were never there.

"You'll have to practice that," Fey told Willow. "But until you master it, we can do the incantation for you."

"There's one built into your uniform as well," Joy informed her. "You don't have to do anything to activate it, but it will hide your scent."

"My scent?" Willow asked, raising her eyebrow and turning to look at Joy. "Are you saying I smell?"

Lilith smacked her arm, snarling. "Stop fucking moving. If I mess up any of the lines, they won't work right."

"Some Shifters can smell us," Joy explained. "It took the Blades a while to work that one out, and a few of us supposedly died in the meantime. We need to stay anonymous, need to stay hidden. But if a Shifter can smell you in your uniform, they can track you later when you're just walking through the city. When you're not ready. Better safe than sorry."

Willow nodded, earning her another smack from Lilith.

"Almost done," Lilith said, dipping her finger a final time, and returning to her task. She burned a final line, curving an arch through the sigil for perception, and immediately Willow's eyes widened as her nostrils flared.

"Oh my Goddess," she whispered in amazement. "I can smell the bacon in the icebox. And I have never been so hungry in all of my life."

Lilith laughed, using a cloth to wipe the ink from her hand.

"Welcome to the Blades, sister," she said, smiling. "Now you look just like a proper assassin."

CHAPTER 14

The setting sun cast a golden hue over the gardens as the final remnants of daylight bled from the sky. Fey loved this time, the moments between day and night, and this was her favorite place to spend it.

Shortly after the War of the Fallen had ended and the Eternal City was being built, the first Queen had commissioned this park. In the center of everything, far from the palace proper, far from the twin rivers that flanked the city. It was a place for all the citizens of the city to enjoy regardless of Faction or status.

At the center of the park sat the Dual-Faced Goddess Statue.

Fey sat on the bench before it, staring up at her Goddess, letting peace settle through her.

The statue was a massive thing, nearly twenty feet tall, and made of solid metal. Split down the center, half depicted a woman in gold, her face upturned to the sky, hand resting gently on the swell of her stomach. Her face was serene, soft, and feminine. This was the Mother Goddess, the giver of life. The Goddess most denizens of the realm prayed to.

The statue had another face, in silver. The same features, the same feminine lines, but no serenity would be found here. No forgiveness.

Her eyes were narrowed in fury, her face a mix of rage and beauty. Her hand didn't rest on the swell of her curves but instead clutched a sword before her, sharp and dangerous.

This was the Goddess Fey worshiped. A fighter. A destroyer. This was vengeance given physical form.

And yet—here, in this one place, they existed as one. A single entity, with two heads, but one body. The duality of the Goddess herself. Creator and destroyer.

The garden darkened as the sun dipped further below the horizon. Fey sighed.

It would be stupid to go back there. It was reckless, and it was stupid. But right now, it didn't feel like they had any other options, and stupid was better than nothing.

After their night at the club, Fey had dug up everything she could about the owner, going through the Crown's extensive incidence lists and making a dossier of everything she could find.

Alastair Salvatore—that was the name of the Vamp that had her purring in the palm of his hand that night. The Vamp she was having trouble not thinking of when her fingers slipped between her legs at night. He'd purchased the property just over ten years ago as an abandoned factory building and quickly turned it into one of the city's hottest nightclubs. In the last few years, the neighborhood around it had been transformed from a slum into an up-and-coming fixture of the city—the nightclub bringing new life to the area and quickly becoming a favorite with the students from the university just a few blocks away.

There had been a few incidents at the club, but fewer than Fey had expected. A Wolf Shifter he'd hired had been arrested and convicted of assault just a few months ago, and a note in the file claimed it was Alastair himself who had brought the man in for justice. And there had been a small fire just after the club's opening, though no one had been hurt. But other than that? The Crown had surprisingly little criminal activity on record about The Last Drop. Or on Alastair himself, for that matter.

A shadow fell on the bench beside her, and Fey glanced up.

"Hey," Lilith said, looking down at her. Fey squinted against the light of the setting sun, and Lilith grinned. She held a strawberry ice cream cone in one hand, and it dripped down the side.

"Hey," Fey answered.

Lilith didn't make a sound as she slipped into the seat beside Fey, curling her legs beneath her as she sat, and licked some of the melted cream from her cone. Around them, couples walked through the park, stopping to admire the art. A few Shifter children played nearby, some of them halfway in their animal forms, still learning the basics of their transformation.

It felt... weird, sitting with her sister in public like this. Most of their time was spent in their quarters, and the rest—well... when they were out together in public like this, they were on a mission. Masked.

"What are you doing here?" Fey asked, curiously.

"I had a date," Lilith answered, taking a bite of her ice cream, pink bits of strawberry clinging to her lips. "Figured I would grab a little treat on the way back to the palace."

Fey snorted. "Must not have been a very good date if you're done before sundown."

"Oh, I disagree," Lilith purred, smiling devilishly. "I think it was a very, very good date."

Fey couldn't help it. She laughed, shaking her head.

"Do I even want to know what you're doing out here, in the middle of the Demon district?" Lilith asked, her voice teasing.

Goddess Park sat closest at the intersection of the Demon and Shifter districts, and the streets surrounding it were mostly factories and food stores, spotted with a few low-income housing complexes. There wasn't much around the area if you were looking for things to do.

"This is my favorite part of the city," Fey told her. She gestured at the statue before them. "This is the first place I came to when I moved here."

Lilith frowned up at the statue, licking sugar from her lips.

"We had a traditional Goddess statue in our home when I was growing up," Fey said. "You know the one? She's on her knees, palms uplifted. Subservient."

Lilith nodded.

"I hated it. She looked so small, so... powerless, kneeling there like that. It wasn't until I saw this—saw her shown like this—that I finally felt like I *saw* her. Like I saw the Goddess I felt inside me, the one that I could resonate with."

Lilith smiled. "Yeah," she said. "I get that." She licked a trickle of strawberry ice cream that was melting down her cone, racing toward her fingers.

Fey shrugged. "I like to come here when I want to feel close to Her. When I have to do something I don't want to do."

"And what is it that you don't want to do?" Lilith asked, teasing.

Fey sighed heavily and stood up to leave.

"I have to go make a deal with the devil," she told Lilith, turning to walk away. "See you at the palace later, okay? And if I'm not back by morning... send Joy out to save me."

Fey hoped Mr. Alastair Salvatore was the forgiving type...

But she doubted it.

IT WAS BARELY 8 pm by the time Fey arrived at The Last Drop, and the club was almost unrecognizable from the last time she'd been there. It wasn't busy yet, and the few people already there were content to sit at the bar or in various booths along the walls, sipping at their drinks and chatting. The dance floor was empty, and Fey was pleasantly surprised to find that the music and lighting were more reflective of an upscale bar, rather than a popular dance club. They must turn up the sound and turn down the lights once the place starts to fill up.

The bartender watched her approach with curious green eyes. The sleeves of his T-shirt were rolled up and stretched over his thick biceps. With his messy brown hair and five o'clock shadow, he looked more like a model than a bartender.

"What's your poison?" he asked in a purring voice, giving her a crooked grin when she sat on an empty stool in front of him.

"Vodka seltzer," Fey ordered. He nodded, and when he set the drink in front of her a few moments later, Fey's eyebrows shot up. Calling it a vodka seltzer was a lie. The drink he set in front of her was a full glass of vodka, with only the barest whisper of mixer, and it smelled strong enough to strip paint. Fey appreciated that in a drink, even if she didn't plan on drinking it tonight. It was just for show, after all—a prop.

The bartender smiled wider at her raised eyebrow, revealing a twin set of dimples in his cheeks. And a sharp set of incisors. "You look like a girl who can appreciate a strong drink," he explained.

She smiled back in response and slipped a full silver mark across the bar in appreciation, bringing the drink to her lips and feigning taking a sip. The bartender watched her, and when she set the glass down on the bar, his eyes lingered on it, narrowing slightly.

"We don't get a lot of Witches in here," he told her, gaze moving from her drink to her face. He leaned on the bar, watching her.

Fey raised an eyebrow. "Are we going to have a problem?" she asked, letting the barest hint of a threat darken her voice.

The Shifter just smiled lazily, flashing sharp teeth in the process. "Oh no," he assured her. "No problem at all. Just curious if the Crown sent you to take one of us out of here in handcuffs." His smile grew, turning slightly feral. "And if you're looking for volunteers."

His voice held enough sexual purr that Fey's toes curled slightly. Fuck, was every male here nothing but walking sex appeal? No wonder this place was so popular.

"Why do I get the feeling you flirt with every woman who walks in here?" she asked, teasing.

The bartender laughed. "No, no—I definitely have a type." He leaned a little closer to her, and Fey couldn't help the slight blush that rose to her cheeks. He drummed his fingers on the wood of the bar top, and she noted that his fingers ended in claws. Sharp. Dangerous.

"Actually," Fey said, trying to ground herself. It would be too easy to get distracted, too easy to give in and finish her drink, to leave without doing what she came here to do. She feigned another sip from her glass. "I'm here to see the owner. Do you know if he's in tonight, or when he might—"

CRASH.

The sound of a door slamming above was loud enough to shake the floor, and the bottles on the bar wall rattled. Fey winced. Well, that answered her question.

The bartender's eyes tracked something behind her. "Oh, he's here alright," he said, a smile curving up one side of his face. "And I get the impression he's been looking for you, too."

He shot Fey a sympathetic look.

"Well, well, well," a voice snarled from behind Fey as Alastair stalked across the room, radiating fury. A few patrons glanced up, only to quickly look away again, fear in their eyes. He wore a suit again, identical to the one she'd seen him in before. Dark, and expensive. He moved with a slow, deliberate grace and didn't stop until he was standing directly behind Fey's stool, towering above her. "This is a pleasant fucking surprise, don't you think?"

Fey's heart rate jumped at the sound of his voice, but she kept her face impassive, placing her drink down on the bar with deliberate care and slowly turning around in her seat.

"Hello, Alastair." She rested her elbows on the bar top and tilted her face up to smile at him.

He looked furious. Though Fey supposed to anyone else he might have looked casual, standing with his hands in the pockets of his slacks. But his eyes flashed with anger, and a muscle in his jaw twitched as he looked down at her, his gaze drinking in every detail of the Witch before him.

A woman's appearance was just as much a tool as any other weapon in her arsenal, and Fey had spent time perfecting her look before she arrived here tonight. In place of the skintight dress he'd seen her in last time, she wore a pair of dark pants and a white cashmere sweater, baggy enough at the neckline that it fell from her shoulder and displayed the full expanse of her collarbones. She'd wanted to accentuate her neck, so she wore her hair up in a high ponytail, leaving her cream-colored skin on full display.

She hadn't bothered with a healing elixir after she'd last seen him, and the faintest remnants of a bruise still graced the side of her neck—a reminder to him of what they'd done in those few minutes they were alone. His eyes lingered on it.

But from the way his teeth ground together as he looked her up and down, Fey couldn't tell if he was mentally undressing her, or skinning her.

"I have to say," he said, when he finished assessing her, his golden eyes finally settling on hers. "It takes a lot of fucking balls for you to walk back into my club after what you did."

Mentally skinning me, Fey decided.

"I think you of all people would know whether or not I have balls," Fey countered. The bartender developed a sudden coughing fit that sounded a lot like laughter.

"Jasper, you have five seconds to fuck off somewhere else," Alastair snapped, glancing over.

The bartender, Jasper, only shrugged, grinning. "I've got nowhere better to be, boss." And then, as if to emphasize his point, he poured himself a drink and brought the glass to his smile to sip it.

Alastair snarled, then turned his gaze back to Fey. He took a step towards her, and she wondered vaguely if he would kill her in front of all these witnesses.

I should stop pushing him like this, Fey thought. *I need to stop pushing him like this.*

But he made it *oh so* fun.

Instead of murdering her in cold blood, though, he leaned in, placing a hand on the bar on either side of her, caging her in place with his body. "So why *are* you here, Witchling?" he asked, his face barely an inch from hers. "Have you come back to beg for my forgiveness? Or... did you forget something the last time you were here, hmm?"

Fey's pulse raced as he leaned even closer, whispering directly into her ear. "I found the gift you left on my desk for me."

He leaned back just far enough to look her in the eyes, and his tongue slid across his bottom lip suggestively. Oh, right. She had forgotten about the pair of panties she'd left behind on his desk.

Oops.

"Actually," Fey started, fighting to keep her voice calm. "I came back because I need your help."

Alastair blinked. He stared at her in absolute wonder for a moment, his face mere inches from her own, before barking out a laugh and stepping back.

"You need *my* help? After you broke into my office?" Alastair ran his hand through his black hair, ruffling it and shaking his head in amazement. "You must be fucking insane, Witchling. Do you even have any idea who the fuck I am?"

Fey shrugged like it didn't matter, like she didn't care. And she didn't. She was a Blade, and there wasn't a Vamp out there in the realm who would outrank her.

Baffled, Alastair said, "Give me one fucking reason why I should even consider helping you."

"Because I'm willing to bet that deep down you're actually a decent guy," Fey offered, and Alastair threw back his head to laugh.

"You'd lose that fucking bet," he chuckled.

"I don't think I would," Fey answered. Her temper was rising, and she couldn't help the bite in her voice.

"And why's that?"

"Because of what happened to Alicia," Fey countered.

All the air in the room seemed to vanish at those words, and Alastair went very, very still.

"You're going to want to think long and hard about the next words out of your mouth," he whispered.

"You remember Alicia, don't you?" Fey continued, ignoring the warning. "She was a bartender of yours about two years ago, before she went missing."

Someone was growling, and the danger in that sound made the hair on Fey's arms stand at attention. It was the bartender, Jasper.

"Keep her name out of your mouth," Jasper snarled. Gone was the flirtatious smirk, gone were the bedroom eyes. A predator stood behind the bar, staring at her, and Fey could see the beast that lived under his skin clawing to be let out.

She didn't care. Fey gave him a cold smile in return and let her own monster show through, just a little.

"Everyone knew she was murdered," Fey continued, turning back to address Alastair, ignoring the snarling Wolf, ignoring everything else to address him, and only him. "Even before the body turned up. And everyone knew who did it. Her boyfriend had a history of hurting women who wouldn't listen to him."

Alastair was so still, so very still, as she continued.

"So no one was surprised when he disappeared a few days later. Even the Crown assumed he had run to escape justice. To escape the Blades."

Alastair laughed, cruelly. "Like the Queen's Blades give a shit about what happens to Fallen like us?" he sneered.

Fey ignored him. "But he didn't run away, did he? And pieces of him started to turn up, all around the city, at every dive bar, at every seedy restaurant this asshole liked to frequent. A message from someone powerful. A message to all the abusive fucks out there that no one, *no one*, hurts someone under *your* protection. Isn't that right?"

The growling from Jasper stopped.

"What makes you think I had anything to do with it?" Alastair asked, voice low and dangerous.

"Everyone knows who that message was from," Fey said. It was true. The dossier she'd assembled made it very clear the Crown knew about it but didn't care. Just trash taking care of trash. "Rumor has it that no one hurts a woman in this club if they want to live. So, yeah, I'm willing to bet the Vamp who tracked down that murdering piece of shit and cut him into pieces might be a decent guy under all the bluster. And he might be willing to hear me out."

Alastair smiled, and for one brief moment, Fey felt hope.

"And like I said," the Vamp purred. "You'd lose that bet."

Hope is a dangerous thing. It fractured in Fey's chest, and she could feel the sharp edges of it cutting her heart.

"Even if what you're saying is true, even if I did all of that, it doesn't mean I'll help you," Alastair told her. But there was something there, something in his eyes that let Fey know she had a chance.

Or... maybe that was just her desperation. Maybe that was just her hoping, beyond hope, that someone, anyone, would be willing to help.

"Please," she said as Alastair turned away. The words sounded so weak coming out of her mouth. But he stopped. "Please, I...I don't have anywhere else to turn right now. I'm at a dead end and I...I just... please. Please, just hear me out."

Fey hated the weakness in her voice when she said it, hated the pleading tone to her words, but it was the truth. All of it. She was out of options, out of time. And she was willing to beg if it would help get her answers. Even if she couldn't look at herself in the morning.

She'd do anything for Alice.

Alastair turned and stared at her, assessing. Then he sighed, long and loud, tipping his head back to do so.

"Fuck the Goddess, I must be out of my fucking mind, too," he said, raising his hands in mock surrender. "Fine. Fuck it. You get two minutes."

Hope, that stupid, treacherous emotion, flared to life again. Fey tried not to look too pleased, tried not to smile as she looked up at him and nodded.

"Two minutes," she repeated.

"Meet me in my office. I'll be right there," he said. His eyes flicked up to hers with a dry amusement when he added, "You remember where my office is, don't you, Witchling?"

It took effort not to bare her teeth at him. Accepting the dismissal, she stood, moving toward the stairs that led to the second floor. Behind her, Alastair leaned against the bar, speaking in a low voice to the bartender.

CHAPTER 15
ALASTAIR

She had left.

The fucking Witch had left him high and dry, and now she was back, acting like she hadn't given him the worst case of blue balls in his life. Acting like she hadn't been grinding against his fucking hand the last time she'd seen him.

He'd practically raced through his work with Ferus that night—he'd been itching to get back to his office, itching to get back to her. And when he'd returned, what had he found? An empty fucking office.

Well... empty, save for a pair of black panties conspicuously left in the middle of his desk. Panties soaked with her scent, with her proof that she'd enjoyed what he had done to her.

At first, he couldn't believe it. She'd been putty in his hands, even without the persuasion, and he knew she'd been enjoying herself. Hell, she'd been close to coming for him, so fucking close, before Ferus had interrupted them. It would have been the first of many he was willing to give her that night.

Alastair had been in a rage when he'd found her gone. Even more wrathful when he'd noticed the gift she'd left behind to mock him. He wasn't proud of the surge of arousal he'd felt at finding her soaked panties. Wasn't proud of how hard he'd come that night with them wrapped around his throbbing cock.

Shaking those thoughts from his head, Alastair tried to focus as he headed back to his office, back to the Witch waiting for him there. Years of running seedy bars and clubs had given him a sixth sense for trouble, and this Witch was trouble.

He'd hear her out and be done with her. The last thing he needed was more trouble. No, scratch that, the *second* last thing he needed was trouble. The absolute last thing he needed was a Witch who had somehow wrapped him around her little pinky in the few minutes they'd spent together. A Witch he hadn't been able to stop fantasizing about.

She was sitting on his desk when he finally got to his office, her long, elegant legs crossed, feet dangling in the air.

Alastair stopped on the threshold, frowning at the open and unlocked door, at the Witch perched nonchalantly on his desk. She looked up at him with wide, innocent green eyes.

"You really shouldn't leave your door unlocked," she said, voice dripping with sincerity. "Who knows what sort of criminals could get in?"

Alastair snorted. It *had* been locked. And, just like before, it hadn't presented any sort of barrier to her. "Clever trick, Witchling," he said. He didn't close the door behind him, but he made a sound of appreciation as he looked at her on the desk. "This certainly brings back memories," he purred.

She had the decency to blush before hopping off his desk. Her sweater shifted up as she did so, and he caught a glimpse of her ass in those skintight pants.

He couldn't help the mental image that jumped into his head. The image of him on his knees, peeling those pants from her long legs. He imagined propping her back up on that desk and worshiping her with his mouth until she screamed...

Alastair cleared his throat.

Yeah, those were exactly the sort of thoughts he didn't need right now.

"Sit," he said, and she did, slipping into the chair before his desk and settling against the backrest.

She looked different like this. More comfortable. He'd loved the look of that tight dress on her, but this looked more... *her*. Relaxed.

"So," Alastair started. He stood over her, and she had to crane her neck up to look at him. It was petty, Alastair knew, but today he was feeling pretty fucking petty, and he sure as fuck was going to lean into it. "You have two minutes, Witchling."

Her eyes flashed with a spark of anger. "My name isn't *Witchling*. You don't hear me calling you *leech*, do you?"

He raised an eyebrow at her. "Cute. So, what should I call you? Thief? Cock tease?"

"Fey," she snapped. "My name is Fey."

"*Fey*." He liked the way it sounded. Liked the way her breath hitched when he said it. "You have two minutes, *Fey*."

"Are you always like this?" she snapped.

"Like what?"

"Like a fucking ass."

Oh, he liked this. He liked playing with her.

"Let me be very clear, *Fey*. You came here to my club, and you broke into my office. Now you're here again, uninvited and demanding my help. So, I think I'll act however the fuck I want."

He reached out, running a finger down the crook of her neck, delighting in the way her pulse leaped in response. "You should be thankful. There are women here every night who would beg for two minutes of my undivided attention. And I think you remember what I can do in such a short period, don't you?"

She swallowed.

And someone from the doorway cleared their throat, loudly.

Alastair pulled his hand back, all sexual tension vanishing from the room as though it was never there. "Come in," he said, shoving his hands into his pockets, the pinnacle of professionalism.

Right.

Jasper entered the office, two drinks in hand. He set a whiskey neat in front of Alastair, and something deliciously red and full of crushed ice and cherries in front of the Witch before nodding at them both and leaving. If he'd noticed the pulse of desire in the room, he gave no indication, but to his credit, Jasper made sure to close the door behind him as he left.

And then it was just the two of them.

Alone.

Again.

Alastair took his drink and moved around the desk to his chair. He needed some space, needed some distance from this little Witch and her intoxicating scent. She was riling him up again, and *fuck,* he wanted to play with her.

Seemingly uninterested in him or why he'd moved away, Fey frowned at the drink in front of her.

"Go on," Alastair urged, nodding toward the drink. He took a sip from his glass, feeling the whiskey burn away a little more of his willpower.

"What is it?" she asked suspiciously. She plucked an obscenely red cherry from the glass, spinning the stem between her fingers, before dropping it back onto the ice.

"Jasper made it especially for you. It's called a Shirley Temple," Alastair answered with a condescending smirk.

When she raised an eyebrow at him, he laughed. "You might be fooling other people into thinking you were drinking earlier, but not me. And not Jasper. He was very offended you didn't have any of the drink he gave you down at the bar."

"How did—" she started, but Alastair held up a hand to stop her.

"You don't have a drop of alcohol in your system, Fey, and you didn't the other night either."

"There's no way you could have known that."

"Oh?" Alastair smiled. "I tasted you, remember?" His voice was dark, and he couldn't help the surge of desire racing through his veins at the memory. "And you want to know what I tasted in your blood? Power. Power, and fire."

From the way her pupils dilated, from the way her breathing hitched, Alastair knew the memory was affecting her as well.

"But you know what I didn't taste? I didn't taste any alcohol. Not one drop," he finished. He motioned to the drink again. "Try it. You'll offend Jasper if you don't. It's nonalcoholic... and I think the color suits you." He raised his glass to his lips again to hide his smile.

She considered the bright red drink before her but still hesitated.

"It's not poisoned," he insisted. "And ... wouldn't you be able to tell, anyway? I thought Witches could sense poison."

"Only Earth Witches," she admitted, "Which I'm not." For a moment he thought she would refuse the drink. He couldn't blame her. He was just some male she didn't even know, even worse some *Vamp* she didn't even know. But there was a challenge in his voice, a tacit dare hanging in the air between them, and he wanted to know if she'd rise to it.

Finally, eyes locked on his, she plucked the drink off the table and took a sip.

Her eyes widened, ever so slightly, as she tasted it, and he swallowed a laugh.

"It's... sweet. Like candy," Fey said, sounding almost amazed. She took another drink, more of a gulp, and Alastair found it very hard to pry his eyes away from the way she licked her lips, chasing the taste.

He smiled at her. "See? Jasper knows his shit."

She smiled back at him, just slightly, but it was enough.

"So," Alastair prompted. "You said you needed my help?"

Fey nodded, setting her glass down carefully. "My sister. She, uh, she was murdered. Almost two months ago."

Alastair leaned back in his chair, watching Fey closely. She was hard to read, this Witch, but he saw the pain flash in her eyes for just a moment before she shut it down. Her face hadn't changed, hadn't shown any real emotion, but it had been there, even for a fraction of a second.

"I'm sorry," he told her. And he meant it.

"This was the last place she was that night. Before she was killed," Fey finished.

"And you think someone here had something to do with it?" Alastair asked.

She shrugged a single well-muscled shoulder. Her sweater slid a little further down her arm, and Alastair found his eyes drawn to the skin there. "I don't know," she told him honestly, toying with her glass. She plucked a cherry from it by the stem and popped it in her mouth, chewing it thoughtfully. "But I'm out of leads. I'm at a dead end, and I feel... I feel—" She sighed, clenching the cherry stem in her hand. "I can't let it end, not like this. Not without knowing what happened. *Why* it happened."

Alastair didn't say anything. He just watched her, face impassive.

Finally, he shifted, leaning forward across the table to grab a pen and pad of paper.

"What was your sister's name?" he asked.

"Alice," Fey told him. "Alice Kelly."

"Age?"

"35. Dark skin, and short hair. As in 'cut above her ears' short."

He jotted it down. "Do you know what she was doing here that night?"

Fey shook her head. "Not really. I think she was meeting someone, maybe. She was—" The Witch stumbled, like it wasn't easy to explain. "She was investigating something. Something big. She had some sort of lead, we think, someone she was meeting about it, but..." A shrug. "That's all we know."

"We?" Alastair asked, glancing up from his notes and raising an eyebrow.

"Me and my other sisters," Fey clarified. He nodded, still writing.

"Do you have any idea what she was investigating?"

Fey nibbled on her lip, as though deciding whether to answer. "Yeah... we think she was following the trail of a drug dealer. Devil dust, probably."

Alastair's pen skipped, but he kept writing.

More fucking drugs in his club.

"Do you know the date and time she was here?"

She did, and she told him. She didn't tell him how she knew. Didn't tell him that her sister had spent hours combing through security footage of the city, finally finding footage of her entering the club at a quarter to 11 that night and leaving almost an hour later.

The entire time, Alastair kept writing. Finally, he set his pen down and gave her a heavy stare.

"How was she killed?" he asked, voice soft.

Fey didn't answer. She just looked at him blankly.

"You won't tell me how she was killed?" Alastair asked, incredulously.

"No," she answered, face betraying nothing.

Interesting.

"So, you don't know what she was investigating, you don't know who might be involved or why she was here, and you won't tell me how she was killed... For someone who needs my help, you're not very generous with the details," Alastair told her, tapping the pen against his notes.

Sometimes the easiest way to get someone to talk was just to give them space and wait. So, Alastair watched her. Watched and waited.

And, finally, it worked.

"This is why I was in your office," Fey admitted. "I was hoping I could find anything at all that would help us find out what she was doing here."

It wasn't a lie, though it might not have been the full truth. Still, it was enough for him to get started.

"I'll do what I can," Alastair told her. "I'll make some inquiries, check our video feeds, and see what I can find out."

She nodded. She even looked like she might thank him.

Or she did until he bared his fangs and said, "If that's all? I think we're done here... Unless, of course, you want to stay a little longer." He set his notes aside and stood, slowly circling the desk to stand in front of her. With her seated, her eyes right at waist level, she didn't need to guess at how her presence was affecting him. "I told you the last time you were here that I'd enjoy making you beg, Witchling."

"Fuck you," she spat at him, but her eyes lingered on his lap.

Alastair reached out, taking her face in his hand. Her pulse was quick against his fingers, and as he traced the curve of her bottom lip with his thumb, her breath hitched.

"Your two minutes are up, Witchling," he purred. "Time to get the fuck out of my office."

CHAPTER 16

At least the Vamp worked quickly, Fey thought.

Less than two days later, in the middle of fight training with her sisters, she got a text from an unknown number. A single line.

I have your info. Meet me at the club.

No need to say who it was from, no setting up a time to meet, no hint at what he'd found.

She stared at the message, dabbing the sweat from her forehead with a towel. Across the training room, Willow let out a snarl, followed by an audible shriek as Lilith flung her to the mat.

"Plant your *feet*," Lilith snapped. "How the fuck are you supposed to defend the realm if you can't even plant your feet?"

Another shriek, this time from Lilith, as Willow tackled her legs, bringing her to the ground.

"Who's that?" Joy asked, panting at Fey's side. She looked over Fey's shoulder at the message, as they both struggled to catch their breath.

"That," Fey told her with a smirk. "Is the owner of the club we visited. Alice's club."

Joy's eyebrows rose high enough that they nearly disappeared into her hairline.

"I asked for his help," Fey explained. "And it looks like he might have come through for us."

"Do you need backup?"

Fey slipped the phone back into the pocket of her exercise pants. "I'll tell you what—if I'm not home by morning, feel free to level the whole damn building, okay?"

Joy smiled. "Deal."

Snarls and swearing filled the gym as Lilith and Willow continued to wrestle, both refusing to tap out.

"And make sure those two don't kill each other while I'm gone," Fey said with a sigh. Joy just laughed.

***

"You Fey?"

The massive Shifter guarding the door of The Last Drop stared down at Fey when she arrived at the club. He spoke in such a low, growling voice, Fey vaguely wondered if he spent most of his time off work in his other, furrier, form. Maybe he wasn't used to speaking in something other than growls and howls.

"That's me," Fey answered, and the male grunted, moving aside, and opening the door for her. It was still early enough that the club wasn't open yet. Fey went to move past the giant male but jumped, startled when he tipped his head back and *howled*.

A moment later, another Wolf from inside the building howled in answer.

The Shifter grunted again. If he'd noticed her startle, he didn't show it.

"Boss is up in VIP. You need an escort?"

It was...sweet, almost.

"I'm good, big guy," Fey said, patting him on the chest and shooting him a patronizing smile. "But thanks."

The place was empty, and from the looks of it, most of the staff hadn't shown up for their shifts yet. Fey saw no sign of the handsome bartender she'd seen before and wasn't sure if what she felt was disappointed or relieved.

For the first time, Fey noticed the complete lack of windows in the club. It wasn't unusual, she supposed, since nightclubs thrived when there was barely enough light to see your hand in front of your face. But, still, it made a macabre sort of sense to her. What's the point in windows, anyway, when your owner can't be caught in the daylight?

Sure enough, just as the Wolf had promised, Alastair was seated in the empty VIP section, drinking, and watching her as she crossed the room toward him. He said nothing when she approached, just motioned her to sit down opposite him.

"I have the information you wanted," he told her as she slid into the booth.

For a moment Fey thought he might ask for something in return, some form of payment. But he only stared at her for a few moments, before reaching under the table and producing a crisp tan folder. He slid it across the desk toward her, and Fey took it, her mouth dry.

Inside there were photos—blurry, but still high enough resolution for her to make out enough detail. Photos of Alice. Alice, sitting in a booth she recognized from downstairs in the club. Alice, drinking something, staring into the distance.

Alice, speaking to a male.

"Do you recognize him?" Alastair asked, leaning forward to tap his finger next to the photo. It was hard to make out his face, but he had long dark hair, a bushy beard, and thick-rimmed glasses.

"No," Fey shook her head. She was... disappointed. As though she'd expected to recognize whoever it was, as though she'd expected it to be someone she knew.

But Alastair leaned back in his seat, nodding like it confirmed what he already knew.

"His name is Phillip," he said. "Phillip Danvers. And he's a ghost."

She glanced up at him in confusion, and he waved the word away. "A nobody," he clarified. "A nothing. He's not a regular here, so I had no reason to look out for him, but after I pulled the security cameras from that night, I sent out some feelers."

Fey nodded, and he kept going.

"He's not a drug dealer."

Now that? That was a surprise, and it must have shown on Fey's face because Alastair shrugged.

"I know that's not what you were expecting, and I'm sorry, but he's not."

"I don't understand," Fey told him. "Alice was looking into some sort of club drug—so he's not the dealer?"

"As far as I can tell? No."

"So, what is he? A whistleblower?"

Alastair shook his head and sighed.

"As far as I can tell, Witchling, this guy is about as far from being involved in the drug trade as you can get. He's squeaky clean—and that's not something I'm used to finding when I send my hounds out to hunt down someone's secrets. He's a professor, of all fucking things, at the City University, in the Med Witch department. No ties to any gangs, no ties to the dipshits in Prey for the Crown, no ties to anything even remotely shady as far as I can tell. He's never been arrested, never had a complaint filed against him with the Crown. The guy is as clean as they come."

Fey was shaking her head. It didn't make any sense. "I don't understand. If he's clean, why was she here meeting him that night?"

Alastair considered her. "Is it possible she was seeing him?" he asked. "Romantically?"

The question immediately conjured an image of Joy. The touches that passed between her and Alice. The smiles, the secret glances. The nights spent in each other's bedrooms, close enough that Fey could hear them. "No," Fey shook her head. "No. She had someone else."

Alastair's stare was intense. "That doesn't always stop people," he said, carefully.

But Fey only laughed. "It would have stopped her. She was happy, Alastair. She was..." Fey searched for the words. "Understood. She had someone who understood her, really understood her. Someone who loved her. She didn't need anyone else."

Alastair nodded like he knew how important that was. Hell, maybe he did.

"Even if she strayed, trust me," Fey insisted. "It wouldn't have been this guy. It wouldn't have been..." She nibbled her lip. "It wouldn't have been any *guy*."

Alastair's lip twitched. "She wasn't into males?"

"Can you blame her?" Fey asked, her smile sharp as a knife.

"Oh, I don't know." Alastair's eyes sparkled. "I think some of us can serve a useful purpose if we know what we're doing."

Fey rolled her eyes. She didn't want to flirt with him, not tonight.

"So..." She looked at the man in the photo, memorizing his face. He looked... so ordinary. Normal. "He's not a dealer. Not a whistleblower. What was he doing with Alice, then?"

"That's a question for you to answer."

Fey huffed, shuffling through the photos, flipping through them, looking for something, anything. She stopped on one, leaning forward over the image to look closer.

"What's this?" she asked, pointing.

"He gave her something," Alastair told her. "My cameras aren't good enough to pick up what it says, though. A stack of papers, it looks like."

Fey stared at the photo, a still image of the man, Phillip, handing a few sheets of paper to Alice. Fey flipped to the next image.

The man was leaving, and Alice wasn't watching him go. She was staring at the pages in front of her.

Shaking, Fey flipped through the remaining photos. Alice, reading. Alice closing the packet. Alice sitting there, thinking.

There was a look on her face, one almost indescribable. But Fey knew that look.

It was betrayal.

This was it. This hadn't been a waste at all. Whatever that man had given her, that was the answer to their questions. That was the reason Alice had been killed.

All they had to do was find Phillip Danvers and find out what was on those pages.

"Thank you," Fey told Alastair. "Can I keep these?"

"Of course," he said, motioning to the photos on the table with elegant fingers. "They're yours."

But she didn't move to gather them. Didn't move to put them away.

"Something tells me you're not doing this out of the kindness of your heart," Fey said, finally, her voice barely a whisper. "So, tell me, Alastair—what do you expect in payment for this information?"

She hesitated to ask. Hesitated to know what she'd give him for this, what she'd hand over willingly, happily, regardless of how she might feel afterwards.

Alastair shrugged. "I want a lot of things, Witchling. I want every drug dealer within five miles of this building dead. I want the freedom to do whatever the fuck I want, without having to answer to anyone." He looked at her, then, his eyes afire with intensity. "And I want you looking up at me with those perfect green eyes while you suck my cock."

Fey clenched her teeth together. This was it, then.

"But we don't always get what we want, do we?" He smiled, and it was almost a little sad. "So, consider this a gift. And if you need to think of this as transactional, remember I don't like trash in my club. And I'm more than happy to do my part to get rid of it. This guy might be a ghost, but if had something to do with your sister's murder, well..." He cleared his throat. "I don't need that kind of shit around here, you know?"

"No payment?" Fey asked.

"Consider us even," Alastair smiled at her. "No payment necessary."

It was... a relief, Fey realized. She gathered the photos into a pile, slipping them back into the folder.

"Thank you," she told him, again.

He smiled at her and turned back to his drink.

"Come back and see me anytime, Witchling," he said. "I don't need any payment for this, but I'll be right here if you're ever looking for some fun."

CHAPTER 17

Joy and Lilith stared down at the photos spread out on the table, silent and still.

"What were you up to, Alice?" Joy asked, her voice heavy with pain, as she traced the image of Alice sitting in the booth at The Last Drop with her finger.

"So, what do we know about this guy?" Lilith asked.

Fey shrugged. "Joy pulled some information about him and his work. Alastair said he was clean. He works at the university—some sort of Med Witch professor, I guess."

The City University was funded through the Crown, and though it was open to all Factions and genders, it was mostly attended and staffed by males from the Witch Faction. Without any elemental power, the prospect of advancing the realm through research and knowledge was an attractive career option for many of them.

"*Alastair*, huh?" Joy asked, her eyes sparkling with barely constrained laughter. "You're on a first-name basis with the club Vamp now?"

"Fuck off," Fey answered. "He's helping us, okay?"

"Why *is* he helping you, anyway?" Lilith asked, smiling. "You donating a little blood to the cause, sister?"

"And you can fuck off, too," Fey answered. Lilith laughed.

"I have to say, I didn't peg you for a Fang Chaser, Fey." Lilith continued, ignoring the scowl Fey shot her. "Tell me, how big are his fangs, anyway? Is it true what they say? That it's proportional to his—"

Fey swung a wild punch, and Lilith dodged it easily, laughing and hopping aside.

"I'm not fucking a Vamp," Fey snarled.

"That sounds like something a Witch who was fucking a Vamp would say," Joy told her.

"Fey's fucking a Vamp?" Willow asked, walking into the room and heading straight for the kitchen. She pulled a box of cereal from the pantry and hummed to herself as she filled a bowl.

"Fuck all of you," Fey answered. "But Lilith in particular."

Lilith snickered.

"Where have *you* been, little sister?" Joy asked, watching Willow.

"In Lilith's library," Willow answered, pouring milk into her bowl. "Reading about some of the other Blades."

"Find anything fun?"

Willow nodded enthusiastically, spooning cereal into her mouth. "Oh yeah. Did you know the Queen *can't* be poisoned?"

Lilith smiled. "We did."

"But tell us why, sister," Joy prompted.

"You can't poison a Witch with Water and Earth," Willow answered, smiling proudly. "An Earth Witch can sense poison, and a Water Witch can heal it if she knows what it is. Something about the combo—*boom*, poison resistant."

Fey remembered this, remembered the enthusiasm she felt after her induction, with the sudden knowledge that was available to her. It's curious how much of their history was kept under tight lock and key, available only to a select few.

"So, what're you all up to?" Willow asked around a mouthful of cereal.

Joy beamed. "We're going to dress up like college students and track down some sketchy professor—want to come?

Willow smiled widely. "Totally!"

Fey rolled her eyes, stacking the papers in front of them. Joy had managed to gather quite a lot more information about the professor who had met with Alice, including his class schedule and a copy of his university ID, complete with an ID photo.

Spooning another bit of cereal into her mouth, Willow gestured at the picture on the table, the one from the professor's ID, showing him with a goofy grin half hidden in his beard and thick black glasses. "Hey...why do you guys have a photo of Phillip Danvers?"

Fey's heart skipped a beat at the same time that Lilith hissed.

"You know who this is?" Fey asked, pointing at the photo.

Her voice came out with more intensity than she'd intended, and Willow froze, the spoon hanging from her mouth.

"It's okay, you're not in trouble, Willow," Joy soothed, walking over to put a comforting hand on Willow's shoulder. "Right, Fey?" she added, pointedly shooting a glare toward Fey.

"No, sorry—you're not in any trouble, sister. I just..." Fey took a deep, calming breath. Her thoughts rattled loudly in her skull. "I need to know how you know this man, Willow. It's important, okay?"

Willow nodded slowly, swallowing her mouthful of cereal.

"Do you know how we can get in contact with him?" Joy asked, gently.

"Well," Willow sighed. "See, that's going to be a problem."

Fey's hands clenched at her sides. "Why is that a problem, Willow?"

Willow smiled sadly. "Because Phillip Danvers was my first assignation as a Queen's Blade. He's dead, Fey. Very, very dead."

CHAPTER 18
WILLOW

"Um, excuse me?"

Sean looked up, blinking. A Witch stood in front of him, in a short flowy sundress, clutching a stack of books to her chest and chewing at her bottom lip.

"Uh... hey, yeah." He shuffled some of the books on his lap nervously. "What's up?"

She was breathtaking. Almost literally, as Sean found it hard to draw a proper breath while looking at her. Her curly brown hair surrounded her adorably round face like a halo and the way the top of her dress clung to her curves...

Sean swallowed audibly.

"I just moved here from the fifth octant," the girl was saying to him. "And I'm supposed to meet with my advisor, Professor..." She struggled with the books and papers she clutched against her chest, jostling and bouncing her breasts as she searched for a scrap of paper. "Ah! Here it is —Professor *Danvers*. Do you know where his office is?"

Sean's face fell. "Uh, yeah, I do, but I'm so sorry to tell you this— Professor Danvers went missing a few days ago. No one's seen him, and no one knows where he is."

"Disappeared?" A blonde woman appeared at the girl's side,

frowning. She was equally beautiful, though a few years older, and wearing significantly more clothing. "It wasn't anything... dangerous, was it?"

She sounded so concerned, so scared, that Sean found himself jumping to reassure her.

"Oh, no, no, I'm sure it's nothing dangerous," he insisted. "The city is safe, honest—and nothing bad happens on campus. There's nothing to be worried about."

"See?" The brown-skinned angel in front of him beamed. "I *told you* it was safe here." She juggled with the books in her arms once more, holding out her entire arm to offer him her hand. "I'm Willow," she said, smiling. "And this is my sister."

Sean blinked, standing to shake her hand, and looking between the two of them. The white-skinned blonde woman certainly didn't look like she could be her *sister*. But he knew enough about Witches to know they had a strange sense of family. Didn't members of the same coven sometimes call each other sister?

"I'm Sean," he introduced himself.

"So," Willow asked in a loud stage whisper. "What *did* happen to him, then?"

Sean shrugged. "No one knows, yet. But I don't think he's originally from the city, so he probably just went home and didn't bother to tell anyone. He has a husband, I think, in one of the inner octants, so he probably just had a family emergency and had to take off with no notice, you know?"

That was the gossip, at least, after Professor Danvers failed to show up to his last few classes.

"And you're sure it's safe here?" the blonde pressured, frowning. She put a protective hand on her sister's arm.

"Oh, totally. The safest place in the city. You don't have anything to worry about. Your sister will be safe here." He gave her his most sincere smile, the one he used whenever he picked up a girl from her parents' house for a date, and the woman visibly relaxed.

"Well," Willow sighed. "I guess I won't be meeting with Professor Danvers after all... Did you know him? Like, personally?"

"Yeah, uh, I did. I mean, I do. I'm taking his class in Medicinal

Chemistry this quarter, and I had him for History of Medical Witchcraft last year. He's a great professor, really engaging."

"And... is he nice?"

"Oh, totally," Sean continued. Her sister pulled out her cell phone, frowning at something, and wandered a few steps away to take a call. It gave them a little space to chat, and Sean silently thanked the Goddess. He could talk to this girl all day. "If he's your advisor, you'll have no problems. The guy is a total softy. And open-minded—he sponsors all sorts of university clubs, even for the Shifters."

"Are... are you a Shifter?" the girl asked, eyes wide.

He tried not to smile, tried to ignore the giddy feeling in his chest. Of course, she had no idea if he was a Shifter. If she was from one of the outer octants, she probably hadn't ever met a Shifter before. Outside the Eternal City, Factions kept to themselves, and fraternization between them was rare—even rarer the further away from the city you got.

He could be the first Shifter she'd ever talked to. The thought made him smile.

"I am," he answered, and her mouth formed a shocked circle that was just too adorable. "But don't be scared. We're harmless." He dropped his voice to make sure her sister couldn't hear him, but she seemed preoccupied with her phone, ignoring them entirely. "Me, especially. I'm not even a predator."

"What... what are you?" Willow asked. And then, immediately, she blushed. "Goddess, is that rude to ask? Did I just, like, totally insult you?"

Sean laughed. Goddess bless him, could this girl get any cuter? "No, it's fine. I don't mind at all. But to answer your question, I'm a Deer Shifter."

"Do you... do you have horns?" Willow asked, and she sucked her bottom lip between her teeth, almost involuntarily.

Sean's blood heated. This gorgeous Witch sounded so intrigued, so interested... in him.

"Yeah," he told her, his voice husky. "Yeah, I have antlers."

"Wow," she whispered back. "Antlers."

"We should go," her sister interrupted, finally coming back over. "If your advisor has gone missing, maybe we can go speak with the dean and find out who you're supposed to meet with instead?"

"Yeah, okay," Willow told her, and Sean felt his luck finally run out. Oh, well... he had class in a few minutes anyway, so it wasn't like he could have stayed chatting with her all afternoon. He leaned down to start gathering his books and his notes.

"Hey, Sean?"

Sean glanced up, and the Witch was looking at him with big, inviting eyes.

"Would you mind showing us around?" Willow asked. "We don't know the campus, and you seem just like... so smart." She blushed and looked away. "If you're not busy or anything, I mean?"

What the hell, he could miss one class, right?

"Uh, sure," he said, trying not to blush as the girl beamed at him. "Why not?"

"Maybe we can stop by Professor Danvers's office, just in case he came back? And you could tell us a little more about him and these clubs he sponsors."

Sean smiled. "Yeah, totally. I can do that."

CHAPTER 19

"Y ou gave him your number?" Fey asked incredulously, eyebrow raised.

"What?" Willow snapped. "He was nice, Fey. And you should have seen how he blushed when I asked about his antlers."

"It was embarrassing," Joy admitted, but her smile was warm. "The poor guy was so smitten with her, we couldn't have gotten him to shut up if we tried."

Fey had to hand it to them—they'd managed to gather a rather absurd amount of information about Phillip Danvers in only one day at the university. Most of it, they already knew from Joy's research and what Alastair had told them.

But Alastair's sources had been wrong about one thing: Phillip Danvers *was* a member of Prey for the Crown—a group of Shifter extremists dedicated to overthrowing the Witch regime and installing a government representative of *all* Factions. Or, if not a card-carrying member, he was at least sympathetic to the cause.

"He lets a group of PFTC members meet in his classroom every week, after hours," Joy explained. "We tried to get an invite, but—"

"But no one was going to give two Witches access to an anti-Witch group," Fey finished with a frustrated sigh.

"Exactly."

Willow had even swiped a copy of Professor Danvers's doctoral dissertation from his office. They'd found it 'mysteriously' unlocked when the Shifter had taken them by it and convinced him that there was no harm in looking around.

Fey read the cover, *An Investigation on the Ethical Ramifications of Allium Therapy in the Treatment of Sanguine-Focused Elemental Magic* by Dr. Phillip Danvers, and felt her eyes drift out of focus. She flipped through the pages of the book absently, stopping to read bits and pieces every few paragraphs.

'*While effective in the dissolution of any individual power sets, the use of Allium has historically been confined to only one elemental practice. I refer, of course, to that of Sanguine-Focused craft, colloquially called 'Blood Magic'.*'

"What is 'Allium,' anyway?" Fey asked aloud. She flipped to another page, skimming it.

Joy shrugged, clearly as in the dark as she was, but Willow perked up in her seat.

"Allium? It's a poison," she said excitedly. "They used to use it ages ago, to dampen Blood Magic. There's a whole book about it in Lilith's library."

"Blood Magic?" Fey mused. Of all the elemental gifts, only Blood Magic—the power to bend people and minds to a Witch's will—was forbidden. It was a thankfully rare power and one that had been actively destroyed from the bloodlines. Fey flipped back to the title page of Phillip's dissertation. "An Investigation on the Ethical Ramifications of Allium Therapy in the Treatment of Sanguine-Focused Elemental Magic," she read. "Okay... so, what, this is about how they used Allium to fix Blood Witches?"

"Well," Willow made a face. "'Fix' is a pretty shitty description, honestly. Allium cut off access to their power, completely. One day you have power over blood, and the next—bam, nothing, no gifts from the Goddess at all."

Fey felt ill just thinking about it. She remembered her dream, remembered the feeling of being cut off from her power. It made her stomach roil.

"They don't use it anymore, though," Willow said. "Someone came up with an antidote for it, and that was that. No use in giving it to treat Blood Magic if a Witch could just go out and find the antidote somewhere on the black market."

"So, what do they do now?" Fey asked. She immediately regretted asking. She knew what happened, now, when a Blood Witch was identified during their Awakening.

Knew, because she had been sent to kill one, once.

Blood Witches were too dangerous to let live. Too dangerous to be allowed to stay in their society. It was better for everyone if they were taken out before they got full control of their powers.

Fey tossed the book aside, not wanting to look at it anymore.

"You don't think Alice was chasing a Blood Witch... do you?" Willow asked. If Fey didn't know any better, she'd think that was fear in her sister's voice.

Joy shook her head. "No. No, I don't think so. There hasn't been a new Blood Witch identified in years, and I just don't think it's possible that one could slip through the Awakening without being noticed." Joy rubbed the palms of her hands against her eyes. "And even if she'd found one, why hide it from us? Why contact a *professor*, for that matter? The solution to a Blood Witch is death—Alice knew that. She wouldn't go looking into some... archaic cure."

"Agreed—I think the Blood Witch angle is a dead end." Fey sighed. "So... where does that leave us?"

"Prey for the Crown," Willow offered. "Look, I know they're kind of a joke. I met with them, I get it. They're..." She searched for the words. "They're kids. Just teenagers, looking to make a difference. I don't even think they're dangerous, but... I mean, what else could it be?"

"Maybe Phillip wasn't a member of PFTC at all," Joy mused. "Maybe we were closer to the truth when we thought he was a drug informant—what if he was feeding Alice information about PFTC meetings, giving her names, locations for events and attacks?"

"That..." Fey let the idea settle in her mind, let it fit itself like a puzzle piece with what else they knew. "That could be it."

"And she didn't tell you guys because...?" Willow asked.

"Because she didn't need to," Joy offered. "Because there wasn't a reason to tell us yet. Or, maybe, she didn't know who to trust yet?"

"Maybe she had reason to think someone close to the Queen was working with PFTC." Fey finished.

"Could that have been what Phillip gave her?" Willow asked. "What if he gave her some evidence that someone we trust was actively working to take down the Crown?"

Joy smiled sadly. "Well, if that's the case," she said, "then I think we have a lot more to worry about than just one murder."

"What if she *did* tell someone?" Willow asked. "Just hear me out— what if Phillip *was* involved with Prey for the Crown, and Alice was feeding information about him and the group to Dameon? I *was* sent to kill him, right? Doesn't that make way more sense than a plot to take down the Queen from within?"

Joy nodded, considering.

"We need more information," Fey insisted. "This is all just us guessing at this point. We need some evidence that Phillip was working with Alice on this, or that he was actively involved with PFTC, or... *anything*."

"Can't you just... you know, *ask?*" Willow suggested. "If Dameon sent her to gather information from Phillip, you could just ask him—"

"It's treason," Joy interrupted. She sighed. "Sorry, little sister, but there are rules to what we can and can't do, and questioning an assignation? Especially one we weren't even told about? That's treason against the Crown. It's questioning the Queen herself, and Dameon... Dameon doesn't react well to any threats against the Queen, even from us."

They lapsed into an uncomfortable silence.

"What did you do with Alice's stuff after..." Willow's voice trailed off.

It was hard to speak around the lump in her throat, but Fey managed. "We put everything together into boxes... everything that wasn't—"

Burned. She couldn't say it. The sentence hung in the air and died without another word.

"I'd like to look through it all if that's okay," Willow offered in a small voice. "I think you could use some fresh eyes on this, and I could—"

A knock on the door was the only warning they had before it opened, and Dameon walked in.

Fey sighed. Playing detective with Alice's death would have to wait.

Dameon was holding a black envelope.

CHAPTER 20

Devil dust had been a thorn in the Crown's side for years, and its quick popularity was making it almost impossible to keep in check. As a club drug, it was innocent enough. A little mixed in a drink, and you were euphoric, alert. Able to dance and fuck all night, and perfectly content to do either.

A little more? Pain no longer bothered you, exhaustion no longer seemed to slow you down. You were untouchable, a veritable god.

And a touch too much?

Fey had seen firsthand what the aggression from too much devil dust could do. Months ago, a group of Demons had gotten their hands on some, using it to help fuel an attack on one of the aristocratic Witch families in the third octant. It had been a bloodbath. And when they'd torn through the family, leaving no one behind, the Demons had turned on each other. Two had survived the night.

Like so many things, devil dust was fine in small doses, but oh so dangerous in the wrong hands and the wrong amounts.

"This is the place," Joy said, pointing out the building to them. She'd come the night before, after Dameon had delivered the address, to stake out the location and prepare for tonight.

The real issue with devil dust was it was impossible to stop it from flowing into the city, impossible to stop it from circulating among the population. It was relatively easy to make and even easier to sell. There was a lively, growing market for it, and the Queen was terrified about large doses of it ending up in the wrong hands.

Like Prey for the Crown, Fey thought. The group was, historically, non-violent. They wanted change, not bloody revolution. But the idea of so many Shifters, even the non-predators, ingesting enough of the drug to make them as deadly and bloodthirsty as those Demons had been? Yeah, that was scary enough to keep Fey up at night.

So, when Dameon had located a manufacturer right here in the city, when he had found an entire building's worth of devil dust?

That was something that demanded their attention.

Willow stared down at the warehouse below them. They were stationed on an adjacent rooftop, and from here they had a clear view of the single-story building below. And the guards that patrolled the perimeter.

The other side of the building faced a drop-off into the Western River. It was an almost certainly fatal drop, and even at this distance, Fey could hear the sounds of the river churning from where it hugged the edges of the Demon district.

"It doesn't look much like a drug den to me," Willow said. "It looks like a shoe factory."

Lilith snorted. "What *does* a drug den look like, little sister?" she asked in a mocking voice.

Willow shrugged. "I don't know. More... shabby? Dirty? Maybe some rave music and strobe lights?"

Joy giggled, but Lilith rolled her eyes.

"I'll be sure to tell Dameon the drug den wasn't sufficiently shabby enough for you. Maybe the next one he sends us to destroy will be better, huh?"

"How many guards?" Fey asked, and Joy frowned down from their vantage point to confirm.

"Three. Two patrols, one on the door. All Demons."

"See, sister?" Lilith cooed. "How many shoe factories have armed Demons patrolling them at night?"

Willow just shrugged. "Maybe the really expensive ones. Like, designer shoes." She chewed on her lip for a moment. "I've never fought a Demon before."

"They're easy," Joy assured her. "They're the weakest of all the Factions, furthest from the Goddess. Some of them can summon up a little elemental power, but it's nothing compared to what we can do."

Willow was shaking her head. "I heard they were like... all-powerful. Like... 'pull your skeleton right out of your body' powerful."

"Those are just *fairytales.*" Lilith rolled her eyes. "Scary stories to keep Witches up at night. If they were *ever* really that powerful, they sure as shit aren't anymore, especially the ones here in the city."

"All the powerful Demons live in the eighth octant," Joy explained. "Far away from here. And even then, I doubt they're even close to as powerful as the stories say they are. Trust me, little sis. This will be easy."

"Okay. Okay." Willow took a deep breath and smiled. "So... what's the plan?"

It was her first assignation with them all. And, as expected, Joy was in the mood to show off.

"Do you have eyes on the closest patrol?" Joy asked, glancing at Fey. The corner of her mouth curved into a smile.

Fey nodded. The Demon was slowly making his way around the building toward them and would be nearly directly below them in a few seconds.

Joy turned to Willow with a sparkling smile. "Ready to see our Fey in action?" she asked.

Willow's eyes widened, and Fey took a deep breath, closing her eyes and letting herself sink into her power. Relaxing her body, she let herself become a vessel.

Water. It was the element of life. The element of healing. But every creation from the Goddess has its shadow, its mirrored counterpart, and since life could never exist without water, it was, in its absence, just as easily an element of death.

The air was cold around them, the first touch of winter. But more importantly, the night was wet. It had rained earlier, and the air was heavy with it.

Water and air. Fey breathed them in, her power rejoicing under her skin.

The Demon was coming. His steps echoed in the dark alley below them. Twenty feet away. Fifteen. Ten.

Eyes closed, entirely focused, Fey could almost see him. She could hear his steps, his heartbeat, his breath. He took a deep inhale, filling his lungs with the cold night air.

Throat first, Fey thought. It was a trick she'd learned early on. Take out the throat, and they can't call for help. Can't scream while she takes them out, piece by piece.

Perfectly still, eyes closed, Fey commanded the water in the Demon's body to freeze.

Willow watched, wide-eyed, as the Demon below them stopped. He made a noise like he was choking, reaching his hands up to his throat. But he didn't scream, didn't yell to raise the alarm as he scratched at the outside of his throat, fingernails raking rivets into his skin, drawing lines of blood.

"Our bodies are over 60% water," Fey whispered, eyes still closed as she concentrated. The Demon's throat was fully frozen now, but she wasn't done. The ice spread down his larynx, creeping into the soft tissue of his lungs. "Did you know that, little sister?"

Willow swallowed audibly.

Fey could feel him suffocating, could hear him thrashing against the ground. The ice continued to spread. It filled the tiny spaces in his lungs, turning the tissue into ice. It coated his heart, slowing the frantic beating and spreading to the inner chambers. It spread up his arteries, creeping into his brain, through veins and capillaries.

The ice had started to creep into his fingertips when his heart gave one final, feeble jolt and stopped. The Demon's body slumped to the ground, curled around himself, ice crystals forming delicate patterns on his lips.

When Fey finally opened her eyes and looked at Willow, she wasn't surprised by the horror she saw in her sister's face. Not surprised, but maybe a little disappointed. Hurt. But this was the truth of what she was. This was the truth of her power.

"I didn't know Water Witches could do that," Willow said, softly.

"They can't," Lilith answered. "At least, no one's ever heard of it before."

"Our Fey is one of a kind," Joy crooned, her voice full of pride.

Willow considered this. Considered Fey, and the half-frozen body in the alley. Then she smiled.

"That's so fucking cool," she said finally.

The ache in Fey's chest lessened, and she grinned.

"It's harder the further away I am," Fey explained. "Easiest if I can touch them. And it's much easier to freeze than boil. Trust me I've tried."

Willow's eyes were wide. "You've *boiled* someone from the inside?"

"No," Fey corrected. "I said I've *tried*. I could, maybe, if I had any control over Fire, but..." She shrugged. "Air helps with freezing. And unless it's been raining, there's no way I can do it from a distance."

"Come on, let's get down there. We need to drag him out of sight before anyone sees him," Lilith said.

Joy hopped down from the roof, using air to float gracefully to the ground. She hooked her arms under the Demon and pulled him into the alley, depositing him unceremoniously behind a trash can.

"One down, two to go," purred Lilith.

They moved, four specters of death creeping through the night.

LILITH TOOK THE NEXT DEMON.

He passed right by them, unaware of what lurked in the shadows, the danger that was watching and waiting. When she slit his throat, he barely made a sound before crumbling to the ground. Willow dragged his body back into the alley with the other guard.

Joy took down the Demon guarding the door, her power pulling the air from her lungs before she even knew there was anyone there. She died silently, suffocating at their feet as they moved past her and through the doors.

There was no alarm when they entered the warehouse, no sudden shriek of a siren. It was quiet inside.

Lilith summoned a sphere of Fire, holding it out in front of her to give them enough light to see the building.

It was... incredibly unremarkable.

"Isn't this supposed to be some big drug stash?" Willow asked, her voice barely a whisper.

Fey nodded, frowning. Willow had been right earlier—this didn't feel like a criminal enterprise. The one-story building was just a single, enormous room full of wooden crates. Unremarkable, innocent-looking crates.

It really could have been a shoe factory, Fey thought, looking around. It looked like a storage facility.

Lilith shrugged her backpack to the ground, nodding to Joy to open it. Inside were stacks of plastic explosives, long white bars that just needed a spark to ignite. Lilith held her ball of Fire away from the bag, careful not to get too close to it.

It was a simple assignation. Take out the building and its contents, and leave. A few charges of plastic explosive set in the right places around the building, and *boom*—no more devil dust.

Fey didn't hear the Shifter approach until it was too late.

"Don't you fucking move," a voice snarled in her ear. His breath was hot and putrid. He held a knife to her throat, but his hand shook hard enough that the metal blade nicked at her skin.

"You tell your friends to drop their weapons, drop whatever it is they are holding, and I'll make sure you all get out of this alive," he told her.

It was an effort for Fey not to laugh.

"Sister?" she called out, ignoring him entirely. Her eyes met Willow's in the dark. "A little help, please?"

The knife at her throat glowed red hot, and the Shifter yelped in shock, dropping the blade before the metal had even started to melt. Fey dropped to the ground and rolled to the side as Willow struck, hitting the Shifter like an avalanche. She was a ball of knives and fists and fury. The Shifter screamed as she hit him, and they crashed noisily into a stack of wooden crates.

The male was dead before he hit the ground, but the momentum of Willow's attack shook the boxes. "*Shit,*" Willow hissed. She leaped away from the dead Shifter, but it was too late. The stack tilted and swayed, and several crates tumbled to the ground with a *crash*.

The sound echoed through the building, and Fey winced.

"Oh great, just fucking great." Lilith snapped. "So much for the element of fucking surprise."

Willow frowned at the mess on the warehouse floor, cringing. "Oops," she said.

"Oops?" Lilith mocked. Then she turned, scowling at Joy. "And what was that, Joy? *Who* was that? You said *three Demon guards*. It was your job to case this place. You didn't say anything about Shifters!"

Joy knelt next to the dead body, frowning. "I don't think he's a guard," she said, softly. She touched his face. "I don't know who he is."

Fey looked down at the body and couldn't help but agree with her assessment. He was a thin, spindly thing, barely more than a kid. A civilian. He didn't look anything like the predators they'd encountered outside.

He looked like... like prey.

That was it. He was a prey Shifter.

So, what was he doing here?

Lilith shook her head angrily. "I guess it doesn't matter who he was now, does it?"

Several of the crates that had hit the ground had broken open, spilling pieces of wood and glass shards over the floor. Something wet trickled from a box, spilling onto the ground, mixing with the grime on the warehouse floor.

Fey reached down and plucked a small glass bottle from where it had rolled from a crate to rest at her feet, holding it up. The liquid inside was golden, and it sparkled in the light like it was full of tiny, shimmering stars.

"Devil dust?" Joy asked, head tilted as she stared at the bottle in Fey's hands.

"I guess," Fey said. It was mesmerizing. Inviting. "I didn't expect it to be so..."

"Pretty?" Willow finished for her.

"There must be gallons of the stuff here," Fey said, gesturing to the crates that filled the building. "No wonder the Crown wanted this place leveled—there's enough drug here to dose the entire realm."

"Not for long," Lilith snorted. "Come on, help me place the rest of this. We need to get out of here. We've made enough noise to wake the dead, and I don't want to be blamed if another dumbass civilian gets themselves killed trying to investigate."

Lilith tossed a bundle of explosives toward Joy, and she caught it easily. Fey gave the golden liquid one last look before tossing it on the ground.

It took just a few minutes to place the rest of the explosives under Joy's careful supervision. There's an art to explosives, to leveling a building while limiting damage to the surrounding area. It wouldn't do to set the block alight, wouldn't do for the Queen's Blades to level part of the city. This mission was simple and surgical: Take down the building and everything in it but leave as little damage to the neighborhood as possible.

By the time the explosives were set and they were on their way back to the palace, the building burning behind them, the mesmerizing golden liquid was a distant memory.

CHAPTER 21

ey couldn't sleep.

She tossed and turned, pushing the sheets away, only to pull them back over herself a moment later. She couldn't get comfortable, couldn't get settled in her skin.

The adrenaline from their mission that evening had faded hours ago after they'd finished their report to Dameon, and she should have fallen into a deep, exhausted sleep after her bath. But something gnawed at her, something had her shifting uncomfortably on her bed, unable to lie still.

She was thinking about him.

She didn't want to, especially not after tonight. She was exhausted, and all she wanted to do was sleep. She didn't want to have her head full of thoughts of Alastair. Alastair kissing her. Alastair touching her.

Alastair's hand around her neck.

I'll be right here if you're ever looking for some fun.

Fey snarled and rolled over again in bed, kicking at her sheets.

He'd awakened something inside her that night in the club, and instead of fading over time like she'd hoped it would, it was growing. She'd tried taking care of the problem herself, her mind full of thoughts of him, her fingers between her legs. But even as she'd shuddered her release, biting her hand to stifle her cries, the ache had returned with a vengeance. It wasn't enough.

Fey growled in frustration, turning over again.

It wasn't any use. She was going mad lying here in the dark with nothing but her thoughts to occupy herself, and a dull constant ache between her legs.

There wasn't anything left to do.

Fey was a fixer. The Crown employed her to fix problems. Well, tonight she had a serious fucking problem. And she intended to fix it.

Before she could question the wisdom behind her decision, before she could stop herself or second guess what she was doing, Fey got out of bed, grabbing a pair of pants and a top from her closet.

She threw the clean clothing on and left, heading to The Last Drop.

CHAPTER 22

*T**his is a terrible fucking idea,* Fey thought to herself, her steps loud on the cobblestone street as she made her way through the city. But she didn't turn back.

It was nearly 1 am by the time she arrived at the club, and the line outside stretched around the block. She grimaced at the sight of it. There was no way she was desperate enough to stand in line just to see him. That was too much, even with the itch under her skin that drove her to come here in the first place. She was desperate, but not *that* desperate.

Absently, she walked past the people waiting, heading toward the door. She hadn't brought her phone, so it wasn't like she could message Alastair that she was downstairs. Maybe the bouncer would let her up to see him, maybe he could—

"Hey, babe!" someone shouted at her as she walked by. "Line starts back there!"

It was just some piece of shit Fallen standing in line, drunk and belligerent, but the words made her heart stop in her chest.

Hey, babe. A different voice said in her memories. A gentle voice. A voice full of love and safety.

It was how Alice had always greeted her, a warm smirk on her face.

She never knew why Alice called her that, but it had always made her feel special. Loved.

Hey, babe.

This was a mistake. Suddenly, everything around her was too much, too loud, too bright. The tight, sequined clothing worn by the people waiting to get into the club was overwhelming, the bass-heavy music she could hear from inside was jarring and out of sync with the pulse thudding in her ears. It was all too much. She needed to leave, she needed to go, she should run, run, run, get out of here as fast as she—

A hand grabbed her arm, and Fey felt her power fill her like a tsunami, a maelstrom of fury and death, as she turned on the male holding her with a snarl.

But... she knew him. The Wolf Shifter who held her arm—not tight, not holding her in place, just a comforting touch—was someone she recognized.

"Evening Fey," he greeted, in his low growl of a voice. It was the massive Wolf Shifter who had let her in before, the one who was waiting for her at the entrance the last time she'd seen Alastair. "That man bothering you?"

Her heartbeat calmed.

"Hey again, big guy," she said. Her voice was a little breathless, and tense, but the world around her felt a little less overwhelming with his massive hand on her arm, grounding her. She took a shuddering breath, and the power she had drawn into herself started to fade.

He was looking past her at the people in line, his eyes focusing on the guy who'd yelled to her, who'd called her babe. Then his eyes flickered to another Shifter standing at the door, and suddenly the male was being pulled out of line, pulled away from the club.

It was such a small thing, and wildly unnecessary. But the gesture made Fey smile. It was almost chivalrous.

"Thanks," she said.

"You can go in." He nodded toward the door. Already another Shifter had appeared to let people in. They were remarkably well coordinated. "The staff knows your scent, and the boss says you're welcome anywhere, at any time."

"My... scent?" Fey asked, raising an eyebrow.

The massive Shifter nodded, clearly seeing nothing strange or unusual or even remotely creepy in that statement.

"Ok... thanks," she said again. And, sure enough, when she approached the door to the club, the Wolf there nodded a greeting and stepped aside to let her pass without a word. No one from the line dared protest this time.

The club inside was even more overwhelming than she'd remembered, and Fey suddenly recalled why she'd hated this place the first time they'd come. The music was loud enough to shake her bones, and she could feel the bass in her teeth. People rubbed against one another on the dance floor, more sex than actual dancing, and it took more of Fey's skill than she'd like to admit getting through the crowd without being groped. She made her way through mostly unclothed bodies to the bar in the back. Toward a familiar face.

"Hey, Jasper," Fey called over the music. She leaned on the bar top. There were no open stools and barely enough room for her to squeeze herself up to the bar.

Jasper looked up from pouring a drink and nodded a greeting toward her. He set the drink on the bar, pushing it toward a customer and palming their coin before he waved her closer.

Ignoring the other patrons, Jasper flipped a latch under the bar top, and a portion of the bar opened like a door. Before Fey could protest, Jasper reached out, catching her by the waist of her pants and pulling her behind the bar, closing the swinging door behind her.

"The boss isn't in," he called over the music, leaning over her, his lips close enough to brush her skin. Fey's breath hitched as his words tickled over her ear.

"That's okay," she said. She needed to get out of here, needed some distance between her and the Shifter looming above her. Her body was too sensitive, too needy to have a male that hot standing this close to her.

Fuck, she needed to get laid.

"I think I'm just going to—" she started, but he cut her off.

"He isn't in *yet*," Jasper said over her. His fingers lingered for a moment on her waist, just long enough for her to think she'd imagined it before he leaned over her to grab a bottle and a clean glass from the wall behind her. "He had a family thing. But he should be here soon."

He poured a generous serving into the glass and held it out to her, eyebrow raised.

Fuck it. She wasn't working tonight, was she?

Fey took the glass, knocking back the shot. Jasper's answering smile was all wicked approval. He leaned over her again to grab another glass and poured her another shot before adding a healthy pour to his glass. Jasper ignored the customers around them vying for his attention, and within a few seconds, another Shifter appeared at the bar to take orders. They drank their shots together, Fey coughing at the burn in her throat.

"So, what did I do to deserve this special treatment?" Fey asked, straining to be heard over the music.

Jasper grinned. "The boss likes you. That means a lot to us here."

Fey tried to hide her smile.

"I'm glad you came back," he told her. "Especially tonight..."

When she just raised an eyebrow at him, he laughed and continued, "The boss has been biting everyone's head off since the last time he saw you. Ferus even sent a few girls to his office the other night to distract him, take some of his edge off."

Fey's lips thinned. She had no right to be jealous, had no right to care where he stuck his dick. But anger crept into her chest before she could help it.

"He sent them away," Jasper said, his smile growing wicked. "I think he's had a taste of something he liked, and he's not willing to settle for anything less."

The Wolf was still so close to her, his body right against her own, and Fey was sure he could feel the heat from her blush. Was Jasper flirting with her?

"Not that I blame him," Jasper said. His fingers caressed the glass in his hand. "You seem like the sort of woman men would crawl over broken glass to bed."

Oh yeah, he was flirting with her.

"So, you have a few choices here," he told her. "You can hang out behind the bar with me—" He glanced around them at the crowds. "But I don't think it's your scene, yeah? Or you can head up to the VIP area—they know who you are, and they'll let you in, no questions asked."

"Or?"

"Or," Jasper continued. "You can head up to the boss's office and wait for him there. It's quiet, and you won't be bothered." His eyes glittered. "His office is unlocked, and he should be in soon. Faster, even, if someone gets ahold of him and tells him you're here."

"Unlocked, huh?" Fey said with a smirk.

"Yeah, I think he's lost his faith in them. Seems like someone kept managing to get in, anyway." He winked.

"And what do you recommend?" she teased.

Jasper chewed his lips like he was giving it serious thought. Then he poured himself another shot.

"I think you should head up to his office," he said finally. "And fuck his brains out."

For just a brief moment when Jasper smiled at her, it was a predator's smile, something feral and dangerous, and Fey felt heat fill her body. This was the Wolf under the skin, the beast he really was. But then she blinked, and he was taking the shot he poured himself, the smile gone. Vanished, like it hadn't been there at all.

Before she could say anything, he was leaning past her again, opening the bar top to let her out.

"Thanks," she shouted over the music.

Jasper just winked.

———

It should have been a struggle to get across the crowded dance floor, but the moment Fey stepped out from behind the bar, the crowd seemed to shift to let her through, and before long Fey noticed the Shifters moving in the crowd around, herding the patrons to make room for her.

She recognized the Wolf waiting at the VIP rope by his voice immediately.

"Welcome, Fey."

"Hello Ferus," she purred. She took in the sight of him, even bigger than the massive Shifter she'd met outside.

Ferus lifted the rope without another word, letting her through.

Jasper was right—Alastair wasn't in his office when she entered, and the door was unlocked. The room smelled like him, she noticed immediately when she entered. Like cloves and wood smoke and whiskey. She took a deep breath, filling her lungs with it.

It was quiet here, the sounds from downstairs barely audible. It was... cozy.

Fey trailed her fingers over the books filling the wall shelves. She recognized a few, but most of them were... different from the books she was familiar with. Plucking one from the wall, she frowned at the cover.

Frankenstein by Mary Shelley.

Then, with nothing better to do than wait, she curled up in the armchair and began to read.

CHAPTER 23

Fey didn't have to wait long. Within the hour, the door to the office opened, and in he walked.

Alastair was furious. It radiated off him as he stalked inside his office, as he angrily ripped off his suit jacket and reached up to loosen his tie. Tension rolled off him in waves, and Fey recalled what Jasper had said, that he had some sort of family engagement tonight.

Some family, Fey thought to herself.

Alastair sensed her almost immediately, and he stopped dead, his hand on the knot of his tie. His nostrils flared, and his eyes snapped to where she lounged in his chair, legs curled up against the armrest.

The fiery rage in his eyes flickered and extinguished, and his lips curved into a slow smile.

"Alastair," Fey greeted him, slipping a scrap of paper into the book to mark her place. Her voice was cold and casual, but his presence made her pulse jump.

His smile grew. "Well, well, well," he purred. "This is a surprise." He continued to loosen his tie, pulling it off his neck smoothly and tossing it aside, eyes locked on her as he stalked closer.

She held the book up for him. "What is this?" she asked.

"A book," he answered. "Don't they teach you Witches anything?"

Fey snorted. "This isn't like any book I've read before."

Alastair glanced at the cover. "Oh. Yes. I collect literature from before the war. This one is a unique piece. One of my favorites, too."

Fey frowned at the book in her hand. "This is from before the War of the Fallen?" she asked. It was amazing to her to imagine a story that existed for so long, traveling through hundreds of years to end up in her hands.

Alastair chuckled. "No, it's even older. This book is from before the Great War—the war of the ancients."

Fey just blinked at him, and Alastair sighed. "They really *don't* teach you Witches anything, do they?"

Fey shrugged, setting the book down. "I know enough to get by," she said. "My schooling was more physically focused."

Alastair stood over her.

"Is that why you're here, Witchling?" he asked. He reached down, tracing a finger over her cheek. "To raid my library?"

Fey's breath hitched, and she leaned into his touch without thinking.

"Oh, Witchling," he chuckled darkly, a smug smile forming on his lips. "Don't tell me you finally came here to beg for me."

"My name is *Fey*. Not Witchling," she managed to snap.

"Fey," he purred, rolling the name around in his mouth. He said it like a prayer, his finger trailing down her neck.

Goddess that was so much worse.

"I don't think I need to beg," Fey told him.

"Oh?" he cocked an eyebrow at her. His eyes glittered in challenge. "Stand."

Fey didn't move, didn't shift from her seat, and Alastair's smile slipped into something darker, more dangerous.

"*Stand*," he repeated, and the persuasion in his voice brought Fey to her feet before him without a thought.

His eyes focused on her lips, his stare glazed and full of heat.

"Use persuasion on me again," Fey warned, "and I will gut you, Alastair. I will fucking kill you. I won't even hesitate. You know that don't you?"

"Oh, I know," he answered. His eyes never left her lips. "Do you remember what I told you I tasted in your blood, *Fey?*"

Fey swallowed hard. His voice was low and guttural, and it sent a heat through her body.

"What?" she asked.

"I tasted *power*," he said, and every word was full of hunger. Desire. He moved closer, pressing his body against hers. "Is that why you're here? Did you come here tonight to kill me?"

"I—" Fey couldn't think. He felt so good pressed against her like this. That ache under her skin, that ache he'd ignited, thrummed in response to his presence.

"Tell me what you want, *Fey*", he repeated. "Because I would be so glad to be of service."

"I ... I want..."

But she couldn't. She didn't even know what she wanted. She didn't know what her body was demanding. She only knew that she *ached* and somehow, he could make it better.

Alastair watched her, unrushed. And when she still didn't answer he reached up to brush the hair from her face. Even the light touch of his fingertips against her skin sent a wave of heat through her. "Why don't I tell you what I want, hmmm?" he said, his voice soft and dark.

His body shifted against hers, and she couldn't think anymore. She just nodded, swallowing hard.

"I want to kiss you, Fey."

He leaned forward, towering over her, his lips brushing against hers softly, like a promise. Like a question.

"Yes," Fey answered.

He kissed her. Gently, nothing like before. A sweet, soft kiss at first. And when she opened her mouth to him, he deepened into it with a groan, sweeping his tongue over her bottom lip.

Fey was falling into him, swept up in the kiss. She wrapped her arms around his neck, pulling him closer. Her tongue grazed his fangs and a shiver of fear coursed up her body. He laughed darkly, pulling back to kiss her cheek, her jawline, her neck.

"And I want to taste you," he whispered into her ear. Fey whimpered, her toes curling. "I want to taste every part of you, Fey."

His tongue darted out to lick her earlobe. She bit back a moan.

"I want to know what it tastes like to have you come on my tongue. Would you let me do that, Fey?"

Oh fuck, Fey thought, her head spinning. She couldn't answer him, couldn't trust herself to speak.

"And after that," he whispered, pressing gentle kisses down her neck to her collarbone. "After that, I want to bend you over my desk and fuck you until you forget who you are."

"Yes," she gasped.

"Is that what you want, too, Witchling?"

"Yes," she repeated.

His teeth sank into her neck—not enough to draw blood, but a warning. A reminder that he wouldn't be gentle.

And Goddess help her, Fey didn't want him to be.

CHAPTER 24
ALASTAIR

She was intoxicating.

Alastair ran his tongue along the length of her collarbone, savoring the taste of her, the way her body arched into his.

Intoxicating, and oh so responsive.

Her hands grasped his back as he rolled his hips against her, wanting her to feel how hard he was already. He wanted her to feel how much he desired her. She gasped, gripping him tighter.

"You're wearing far too much clothing," he chided. His hands moved up her body, reaching under her shirt. Her skin was like silk under his fingers, and he growled when he found nothing but flesh. She wasn't wearing a bra, wasn't wearing anything under her sweater.

Fey laughed, clearly enjoying his reaction, and he silenced her with another kiss. Harder, this time, a clash of teeth and tongues that she responded to greedily.

He brought his hands to the back of her thighs, gripping her hard and lifting her. She wrapped her legs around him, and when his cock pressed against the apex of her thighs she gasped. He carried her from the bookshelves to his desk, setting her on the edge.

"You have no idea how much I've thought about this moment,"

Alastair told her, breaking the kiss and sliding his hands to the waist of her pants.

"Oh?" she mocked, with a smile. Her lips were flushed red.

He slipped a hand to her crotch, pressing his fingers against her and making her gasp and arch her back.

"Oh," he answered. He unfastened her pants, pulling them off her long legs. His fingers traced their way up the inside of her thigh, but he kept his eyes on her face, lost in the way her mouth opened, the way her eyes unfocused.

When he reached her panties, he trailed his fingertips along the wet fabric. Her legs twitched.

"Tell me, *Fey*," his hands peeled the underwear from her body, pulling them down her thighs and tossing them aside. "Do you taste as good as you look?"

He didn't give her time to answer. His hands went back up her shirt, his mouth going to her jaw. He kissed and bit the skin there, pulling her sweater up and throwing it. He spared a moment to glance down at her, nude and perched on his desk.

"*Fuck*," he breathed.

She was perfect. Lithe, muscled, and perfect. His fingers traced a puckered scar on her toned stomach, following it up to another at her ribs. They marked her body like constellations. Good. That meant she could take a little pain.

His mouth returned to her neck, his hands caressing her breasts. Softly at first. Then he scraped his fangs across her neck, just above her pulse, as he twisted one of her nipples between his fingers.

Fey arched her back, wrapping her legs around his waist to bring him closer. He was still fully clothed, but he didn't care. He encouraged her to press against him, feeling her move against the hard length of him straining to escape his pants.

"What do you want, Witchling?" he asked. He pressed his cock against her, gripping her hard.

She moaned, seemingly beyond words. His lips moved to her chest, and he moved back just enough to take her nipple into his mouth.

"Tell me what you want."

She gasped as he bit down. "You, Alastair," she whispered.

He chuckled.

"Oh, no, no, no, Witchling. That wasn't the deal, remember?" He bit down hard, leaving a mark on the perfect white skin of her breast. His tongue traced the edges of his bite.

"Don't you remember?" He moved further down her body, kissing his way down her stomach, and coming to his knees before her. He traced her scars with his tongue, mesmerized by the way she gasped and twitched under his attention.

He reached her hips and looked up at her.

"Do you remember?" he asked, his tongue snaking out to lick the arch of her hipbone.

She shuddered, eyes wide and glassy.

He kissed his way to her center, running his tongue up her once. His eyes never left hers, and when he paused at the top of her core, she whispered one word.

"Yes."

With a growl, he unleashed himself.

CHAPTER 25

This was what her body had been craving, Fey thought, shuddering beneath Alastair's tongue.

She'd had lovers before, but Alastair looked at her like he would die if he couldn't taste her, would die if he couldn't touch every inch of her body. He touched her like he was worshiping her, like every caress was a prayer.

He groaned as his tongue slipped into her, his hands holding her in place by her hips, and she lost herself in the feeling of his mouth on her. She'd have bruises where he gripped her hips, but she didn't care.

He found her clit, and his tongue circled once like he was teasing it before he closed his mouth around it.

Fey's body jolted, and he chuckled against her skin. One of his hands released her, and a moment later she heard a zipper. Shocked, she glanced down at where he knelt on the floor between her open legs. Alastair's hand gripped his cock from where he'd freed it from his pants, and he stroked himself as he licked and teased her.

"Do you like that?" he asked, looking up at her as she watched. He fisted his cock for her.

Wordlessly, she nodded, and she felt his smile against her skin.

"And what about this?" Alastair asked. His hand moved from her hips to her pussy, and he slipped a finger inside of her.

Fey fell back against the desk, her back arching like a bow. He growled his approval, and added another finger, his mouth never leaving her.

She was losing herself in this feeling, the combination of his fingers and mouth on her.

"Alastair," she warned, feeling her pleasure building. Her hands gripped the edge of the desk, fingernails digging into the wood.

He groaned again, curling his fingers inside her.

"Come for me, Witchling," he urged. His tongue danced over her clit as his fingers worked inside of her.

She did, her body flexing off the desk, head thrown back as she screamed. She gripped his head in her thighs, and he devoured her, using his fingers to guide her through her climax, mouth clasped around her clit.

Fey had never come so hard in her life, and when she finally relaxed enough to release his head from between her thighs, she collapsed back against the desk, breathless.

His clothing made little noise as he removed it, standing between her legs and leaning over the desk to cover her body with her own.

Alastair's face was wet with her arousal, and she could taste herself on him when he kissed her.

"You taste even better than I imagined," he whispered against her lips. His hands moved to her wrists, and he brought them up above her head, pinning her to the desk with one massive hand.

His other hand moved down her body, returning to between her thighs.

Fey gasped as his fingers entered her again.

"I'm not done with you yet," he said, and his words felt like a threat. "Oh no. Not after how long you made me wait for this. How long you made me wait to taste you."

Despite the earth-shattering orgasm she'd just had, Fey's body wasn't done either. His fingers moved inside her, and her body roiled in response.

"Beg me," Alastair said, moving his mouth to her ear.

His fingers moved inside her in a slow steady rhythm, and Fey barely heard him above the noises she was making.

"What?" she asked, breathlessly.

His fingers dug into her wrists, and between her legs he pushed a third finger inside her, stretching her. She gasped at the sensation.

"Beg me," he repeated.

He was fucking her hard with his fingers. Her body was wet enough to allow it, responding to his touches in a way she'd never responded to anyone before.

"Come on, little Witchling." His hand left her wrists, grabbing a fistful of her hair and wrenching her head back against the wood, forcing her body to arch. "Beg me to fuck you."

His fingers moved faster, harder inside her, and already Fey felt herself building to another release.

She wanted to tell him to fuck off. Want to tell him to get off of her and go fuck himself.

But that's not what came out of her mouth. His hand tangled in her hair, his fingers working her closer and closer to orgasm, and his fangs scraping against her neck, the word that came out of her mouth was *"Please."*

"Please what?" his voice was teasing, but his fingers fucked her even harder, almost painfully hard.

"Fuck me, Alastair," Fey panted. "Please. Please fuck me."

He groaned in relief. His fingers slipped out of her, and he brought them to her lips.

"Open," he ordered, eyes flashing. Without protest, Fey opened her mouth and let him slip two fingers inside her, sucking her juices from his fingers.

He smiled as she closed her mouth around his fingers, and she felt him shift between her legs, felt his cock nudge her entrance.

"Good girl," he whispered. And he pushed himself inside her.

Three fingers had stretched her, but this? This was enough to break her apart. Fey screamed as he entered her, inch by inch, her hands clawing at his back. It hurt, Goddess knew it hurt, but it was like nothing she'd felt before.

He swore against her skin, and she wondered if he felt the same.

"*Fuck*," he snarled. She bit the space between his shoulder and his neck to stop from screaming again. "Witchling, you're so fucking tight."

When the last inch of his cock buried inside her, he paused for a second, letting her adjust to the sensation of him filling her. Then, his face hovering above hers, their eyes locked, he started to move.

This is what sex should be, Fey thought as he moved inside her. Her body was on fire, every nerve firing. Already she was cresting to another peak.

The desk creaked underneath them as he fucked her. Alastair's hand gripped her thigh tight enough to hurt, holding her in place, and his other hand found her neck and squeezed.

"I want to make you hurt, Fey," he said. His hand tightened around her throat and his cock was agonizingly hard inside her. "I want you covered in marks from me. And when you come back for more, I want to taste every mark I left on you."

He was moving faster, pounding into her. The desk moved with each thrust. Fey couldn't think, couldn't catch her breath. Her body was coming apart, and she wanted this, wanted him to hurt her.

"I want you to remember this," he groaned against her skin. "I want you to remember every place I touched you."

She tried to talk, tried to say his name, but he moved his hand to her mouth, covering her words.

"Come for me again, Witchling," he commanded.

And she did.

Fey nearly blacked out from the force of it, and if his hand hadn't covered her mouth she might have screamed loud enough to be heard in the club, music be damned. He fucked her through it, moving his hips in slow sensual strokes and whispering filthy things in her ears.

As she came down from her peak, his rhythm became faster, more erratic, and when she whispered his name against the hand that held her, he groaned his release, spilling himself inside her before collapsing.

They lay there together, entwined on his desk, breathless and sweaty. Might have stayed there all night if the desk hadn't creaked again, under the weight of them both. Creaked, and *shifted*.

"Alastair?" Fey said in warning, but before he could respond the desk gave an audible *crack* as a leg snapped and flung them both to the floor.

Alastair swore as they fell, rolling so he landed on his back, cradling her safely against his chest.

"What the *fuck*?" he snarled, lifting his head to look around in shock, and she laughed.

"You broke the desk!"

He blinked at her in confusion, then blinked at the desk, now toppled on the ground.

"Fuck," he said, finally. He let his head fall back against the floor. "Fuck me, that was an antique."

Fey laughed again, harder than she probably should have, and his arms slipped around her back, holding her tight against him. His fingers traced patterns on her bare skin, pausing at each of her scars. Not in disgust or surprise, but something akin to curiosity. Reverence.

Curled against his chest, Fey let him. Let him trail his fingers over each of her battle scars. She had the strangest feeling that he was memorizing them.

She could have fallen asleep there, draped over him on the floor. Could have, but shouldn't.

She shifted in his arms to sit up, and his hands tensed around her, grunting a wordless objection.

"I have to go," Fey said with a smile.

"No, you don't," he responded. His eyes were closed.

"I do. And you have to go back to work. You have a club to run."

"Fuck them," he said. "They can handle one night without me. And fuck them if they can't. Let the building burn for all I care."

"I have to go, and you know it." She stood, stretching her limbs, and began searching for her clothing.

Alastair propped himself up on his elbow, watching her move around the room, digging through the mess the broken desk had made.

"What?" she asked, finding her panties and pulling them over her hips.

"You're exquisite, you know that?" Alastair said. He sounded amazed. Fey snorted, reaching for her sweater. He reached out to grab her wrist, holding her.

"Stay here with me tonight," he said. "I shouldn't have done this here. There's a bed upstairs." He nodded to the ceiling. *Good to know*, Fey thought to herself. "Sleep here. I'll make it worth it." His eyes glittered, and Fey clenched her thighs together involuntarily.

"Maybe next time," she said, gently peeling his fingers from her wrist.

"Next time?" He asked, grinning. "So, there will be a next time?"

"Don't get too ahead of yourself," Fey warned, but it was an effort not to smile back at him. An effort not to take him up on the offer and let him take her upstairs to a bed where he could ravish her all night.

Fey felt good. For the first time in a long time, she felt at peace in her body. Maybe there *would* be another time. And maybe another after that. It wasn't common for a Witch to become involved with a Vampire, but it wasn't forbidden. And that sex? That had been just what she'd needed. It would be hard to say no to that again...

The contents of his desk had spilled over the floor, and she couldn't seem to find her pants in the mess. She piled things together, organizing the chaos. A small bag caught her eye, and Fey plucked it from the ground, shaking the powder inside.

"What's this?" she asked.

Alastair grunted from where he lay on the ground. "Devil dust. We pulled it off a dealer a few weeks ago." He eyed the bag in her hand nervously. "It's foul stuff. You should put it down, trust me."

But Fey wasn't listening. The color had drained from her face as she stared at the bag.

"This?" she asked, breathless. "This is devil dust?"

Alastair nodded, but she wasn't looking at him. "It is," he confirmed, suspicion in his voice. "Why?"

"It's not gold," Fey whispered.

"No," Alastair answered. His voice was slow and soft. "It's not."

Fey's head was spinning. There wasn't enough air in the room suddenly. "Alastair, is there a drug that's gold? Liquid gold, with," she faltered. "With light swirling inside?"

"Fey," he started.

"Just answer the fucking question." Fey snarled at him.

Alastair swallowed. He knew the answer. Suspected she did too. And it meant something more to her than he could understand.

"No, Witchling. As far as I know—and, trust me, I *would* know—there's no drug out there like you're describing."

She was going to vomit. Thoughts were tumbling through her head faster than she could keep up.

It wasn't devil dust, what they'd found in the warehouse. Wasn't a drug at all. Why had they thought that? Where had that information come from? And why were they sent to destroy it? What could be so dangerous that the Queen sent her Blades to get rid of it?

Something bigger was happening here, a puzzle she had only the vaguest idea of, too many pieces that she didn't have yet.

Fey tossed the devil dust on the broken remnants of his desk.

"I have to go," she said, yanking her pants from underneath the desk and pulling them on. She shrugged her sweater on, pulling it over her breasts.

"Wait, Fey—" Alastair started, but it was too late. She was already heading out the door.

And then she was gone.

CHAPTER 26

Joy stared at the wall, seeing nothing and saying nothing. Energy crackled in the air.

Finally, she took a long, deep breath. The air in the room moved with it, drawing in toward her, and back out again.

"It wasn't a drug," she said, finally.

Fey nodded. She sat on Joy's bed, her arms wrapped around her knees, hugging her legs to herself. She'd come to Joy immediately upon returning to the palace. Lilith had been in the training gym and joined them, but Willow was fast asleep, spread out on her bed like a starfish. They'd agreed to let her rest.

"Then what was it?" Joy mused. "What could be so dangerous the Crown would send *us* to wipe it off the face of the earth?"

This was Joy's process, Fey knew. This was how she connected the dots, how she stepped back to see the bigger picture. They were looking at a puzzle with too few pieces, but if anyone could see the pattern here, it was Joy.

"A weapon," Lilith reasoned. She lounged in an armchair next to the fireplace. Her whetstone sat on her lap, but for once she wasn't sharpening her blades. She was tense and still.

Joy nodded absently. "A weapon," she repeated. "That would make sense. Something bad enough to scare the Crown. Something they didn't want in the wrong hands. Something better off destroyed."

"Why lie about it, though? Why tell us we were after some sort of drug?" Fey asked, unable to keep the resentment out of her voice.

"Did they lie?" Lilith challenged. "Where did you get the idea that it was drugs, anyway?"

You, not *we*, Fey noted and shot her sister an irritated look.

"Dameon," Joy answered. "When he briefed us the night before. I don't remember if he said it outright, not explicitly, but he implied it. Implied we were going after a big devil dust supplier."

"Implied," Lilith repeated. She threw her hands up. "Don't shoot the messenger, but we can't accuse our handler of *lying* just because he 'implied' something. Maybe *we* misunderstood."

Joy pursed her lips together. "That's possible. It's also possible he misunderstood. Maybe he gave us the information he had available to him?" Joy let the words hang in the air for a moment before she added. "And it's possible he deliberately misled us."

"Why?" asked Lilith. "No, don't give me that look, Fey, I'm being fucking serious, here. *Why* would he lie? Why would he even *need* to? We are the *Queen's assassins*. She points us in a direction and sets us loose. We do what we're told. He doesn't even have to tell us *anything*. Dameon wouldn't lie to us because he has *no reason to*. We're not worth being lied to."

Lilith huffed. "We're attack dogs, like it or not. All of us. And you don't have to tell an attack dog why they bite—only *who*."

Fey let her legs go, putting her face in her hands in frustration.

"Am I wrong?" Lilith challenged.

"You're not wrong," Joy said calmly. "It's not our job to question where the Queen sends us."

"It's *treason* to question it," Lilith reminded them. "We took our oath to obey the Crown, unquestioningly. And you both sure as fuck sound like you're *questioning*."

"I can't help but think something is going on here," Fey said. She felt exhausted. It must be past dawn by now, and she hadn't slept at all. "I feel like we're walking into danger, and we won't even realize it until the snare closes around our neck."

"That's your problem, Fey," Lilith sneered. "Always thinking. You weren't inducted into the Blades to *think*."

"That's enough, Lilith," Joy murmured. She still stared at the wall half lost in thought. "There's no need for cruelty."

"I'm not trying to be cruel," Lilith insisted. "I just—"

"I said that's enough." Joy turned to her at that, her eyes blazing. The air in the room surged, and the photos Joy had hanging on her walls, photos of her and Alice, shook. Lilith stopped.

The air stilled, but their conversation hung heavy in the room, too many emotions floating around them. Too many questions.

"I'm sorry," Lilith said, finally. "Fey, I'm sorry, I didn't mean—"

"It's fine," Fey insisted. "Really. You're not wrong. We're not supposed to question our orders, we're not even supposed to talk about her. But here we are. Trying to piece it all together with what little clues we have."

"I just—" Lilith huffed a breath. "I don't like this. I don't think any good will come of it, trying to unravel this. I think we should stop this, stop trying to figure any of this out. I'm scared of where it will lead us. Scared of what it will do to us."

Fey sighed.

"I'm scared too."

CHAPTER 27

The day passed in a fuzzy, exhausted haze. Joy was called on for another assignation and took Willow along with her. Lilith disappeared shortly after, and Fey couldn't help but think she was finished helping them. Lilith could live without knowing why Alice had died.

But Fey couldn't.

So, she spent the day in the training gym, pushing her body to its limits. After her night with Alastair, her muscles had been pleasantly sore, but she didn't want to feel pleasantly sore today. She wanted to hurt. She wanted her body to match how she felt. She wanted to be distracted.

By the time the afternoon rolled into the evening, her muscles were a quivering mess. Finally, blissfully lost in the agony of pushing her body too hard, Fey went to the Med table on shaking legs and selected a bottle from their stock.

This wasn't the first time Fey had used training to escape her thoughts and emotions, and she'd learned the perfect combination of elixirs to dull the pain just enough that she could fight, if necessary.

She didn't want to take all the pain away, but a little something to relax her muscles so she could move again, a little something to dull the screaming in her limbs to a mild protest—that was the balance she was looking for.

Fey sighed, breaking the seal on the elixir bottle and preparing to pour it into the basin before her.

Then she stopped. Stopped, and looked at the contents of the bottle, *really* looked at it, for the first time in years.

She'd never bothered learning the art of making healing elixirs. Never gave much thought to how they worked, how they were made, despite being a Water Witch. That gift seemed so far outside of her own skills, so distant from what she was capable of.

Sana, head of the Water Coven, was the sort of Witch who concerned herself with healing elixirs. And Fey was no Sana.

It was easy to take them for granted. Easy to not think twice about the healing droughts delivered to their training room each week.

But tonight, her mind swimming with thoughts and fears, Fey stared at the bottle in her hand. The contents were a crystalline white, with opalescent magic swirling inside, circling within the bottle like a storm. Others on the shelves were blue, green, any color imaginable, all full of magic waiting to be released.

An elixir.

That's what it was—that's what they'd found in the warehouse. It hadn't been drugs, hadn't been a weapon.

It was an elixir. Crates upon crates of golden elixirs, gallons of the stuff. Enough to fuel an army.

Her mind reeled, and another piece of information slipped into the puzzle.

Phillip Danvers had been in the Med Witch department, hadn't he? And the Shifter Willow had met, he'd said Professor Danvers had taught Medicinal Chemistry... He would have been an expert on elixirs, would have known just as much about them and their properties as any Water Witch trained in elixir magic.

Phillip Danvers had met with Alice. Given her something, something that had shaken her.

It was all connected, somehow, wasn't it?

Fey felt dizzy.

She had to go back, back to the warehouse. Maybe there was some left, some that had survived the blast. It was a long shot, but if they had just a single bottle of the elixir they'd found, they could take it to Sana and have it identified.

She called Joy on her way back to her room, but the call rang through. She tried again, and again it rang and rang until finally clicking to voicemail.

"Joy, I need you to call me as soon as you get this," Fey said into the phone, pulling off her training clothes and grabbing her leathers. "It's all connected, the club, the warehouse it's—"

She stopped, suddenly.

Something was happening here. Something big. And, until they had a bigger picture, until she knew what was going on, she didn't want anything recorded. Didn't want to reveal anything.

Her mouth dried.

"Just call me," she said, finally, and ended the call.

Fey slipped her phone into her pocket and pulled her mask over her face.

There was only one place she could go for answers, and she prayed to the Goddess she would find something still there.

———

THE SUN HAD ALMOST SET by the time Fey reached the ruins of the warehouse. She kept to the shadows, moving out of sight, until she reached the building. Or, rather, where the building had once stood.

Someone had cleaned up much of the mess they'd left, shuffling parts of the broken building into piles of rubble and debris. A few walls still stood, blackened and burnt from the explosion. The sound of the river running below was even louder now, with no building there to muffle the sounds.

The streets around the building were empty, and there were no more guards on patrol here, not anymore. Fey wandered through the piles of debris, shifting pieces of broken wood and glass with her boots, looking for...

Well, that was the problem, wasn't it? She wasn't sure what she was looking for.

But something gnawed at her, some intuition that there was something more here. Something they were missing.

There were no elixir bottles, no remnants of the 'devil dust' they'd been sent to destroy. What remained of the building looked exactly as it should have—an abandoned, destroyed warehouse, stripped down to its skeleton.

Was there even a point to coming here? Fey moved further into the rubble, further into the remains that were still standing. There was nothing here. Nothing at all that—

Something shifted in the debris, and Fey froze instinctually, crouching against a half standing wall and letting the shadows hide her.

Someone else was here.

More shuffling, just out of sight, somewhere deeper in the skeletal remains of the building. Then a voice.

"No, it's gone." A male voice. Gruff. "Picked clean."

Fey's breath caught in her throat, and carefully, oh so carefully, she shifted forward, moving silently across the rubble-strewn floor. It took practiced maneuvering to make her way toward the voice, keeping to the shadows for cover.

"If they were, they're long gone now."

Fey could only hear one voice, one body shifting through the rubble. Someone talking on the phone, then. She leaned closer, straining to hear the conversation. Strained hard enough that she didn't notice the small fragment of glass under her boot, shifting under her weight, until it cracked with an audible snap.

The shifting on the other side of a pile of debris stopped.

Fuck.

A shadow passed over her, blocking the golden light from the setting sun, as a figure strode around the pile and loomed over her.

"You're not supposed to be here," the figure told her in a gruff voice. It was too dark to see him clearly, with the last remains of sunlight at his back.

But sometimes it's best to attack first and ask questions later.

Fey struck, shooting up from her crouch and knocking the male backward with a kick to the chest. She didn't move to kill, didn't draw the blades strapped to her thighs. After all, she had no idea who this person was, what they were doing here in this Goddess-forsaken warehouse. They could be another lifeline, another clue as to what the fuck was going on here.

The male was huge. Big enough that her kick had only sent him stumbling backwards a few steps. But Fey was already readying herself to go again, arms up to fight.

"That was a mistake," the man growled.

And he began to shift.

Watching a Shifter change between forms is something that never gets easier with time. It never loses the horror, the twisting sickening feeling that rises in your guts. It unleashes a fear, primal and ancient, of watching a monster being born.

The man on the warehouse floor roared as his face split in two, his jaw elongating and his skull cracking open. Fur flowed out from under his skin, black and smooth, and his thick arms twisted and bent as the muscles and bones broke and reformed.

It took just a few seconds for the shift to finish, and Fey watched, horrified, as a large cat emerged from within the skin of the man in front of her.

Fey had fought Shifters before. Fought and killed more Shifters than she could count on both hands. But she was alone tonight. Alone, with no backup, no sleep, and a seven-foot Panther rising to meet her.

The Panther snarled, revealing fangs sharp and big as fingers, and crouched to pounce. There was no time to run, no time to hide.

Fuck.

She rolled as the cat struck, barely getting out of the way in time. The Shifter didn't even pause before turning to launch at her again.

It hit her with enough force that Fey felt the air rush from her lungs. The two of them hit the ground, snapping burnt wood beneath them as they fought. Claws ripped into Fey's arm, and she screamed. It was a lucky hit for the Shifter—luckier, still, that it clipped her sigil for healing, tearing through the intricate pattern.

Fey immediately felt the sigil's loss, and every ache and pain in her body roared to life. The sigils kept them strong, powerful, and healthy. Without her healing sigil, every wound she took in this fight would be slow to re-knit, slow to heal.

She managed to get her forearm up between her and the Shifter's body, pushing against his neck to keep those gnashing fangs away from her face, but the claws tore into her, ripping into her shoulder as she fought.

The damage a large predator can do in just a few seconds is immense. By the time Fey had managed to pull her blade from its sheath and bury it in the Panther's side, her shoulders were covered in deep wounds.

The Shifter yowled when the blade sunk into its side, rolling away from her and scrambling for safety. She struck it again, slicing at its ribs, until finally it stumbled and collapsed.

Panting, Fey stood. She would live. Blood coated her arms, gushing from deep wounds on her shoulders and biceps, and it would take weeks for her to heal from this without her sigil. But she would live.

The Shifter would, too, Fey realized. The Panther whimpered at her feet, close to unconsciousness, but she hadn't hit anything vital. He would live, and she might finally get some answers—

Someone hit her hard from the side, knocking her to the ground. Something smaller than the giant cat she'd just fought. Fey turned, scrambling to her feet, trying to locate her new enemy.

But something was wrong.

The world had been caught in a gentle dusk, the slowly setting sun basking everything in a gentle glow. But now? Something was in her eyes, clouding the light, something rough and gritty. Her body was awash with pain, all her nerves alight with agony. Fey scrambled to rub at her eyes, trying to move backward away from whatever was attacking her.

Too late. A foot found her rib cage, and Fey screamed as she curled over her body in pain. She barely had time to react before she was kicked again, the force of it flinging her several feet across the soot-coated ground.

Pain wracked her body, clouding her remaining senses. Everything was darkened and shadowed, hazy as though covered in dark mist. She couldn't see the danger around her, couldn't see where the next attack might come from.

But she could see something in the distance. Even through the shadows clouding her vision, she could see the golden glow of the sun dipping below the horizon.

Below the cliffside leading to the river below.

Fey pulled her power to her, releasing a blast of air in all directions around her. A roar of pain and crash let her know she'd hit her mark.

Scrambling to her feet, Fey pointed herself to the light on the horizon and ran. Her body was hot and heavy, and something was wrong, very, very wrong. Agony flooded her body as she moved, and the air was thick and far too heavy, impossibly thick in her lungs.

Smoke, she realized.

The world was hot around her, and Fey realized the world around her was burning. She was burning.

She was on fire.

Sounds behind her alerted her to danger a moment before she was attacked, giving her just enough time to dive to the side. The world spun, smoke clouding her gaze, but Fey screamed in rage and desperation and kept running.

This would not be how she died. Not like this, not blinded and running like a coward. She wouldn't die today, she wouldn't—

The ground below her vanished as she reached the edge of the cliff face, and with a scream, Fey tumbled down into the emptiness, down, down, down to the river below.

PART TWO

CHAPTER 28

She was in a dream.

No, Fey thought, panic surging through her. *Not again. Please Goddess, no, not again.*

The steps to the temple entrance stretched before her, an endless staircase of cold white marble leading *up*,

up,

up.

She tried to turn around, tried to go back—wherever *back* was, here —but there were too many people. Too many girls crowding the steps, too many bodies moving upward, pushing her up the stairs. She was caught up in the stream of bodies, unable to move against them, unable to get away.

This isn't what happened, something inside her was insisting. A voice, her voice from somewhere deep inside herself, but it was distant and growing more distant with each step she was forced to climb. It was fading to a whisper, a plea from somewhere far, far away, until it finally faded to nothing.

When she reached the top of the stairs, the other bodies around her vanished, the stairs at her back vanished, and it was just her and the White Priestess standing in that room, once again.

"Water," the old woman demanded, extending an aged finger toward her. She said it with a voice full of scorn and anger, a voice completely unlike the one from Fey's memories.

Fey didn't understand what she wanted, what she was asking for.

"Water!" the woman shouted, pointing. Her face contorted with rage, her mouth an open sneer revealing age-blackened teeth.

Fey opened her mouth to protest, to beg for some sort of explanation, but no words came out. Instead, water flowed out from between her lips and down her chin, and Fey brought her hands to her mouth, horrified.

She closed her mouth tightly, clasping her fingers across her lips, but the water continued to flow from her, spilling down her front and pooling on the marble floor.

It came from everywhere. Water spilled like tears from her eyes and flowed from her ears, from her nose. It seeped from her very skin, and when she screamed, it was nothing but a strangled gurgling against the flow of water.

———

FEY'S EYES SNAPPED OPEN, her heart pounding against her ribcage. She tried to sit up, but she couldn't move her body. She was heavy, far too heavy, and *Goddess spare her* she *hurt*.

For several long seconds, there was nothing but the pain. No thoughts, no awareness, nothing but the oppressive, suffocating pain that filled every inch of her body.

Slowly, oh so slowly, she became aware of the world around her.

She was in a bed—she could feel that much. But she couldn't move her head to look around at her surroundings. Couldn't move anything at all. Her muscles were heavy and leaden, and just thinking about moving them hurt.

Fey tried to speak, instead, but her throat burned like fire, and all she managed to make was a terrible, strained croaking sound.

Someone was next to her, curled by her side near enough to be touching, and when Fey tried to speak again, the person stirred.

"Fey?" a voice asked, heavy with sleep.

Willow's face appeared above her, eyes red-lined, her hair unkempt and messy from sleep. Seeing Fey awake, her eyes widened.

"She's awake!" Willow shouted, not taking her eyes from Fey's face. "Guys? Guys, come here, she's awake!"

Fey made another pained sound, and Willow winced.

"Don't try to talk," she insisted. "Your throat was damaged from the fire. You could hurt yourself."

Fire? Fey's head was spinning. Memories were jumbled together, hazy and indistinct. Then she remembered the ambush, the Shifter, the desperate leap to the water below…

She opened her mouth again, but Willow just shook her head frantically.

"Don't talk!" she insisted. "You're going to hurt yourself. You have to be still while your body heals, you're—"

A door opened somewhere in the room, and suddenly they were all there. Her sisters. Joy and Lilith joined Willow above her, staring down at her.

"You're alive," Lilith whispered in astonishment.

"Oh, thank the Goddess," Joy sobbed, tears streaming down her face.

I am alive, Fey realized.

And then she closed her eyes and tumbled back into the void of unconsciousness.

FEY SPENT the next few days slipping in and out of sleep. When she was awake, her sisters helped her eat, giving her healing elixirs left by the Med Witch who had attended her before she woke. They soothed the constant ache in her throat, but still, she couldn't speak in those first few days.

Bit by bit, she returned to her body. She'd been hurt badly. Whether from the fight or the fall, they weren't sure. She'd been found near death, her body broken and burned, washed up on the shore of the river. She'd lost her mask in the water, but the civilian who'd found her had recognized her uniform, recognized the mark on her forearm: a member of the Queen's Blades, hurt and in need of aid.

She'd been rushed to a Med Witch, barely alive, and once her sisters had been contacted, they'd brought her here, to one of their safe houses in the city.

"What happened to you, sister?" Joy asked her the second time Fey had woken.

But Fey had just shaken her head. Unable to talk, unable to explain anything. And Joy hadn't asked again.

It was two weeks before Fey could get out of bed. Even with the best Med Witches in the city, even with the constant care of her sisters and the sigils covering her skin that promised strength and fast healing. Someone had repaired her healing sigil, but even with its power, two and a half weeks passed before she could speak without pain.

"It was an elixir," were the first words Fey spoke, the most important words, the ones that had been burning in her mind for weeks while her body rebuilt itself. Her voice was strained, the pitch deeper and huskier than usual. "In the warehouse. Not devil dust. An elixir."

Joy's eyebrows rose in shock, but Lilith's face darkened.

"You're still going after this?" Lilith asked at the same time Joy breathlessly said, "What do you mean, an elixir? Fey, who attacked you?"

Fey shook her head. "I don't know," she whispered, and though the words hurt her throat, the pain of not knowing who their enemy was hurt more. "A Shifter? I didn't recognize them. Panther, I think. Something big, with claws."

Sharp, deadly claws and her arms and shoulders would carry the scars to prove it.

Lilith stood from the bed. "No," she snapped. "No, Fey, this is enough. You can't do this anymore. You can't keep doing this to us."

Joy turned toward her, frowning. "Sister," she said in a soft, consoling voice.

Face twisted in rage, Lilith spun toward her. "No! Don't you *dare*, Joy. I'm not going to sit back and be quiet about this anymore." Turning her fury on Fey, she shouted. "You could have *died!*"

The words filled the air between them, and Fey blinked, shocked at the anger, the emotions in Lilith's voice.

While she spoke, Lilith's hands shook. Her face was cracking, breaking with an emotion too powerful for words. Under that anger, that fury... pain. Fear. "You could have *died*," she whispered, voice breaking. Her cheeks glistened, and Fey realized with shock that her sister was crying.

She'd never seen Lilith cry before. Not once.

Fey's hand rose to touch her face, and she realized she was crying, too.

"You went out there on your own. You went chasing this, this—" Lilith gestured around her, like couldn't find the words. "This stupid fucking *mystery* of yours. And you almost *died*, Fey. Even after you were found, even after we brought you here, we didn't know if you'd make it. No one could tell us if you were going to make it!"

Fey opened her mouth to speak, but Lilith cut her off before she could even think of what she would say.

"No, you don't get to explain, you don't get to talk. You *left us*, Fey. You left us and you almost got yourself killed." Lilith was openly sobbing now, her shoulders shaking from it. "I *told you* to let it go, but no. You had to keep looking for problems, you had to question our orders, and you did it *on your own.*"

Lilith rubbed at the tears on her face with her hand in a furious motion. "I told you to let it go. I *told you*." She shuddered with the strength of her anger, her pain, before turning her back on them and storming to the bedroom door.

"You're going to end up just like her if you keep this up," Lilith said, stopping in the doorway for just long enough to fling the words back into the room like a curse. "You're going to end up just like Alice. And I can't handle that, Fey. I can't live through that again."

Lilith left them there, and a moment later they heard the front door of their safe house apartment slam behind her.

Joy sighed heavily.

"She'll be okay," she insisted—reaching out to rest a comforting hand on Fey's. "She just needs some time. She was scared. We all were."

"I'm sorry," Fey sobbed. She wasn't sure exactly what she was apologizing for. There was so much. So much she'd done wrong, so much she'd fucked up. Lilith was right—she could have died, could have been torn away from her sisters just like Alice, and her absence would have left another hole in their hearts that nothing could fill.

But Joy just squeezed her hand and smiled that bright smile of hers. That smile that felt like a sunrise after a dark, terrifying night.

"It's okay. It'll be okay, Fey. You're alive, and that's what matters. You're alive, and you're here with us."

CHAPTER 29

ALASTAIR

"More," Alastair ordered, tapping the bar next to his empty glass.

Jasper hadn't even bothered putting the bottle away after he'd poured Alastair's last drink. Wordlessly, the Shifter uncorked the bottle again and poured his boss a generous serving of scotch.

Alastair brought the glass to his lips and tipped it back. It was almost impossible for a Vampire to get drunk with their metabolism but tonight he was going to give it his best try.

The pleasurable burn of the liquor sliding down his throat was almost enough to make him moan. But it was short-lived. Heat pooled in his stomach for a fraction of a second and was gone.

Sighing, Alastair put his glass back down, and this time he didn't even need to ask for more. Jasper was already pouring another before he'd even set the glass fully on the table.

Saturday night was their busiest night, and the club was closed. Closed, for the first time since he had bought the place and turned it into one of the Eternal City's most successful nightclubs. It would cost him, losing all that income from tonight, but he didn't give a fuck about the money.

Tonight, all he cared about was trying to get rip-roaring drunk.

The next shot stayed in his stomach even longer, and the warmth from it was a pleasant escape for a few seconds.

"More."

Alastair wasn't some love-struck puppy. He wasn't some pussy-whipped teenager. So, when Fey had left that night—the night they'd fucked on his desk—and hadn't returned within the next few days, he hadn't been some heartbroken sniveling mess. He'd given her the space and independence a powerful Witch deserved.

When a week passed, and he still hadn't seen her, he'd sent her a message. Then called. He wasn't *lovesick*. He wasn't *pining* for her, or any shit like that, for fuck's sake. He was worried, alright? The way she'd looked when she'd left, after finding that baggie of devil dust, it worried him.

It's not like he was fucking obsessed with her, or anything.

It's not like he couldn't stop thinking about her. Like she occupied his every waking thought.

Like he couldn't stop remembering the way her skin felt. The way she moved on him when he fucked her with his fingers. The sounds she made, the perfect fucking sounds she made, when she came. The sweetest sound he'd ever heard.

It's not like he couldn't stop thinking about the way she'd said his name, the way she'd whispered it against his hand, her body taut with pleasure as she came on his cock in a way he'd never forget.

It's not like he'd spent the next day smelling her on his skin, his face, his clothes, and *fuck* it left him hard just remembering it.

Alastair's next drink tasted like a lie, but it stayed in his system longer than the last one.

Ok, so maybe he had been a little fucking obsessed. And a little frantic when she didn't come back. Maybe he'd been worried, too, maybe he was a lot of fucking things. Maybe when she hadn't returned his messages and his calls, when she hadn't come back two weeks later, he'd been worried enough to set his hounds on her scent, worried enough to send out feelers looking for any information about Fey and what trouble she might be in.

Maybe he'd wanted to help.

But now?

Now he was fucking pissed.

The packet in front of him was thinner than most he received from his hounds. Thinner, even, than the packet of information he'd received about Phillip Danvers. The packet *she'd* convinced him to get for her.

No. The packet his hounds had delivered, the packet containing every piece of information they could find about Fey, had only been one sheet of paper.

Because as far as his sources could tell, no Witch going by that name even existed.

CHAPTER 30
LILITH

The electric buzz coming from the fluorescent lights grated on Lilith's already foul mood. She sighed angrily, drumming her long fingernails on the restaurant counter and scowling at everyone who made the mistake of glancing her way.

The other Factions were smart enough to give Witches space in public, smart enough to treat them with the healthy combination of fear and respect they deserved. They *were* the Goddess's most cherished children, after all. But the patrons here were taking it to the next level, and Lilith was sure that when they looked into her eyes, they saw *murder* written there.

Fucking Fey, Lilith thought to herself. And then, after an uncomfortable level of guilt flushed under her skin, she tried to shake it off by refocusing her anger.

Fucking Alice.

This was all Alice's fault, after all. It was Alice who had left them with this stupid "mystery" that Joy and Fey couldn't seem to let go of. Alice, who had gotten herself killed. Alice, who should have known better. *Done* better.

Lilith didn't mourn. No, she *fumed*.

How could she have gone and gotten herself killed like that? How could she have been so stupid, so reckless? If she'd just reached out to them for help, if she'd just tried to *talk* to them...

And *Joy*. Everyone knew that she and Alice had been fucking, which was fine, whatever. It's not like Lilith cared or anything. But there was a big difference between fucking and feelings, and Lilith had tried to get her sisters to understand that, tried to stop them from falling so head over heels in love with each other...

Lilith gnashed her teeth together and snarled loudly enough the couple seated near her shot her a frightened glance. She narrowed her eyes back at them, giving them a sneering smile that had them both quickly looking back at their slices of pizza.

Good.

If Alice hadn't gotten herself killed, Fey wouldn't be caught up in this new obsession of hers. Wouldn't be trying to drag all of them down with her. And they wouldn't have argued then, would they? Lilith wouldn't have yelled at her, wouldn't have stormed off, and spent the night and half of the next day away from her sisters, would she? It's not like she needed to apologize or anything. She was only *trying* to help, trying to get her sister to see reason, to—

"Order up," came a call from the counter, and the kid working the register at "Shifters' Best 'Za" set her pizza boxes down at the pickup counter.

About damn time.

Lilith slapped a silver coin on the counter to cover the tip before grabbing the tower of pizza boxes and heading for the door.

She couldn't remember Fey's favorite pizza topping, so she'd ordered a large of everything that looked good. One of them *had* to be Fey's favorite, right? And judging by the smell of the place, and how packed it was this early in the evening, these pizzas just might be good enough that Fey would consider forgiving her.

Not that she *needed* forgiving. Not that she'd done anything wrong.

Lilith struggled with her armful of pizza boxes, trying to maneuver the exit door open with her hip. Before she could manage, though, the door opened from the other side, and she stumbled, nearly falling against the person standing there.

"Watch it, you—" Lilith hissed. But she paused, her lips parted slightly, as she looked at the male in front of her.

The Shifter who held the door open was all kinds of *Fine*, with a capital F. The guy had to be almost six and a half feet tall, all muscle, and just a hint of menace. Just her type.

And wouldn't you know it? He seemed to be thinking the same thing about her, judging from the way he looked her over. His green eyes flashed as he took her in, gaze traveling down her body in that slow, dangerous assessing stare she'd seen in Wolf Shifters before, and his nostrils flared as he took in her scent.

"Thanks," she said, her voice a little breathless.

His eyes snapped to hers when she spoke, and the predatory spark in them had her feeling like a cornered rabbit with nowhere to run. Her pulse quickened, and the tip of her tongue snaked out to lick her lips. Dangerous. Oh yes. He was just her type.

"No problem." He grinned down at her, showing a bit too many teeth. But he didn't move, didn't shift out of the doorway to let her by. "Do you need some help with those?"

The crooked smile accompanying that question made Lilith seriously consider tossing the pizzas in the trash and asking for his help locating the nearest bed. Hell, even a wall in the alley would work, for a face like that.

But... her sisters were waiting, and cold pizza wasn't much of an apology gift, was it?

"Not today, puppy," Lilith cooed, shouldering him aside and slipping out the door. Sure, maybe she brushed against him a bit more than was necessary, and maybe she lingered for just a moment to feel his hard chest pressed against her upper arm, but who could blame her? The guy was a snack. "I can take care of myself."

"Oh, I don't doubt it," he called after her.

Lilith shot him one last look over her shoulder, smiling at how intensely he watched her walk away.

JASPER WATCHED Lilith until she turned the corner, disappearing around the block before he stepped away from the door and let it fall closed.

The street was swarming with scents tonight, but the wind was on his side. He took a deep breath, filling his lungs with the smell of pizza and the faint odor of jasmine and...

Leather. Huh.

He started after her, carefully tearing apart her scent piece by piece. When Alastair had told them all to keep an eye out for the red-haired Witch and her friends, he'd shown the Wolves who worked at his night-club photos of each of the four of them, pulled from the security cameras. But photos gave such little information that they were almost useless to Shifters like him.

No, they had a much better way of identifying people.

Jasper had spent enough time with Fey to recognize her by scent. Fuck, Alastair had smelled so strongly of her the last time she'd come by the club all he'd wanted to do was bury his face in his boss's clothes and soak up every sweet trace of her. He'd spent that entire night constantly having to rearrange himself to hide his erection, and he hadn't been the only one that night. Even Ferus had been on edge, snapping at everyone who came near him, and drinking more than usual to keep his calm. Wolves were drawn to power, drawn to the safety of forming a pack centered around a strong leader. Fey's scent had them all practically drooling around her, and Alastair had no idea what it had done to his bar staff to walk around that night smelling so strongly of her, so strongly of sex...

And under that mouthwatering smell? Jasmine. And just a faint hint of leather.

The smell pulled at something deep in his chest, something he didn't fully understand. He swallowed down the questions it raised.

It was dumb luck he'd gone out tonight to grab a slice of pizza for his niece before work. Pure luck he'd managed to catch a whiff of that scent on the wind.

Jasper tipped his head back, taking a deep breath of the cold night air. Oh yeah, it was her alright. Under the other Witch's scent, there was Fey's smell, fresh and thick.

It didn't take much effort to follow her, not with the scent in his nose and the streets crowded enough to blend in easily. After all, there was a time in his life before Jasper had tended bar, a time before Alastair had convinced him to go straight, a time when stalking marks was all that kept him and his family eating. And that skill set did not fade, even after all these years.

The Witch led him a few blocks out of the main thoroughfare of his neighborhood, to a small apartment building. He paused, hidden well enough from view, and watched as Lilith fumbled with the building's door and key code before disappearing inside. Watched and listened.

The street was buzzing with noise, and the building Lilith had entered held several well-illuminated luxury apartments. But though the lights were on, the curtains were all closed, and as Jasper listened, his hearing nearly as well developed as his sense of smell, he knew one thing with certainty.

Only one of those apartments was occupied.

Curious.

Pulling his phone from his pocket, Jasper kept his eyes on the building as he dialed the number from memory and listened to it ring.

"Hey boss," he said into the phone when it picked up. "Guess who I just found."

CHAPTER 31

"Take a deep breath," Fey drew in a deep lungful of air and held it. The Med Witch beside her pressed the flat of her palm against Fey's back and nodded almost absently, feeling the air inside her.

"Good, that's good. Okay, breathe out."

Fey exhaled noisily. She'd endured almost an hour of poking and prodding and was quickly reaching her limit. It wasn't the Med Witch's fault, though it was an effort not to snap at her to hurry it up. Having a stranger touch her, run their hands over Fey's wounds and weak points, made her skin crawl. And this was the same Witch who had seen her immediately after she'd been pulled from the river, the Witch who had seen Fey at her most broken and vulnerable.

Something about that—knowing this stranger had held Fey's life in her hands—made her feel weak in a way she wasn't used to. A way she didn't like.

It was a relief when the Witch finally stepped back and clasped her hands together.

"Well," she told Fey with a practiced but comforting smile. "The good news is you're almost completely healed. No scars from the fire, and the bones are mending nicely. It's a miracle, considering how badly you were hurt."

"How much longer will I be like… *this*?" Fey gestured to her body on the bed. She'd lost a lot of muscle mass and standing even for a few minutes at a time was exhausting. She'd spent three weeks stuck in bed, and if she didn't start training again soon, she was going to lose her mind.

"That's the bad news," the Med Witch told her with a sigh. "You lost a lot of power healing yourself, and you need to work to build your power reserves back up."

"I didn't heal myself," Fey insisted. "I don't know any healing magic."

"*You* might not, but your body does," the Witch insisted. "Our elements aren't just something we control—it's not a switch you can turn on and off. It's a part of you. Whether you made the choice or not, your power started to heal you the moment you got hurt. But losing your health sigil *and* taking so much damage?" She shook her head. "Anyone else would have died. All of my medical experience is telling me you *should* have died. You must have a remarkable power reservoir to draw from to recover from the wounds you sustained as quickly as you have."

Fey sighed, letting her head fall back against the pillows behind her.

"So, how do I refill this power reservoir? How do I get *better?*"

The Med Witch smiled. "You *eat*. No more of these medicinal soups your friends seem insistent on feeding you, no more watered-down juice, no more light meals. Your power had to draw heavily on your body to fuel that healing, and you've lost a lot of muscle. You need to rebuild that mass, so—consider this your excuse to eat whatever you want, as much as you want, for the next few weeks until you get that mass back."

"Whatever I want?" Fey asked with a smirk.

"Anything. You want rice? Eat an entire pot. Chocolate? Eat your weight in it, if you can. Power requires fuel, and the stronger you are, the more fuel you'll burn throughout the day, just keeping yourself alive. You were probably underweight before, and you were only using a portion of your power every day. Now? You burned through a lot of calories to keep yourself from dying, and you're *still* running a deficit. Eat."

"And can I start exercising again?"

"Absolutely. You can start today if you want. But be patient with yourself. Even light exercise is going to be too much for you until you build that muscle mass back, so take lots of breaks during those first few days. And *eat*."

Joy beamed at her and Fey from where she stood watching in the bedroom doorway. "We can do that. Thank you, again, for everything. You brought our sister back to us, and we'll never forget that." The Med Witch nodded and gathered her things together.

While Joy showed the Witch out, the two of them chatting about Fey's progress, Fey maneuvered her way to the edge of the bed. She stood, ignoring the dizziness that swept over her, and walked out of her room and to the kitchen on shaky legs.

She had lost a lot of muscle, and her body felt all sorts of wrong. Her arms and legs felt like spindly appendages that could barely keep her upright.

"The Med Witch says you need to make me breakfast," Fey told Willow as she entered the kitchen. Willow was standing at the sink, a novelty mug full of coffee cupped in her hands. "And ice cream. I need a *lot* of ice cream. Those were her orders."

"Well, if the *Med Witch* says so..." Willow shot her a playful grin and bounced over to the icebox. She began to pull ingredients out, piling things on the countertop. Eggs, ham, mushrooms, peppers, cheese. "I make a *mean* bacon and vegetable omelet, Fey."

Fey sank into a chair at the kitchen table, smiling. "I'm sure it's delicious, sister."

"I didn't say it was delicious. I said it was *mean*."

The front door clicked open, and a few moments later Joy joined them, pulling up a chair to sit beside Fey. She looked exhausted.

They all were.

They must have felt it through their shared mark. Felt every wound, every injury Fey had endured. And in the hours before they found her, the hours that she floated down the river, her body broken and dying, what had that been like for them?

"Any word from Lilith?" Fey asked. After storming off the other day, their sister hadn't returned.

Joy shook her head. "She just needs time, Fey. You know what she's like... she'll burn herself out in a day or so and be back here like nothing ever happened." Joy placed a comforting hand on Fey's. "Trust me. I've known Lilith a long time—the whole time I've been a Blade. She just needs to vent, and then she'll be back before you know it."

JOY WAS RIGHT, as always.

Lilith returned a few hours later, her arms loaded with enough food to feed the entire Queen's army.

"I got us pizzas," Lilith announced, setting the massive stack of pizza boxes on the coffee table and dropping onto the couch beside Fey.

After enduring a full plate of Willow's bacon and vegetable omelet —which had been doused in hot sauce and was very, very *mean*—they had retired to the living room, all three of them, to watch bad TV and relax. Fey couldn't stand the idea of spending another second in bed, so even though she was exhausted, she had refused to leave the couch. Joy had found a soft, knitted blanket from somewhere in the apartment and brought it to her, and Fey had used it to create a blanket cocoon, wrapping herself in the luxuriously soft fabric and taking up far more space on the couch than was necessary.

"Ooh!" squealed Willow, leaning forward to flip one of the pizza boxes open. She grabbed a slice and settled back on the couch, wriggling in pleasure.

Lilith made no move to grab any pizza for herself, but when Fey took a paper plate and loaded it with everything that looked good, she shuffled herself just back enough on the couch so Fey could lean against her shoulder while she ate.

This was the closest Lilith would ever get to apologizing, Fey knew. And it was enough. Fey smiled, leaning back into the couch and resting her head against Lilith's shoulder as she chewed a slice of pizza.

Apology accepted.

They spent the next hour eating pizza, flipping through the channels for mindless TV, and chatting. At some point Fey drifted off to sleep, still exhausted from the trauma her body had gone through, still healing.

CHAPTER 32

Fey awoke to the scream of an alarm.

Ordinarily, the sound of the perimeter alarm being triggered would have had her awake and armed within seconds. But her weakened state made her slow, and coming out of her deep sleep felt like fighting through mud.

Fey groaned, rolling to her side to speed her rise to consciousness. She was still partially wrapped in the blanket, and someone had placed a pillow under her head while she slept. The alarm screeched incessantly before abruptly going silent.

It was one of Joy's additions, the alarm. She'd installed them in every one of their safe houses, even before Alice's murder. But the alarm was never triggered on the night of Alice's death. Just another mystery about that night that had never made sense.

In the sudden quiet the alarm's absence left, Fey heard the apartment door open and slam.

"Joy?" Fey called out. "Willow?"

Nothing. Somewhere in the building a crash sounded, and the spike in adrenaline burned the last modicum of sleep from Fey's body. She cursed, flinging the blanket off herself and getting to her feet.

Her uniform was nowhere to be found, but someone had left her blades next to the bed, and Fey retreated to her bedroom to grab them, comforted by the weight of her familiar weapons. She didn't bother to put on pants, didn't bother putting anything on over her loose T-shirt and panties. Nothing here would deflect much of a weapon, anyway, and getting dressed meant losing even more time.

The apartment was empty. In the time it had taken her to wake up enough to even realize the alarm was sounding, her sisters had managed to arm themselves and leave to assess the threat. They hadn't bothered waking her, probably believing in her state that she was more likely to be a liability than a resource.

Fuck that.

After eating an entire pizza on her own and making a substantial dent in another, Fey was already feeling stronger. If they were in danger, she sure as fuck wasn't staying here snuggled in a blanket cocoon. Taking a deep breath to steady herself, Fey leaned against the apartment door to listen and quietly eased the door open.

The hallway was empty.

This particular apartment complex of theirs had three floors, and each floor housed four fully furnished units. The entire building was empty, though, save for them, and all their safe houses around the city— around the *realm*, really—were the same. The Crown owned and maintained these buildings to give the Queen's Blades and royal family a place to lay low when necessary.

An alarm meant someone had entered the building by force. Only a handful of people knew the locations and door codes to their safe houses—Dameon, of course, and the Queen and the treasurer responsible for all the building payments and upkeep. Their safe houses were a closely guarded secret. That remained one of the biggest mysteries surrounding Alice's death. She'd been at a safe house, should have been safe and protected. But someone had found her there, someone had known the location and set up the explosives that took her out without triggering any of their alarms.

Somewhere in the building, Fey could make out the faint sounds of fighting, followed by a very audible *crash* as something made of glass shattered. Sprinting to the stairwell, Fey leaped over the handrailing, calling on Air to slow her fall just before she landed on the first floor.

The sound of fighting was clearer now, and Fey readied herself for violence as she flung the door open to the lobby.

Nothing, however, prepared her for what she saw there.

Willow and Lilith were in their fighting leathers, masked but with no cowls covering their hair. They, at least, must have reacted to the alarm immediately and had taken the time to outfit themselves for a fight.

The furniture around the lobby lay splintered and broken against the perimeter of the room, and it looked like a tornado had hit the interior of the building. Even the floor tiles were damaged, and scorch marks marred the ceiling. The floor-to-ceiling windows and glass front door had all been shattered, and though they remained in place, not a single piece of glass wasn't covered in spiderweb fractures.

But it was the intruder who stopped Fey in her tracks, the intruder who almost made her knees buckle in shock.

"*Alastair*?" Fey whispered, stunned.

The Vampire had Lilith pinned to the wall with one massive hand crushing her throat, her feet dangling helplessly above the floor. Willow was clasped to his back, her legs wrapped around his midsection. One of her hands gripped his hair, pulling his head backward, and the other held her blade to his throat.

"Let my sister *go*!" Willow screamed. Lilith's legs kicked ineffectually at the wall behind her, her eyes vaguely unfocused and panicked. She was suffocating, Fey realized.

"*Tell me where she is!*" Alastair roared, his persuasion rolling through the air in a wave of pure power.

"No one knows who the fuck you're talking about, you absolute psycho!" Willow shouted back at him. "Let her go!"

Rage twisted in Fey's chest, power swirling through her and rising.

"Drop her right now, Alastair," Fey snarled, and the Vampire's head whipped towards her.

"Fey?" he asked. His hand immediately loosened around Lilith's throat, and she drew a deep, strained breath. The blade Willow held at his throat was now pressed tight enough to his skin to draw a line of blood, vivid red against the pale white of his neck, but he didn't seem to notice. His eyes were entirely focused on where Fey stood, and his gaze held an intensity that burned into her.

He stared at Fey like she was the only person in the room, eyes heating as he took in what little clothing she wore. Stared at her right up until the very moment Lilith wrapped her hands around his wrist and called Fire.

Alastair howled in pain as Lilith's hands burned into his wrist and he flung her aside. Lilith hit the ground hard, but still managed to roll skillfully into a crouch, agile as a cat.

"You'll have to do a hell of a lot better than that, handsome," Lilith told him in a mocking voice, drawing her blades from their sheaths at her side. "Willow, be a dear and go ahead and slit this asshole's throat."

"Gladly," Willow replied, adjusting her arm, but Alastair's hand closed over her wrist faster than Fey's eyes could register, holding the blade an inch from his skin. Fey's chest tightened, knowing her little sister wasn't a match for a Vamp as strong and quick as him. It would take no effort at all for him to snap her delicate wrist like a twig.

"That's *ENOUGH*!"

The blast of air that hit them was strong enough to knock all three of them backward, flinging Willow from Alastair's back. She hit the glass door, and the spiderweb cracks spread even further from the impact. Lilith hit the window hard enough to finally break the glass free from the metal frame, and the huge sheet of glass hit the ground outside and shattered. Alastair alone remained upright, though the blast of wind took him down to one knee.

Joy stalked into the room, unclasping her mask and flinging it aside, her uncovered hair trailing behind her like a cape. A storm raged in her blue eyes, and the fury that came from her was palpable enough to feel almost physical.

"What *the fuck* do you two think you're doing?" she snapped, pointing her finger at Lilith like it was a weapon.

"Our *jobs*," Lilith snarled back, struggling to her feet, glass shards cracking beneath her. "This Vamp broke into *our safe house*."

"And what, you just attacked him? You didn't bother to ask what he was doing here? Why he broke in?"

"He's a *Vampire*," Willow whined, as though that was enough of an explanation to absolve them of any blame. She rubbed the back of her head where it had hit the window.

"He's *Fey's Vampire*," Joy answered.

"Wait, no—he's not Fey's *anything*," Fey insisted. All three of her sisters turned to look at her, as though just now noticing her there.

But Alastair hadn't stopped staring at her from the moment he'd seen her.

"Where have you been?" he hissed, ignoring everyone else in the room. He stood, and Fey was pleased to see Joy's power had left him slightly shaky.

"Oh no, we're asking the questions here," Lilith said in a dark and deadly voice, circling him. "Starting with how you found this place. And I'd talk fast, my sister isn't the patient type, and I already promised her she could slit your throat, so..."

Willow smirked, and Alastair finally took his eyes off Fey to look at Lilith.

"*You* showed me where this place was," he purred to her. And Lilith's teeth visibly clenched. "You were so easy to follow, it didn't even take a week to track you down. I've had my staff on alert for you—for *any* of you—since last night, and one of them spotted you this afternoon. In a pizza place."

"Why?" Fey asked, suspicion and anger in her voice. "Why in all hell did you have people out looking for us?"

"I've been calling you," Alastair snarled. A dark red bead of blood welled in the cut at his neck, and as he spoke it dripped down to rest in the grove of his collarbone. "Three weeks, Fey. For *three fucking weeks* you've been gone. *Poof*, like you fucking vanished, without a word."

"Sweetie, maybe you're just not as memorable in bed as you think," Lilith teased, but Fey shot her a warning glare, and she went quiet with a smirk.

"I lost my phone," Fey said, a hard finality to her voice.

It wasn't a lie. At some point, either in the fight with the Shifter or when she'd plummeted off a cliff and into the river, her phone had been lost. Though, she *hadn't* given any thought to Alastair in the last three weeks, hadn't even considered that he would trying to contact her.

"But even if I hadn't, I don't belong to you," Fey continued. "And I don't owe you an explanation for *vanishing*."

"What about a real name? Do you owe me that?" Alastair snarled. "Because you sure as fuck didn't bother even bother with that, did you, *Fey*?"

The room went quiet. A dangerous quiet, the frightening stillness before a storm.

"What do you mean I didn't give you a real name?" The question came out as nonchalantly as she could make it, but even Fey could hear the threat in her voice. Alastair was very close to something he should let go of, for his safety.

"When I couldn't get a hold of you, I got worried. So, guess what I did? I looked into you, *Fey*, and what do you know? *You don't even fucking exist.*"

Fey shrugged, hoping he didn't register the rise in her pulse. Hoping he couldn't hear the deafening beat of her heart. "You said Phillip was a ghost, too—just because your contacts can't find anything on me doesn't mean any—"

"No," Alastair interrupted. "No, they couldn't find any *dirt* on him, but you know what they did find? A job. A residence. A fucking family. But you?" He gestured to her and laughed, a dark cruel laugh without a hint of humor. "You're an actual fucking ghost. You're a nobody. All of you are." He looked around at them, face twisted in anger. "I didn't show up here because you didn't answer the phone after we fucked, Witchling. I showed up here because you used me to get information, and you didn't even bother to give me *your real fucking name*."

"Oh shit, you did fuck him," Willow whispered.

Lilith took a step closer, and Alastair spun toward her, eyes fiery and fangs bared. "Try it, Witch, and see where it gets you."

Lilith took another step, a savage smile spreading across her face. "Gladly, leech."

"Enough!" shouted Fey. She pointed at Lilith. "You, back the fuck down right now, and *you.*" She moved her arm to point at Alastair. "I don't owe you *shit*. But for the record, my name *is* Fey. You said you could smell lies, right? That is my name and has always been my name. Tell me if I'm fucking lying."

Alastair calmed slightly, but only enough to seemingly assess what was truly happening. Knowing Lilith and Willow, they likely jumped him the moment he'd gotten into the building, and in the rush of the attack, Alastair hadn't had a chance to evaluate his situation. He looked around at them, then, really looked at them all one by one. Lilith, rage, and violence contorting her face. Willow, her knife now at her side but its blade smeared with his blood. Joy, who stood among the wreckage of the lobby, was dangerously quiet. Three of them were in their fighting leathers. And all four of them had failed to activate the spell that hid their Blade's marks from view. He took it all in, as he looked at them.

And, finally, Alastair's eyes came to rest on Fey.

"What are you?" he asked, his voice low.

"Exactly what you said," Fey answered. She held her blades at her side, letting him see her—*all* of her. The oversized T-shirt didn't cover her arms, didn't cover the sigils and blade branded there. "I'm a ghost."

Alastair swallowed, then glanced between them all again and asked softly. "Your... sisters?"

Willow growled, baring her teeth at him as he turned his gaze on her, but Fey gave a small nod.

"Yes. My sisters."

She watched him put it together. She saw the moment it clicked into place, and he saw her, really saw her, for who she was.

"I wasn't lying, you know," Fey told him with a sheepish smile, under the heavy weight of his gaze. "I did lose my phone. I had no idea you were trying to reach me."

He nodded, clearly not listening. Then he ran his hands through his hair and let out a long exhale of breath. He looked at the room around them, at the damage they'd caused with their fight.

"Fuck," he said. "*Fuck.*"

Yeah, that pretty much summed it up, Fey thought.

Alastair turned to Lilith. "I shouldn't have had you followed," he admitted begrudgingly.

"No, you fucking shouldn't have," she snapped back.

"I didn't..." He stopped. "I didn't know that you were... didn't know you all were—" He tipped his head back. "*Fuck,*" he said, again.

"Yeah," agreed Fey.

Then, suddenly, he laughed, eyes still closed. "I thought you were a myth, you know that? The Blades? I never believed you were real."

Willow made a noise from behind him.

"We should kill him," she said, decidedly.

"Agreed," said Lilith at the same time Joy snapped, "*Willow!*"

"What?" Willow asked her, sounding indignant. "Fey, he fucking *stalked you*. I don't care what your reasoning is—" She gestured with her blade at Alastair. "That's fucking *creepy*, dude. So, she slept with you, big fucking deal, that doesn't give you the right to track her down like she's your lost pet or something. And now this site is compromised, *and* he knows who we are. A *Vampire* knows who we are. He's a liability, and *I think* we should kill him."

"She's right," said Alastair, glancing back at her. "About being creepy, not about needing to kill me. What the fuck is wrong with you, you crazy Witch?"

Willow bared her teeth at him again. "I'm not crazy, I'm *practical*."

"And she's right that I've compromised this site," Alastair continued. "But I'm not a liability. I won't tell anyone who you are. What you are."

"And how are we supposed to believe that?" Lilith asked.

Alastair shrugged. "Believe what you want. But I have no hate for the Crown or the Queen, and no one I'd sell this information to, even if I wanted to."

"The Fallen King would pay dearly for it," Joy said in a dangerously quiet voice, and Fey winced to think of what would happen if the Vampire Patriarch knew the names and identities of the Queen's Blades. They wouldn't be able to leave the palace, unmasked, for risk of being jumped.

Alastair laughed darkly. "Oh, I know he would. And he's the last person I'd want to help, trust me. There isn't enough money in the world he could give me to piss on him if he were on fire."

"But that could change," Joy challenged. "People change. Five years from now, you might not feel the same way and selling us out might sound very tempting."

"And what will this information be worth in five years, when I'll have no guarantee any of you are even alive?" Alastair asked. "I don't know a lot about your Faction, but I know enough to imagine that the Queen's Blades don't live very long. In five years, you could all be dead, and knowing your names and what you look like wouldn't be worth shit to anyone, not even him."

Joy chewed her lip thoughtfully. Lilith snorted, something she only did when she was losing an argument.

"So..." Willow asked, hesitantly. "We're *not* going to kill him?"

When they all turned to look at her, she snapped, "What? I'm just asking!"

"Do you..." Lilith sighed, exasperated. She sheathed her blades and crossed her arms over her chest. "Do you want to stay for pizza or something?"

Alastair's mouth opened in shock, and Lilith huffed. "You're Fey's boyfriend now, right? And you're already here, you fucking stalker."

He laughed at that, and his golden eyes sparkled when he looked at Fey.

"Boyfriend, huh?" he asked, slipping his hands into his pockets.

"Fuck no," she snapped.

"As tempting as that sounds, no," Alastair said to Lilith, ignoring Fey's quick protest. "No, I should go. And so should all of you. If I could find you, so could anyone," he warned. "Especially with the, uh— mess we've made of this place."

"He's right," Joy said, "We need to go. This site isn't safe anymore. We should head back to the palace. Fey has healed enough to be moved, and it'll be safer there."

Fey sighed, letting her head fall back against the wall. She'd liked this place. The bath was big enough to stretch all the way out, and that was a luxury she wasn't thrilled to give up.

Willow wiped Alastair's blood off her blade. "Fine," she said. "But we're bringing the pizzas."

CHAPTER 33

Healing was an agonizingly slow process.

Fey was excused from her duties and assignations while she got back into shape, and she saw her sisters less and less as they took up the workload without her. Someone had finally reported Phillip Danvers's disappearance to the Crown, and seemingly inspired by the fall Fey had taken into the Western River, Dameon announced with sorrow that the professor had fallen to his watery death, his body having been discovered weeks previously but unidentified until just recently. The Crown sent condolences to his husband.

A tragic accident, and one the university and its students would mourn for the proper length of time and then move past.

The day after the news had broken, Dameon had come for a full day of combat training, and Fey had almost asked him about it. Had even opened her mouth the moment she'd seen him, ready to demand answers to the questions that still burned inside her. But Lilith had taken that moment to stomp very deliberately on her foot and shoot her a glare that reminded her just what her sister thought about questioning their orders.

So she'd dropped it. Dropped the questions, dropped the mystery.

She had lived. Lived, but at a heavy cost to her body, and for the next few weeks at least, she needed to focus on rebuilding everything she'd lost.

Instead of following the mysteries further, Fey trained.

From sunrise to sunset, and often even longer, she trained, pushing herself to her limit. She spent entire days in the gym, toning her body and her powers, building her strength and muscles.

It took time, but bit by bit, day by day, Fey began to feel like herself again. The muscles in her arms and legs grew and hardened with use, and her figure filled out once more. Even her powers felt strong, again, and she spent several hours every night drawing on Water and Air, filling herself with the elements available to her and rejoicing in her power.

By the time the Winter Solstice grew near, and planning for the Queen's Winter Ball was in full swing, Fey was ready to rejoin her sisters and take up her blades again.

THE WINTER SOLSTICE marks the shortest day of the lunar year—the point at which the sun is at its furthest point from our world. For the Witches of the realm, it's a holy day, the first day of Winter, and the day when the Goddess makes Her transition from a giver of life to a destroyer. In the dark months of Winter, She will take more lives than at any other time in the year, and the world will grow as cold and dead as Her heart.

On the morning of the Winter Solstice, most Witches attend services at their Temple to honor the dead. It is tradition to make food —mostly baked sweets and chocolates—and leave them as offerings around the city. For their Faction, it is a time to honor the ones they have lost. A time of contemplation and prayer.

For the Queen, it's an excuse to throw a party.

The Winter Ball was the social highlight of the year for aristocrats in the Eternal City and inner octants, and many socialites spent months each year plying the Queen and her heir with gifts and social visits to earn themselves an invitation.

In the past, Fey loathed these events. Like the Princess's birthday months earlier, her role in the Winter Ball was nothing more than a show of the Queen's strength. Fey and her sisters would spend the party standing guard over the Queen and her daughter, still as statues at her back, little more than props.

But for once, Fey found herself looking forward to the celebration, looking forward to spending the evening alongside her sisters. They were typically situated just far enough behind the throne that they could whisper to one another—their masks hiding any sign of their lips moving.

The idea of donning her fighting leathers again, even just to stand there and look frightening, sounded like a dream to Fey. When the solstice finally came, and the hour of the Winter Ball approached, Fey couldn't help but be excited.

CHAPTER 34

"Introducing the Lady Madeline and her consort, of the second octant."

The herald's voice boomed across the massive room, amplified by her Air magic, and following their introduction, Lady Madeline swept into the room in a crimson and gold gown, a male in matching attire on her arm.

The couple stopped before the dais, bowing to the Queen, and wished her a joyous Solstice. Queen Edelin accepted their greetings with a regal nod, as she had with all the guests so far, and waved them away, bidding them to join the party.

Fey was pleased to learn the Princess had been given leave to enjoy the ball, and for the first year since Fey had become a Queen's Blade, Princess Amalia would not be forced to join her mother on the dais, accepting thanks and welcoming guests. Fey couldn't see her in the crowd, but she hoped the Princess was finally getting to mingle with other children her age, for once.

Queen Edelin, of course, would not be joining in the festivities. She would sit on her throne the entire night, as she did each Solstice, welcoming guests as they arrived and watching over the Solstice Ball in the bored and haughty manner befitting a Queen.

All four Queen's Blades stood behind her, two at each shoulder. Far enough back to give her space for private conversation, but close enough to make most guests nervous. Dameon, captain of her Guard, stood at the foot of the dais, his hand on the hilt of the sword at his waist.

"Introducing Lord and Lady Roberts, and their consort Desdemona, of the Eternal City," The herald announced, and three more guests entered and approached the Queen, bowing formally and offering pleasantries.

"Their consort is a Shifter," Lilith whispered, loud enough for her sisters to hear, but just quiet enough to evade the Queen's sharp ears and Dameon's notice. It was an art they had practiced for just such an occasion. Lilith, somehow, knew all the gossip in the realm and dished it out like small, tasty treats to them throughout the Winter Ball. It was the one royal event she seemed required to attend, the only one she never seemed to be otherwise occupied for. "*All* of their past consorts have been Shifters."

"They must have a type," Joy said, her voice barely audible over the din of the party.

"Oh, they do, a very specific type," Lilith answered. Her voice dropped even lower, the sign of juicy gossip. "I've heard they like to be *hunted*. And that pretty Lioness at their side is more than happy to oblige."

Willow stifled a laugh, and Lilith twerked her eyebrows at her suggestively.

"Have *you* ever been hunted, Lilith?" Fey asked.

"Once or twice," she answered with a casual but barely perceptible shrug. "I can't say I'm a fan. I'd rather be tied up. Less cardio."

Another giggle from Willow, and even Fey couldn't help but smile behind her mask.

Goddess above and below, Fey had missed this. Missed spending time with her sisters, missed the easy flow of conversation between the four of them.

"Look," whispered Joy. "It's the other Queen."

And sure enough, there she was—the Queen's twin sister, Cassandra. She entered before she was even formally announced, her head held high, raven black hair piled on her head in an intricate braid. Unlike other guests, she didn't wear a ball gown or expensive suit, adorning herself instead in the pure white robes of the White Priestesses.

"Introducing High Priestess Cassandra, head of the White Coven and of royal blood," the herald announced, but Cassandra had already started toward the dais. Ignoring Dameon entirely, she climbed the few steps to the Queen, coming to a stop directly in front of her sister. She spoke to her in a hushed voice, low enough Fey couldn't hear what was being said.

Cassandra seemed worried, her brows drawn together as she spoke, but Queen Edelin's expression never changed. She nodded to her sister and said with a finality that made it clear the conversation was finished.

"We will look into it," she said, motioning Dameon to join them on the dais. "Give the Captain of my Guard the details, and we will send someone to investigate. Go."

Cassandra bowed, and Dameon escorted her out of the ballroom, his hand on her elbow and the two of them speaking in low voices.

"She has a daughter, you know," Lilith told her sisters, waiting until the hem of Cassandra's long white robe vanished out the door before speaking.

"No!" Joy squealed.

"Oh yes," Lilith confirmed. "Years before Princess Amalia was born. It was quite the scandal—a White Priestess, pregnant with a potential heir to the throne? The realm was in *shambles* over it."

"What happened?" Fey asked.

Lilith shrugged. "She wasn't Goddess blessed, was she? Her Awakening came and went, and she couldn't wield all four elements. And by then the Queen had a girl of her own, so... I guess everyone just forgot about her."

"That's so sad," Willow said.

"That's life, little sister," Lilith said, then her eyes focused on a new target. "Oh! Wait until you hear about *them*," she crooned, as another couple approached the dais, and Fey could feel her sisters practically buzzing with excitement.

Dameon returned shortly after, without Cassandra. But he made no move to recall them from the Queen's side, so whatever help the

Queen's sister had requested wasn't important enough to require their expertise.

The evening sped by—hours passing quickly under the spell of Lilith's gossip. Even the Queen seemed to relax as the night went on, and Dameon eventually left his post at the base of the dais to come sit next to her, lounging on the Princess's throne. It was the first time Fey had ever seen them behave like this in public.

"Oh, you have got to be fucking kidding me," Lilith said, suddenly, her voice louder than before, loud enough to be overheard.

Fey followed her gaze to the entrance, and her mouth dropped open.

"Is that?" started Joy, and next to her, Willow started to laugh almost hysterically.

"Yes," snarled Fey, rage twisting her words. "Yes, it is."

"Introducing the Vampire Patriarch, Cassian Salvatore deSanguine," The herald announced. "And his eldest son, Alastair Salvatore, of the Eternal City."

The Vampire King was younger looking than he had any right to be at his age, though old enough that his once black hair had gone silver. He stood tall, his back straight in the way of royals, and at his side, dressed in the colors of the vampire royalty, was Alastair. *Her* Alastair.

"I told you we should have killed him," said Willow, between laughs.

CHAPTER 35

It had taken every ounce of her restraint for Fey to remain at her post on the Queen's dais as the final guests of the evening were announced and the party reached its apex. Her hands clenched and unclenched at her side, and her fingers itched to draw her blades, if only to find some level of comfort in the feel of them in her hands.

At some point over the last hour or so, the shock of Alastair's parentage had gone from infuriating to hilarious to her sisters. And now, instead of a constant stream of gossip, Fey had to endure their endless teasing.

"A *prince*," cooed Lilith, and a barely stifled giggle escaped from behind Willow's mask.

"*Shut the fuck up*," Fey hissed back at them.

"Of course, Princess," Joy whispered back, and this time the giggles were audible enough that the Queen shot them an irritated glance over her shoulder. They managed to get themselves under control, but a few moments later, the Queen gestured Dameon closer, and they held a whispered conversation amongst themselves before she dismissed him with a wave. Dameon stood.

"Uh oh," Joy whispered. "Busted."

"Our Queen informs me that you are relieved for the night,"

Dameon announced when he approached the four of them. "You are free to return to your chambers or stay and enjoy the festivities. Just remember that you are an extension of the Queen herself and are not to speak or interact with any of the guests."

They bowed their heads in acknowledgment, keeping their gaze lowered to the ground until he left.

The command wasn't unexpected, though it *was* unnecessary. Of course they were not to socialize with the other guests, not to reveal anything about themselves that could put that anonymity in jeopardy.

Under other circumstances, Fey might have stayed. This was the part she enjoyed about these parties. As the hour drew late, and the guests lost themselves in drink, she could pick up juicy tidbits of gossip just by being in the right place at the right time. She knew how to lose herself in the shadows of the ballroom, and it was easy to eavesdrop when liquor made the guests louder, and bolder, than usual.

But tonight? Tonight, she wanted to hurt something, and she had no intention of staying to listen to any trivial aristocratic gossip. No. She'd head straight to their training room, and she'd likely stay there until her knuckles were bloody and she could barely walk.

There is an art to hurrying without appearing to rush, and Fey was a master of it. She maneuvered her way through the crowds of guests, appearing to be entirely unrushed and at ease, a deadly shadow floating amongst them, but all the while she was clenching her jaw tight enough she feared she might break a tooth, moving as quickly as she could.

She had managed to escape the main ballroom and was almost to the hallway outside of one of the smaller, less crowded, entertaining rooms when a voice from the shadows stopped her.

"Why hello, Witchling."

Her head snapped up at the greeting, and there he was: Alastair Salvatore, Prince of the Vampires.

He leaned against the wall near the exit, a glass of amber liquid in one hand, the other in his pocket. In his red-lined black suit, his usually messy hair brushed back off his face, he did look every bit a Prince.

"Don't talk to me," Fey snarled at him, and she kept walking out the open door and into the hallway.

It was darker here, lit only by a few well-placed oil lamps, and would continue to get darker the further they traveled from the main ballroom. It was a clever way of ensuring guests remained in a centralized area, without them even knowing they were being herded there. It also meant the hallways were all too often occupied by couples, moved by drink and looking for dark unoccupied places where they might lose themselves in some heavy petting. The walls of these hallways were even designed with little hideaways—perfect alcoves for drunk fondling.

Thankfully, it was still early enough in the festivities that the hallway was unoccupied, and Fey dropped all pretense of ease and walked swiftly down the hall, nearly running to get away from the noise and crowd. To get away from *him*.

"Oh, come on now," Alastair said from close behind her. He was following her, and she could tell he was smiling from the tone of his voice. *Fucking Vamp speed*, Fey thought sourly. "Surely you can stand saying hello to me?"

Fey stopped, rage ratcheting through her body.

"You can't talk to me," she hissed through her teeth. "Because I'm not to speak to the guests, *Prince*."

He stepped in front of her, blocking her way, his mouth twisting in distaste.

"Don't call me that," he said.

"And why not?" Fey asked. Her voice was louder than she intended, but she couldn't stop herself. Anger made every word she spoke louder, bolder. "That's what you are, isn't it? Prince Alastair Salvatore, heir to the Vampire throne."

She bowed to him, mockingly, drawing her blades and holding them straight out from her sides in the formal bow of the Queen's Blades.

"Or should I call you Prince deSanguine?" she asked, her voice dripping with venom as she rose. "Is that what Your Grace would prefer?"

"DeSanguine is a title," Alastair snarled. "Not a surname. Fey, I never lied to you."

Fey laughed a dry laugh. "You never *lied to me*? Fuck you. You accused me of using you just because you thought I gave you a fake name, Alastair *deSanguine*."

"It's a *fucking title*. My name is Alastair Salvatore. It has always *been* Alastair Salvatore. And I'm not the heir of shit. I never inherited the title, my sister did. And it's going to skip me and go straight to my brother. My father just drags me to these stupid fucking things every decade or so to show me off and remind the royalty of what a catch his unmarried son would be."

"Salvatore deSanguine doesn't have a daughter," Fey snapped back at him, and something in Alastair's eyes shattered like glass.

"No," he whispered, looking down at the glass he held in his hands. "No, he doesn't, not anymore." He tipped his head back finishing his drink, and for a moment Fey thought he might fling the empty glass against the wall.

"I didn't fucking lie to you," he said instead, hissing the words through clenched teeth.

"You told us we could trust you, told us you had no reason to sell us out. And you're the son of the person who would pay the most to see us fucking dead." Saying it aloud made it hurt even more, the words twisting to form knots in Fey's stomach. "That sounds like a pretty good fucking reason to sell us out, Alastair."

"Fey, I hate the bastard as much as you!" Alastair snarled back at her. "More, even! I *told you* I had no intention of ever telling him anything, and I fucking *meant it.*"

Fey forced herself to take a deep breath. They were being loud. Too loud. And she couldn't risk someone coming out here to find the source of their shouting. She had no idea what Dameon and the Queen would do if they found her here, talking to the son of Salvatore deSanguine. It was hard to imagine a worse guest she could be caught speaking with unless it were the Fallen King himself.

"Come here," she sighed, pulling him toward a floor-length tapestry hanging on the wall. She lifted the fabric, revealing a hidden space built into the marble barely bigger than a closet. "Get in. We can't be seen speaking like this."

Alastair did what she asked unquestioningly, setting his empty glass on a small decorative table and ducking under the tapestry and into the alcove. Once he was inside, Fey slipped in after him, letting the tapestry fall back into place on the wall. Another clever design from the architectural geniuses who had built this place. The fabric of the tapestry was thin enough to let light pass through, thin enough to see people walking by, but the darkness of the alcove left them completely hidden from view.

The moment she stepped into the alcove with Alastair, Fey realized she'd made a terrible mistake. There was no room here, no way to keep any sort of distance between the two of them, and he was...

He was...

His presence was like a tuning fork and every one of her nerves vibrated in response. He hadn't moved to give her any room when she'd ducked inside, and Fey found herself with less than a few inches between them, and Alastair looming above her. He smelled like expensive cologne tonight, and she realized for the first time the scent she'd smelled before, the smell of cloves and wood smoke, wasn't something he put on. That was *his* scent, the smell of his body.

Fey swallowed, her mouth suddenly dry.

"How did you know it was me?" she asked, trying to distract herself from how close he was and dropping her voice to a whisper. They wouldn't be seen here, but they still had to be quiet.

He stared down at her, head cocked to the side in confusion, and Fey clarified. "In the party back there, you called me Witchling. But I could have been any one of the Blades, so how did you know it was me? How were you so sure I wasn't one of my sisters?"

Alastair snorted. "How did I know it was you? How could I *not* know?" He motioned to her fighting leathers with a flick of his fingers, stepping closer. Fey tried to shrink back, to keep that much-needed space between them, but her back hit the wall almost immediately. *Oh yes. Leading him here was a mistake.* "Every single person at this party could be dressed in that same outfit, and I'd still know which one was you, Fey."

"How?" she asked again, her voice a little breathless. He was close enough that she had to tilt her head up to look him in the eyes.

His hand rose to grip her face, and the fabric of her mask dug into her skin. "Because you're a knife in a room of cowards. You're an apex predator, head and shoulders above every person in that party." His voice was a sensual purr, and Fey whimpered in his hold. "I can sense you, Fey. You feel like heat and fire and *power*. There's not a single person in the world who could hold a candle to it."

He bent his head down, kissing her, his lips pressing the gossamer material of her mask hard against her lips. Kissed her like she belonged to him, kissed her like she was his everything, like she was the Goddess come to life.

Kissed her until he felt the tip of her blade press against his stomach.

Startled, Alastair pulled back enough to glance down at the knife between them. Fey's hand was steady, and though she pressed the tip of her blade into him enough to hurt, she wasn't pressing enough to draw blood.

Yet.

"What are you doing here, Alastair?" she asked. Her head was spinning from the kiss, but she drew on every ounce of restraint she had to keep herself steady.

"I told you. My father drags me to these things—"

"No, what are you doing *here*?" With her free hand, Fey gestured to the darkness around them, to the space—what little there was—between them. "What are you doing here, with me? What do you even want from me? You know what I am now; you know—"

She stopped. Some emotion she couldn't identify was stuck in her throat, and it was hard to form the words around it. Instead, she tightened her grip on the hilt of her blade and pushed it harder against him, drawing a small bead of blood that spread over the fabric of his dress shirt.

Fey expected him to move away, to take a step backward and put a little distance between the two of them. The distance that she needed if she was going to catch her breath. She expected him to shout, to curse. Expected him to do anything but what he did.

Staring down at the knife between them, at the welt of dark blood on his dress shirt, Alastair smiled.

Fey blinked at him, in surprise.

"Aren't you scared of me?" she asked.

"Scared? No," Alastair answered, still looking down at where she held the blade against his midsection. "Fey, I'm fucking *terrified* of you."

The answer startled a laugh from her. "You are crazy, you know that?" she told him, shaking her head and smiling.

"Maybe," he conceded. He brought his own hands up to cover the hilt of her knife, wrapping them around hers. His gaze rose to capture her stare, and she felt like she was drowning in his golden eyes. "I see you, Fey," he whispered. "I see every part of you, and what you are. And I want all of it."

Fey's grip loosened, and the blade clattered to the floor between them. She reached up, pulling her mask off. Then she grabbed his head in both hands and pulled him down to kiss her again.

CHAPTER 36

Alastair groaned into their kiss, moving even closer to pin Fey between the wall and his body, crushing her against him.

Every thought in Fey's head vanished as she felt his body against hers. She wanted to touch him, *needed* to touch him.

Her hands moved from his hair and down his chest, feeling hard muscle beneath the silk of his dress shirt.

Not enough.

Alastair's tongue danced with hers as she fumbled with his buttons, finally getting his shirt open enough to run her hands along his skin. He was perfect, all smooth skin taut over muscle, no scars, no sigils. Her hands slid lower, over his stomach. Lower, over his hips. Lower...

Alastair hissed when she gripped him through the fabric of his pants, pulling back from their kiss a fraction to curse. But it still wasn't enough for Fey. She craned her head up to capture his mouth again, and he kissed her back even harder than before, nipping at her lips with his teeth. Her fingers worked swiftly, unlatching his belt and pulling his zipper down, releasing him.

When she wrapped her hand around his cock, marveling at the thickness, he threw his head back and groaned.

"*Fuck*, Fey,"

His skin is like silk, she thought as she trailed her fingers up the length of him, feeling him twitch under her light touch. A bead of precum glistened at his tip, and the sight of it made Fey dizzy with desire. She gripped him again, wrapping her fingers around the base of him, and he groaned, his hips rocking forward, thrusting into her hand.

Before she could explore his body further, Alastair crushed her back against the wall, knocking her hand away and reaching between them for her clothing. The laces of her pants melted away under his quick fingers, and Alastair pushed her hips back as he slipped his hand under the soft leather fabric of her pants to touch her.

Fey's head rolled back, and she gasped as his fingers slipped down her center. Her hands rose to grip the back of his neck, twisting her hips to give him access.

"*Fuck*," Alastair hissed, his breath hot against her neck, his lips brushing against her too-sensitive skin and making her shiver. "You're already so wet for me, aren't you Witchling?"

She didn't have a chance to respond before he pushed one long finger inside her, and all she could do was moan in answer.

"Such a good Witch," he whispered in her ear, adding a second finger and making her back arch against the wall. "Always so wet for me."

His palm pressed against her as he fucked her with his hand, rubbing her clit while he moved his fingers inside her. It was too much already, and when he used his other hand to lift her, spreading her legs and raising her thigh to his hip so his fingers could curl deeper inside her, she lost it.

Fey bit into her bottom lip to keep from screaming as she came, her hips rolling against his hand as she chased each wave of her orgasm. By the time she came down from her peak, she was gasping, fighting to catch her breath. Still, she whimpered at the loss when he pulled his fingers from her throbbing pussy.

Alastair brought his hand up to his face and licked the two fingers that had been inside her. "I love this taste," he told her. "You're the best thing I've ever tasted, Fey."

He moved so quickly that Fey had no time to react. One minute, she was pinned between him and the wall, pressed against him with one leg wrapped around his hip, and the next minute he spun her around, pushing her face and upper body into the wall and yanking her pants down to reveal her ass.

His hands gripped her hips, adjusting her until her back arched, and she had to press her hands against the wall to balance herself. His fingertips trailed across her pussy again, then continued up the curve of her backside, over her ass and back toward—

Fey whimpered when Alastair's fingers stopped against the puckered skin of her ass. He circled her hole with fingertips still drenched from her pussy, slick against her entrance, and chuckled darkly as she trembled under his touch.

"Not tonight, Witchling," he said, fingers circling her hole again, teasing.

Fey's entire body quivered as his fingers moved away, and he gripped her hips hard enough to bruise. She felt him line up with her entrance, felt the tip of his cock press against her pussy, and it was an effort not to push back against him.

When they'd fucked before in his office, he'd entered her slowly, letting her adjust inch by inch to the impossible size of him. He didn't enter her slowly, tonight. With one powerful thrust, he filled her, pushing his cock inside her to the hilt.

Fey's back arched even more, and her head tipped back away from the wall as she screamed, equal parts shock and pleasure. She'd never felt so full, so stretched open, and it was a wonderful agony having him fill her like this.

Alastair's hand immediately clasped over her mouth.

"Shhhhhh," he whispered into her ear. "You're the one who didn't want us to be overheard." His fingers were still slick from her pussy and his saliva, and his hand was damp on her face. She moaned loudly into it as he started to move his hips, his other arm snaking around her chest to pull her back against him as he moved inside her.

"If you're not quiet, you're going to get us caught," he chided, rolling his hips, and tightening his grip on her. "Unless that's what you want?" His voice was a caress against the soft skin of her neck, and the slow steady rhythm of his cock moving inside her was overwhelming. He peppered impossibly light kisses across her skin as he whispered to her. "Do you want us to get caught, little Witchling? Do you want someone to come by and hear you?"

Fey couldn't think, couldn't breathe, she was nothing but raw energy, every nerve of her body on fire with the things he was doing to her. His pace increased, and she could feel her body tightening in response, rising to another peak.

"I think you do want to get caught," he whispered into her skin, and she could feel his lips curving against her into a smile. "What a dirty girl you are, Fey."

It was lucky he still had his hand over her mouth, lucky he gripped her hard enough that she couldn't even open her mouth to draw a proper breath. Because this time, when she came, she came hard enough that the scream she could have made would have brought every guard in the city running.

She shuddered in his grip, her body convulsing over and over as he moved inside her.

"Holy shit," he whispered, finally taking his hand from her mouth as she shuddered weakly for the final time. "You are so fucking perfect, Fey."

His hips started to move faster, harder, as he chased his pleasure. "So fucking perfect," he whispered again, burying his face in the space between her shoulder and her neck and shuddering his release. Fey arched back against him, loving the feel of it, loving the way he held her even tighter as he filled her.

His hands loosened around her slightly, after, and they both fought to catch their breath. Fey licked her lips, shocked at how intense that had been, how good he had felt. She'd thought maybe their first time had been a fluke, but—

"*FUCK,*" Alastair snarled, slamming his hand against the wall above her head. "A fucking *BED.*"

Startled, Fey pulled away slightly, tilting her head back and to the side to look up at him. His face was contorted with anger, eyes clenched, and fangs bared.

"Alastair?" she asked.

"I couldn't take five fucking minutes to find a *bed*," he snarled, palm pressed flat against the wall. "I fucked you on a desk, and now against a wall, when you deserve a fucking *bed*."

Fey couldn't help it. She laughed, her hand coming up to cover her face as she did so.

"It's not funny," he insisted, opening his eyes to look at her.

Fey wiggled away from him and turned to face him. He was leaning against the wall, arm braced above her, and the way his body was curved above hers, almost protective, made her feel... safe.

"Well," she said, reaching up to push his hair out of his eyes. It had been well-styled, brushed back in a coif before, but now? Now it was a mess. And she found herself liking it better this way. "You'll just have to make it up to me, then. Good thing you know someone who lives here, and knows where all the free beds are, isn't it?"

His lips curved up into a smile. "Oh, yeah?" he asked, arching an eyebrow.

She smirked back at him, pulling her pants back up over her hips. "Yeah," she purred. Alastair straightened, tucking himself back into his pants and attempting to button his shirt. "So, why don't we—"

Voices in the hallway. Fey froze, but Alastair's smile grew even wider and more wicked, his golden eyes sparkling with mischief.

"Uh oh," he whispered. "We better be quiet, Witchling." He reached for her, running his thumb over her bottom lip.

She couldn't help it, she laughed again, softly as she could, her fingers retying the laces on her pants, making it clear to him she had no plans on pushing their luck here any further. This incorrigible asshole.

There were audible footsteps in the hallway now, drawing closer, and Fey could hear the soft cadence of conversation grow more distinct as they grew near. Alastair put a finger to her lips and whispered "Shhhhh" as the voices drew close enough for them to hear.

But she recognized that voice. Her smile slipped slightly, under Alastair's finger, and he drew his hand back, sensing the shift in her and frowning.

Yes. She did know that voice. She'd heard that voice for years.

Dameon.

Fey tilted her head, straining to listen.

That was Dameon's voice.

"I don't care what you *thought*. Coming here tonight was a mistake," Dameon was saying. His voice held an edge of anger Fey rarely heard in it, and it chilled her blood to hear it. "What if someone saw you?"

"It's a party, isn't it?" a gruff voice answered, and something about that voice tugged on a memory. She recognized them, too.

But from where?

"Don't be so fucking brainless," Dameon answered. They were closer now, and though they were still whispering, Fey no longer had to strain to hear them. "Anyone could have seen you."

"I didn't have anywhere else to bring it," the other voice protested with a growl. "What was I supposed to do? Leave it somewhere for someone else to find?"

They stepped into the light of the oil lamps in the hallway, and despite herself, Fey sucked in air audibly in shock, prompting Alastair to wrap his hand around her, pulling her against him.

She did know that voice, and the moment she saw the Shifter with Dameon, the memory of where she'd heard it before came crashing into her.

That same voice, that same growl.

"You're not supposed to be here."

A face, moments before it split open, moments before the male transformed before her into a beast.

Into a Panther.

Fey's heart strained in her chest. Dameon—who hated all Shifters since a Bear Shifter had left that scar across his face—was talking with a Shifter. Dameon was talking with *the* Shifter from the warehouse, the one who'd attacked her, who'd almost killed her. Talking as though they knew each other.

She might have screamed if Alastair hadn't been there, holding her. In fear, in rage, in confusion, she didn't know. But cradled in Alastair's arms, she stayed quiet and watched as they walked right past them in the too-small hallway and continued down the hall and out of sight.

The moment Alastair loosened his grip on her, she was gone—out of his arms, out of the alcove, and running down the hallway. She heard him swear quietly behind her, and he called her name in a soft hiss, but Fey didn't look back.

Tonight, she would get answers. Tonight, she was going to find out the truth, even if it killed her.

CHAPTER 37

Fey followed Dameon and the Shifter deeper and deeper into the palace, keeping enough of a distance between them to prevent them from seeing her. At some point she became aware of Alastair moving alongside her, his steps making no noise against the marble floor.

Shooting him a glare, Fey hissed, "Go back to the party."

Alastair shook his head at her with a sneer and mouthed two words back at her: *Fuck. You.*

She didn't have time to argue with him. Scowling, she continued her chase. If the Vampire insisted on accompanying her, he better keep out of her way.

They passed room after room, heading out of the main palace and into the Western Wing. Fey barely had time to resent Alastair's presence before he made himself useful. They reached a fork in a hallway, a staircase on either side, one leading up and one going down.

Fuck. Fey hadn't seen which way they'd gone, and she looked frantically between the two options, trying to decide which way was more likely. But it was impossible without knowing where they might be going. She was about to take a chance and just guess when Alastair touched her shoulder lightly, cocking his head to listen for a moment before pointing to the staircase leading up.

Of course. They were far enough away now that Fey couldn't hear their footsteps, couldn't make out any sound of their conversation—but Alastair, blessed by the Goddess with preternatural Vampire hearing, could. Nodding, she followed his lead and headed up the stairs.

She wasn't familiar with the Western Wing of the palace at all, and twice more she had to rely on Alastair to point them in the right direction before she started to recognize where they were. The moment she did, she knew exactly where Dameon was heading.

Abruptly, she took off down a hallway leading away from their prey, nearly at a run. Alastair gestured frantically, pointing back the other way to indicate the way they should be going. Fey caught his eyes and shook her head, mouthing two words back at him, just as he had done to her.

Except the words she mouthed were, *trust me*.

Alastair nodded and followed.

Dameon had a room in the Western Wing of the palace. Years ago, before he and the Queen had all but given up on hiding their relationship, Fey and her sisters had brought their reports to that room. If he were taking the Shifter there, then she knew exactly how she could keep an eye on him.

Fey slid to a stop in front of a door. The rooms here were almost always unoccupied, but even still she sent a wordless prayer to the Goddess for luck before she quietly opened the door and peeked inside. She must have been listening. The bedroom inside was empty, set aside like so many others in the palace as a place for visiting aristocrats and important Witches from around the realm to stay while visiting the Queen. And, just as she'd guessed, this bedroom was on the Western wall of the palace, with a view of the palace gardens and Solare.

Perfect, Fey thought, slipping into the room and striding straight over to the window.

"Fey, what the fuck are we doing?" Alastair asked, but Fey ignored him, unlatching the window and pushing it up to open it as far as it would go. It wouldn't be easy to do this, she realized, but she *could* do it.

"*You're* not doing anything," Fey told Alastair. She leaned herself out the window, sitting on the windowsill to face him with the top half of her body outside and only her legs still in the room. *"I'm* going to see what Dameon is up to with that Shifter, and *you're* going back to the party."

Not bothering to wait for an answer, Fey swung her legs over the windowsill and dropped.

There was a small ledge that ran along the exterior of the palace—barely two inches deep. They'd seen Merle use it before, walking the thin lip of the ledge to navigate his way around the palace without being seen.

Fey was no Merle, and while she might not have the effortless feline grace that he did, she was fueled by raw determination, and that would have to be enough. If a cat could do it, then so could she.

A gust of Air kept her in place as she balanced on her toes on the ledge, gripping the exterior wall with her fingertips. Slowly, Fey scooted her way down the wall, passing room after blessedly empty room from the outside, making her way down toward Dameon's old bed chambers.

A scuffing sound on the ledge next to her made Fey jump and almost lose her footing. She turned her head carefully and snarled when she saw Alastair there, balanced on the ledge next to her.

Furious, Fey pointed at him, then at the window they just passed.

Alastair just took one hand away from the wall and raised his middle finger at her.

Fine. If he wanted to get himself killed, so be it. He had no safety net, no power over Air to keep him balanced on the precarious ledge they stood on. Still, he seemed perfectly at ease, and something in the effortless way he maneuvered until he was next to her reminded her of Merle's feline grace.

Swallowing all the profanities she wanted to scream at him, Fey turned away from Alastair and kept moving.

They arrived at Dameon's window just as he flipped on the lights.

Fey pulled back immediately, terrified she could have been seen, and the momentum caused her to lose her grip on the wall. Her body tilted back, falling.

Alastair's hand on the small of her back stopped her fall, and his light push enabled her to regain her footing, her heart hammering in her chest, mouth dry with panic.

She twisted her face to thank him, but the self-satisfied grin on his face and the wink he gave her made her scowl even harder at him, instead.

Aren't you glad I came? that grin seemed to say.

Asshole.

Taking a deep, calming breath to recenter herself, Fey leaned over the window frame and found herself looking straight into Dameon's room.

It was far nicer than the bedroom they'd entered to get here, and Fey whispered a silent thanks to the Goddess that either Dameon or the Queen had a preference for four poster beds. The thick, crimson drapery half obscured her view, but it did a good job of hiding her if someone inside were to glance at the window.

Dameon and the Shifter were already inside, and the Shifter set something down heavily on Dameon's desk. His body blocked whatever it was. It wasn't until he moved aside, to let Dameon by, that she saw it.

A single wooden crate. One she immediately recognized.

Fey's heart plummeted and she knew what was inside that crate even before Dameon crossed the room and flipped the lid open. Knew what was inside even before he pulled a single small bottle from within.

When he held it up to the light, the golden liquid inside swirled and glittered, like it contained a galaxy of trapped stars.

No. No, no, no.

"This is the last of it?" Dameon asked, examining the bottle before slipping it back inside the crate with the others.

The Shifter nodded. "That's all that's left. Everything else was destroyed—either by us or by your pets, I guess."

Fey felt Alastair tense at the term, but she was past caring what some Shifter called her, past caring about anything. Her head was reeling, as she started to piece it together.

It was Dameon.

It had been Dameon all along.

Dameon had sent Willow on the assignation to kill Professor Phillip Danvers, the one person who could have told them what Alice had been up to. Who might have known what this golden elixir was.

Dameon knew the locations of their safe houses.

Dameon knew the keycodes that would prevent Joy's alarms from being triggered.

It was Dameon who set the plastic explosives that destroyed Alice's apartment.

It was Dameon who'd killed Alice.

It all made sense. Alice had been investigating something, something about this golden elixir, and Dameon had killed her for it. Killed her and used Fey and her sisters to cover it up.

Fey couldn't breathe, and her pulse was thundering in her ears. Alastair's hand on the small of her back was the only thing keeping her tethered, the only thing that kept her listening to what was happening in the room.

"Why didn't you destroy this one?" Dameon asked. He sounded only mildly curious, bored, even.

The Shifter shrugged a massive shoulder. "Figured the Queen could use it, you know? It must be something important, right? For you to want to get rid of it so bad."

Dameon's laugh in response was cruel. He took a few steps toward the Shifter, shaking his head in amusement. "If I sent you to get rid of it, why in the name of the Goddess would you think I *wanted* any of it?"

The Shifter shrugged again. "I just thought—"

But Dameon was already in motion, and in the space of a single breath Dameon's sword sang through the air, slicing through the Shifter's neck and cutting him off midsentence. The male's head tilted grotesquely on his shoulders, before falling to the ground with a wet *thud*.

"See, that's the problem with you Shifters," Dameon sighed, as the Shifter's headless body slumped forward onto its knees and then collapsed to the floor. "You don't *think*."

Dameon crouched to wipe his blade on the Shifter's clothes when a voice from the doorway behind him made him turn.

"Dameon?" Willow asked. She stepped into the room cautiously, her eyes going from Dameon to the body on the ground, blood still flowing from the open wound on the Shifter's neck and onto the ornamental carpet.

No, Fey pleaded, terror filling her. *No, Willow, get out of here.*

"The Queen was asking about you, she...she sent me to find you. What's going on here, Dameon? Who is that?" Willow asked.

"An intruder," Dameon lied. He stood, and Fey noticed he hadn't bothered to clean his sword, after all. Angry red drops of blood dripped onto the carpet. "Go find your sisters. There could be more of them in the palace."

But Willow wasn't listening to him. Her eyes had settled on the open crate before he'd even started speaking. On the bottles inside.

Run, Fey prayed, willing Willow to hear her, to glance back at the window and see her. *Run, Willow, please just run.*

Willow stalked past Dameon, reaching a delicate hand into the crate and pulling out a bottle. A worry line appeared between her brows as she frowned at it.

"Dameon, what is—"

Dameon stepped up behind her, slitting Willow's throat before she could finish the question.

Fey screamed.

She barely registered the look on Dameon's face as his head snapped to the window, seeing her there. Barely registered the soft swearing from Alastair as he pulled her tight against him.

"Hold your breath," he commanded. But she couldn't. She couldn't hold her breath, she didn't have any left. She couldn't breathe, couldn't speak, couldn't stop screaming.

Dameon was moving towards them, his blade dripping with blood.

Blood from the Shifter, dead on the ground.

Blood from Willow, who clutched at the wound on her neck as though she could knit it back together.

And then all the colors in the world melted away into a wash of grey, and Alastair was Shadow Walking with her, moving them through a space where walls didn't exist, moving her away from Dameon as he flung the window open and thrust his sword in the space where they had been.

Moving her to safety.

CHAPTER 38

The world was a blur of grey and black shadows as Alastair carried her through wall after wall, moving them through the palace with a speed that made her head spin.

Finally, he stopped, and color seeped back into the world as he released her.

Fey barely registered where they were—another empty bedroom, somewhere in the Western Wing—before she fell to her knees and vomited.

Alastair was saying something, but Fey couldn't understand him. Her thoughts were too loud, the colors of the world suddenly too bright.

She was kneeling there, the room reeking of sick, Alastair's voice falling on deaf ears, when Willow's heart stopped beating. Fey felt it, felt the moment she was gone, like a thread inside her heart snapping, and in an instant the place where she had been was filled with her sisters.

Lilith's shock and rage flooded through Fey like an inferno, followed by a sorrow so deep, so painful from Joy that Fey thought her heart might break and die.

And her own pain answered them. Shock. Horror. And betrayal.

She pushed the emotions down the link to them, filling them with her pain, sharing their loss. Their sister was dead, and they'd only had her for such a short period of time. It wasn't fair. She was so young, so sweet, their little Willow.

Alastair was shaking her, and slowly Fey pulled herself from the pain drowning her and focused on the world around her.

"We can't stay here," Alastair was telling her. "Fey, you need to snap out of it. You're not safe here."

Not safe.

No, she wasn't safe here. Wasn't safe anywhere, anymore.

Dameon had killed her sister. She couldn't trust him, couldn't trust anyone anymore.

"Fey!"

She forced herself to look at him, forced herself back into her body. She took a deep, shuddering breath and nodded.

"It's not safe here for you," he repeated.

"I know," she said. This wasn't her home. Not anymore.

"Is there a safe house you can go to? Somewhere they can't find you?"

Fey shook her head. No, the safe houses were *his*, too. Not hers. Anywhere she could go, anywhere she felt safe, Dameon would know about, and he would find her. But then a memory floated to the surface of her mind. Another place she had once felt safe, years ago. A place no one would think to find her.

"Can you get me to Solare?" she asked. "The army training yards," she explained, seeing his confusion, pointing out the window at where the massive circular building stood somewhere in the dark. "There's a room Alice and I would go, just the two of us. No one will look for me there."

Alastair nodded, understanding. "I can get you there. It won't be pleasant," he warned. "And we'll have to stop a few times along the way, so we need to be careful. But I can do it."

"Ok," she said. She closed her eyes and let herself feel it all for just one more second. All the pain, all the loss. It filled her, touching every cell in her body.

And when it was too much, when it felt like she might be sucked into the pain forever, she called Water… and washed it all away.

"Ok," Fey repeated, opening her eyes. "I'm ready. Let's go."

ALASTAIR HADN'T BEEN LYING. It was an incredibly unpleasant way to travel, and she vomited twice more before they made it to Solare.

"Sorry," he said, gently, holding her hair back while she retched after their final Shadow Walk.

She hadn't had anything left in her stomach after the first time, but her body heaved unpleasantly as it tried to bring something, anything, up.

"It's okay," she answered breathlessly, waving him off. "I'm okay, just—" Her body heaved again, and he winced.

He'd brought them all the way to the empty wing in Solare, and Fey was pleased to find it just as dusty and forgotten as it had been the last time she'd been here, with her sisters.

The first time they'd seen Willow.

Fey's stomach clenched again, a fresh wave of pain and nausea roiling through her. When it finally passed, she managed to straighten, wiping sweat from her upper lip with a shaky hand.

"You should go back," Fey told Alastair. "To the party, I mean."

He raised an eyebrow at her. "You want me to leave you, now, to go back to a *party*? Are you insane?"

She shook her head. What was it Willow had said to him?

I'm not crazy.

I'm practical.

"If you can get back before anyone notices you were gone, then no one has any reason to think you could be involved in what happened tonight. Dameon didn't see you, did he?"

Alastair considered it and then shook his head. "No. He was too surprised to see you there. By the time he looked at me we were already in shadow. There's no way he would know who I was."

"Then you need to get back. That party is your alibi."

"And what about you?"

I don't know.

What about her, indeed? She would be safe here, at least for a few hours while she rested and gathered her thoughts. But then what?

What was even left for her?

"I can't go back," she told him, forming the words slowly. The knowledge of that simple statement broke her heart. "At least... I can't go back and risk getting caught by Dameon. I need..." She tried to organize her thoughts, tried to focus on exactly who she could trust. "I need to get word to my sisters," she said, finally. "Somehow, someway, I need to let them know what happened. Let them know they can't trust him."

Alastair watched her closely. "You're sure you can trust *them*?"

Fey nodded, refusing to even consider it. She had to trust them. If she was suspicious of them, if she decided she couldn't trust her own sisters, then she truly had nothing. For that alone, she had to believe in them, had to believe they would protect her.

"Okay," said Alastair. He slipped his hands into his pockets, and for the first time since she'd met him, he seemed awkward. Unsure.

"Come find me," he said, finally. "I can help. If you need to hide, I can hide you. If you need a new identity, if you need..." He stopped and took a deep breath, running a hand through his hair. "I can help, Fey. Just remember that. No matter what happens, I can help you."

Something dangerously close to tears stung her eyes. "Thank you," Fey whispered.

Then, as though realizing something, Alastair pulled a piece of paper from his pocket and handed it to her.

"Here," he said. "This is Jasper's number. I trust him. If something happens to me, he'll help you out."

Alastair smiled at her. All that confidence and bravado back, as though it had never slipped in the first place. "Stay safe, Witchling," he whispered, and then he was gone, slipping out of the physical world and into somewhere else, somewhere the world was made of shadows, making his way back to the palace.

Fey waited. Waited until she was sure he was gone, waited still as a statue until she was certain, beyond any doubt, that she was alone and hadn't been followed.

Outside, the bell tower chimed the hour, and a startled owl hooted in response. It was amazing to her that the world outside of the palace was unchanged. Her world had been turned upside down, but night still fell, and life in the Eternal City continued without her.

Fey rose and made her way through the abandoned building to her old room.

CHAPTER 39
ALASTAIR

Leaving Fey behind in that dusty, broken building had been the hardest thing Alastair had ever done. But he wouldn't have done it—*couldn't* have done it—if he didn't trust that she knew what she was doing.

When Alastair returned to the party, stopping by the restroom first to put his clothing in order and wash the smell of Fey from his fingers, it was as if he'd never left. People were chatting and laughing, half lost in their cups, deliriously happy, without a care in the world.

Alastair hated them all.

But he hated one of them, in particular, more than all the rest. Hated the male so much it was hard to still the rage growing inside him.

He'd barely made it back to the party and gotten himself a drink before Dameon returned, hurrying to the Queen's side.

It would be so easy, Alastair thought to himself as he watched Dameon bend down to whisper in the Queen's ear, so very easy to snap the male's neck. With Alastair's speed, there wasn't a single person in this building who had the power to stop him.

He'd seen the look on Fey's face when Dameon had pulled that bottle out. Seen her face crumble, devastated. Betrayed. That alone was enough to sign the male's death warrant, but then...

Alastair had liked the crazy little Witch that fucker had killed. Willow—that's what her sisters had called her. She'd been bloodthirsty, yeah, but wasn't he the same? Something about her had made him smile, made him glad Fey had a Witch like that protecting her.

And Fey? Fey had loved her.

And this vile excuse for a male had taken that beautiful, bloodthirsty Witch away from her, away from the world, snuffing it out like it meant nothing.

Alastair's lips curled back in a snarl, and he took a step forward.

No one would be able to stop him in time to save Dameon. He might even make it out alive if he were quick enough. No one would—

"Ah, there you are."

The murderous rage growing inside Alastair stilted, and he exhaled, dizzy with the strength of his anger.

Cassiel Salvatore deSanguine placed a hand on his son's arm, turning Alastair to face him.

"My God," he said, his lip curling in distaste. "Where have you even been? You look..." Words failed his father, as his gaze traveled up and down Alastair's body, taking in the wrinkled shirt, the blood his stomach, and various stains on his pants. Some of which were very obvious against the black fabric. "God above, you smell like a whorehouse."

Alastair raised an eyebrow. "And how would you know what a whorehouse smells like, father?"

"Don't be a smartass," Cassiel snapped. "Just look at yourself. I brought you here to socialize, not sleep with anything that moves."

Alastair just shrugged, taking a sip of his whiskey. He'd long since stopped giving a fuck what his father thought about him.

"Are you still drinking that swill? You can't even get drunk, son. What's the point of it?"

"I like the taste," Alastair answered with a smile. "Why do you think I opened a bar?"

"I can say with complete honesty that I have no idea why you do any of the things you choose to do."

"And let's get one thing straight," Alastair continued, ignoring what his father said entirely. A waitress walked by with a tray of drinks, and Alastair set his now empty glass down on it and plucked a fresh whiskey for himself. "You didn't bring me here to socialize. You brought me here for the same reason you always do. You brought me here to wow the aristocrats with what a *fine, virile* young male your son is. You brought me here to play stud." Alastair gestured down at his clothing. "And who am I not to play the part in its entirety?"

In his peripheral vision, Alastair saw Dameon finish his conversation with the Queen and leave, and he ground his teeth together in frustration.

Fuck. He'd missed his chance.

Maybe it was for the best. Fey deserved that kill. She deserved to be the hand that ended that fucker.

"I should have brought your brother," Cassiel deSanguine said, not bothering to hide the disdain in his voice.

"Yeah," Alastair agreed. "You should have. But he wouldn't have been able to entertain the Witches here *nearly* as well as I can since he prefers cock."

"I forgot how disgusting you can be," his father snapped.

"Tut, tut, father, don't be so close-minded. There's nothing disgusting about liking to suck cock. Maybe if you gave it a try?"

But his father wasn't listening to his teasing anymore, his focus instead on the Queen as she stood and addressed the room. The room stilled and quieted as guests turned one-by-one to watch her.

"We thank you all for your attendance tonight," the Queen spoke in a voice carried by Air so that each and every guest could hear her. "But we will be ending the festivities early. Goodnight and blessed Solstice. My guards will be escorting you all from the grounds. Please do not give them reason to use force."

CHAPTER 40

The day after she was inducted into the Queen's Blades, Fey had run away.

It made her cringe to think back on it now, but back then it had felt like her last resort, the only option available to her. Her whole life, Fey had been alone. From the moment her father had turned his contempt on her, from the moment she realized her mother would never do anything to protect her, she had only had herself.

But when the Queen had placed that brand on her arm, all of that had changed. Suddenly, even in her own head, she wasn't alone. When the initial flash of agony had faded, and the Queen had taken the brand away, she had felt her sisters.

Lilith's dark approval and pride at how well Fey had handled her induction.

Joy's swell of excitement and happiness.

And Alice.

Alice's unconditional love, from the very start. Something Fey had never had before, not even from her own mother. But there it was, real and filling her, from a woman she'd just met a few days ago.

It had been too much.

There is a power in solitude. If you are alone, then no one can hurt you. If you build a wall around yourself, you can make it impossible for anyone to hurt you unless you let them. Impossible for them to love you.

But somehow, these three Witches did. Immediately, unquestioningly, they had loved her. Accepted her.

So Fey had run away. Run from that love and that promise of family. The only family she'd ever known had hurt her, and she had no reason to believe this new one would be any different.

She'd run to the only place she'd ever felt safe, the first place she'd felt like she belonged—her bedroom, in the Solare training camps.

And now, years later, Fey found herself coming full circle.

Even back then her room had been a dump, but now? In the years since she'd been inducted into the Queen's Blades, enrollment in the Queen's army had dropped to a historic low. Fewer and fewer Witches were convinced that so many specially trained forces were necessary, and even fewer were in the desperate straits that Fey had been in when she had joined. Solare had been erected to house thousands of Witches, but with only a few hundred recruits to fill the rooms, only one wing of Solare was currently in use. Fey's bedroom sat in a wing long since abandoned, and the dust and mildew along the walls and floor was proof of that.

She would have been the last Witch to occupy this room, Fey realized, trailing her fingers through the dust on the windowsill.

Every bedchamber in Solare was a tiny thing, barely bigger than a closet, with a single bed, a window that barely opened, and a small uncomfortable desk. Still, to Fey it had been home—her first real home—and even now, with everything going on, it was a comfort to be here.

The day she'd run away from the Blades, Alice had found her. Fey never found out how. Never found out how Alice had even known where to look.

She hadn't tried to convince Fey to come back, hadn't scolded or berated her for leaving. Alice had simply sat in the wobbly wooden desk chair next to Fey's bed and waited. She said nothing, demanded nothing, didn't even look at Fey. She just sat there with her, staring out the window and waiting.

And, eventually, Fey had started to talk. All the fear, all the pain, all the sudden emotions she'd had felt when that Blade's mark had opened that connection between her and her new sisters came pouring out of her. Alice hadn't judged her for running away, hadn't judged her for the way she felt. She only wanted to understand, and when she did, she finally talked.

Alice told Fey stories. Stories about her and Lilith and Joy and their times together. Stupid, inconsequential stories, but they gave Fey an insight into her new sisters. Gave her something to love in each of them. Helped her understand why they were so willing to love her, even if they barely knew her. Helped her realize how much she wanted to love them back.

Fey had come back here to her old room in Solare a few more times during her first year as a Queen's Blade, and each time she knew Alice would come and find her and help her heal through whatever she was going through.

But now Alice was gone.

Now Willow was gone, too.

Fey sat down heavily on her bed, ignoring the cloud of dust that rose up around her, and put her head in her hands. She needed to get some sleep. There were only a few hours now until dawn, and she'd need rest for whatever came next.

But first, she needed a plan.

She briefly considered sneaking back into their quarters to find her sisters, but she immediately scrapped that idea. Her mask had been lost, most likely during her triste with Alastair in the hallway, and there was no way she could get by the Guards without it, especially tonight. Dameon would have to sound the alarm at some point, would have to tell the Queen and the Blades that Willow had been killed. The palace would be teeming with activity, and there was no way she could get to the second most heavily guarded wing of the Palace tonight.

She could rest, then head to The Last Drop once the sun set tomorrow. Now that she was in Solare there would be no way to sneak out during daylight, when the training yards below would be full of soldiers. Alastair could find her a place to lay low while activity in the palace died down, and together maybe they could find a way to get a message to her sisters.

Or… she could go back to the palace right now, find Dameon and slit his fucking throat. Just like he'd done to Willow. She could strap him to a chair and make him swallow plastic explosives, and Joy or Lilith could use a little fire to ignite it…

Fey snarled in anger and frustration, flinging herself down onto the pillow, releasing another cloud of dust around her. That's what she wanted to do, what the anger and rage inside her demanded she do. She wanted to peel pieces off him until he told her everything she wanted to know, until he admitted to all of it.

Fey rolled on her side, pausing when something crinkled under her. There was something under her pillowcase.

Propping herself up on her elbow, Fey reached underneath her pillow and pulled out a piece of paper, frowning at it. It was a handwritten note. A single line, hastily written. An address.

1601 Eternity Rd.

Fey stared at it.

The address meant nothing to her, though she recognized it was somewhere on the manufacturing side of town, near the shipping yards.

But the address wasn't what made her stare. The address wasn't what made her heart sink, made her catch her breath.

It was written in Alice's handwriting.

CHAPTER 41

It had taken her longer to leave Solare and the area surrounding the palace unnoticed than she had expected, and by the time Fey had made her way to the shipping district, there was a distinct brightening to the sky that heralded the coming dawn.

Shit. She was running out of time. Without her mask, she was incredibly vulnerable out here, in the open. Under the cover of night, she could move relatively unseen, using her skills to blend into the shadows was second nature to her after so many years. But once the sun came up, she would be an obvious target, with her bright red hair and fighting leathers. Too obvious, too vulnerable.

Fey wasn't sure what compelled her to come here, what compelled her to leave the relative safety of her old, abandoned room to be here—out in the open, with no plan, no idea of what she might be walking into. If Alice had left that note as a clue to whatever had led to her death, it was months old at this point. Had she met someone here, at this address, before she was killed? Was it an accusation? Alice pointing the finger at her murderer from beyond the grave?

Fey had no idea. And even knowing she should go back, even knowing she should find a way to get to her sisters—the ones still alive, still in need of her protection—she couldn't stop herself from coming here. She was compelled to see where Alice was leading her.

At first glance 1601 Eternity Road looked like every other factory in the shipping district. This whole neighborhood was nothing but shipping containers and factories, and Fey triple checked the address before she was even convinced that she'd found the right building.

There were no guards outside, no security cameras, and while it appeared empty, there were enough signs of occupation to convince Fey it wasn't an abandoned building. The windows were relatively clean, the main entrance marred with muddy boot prints from workers arriving for their shifts.

Down to every detail Fey could find, it appeared to be nothing but an ordinary factory, no different from every other building on this block.

Why would Alice send her here? Fey didn't doubt for a second that the note was meant for her to find. There was no reason for anyone else to be in that room, no other person she could have left it for. And it had been too deliberately placed to have been left by accident.

Fey circled the building one final time. The sky was becoming brighter by the second, and it would be dawn soon. And that meant it wouldn't be much longer at all before the factories around her filled with Fallen workers. She was out of time.

Aside from the front door the employees obviously used to enter and exit, there was one other way in: a nondescript locked door at the rear of the building. An emergency exit, more likely than not. A simple unlocking sigil was all it took for Fey to open it.

This is a bad idea, Fey told herself, her hand on the door handle. Coming here was a bad idea, and going in would be a very, *very* bad idea. She was potentially trapping herself in a building that would likely be overrun with Fallen within the next two hours.

But she didn't have any other ideas, did she? And even a bad idea felt better than nothing.

Taking a deep breath, Fey eased the door open and crept inside.

———

IT WAS EASIER INSIDE to keep to the shadows, to keep hidden. The building was huge, full of equipment and inventory. Full of places to hide.

The main space was exactly what Fey had expected—machine after machine, in assembly line formation, filled the first floor, some equipment tall enough to almost touch the high ceilings. The emergency exit Fey had entered from put her near enough to the assembly line's end, where the final products were collected and boxed. Fey flipped a box open, peeking inside.

Soda bottles. Innocuous, marginally unhealthy soda.

She was in a factory that made soft drinks.

Fey found herself feeling a touch... disappointed.

This? This was where Alice sent her? This was the clue she'd been searching for, for months?

There had to be something more. *Anything* more.

But searching the factory floor, examining each station around the room, yielded nothing suspicious, no additional clues.

No, no no no, there has to be something here.

Fey could feel her time running short. All around her the city would be waking up, and she had nothing. No more clues, no plan of where to go from here.

There had to be an office, on a higher floor. Somewhere the factory managers did paperwork and supervised their workers. Maybe that's where she should go—maybe that's where she'd find something.

A metal staircase snaking up the wall clearly led to the upper floors, and Fey had started toward it when she heard the sound.

Subtle, but there to the trained ear—a single intake of breath. Someone was here, with her, in this building. She heard them shift, just a whisper of a sound, heard the scuff of their feet on the concrete floor.

Fey didn't pause or glance around in the hopes of catching them. She didn't want to reveal what she'd heard, but she did grow a little bolder in her movement toward the staircase, a little more obvious. Let them think they could sneak up on her, let them think that *they* were hunting *her*...

Sure enough, as she crossed the room the sounds of someone

moving behind her grew closer, and Fey grew bolder, still, luring them in, letting them get close enough to—

The scuff of their shoes on the ground alerted Fey her prey had gotten close enough to strike. Whipping around, Fey struck first, diving toward the noise, and drawing her blade.

The rising sun outside did little to illuminate the room around her, and Fey's opponent clearly knew how to use that to their advantage. The moment Fey had turned, they had moved back, ducking into the shadows of the equipment around them, and when Fey launched herself at the space where they had once been, she found herself striking at nothing.

A blur of movement to her right, and Fey struck out again, and this time the tip of her blade snagged skin, earning her a hiss of pain from the darkness. Fey moved again, and again, and again, striking out at the shadowed figure.

But the shadow kept retreating, keeping just out of arm's length. Never attacking, but always one step ahead of her.

With a snarl, Fey feigned an attack, and when her opponent went to retreat again, she was ready. She spun, moving into the path the Shadow retreated to, and angling her blade toward their neck.

Thunk.

Fey hissed in pain as the Shadow lashed out, striking her wrist as she spun and forcing her to drop her blade reflexively. They had known, had seen through the feint, and somehow knew exactly what Fey was planning to do. Had been ready for it.

Before Fey could react, before she could retreat herself to regroup and think of a plan, the Shadow attacked.

It was vicious. Like no one Fey had fought before, a flurry of quick, effortless blows, pushing her back, back, back into the room.

Except... Fey *had* sparred with someone like this before. Had been *taught* to fight by someone who moved exactly like this...

Fey's arms moved up in front of her body, her forearms raised to protect her face and neck, and she didn't see the box behind her until she stumbled back into it, losing her balance and falling, hard, back against the concrete, the breath leaving her lungs in a rush of air. She twisted, coming to a crouch and readying herself to rise again.

"Stay down, Fey," a familiar voice insisted. "I'm not trying to hurt you."

Fey's head snapped up to the Shadow in front of her, just as the sun crested the horizon and the first rays of dawn spilled in through the factory window. And in the warm light of dawn, she could finally see the Witch standing in front of her.

The *ghost* standing in front of her.

"Hey babe," Alice said, a sad smile on her face. "It's been a while."

PART THREE

CHAPTER 42

Fey's world fractured—shattering into hundreds of sharp, dangerous pieces.

"Alice?" she whispered, staring up at her sister in disbelief.

It couldn't be. Alice was dead. Fey had *felt* her die, felt her being ripped away from them through their shared Blade's mark. She'd never forget that pain, never forget the sudden void, the cold absence left inside her where Alice had once been.

But here she was—alive. Safe.

Alice had always worn her hair short, but now it was cut so close to her scalp it was practically shaved. It suited her—the tight black coils of hair just a shade darker than her skin. But her eyes were the same eyes Fey remembered, the same eyes that had haunted her memories. Large, dark eyes, full of love and understanding, even now, as she stared down at her sister below her.

Fey opened her mouth to speak, but nothing came out.

"I'm going to help you up, okay?" Alice said, slowly. "I don't want to fight you, babe. I just want to talk."

Fey didn't answer, couldn't answer, but when Alice offered her a hand to help her rise, she took it, letting Alice pull her up and to her feet.

"I..." Fey started, stunned. "I don't understand how this is possible... You died. I *felt* you die."

"I know," Alice responded, her voice a pained whisper. "I'm sorry, babe, but I had to do it. If there had been any other way..."

"*How?*" Fey asked, the anger in her voice surprising even her.

Alice sighed, closing her eyes. Then she rolled up the sleeve of her shirt and held out her arm for Fey to see. A stark white line ran through her Queen's Blade's mark. A long angry scar, splitting the mark right down the middle.

"You faked your own death," Fey whispered, staring down at Alice's broken mark in shock. Which meant... "You blew up your own apartment, didn't you?"

Alice nodded.

The dangerous pieces of Fey's fractured world shattered a little more.

It was too much. Willow's death, Dameon's betrayal, and now... now *this*. The world felt insubstantial around her, the floor tilting under her feet, and for a moment Fey thought she might faint. Her own Blade's mark felt uncomfortably hot on her own arm, and Fey realized absently that her sisters were awake, were dealing with their own worlds shattering around them in the fallout of Willow's death. She could feel them through their bond. Feel their horror. Pain. Shock. Fey tried to push their emotions down, unable to handle it with everything that was happening around her.

"Come on," Alice said. "We should get out of here before everyone starts to show up for the morning shift. There's a basement below us— that's where I've been staying since...." She trailed off, unable to finish her sentence.

"Do they even know you're here?" Fey asked.

Alice laughed. "Yeah, of course they do. I'm good at keeping quiet, babe, but no one is *that* good. Sam has been taking good care of me, here. But you're not their favorite person right now, so I think it's best we're not on the factory floor when they all arrive, just in case."

Fey didn't question her, didn't question why any of the workers here would even know who she was. It was all too much. She let Alice lead her to a hatch hidden among the floorboards under the stairs, barely noticeable if you didn't know where to look.

The hatch swung upward to reveal a set of wooden stairs that led down into a basement. Alice started down them, gesturing for Fey to follow her.

It was dark in the factory basement, darker still when the hatch shut behind them, and the space felt cavernous in the absence of any light, far bigger even than the factory above them. Alice drew on her power to make a small ball of fire appear in her hand, lighting the room around them just enough for them to safely descend the stairs. She walked to a light switch on the basement wall and turned on the overhead lights, illuminating the entire room.

"Welcome to the resistance," Alice said with a smile that didn't quite reach her eyes.

The basement was massive, even larger than Fey had expected. Lab benches lined an entire wall, their surfaces stacked with bottles, gloves, jars of chemicals, and empty glass vials. Hooks next to the stairs held lab coats in various sizes and various degrees of filthy.

"Is this... is this a lab?" Fey asked.

Alice shrugged. "In a way, I suppose. We've scaled down production recently, so we were able to move everything down here for the time being."

"I don't understand," Fey said, but Alice ignored her. She walked past the lab benches, toward the center of the room, where heavy metal shelves held row after row of...

Wooden crates. Fey drew in a sharp breath.

"I have to hand it to you," Alice said. "You came very close to wiping out our entire supply when you blew up my warehouse." She glanced over her shoulder at Fey, her hands on one of the crates, ready to pull it from the shelf. "That *was* you, wasn't it?"

Fey's heart hammered in her chest. She nodded.

"I thought so." Alice sighed, sadly. She pulled the crate down and walked it over to the nearest lab bench to set it down. "It was a good job. Efficient. I was almost proud."

"You hired guards to watch it at night," Fey whispered. "Someone noticed. It was a rookie mistake if you were trying to keep the place hidden."

Alice winced. "Yeah... that was careless of me. I thought I'd been so damn careful, you know? The guards were just there to prevent someone from sneaking in, some kid stumbling onto something they shouldn't know about. I never thought..." Alice took a deep breath. "There was a kid there that night, wasn't there, Fey?"

Fey swallowed. "Yeah," she said, remembering the prey Shifter who had held a knife to her neck, remembering the way his hands had shook. Remembering his fear.

"Is he...?" Alice asked, turning her gaze to Fey.

Fey nodded.

Alice squeezed her eyes shut, as though in pain. "I... I figured. He didn't come back that night, so we thought... *fuck*." She shuddered. "He was just a kid, Fey. The guards, they knew what they were doing, what the risk was, but him? He was just an idealist kid from the PFTC, in way over his head."

"You're... you're working with Prey for the Crown?" she asked in disbelief.

"I'm working with everyone, Fey. Every Faction, every dissatisfied citizen I can get to listen to me," Alice snapped, her voice turning angry. "And there's plenty of them out there, if you know where to look. Do you have any idea what it's like, for the other Factions? Have you even left the palace long enough to see what the city is really like?" Alice turned toward her, eyes blazing.

Fey felt her own anger rise to her defense. "Of course I have," she snapped.

"Really, Fey?" Alice challenged. "Have you really looked around at the state of the Eternal City lately? Tell me, then... Did you know the other Factions can't own land here?"

She hadn't. Fey blinked, caught off guard by the question. "I don't see why—"

"Only Witches can legally own property within the City. Which means every home, every business, every building within City limits can be taken from a citizen at a moment's notice. No explanation, no time to pack up your store or home and move—if the Witch who owns your house decides they no longer want you as a tenant, you're out on your ass."

"What does it matter if—"

"Did you know poverty in this City is almost entirely centralized in Fallen districts? There are plenty of jobs, plenty of food available for us Witches, but the Shifters? Demons? Most of them are struggling to get by, struggling to get enough food for their families," Alice continued. "Tell me, Fey, when was the last time you went hungry? The last time you had no idea where your next meal was coming from?"

"Don't give me this pious, self-serving bullshit," Fey snarled, the anger that had been building inside her finally coming to a boil. "You benefited from all of this just as much as I did, Alice. And you *never* cared about the Fallen when you were a Blade. You never mentioned poverty or hunger to me then. So, why do you suddenly care now, huh? Why do you suddenly give a shit about the other Factions?"

Her words hung heavy in the air between them as they stared at one another. Alice looked away first.

"You're right," she said softly. "I don't care about them, not really. But I have my own score to settle with the Crown. And so do you."

She opened the crate, but Fey already knew what was inside even before Alice pulled the glass bottle out and held it up to the light.

"Do you know what this is?" Alice asked, looking at the golden liquid that danced inside.

Fey didn't. But she'd been thinking about it long enough that she thought she now had a pretty good guess.

"Allium," Fey answered, thinking back to Phillip Danvers's dissertation.

Alice blinked, turning her attention from the vial back to Fey with curious surprise.

"Now *that*," she said, her lips quirking into a smile, "is a very interesting answer, and I can't wait to hear all about why you think that... But no, Fey. It's not Allium."

She closed her hand around the vial, and for a moment she was so lost in thought that Fey began to think Alice had forgotten all about her.

"You must be exhausted," Alice said finally, opening her eyes. "This

—" She motioned around at the room, at the factory upstairs, at everything around them. "This must be a lot for you to take in, I know. I will tell you everything, I promise Fey, but let's at least sit down and maybe rest a little first, okay?"

Fey wanted to argue, wanted to demand answers from her, but the truth was Alice was right. She was dead on her feet. *Had* been dead on her feet for hours now, and she was running on fumes. Plus, the warm smile Alice gave her… it made her feel like she did months ago, before Alice had disappeared. Like everything was okay, like everything would be okay. Alice's smile had always done that, always made her feel safe. With Alice here, with Alice alive, Fey finally felt safe enough to rest, if only for a few minutes.

Instead of demanding answers, Fey nodded.

Alice led her past shelf after shelf of crates, through that massive space, and to a small room tucked away in the far corner of the basement, with a measure of privacy from the rest of the space. Inside was a single lamp, sitting on a crate, a bedroll, and a few cushions. Alice motioned toward the bed, inviting Fey to sit, while she pulled one of the cushions closer, and made herself comfortable next to her.

"This is where I've been staying." Alice smiled, looking down at the bedroll and its rumpled blanket. "It's not as comfortable as the palace, of course, but it gets the job done. It's warm and dry, and it's somewhere to sleep."

Fey sat on the makeshift bed, feeling a little of the tension in her body ease just at the thought of sleep.

"I've missed you so much," Alice admitted softly. "All of you. You have no idea how hard it was to leave you all like that. How much it hurt me."

Fey tried to respond, but there was a lump in her throat. Tears stung her eyes.

"How?" she whispered, finally. "How could you leave us, Alice? How could you put us through it?"

Fey squeezed her eyes shut against the pain, but all it did was push the tears that had gathered in her eyes out and onto her cheeks.

"I know," Alice said. "I was so scared of you getting hurt, scared of bringing any of you into this…"

"But we were your *sisters*," Fey snapped. The tears were coming heavier now, rolling down her face, and her voice was shaking. "Why didn't you come to us? Ask us to help you?"

Alice crawled forward over the bedroll, pulling Fey towards her and into a tight hug. Fey let her, wrapping her arms around her sister, resting her head on Alice's shoulder, and sobbing.

"You *are* my sister, Fey," Alice insisted. "Please remember that. No matter what happens, you are my sister, and nothing will ever change that. Nothing *could* ever change that, okay?"

Fey sobbed harder, and Alice shifted to hold her tighter with one arm.

'I'm sorry," Alice whispered against her hair. "Fey…I'm so, so sorry."

"It's okay," Fey insisted, swallowing the last of her tears, and shifting back to try to look at her. "It's okay, you're alive and—"

Click.

Fey stopped, registering the sound of metal on metal at the same time Alice pulled back from her. She frowned at the metal cuff now attached to her wrist, confused. Stared at the chain that bound her to the floor, the chain that had been hidden under the bedroll the entire time.

Stared, but couldn't understand what it meant.

"Alice, what—?" Too late. Too slow, bogged down with exhaustion and pain.

Alice's hand whipped out, fast and deadly as a viper. Fey barely had time to see the glint of the knife as it struck, the razor-sharp edge cutting down the inside of her forearm.

Slicing through her Queen's Blade's mark.

"I'm so sorry, Fey," Alice repeated, tears on her cheeks, as she leapt back, out of Fey's reach.

But Fey didn't hear her. She felt the pain, sharp on her arm, felt that connection to her remaining sisters surge and grow taut like a string pulled too tight.

Then felt it snap, as that connection was lost forever.

Her sisters were gone.

Fey stared at her arm and screamed.

CHAPTER 43

The soldiers appeared before the sun had finished rising. Gathering in the early hours of the morning, they moved through the city like ghosts. They visited every block, every street, and where they went, they left a message behind.

A simple poster with an image of Fey's face, a remarkable artist's rendition. No photos existed, not of Fey as the Crown knew her, but whomever they'd hired to depict her had done a great job. They had captured the murderous glare in her eyes. The monster hidden behind the mask.

Below the image were just a few words, in dark bold writing.

FEY VEBBER—WANTED BY THE CROWN FOR MURDER. EX-BLADE. ARMED AND DANGEROUS.

The soldiers posted them everywhere, on every lamppost, on every window, throughout the city. And with the posters came the rumors.

Hushed whispers delivered in fearful voices.

A Blade had been named. A Blade had gone rogue. And what do you do when a monster has been set loose? Who do you turn to when the most feared creature in the realm has snapped their leash?

Fear gripped the city. Panic.

Who could save them from the Queen's Broken Blade? Who could protect them?

It was a relief when new rumors started. When whispers from the palace leaked out into the city.

Fey Vebber was dead.

The Queen's Broken Blade was no more.

CHAPTER 44

JOY

Dameon was speaking to them, but Joy wasn't listening. The words were garbled and meaningless. He could have been speaking another language, for all the good it did him. She was too lost to hear it now.

Joy was drowning, lost in a sea of pain.

Alice.

Willow.

Fey.

They were gone, all of them. Each loss had fractured her heart a little more, each death cutting a little deeper.

Love was an unlimited resource. Joy had known this since she was just a child, long before her Awakening, long before she'd joined the Queen's army, long before she'd been selected to be a Queen's Blade. She had been so full of love, so willing to share it with the world and all its beautiful creations from the moment she'd been born.

Her life before the Blades had not been an easy one. But Joy had always tried to focus on the positive memories, always tried to focus on the love she felt for everything around her.

Once, she had admitted to Alice something she had kept hidden away inside her since she'd joined the Queen's army. She told Alice that she loved everyone, if only a little bit. Even her assignations, even the people she had been sent to kill.

She loved them, and she tried to make their last few moments as painless as possible. Loved them even as she spilled their blood, as she took their last breath from them.

We are all children of the Goddess, all worthy of love. Joy believed that with all her heart. Why would the Goddess have made us exactly as we are, if She herself did not love us? There was not a single being in the realm—regardless of Faction or Creed or past—who was undeserving of love, in Joy's eyes.

Some people treated love as a finite thing, something to be hoarded, to be doled out in snippets only when earned or when required. Her parents had been like that—they kept their love close to their chests, refusing to give any more than what they were given, and each of them refusing to ask for more. It left both of her parents ravenous and starved for love, searching for crumbs of it wherever they could. With whomever they could.

But they had been so wrong. Love cost nothing to give, even if it wasn't returned, and Joy was far too full of love to be so miserly with it. She loved every bug and animal and plant in the realm, all of them creations of the Goddess. She loved Alice, her soulmate. She loved her assignations, if only a little. She loved her sisters. She loved Merle, who brought such beauty and comfort to their little family. Loved him for his soft, happy purrs, for the time he spent with her, satisfied just to be near her, just to share his presence with her.

Love was infinite. But so was pain, and Joy could feel herself shattering under the weight of it.

It was becoming too much for her. It was too heavy, all of this loss, all of this pain. Lilith and Dameon were talking, arguing, their voices raised and full of anger, but Joy was far, far from them both, lost in her sea of pain.

And she worried she might never resurface.

CHAPTER 45

How long had she been lying here? How long had she screamed? Had she fought against the chain holding her? How long, how long had she shouted and sworn, screaming herself hoarse, screamed until her words had turned to sobs? Sobbed until she'd collapsed, exhausted, and slept.

Hours? Days? Fey wasn't even sure. More than once, though, someone had brought her food and something to drink. She hadn't touched any of it. There was no point.

She was dead.

That's what her sisters would think, anyway. And it wasn't far from the truth, was it? Her heart was still beating, but what did it matter anymore? What did anything matter anymore?

Everything she was, everything that defined her, was gone. She wasn't a Queen's Blade. She didn't have her sisters, had lost that incredible connection that they had shared. She wasn't anything, not anymore.

She was empty. A broken husk of a Witch.

Fey heard steps descending the stairs on the other side of the basement but couldn't bring herself to care. Whatever they brought her, she wouldn't eat. Wouldn't drink.

She was already dead. Now she was just waiting for her body to catch up.

The steps grew closer and closer, finally stopping just a few feet away.

"You really should eat something," Alice said. She almost sounded concerned. Fey could have laughed at that, laughed at the idea that Alice cared about her at all.

"Fuck off," Fey told her. The words burned in her sore throat.

Alice sighed and crouched down closer.

I could kill her, Fey realized. Alice was close enough that Fey could have reached out and touched her. *I could kill her and pray to the Goddess she has the key to my shackles on her. I could escape. Run back to the palace, back to my sisters...*

But her muscles didn't move.

What's the point of escaping when I'm already dead? she thought.

"At least let me clean that," Alice said, motioning toward her arm, toward the cut that she'd made. "You don't want it to get infected, and this room isn't exactly clean."

Fey didn't answer. After a long while, Alice sighed again.

"I'm sorry," she whispered, her words barely audible.

Then she stood, turning as though to leave.

"Why?" Fey asked. Her voice was hoarse. She raised her head from the ground to look at Alice's back. "Why do it, then? Why do this to me if you're so damned *sorry*?"

Alice turned, blinking hard, and for a moment Fey was sure there were tears in her eyes.

"I didn't have a choice, Fey. Believe me. They can find you if you're connected, you know. I don't know if our sisters have figured it out yet, but it's how I always found you. And I can't risk that, not yet. I can't risk bringing them here."

Fey sat up slowly, and the room tilted around her as she did so. Her head hurt and there was a dull throbbing behind her eyes that got worse when she moved. As if she could sense it, Alice grabbed a bottle of water from near Fey's food and brought it to her.

"Here," she insisted, holding it out.

I shouldn't drink it, Fey thought. *I should just lay back down and die.*

But she didn't. She took the bottle from Alice, twisting the cap open and drinking half of it in one go. It wasn't cold anymore. It was room temperature and had the plastic aftertaste of bottled water, but it felt so soothing against her throat. Her headache lessened, just a bit.

Alice watched her, silently. Then sank back to the ground to sit across from her.

"Why not just kill me?" Fey asked. "Why even bother keeping me here alive?"

Horror filled Alice's eyes as she shook her head violently, like she could shake the words away. "How can you even ask me that, Fey? I don't want you dead. I could never hurt you."

Fey raised an eyebrow as she held up her arm, mockingly, the shackle trapping her there speckled with dried blood from the cut on her arm.

Alice at least had the decency to wince.

"Okay, well, you've got me there," she said with a sad smile.

"Why?" Fey repeated.

"Because I need you to listen to me. I need you to believe me, and I can't let you leave until you do, Fey," Alice told her, her eyes dark and serious. "I love you, babe. You know I do. But this is bigger than you. Bigger than me. And if you leave here and tell the Crown anything about what you've seen, then all of this—" She motioned to her own arm, to the scar running through her Blade's mark. "All of my sacrifices, everything I've been working to achieve will have been for nothing, and we might never get another chance to save this city.'

"But if I listen?"

"Then you can go," Alice assured her. "If you still want to, after."

Fey considered this, taking another long drink of water.

"Okay," she said, finally. Her voice was starting to sound like her own again, and the throbbing in her head was almost gone. "If I can't leave until I listen to you, then talk."

"Eat something," Alice insisted, motioning toward the plates of food.

When Fey didn't move, Alice sighed in frustration. 'It's not drugged, Fey. Give me a little credit."

Fey still made no effort to move, so Alice grabbed the plate. Taking a piece of flat bread, she scooped up the flavored rice and stuffed it into her mouth, smiling.

"See?" She held the plate out to Fey. "Not drugged. And pretty good, actually."

Fey took the plate from her cautiously, slowly pinching rice into a piece of flat bread, and chewing it. Her stomach groaned in approval. It was pretty good, even if it was room temperature.

"Talk," Fey demanded, swallowing her mouthful of food and scooping up more.

But Alice didn't say a word. Instead, giving Fey a measured look, she reached into her pocket and pulled out the bottle of golden liquid.

"What is it, Alice?" Fey asked, looking at the vial in her hand. "If it's not Allium, is it some sort of elixir? A weapon?"

Alice laughed, sadly. "A weapon? Yeah, I suppose it is a weapon, of sorts."

"What is it?" Fey demanded.

"It's the truth," Alice responded with a shrug.

"No," Fey threw her plate aside, not caring about the mess it left as food scattered on the floor. "No, no more fucking riddles, Alice. You claim that shit is truth? Then tell me. Give *me* the truth, sister. No more running, no more bullshit, no more cryptic clues and addresses hidden in my fucking room. *Tell me* what's going on, so I can leave."

Alice sighed. "Okay," she said, and she tossed the vial to Fey.

Fey caught it reflexively, still staring at Alice.

"You want to know the truth, Fey? Then drink it," Alice told her.

"No," Fey snarled. "You drink it."

"I have," Alice said. "It didn't do anything for me. But you, Fey? I think the Goddess had her reasons for sending you here."

"*You* sent me here." Fey reminded her.

Alice almost smiled. "I left you that note months ago, Fey, the same night I blew up my apartment. But you found it *now*, just as all of this is coming to a head, just a few days before this will all be over, one way or another. Just when we need someone like you. I think you're the final key to all of this. The final nail in the Queen's coffin."

Fey shook her head. "I don't understand."

"You've always been different, haven't you Fey?" Alice asked. "Not just strong, but *different* from who you've been told you are. Your primary element is Water, but you don't heal, do you? You hurt. You kill. Your power hasn't ever been a calm stream. It's a storm."

Fey didn't answer. Just stared at her, waiting for Alice to make her point.

"What if everything you've been told about yourself was a lie, Fey? What if you're more than you think?"

Fey growled. "And, what, this?" She waved the small bottle. "This will change all of that, huh? This will solve everything?" Her voice was angry, full of sour disbelief.

Alice shrugged, but her eyes glittered with mischief. "Maybe. Or maybe I'm wrong. Maybe you drink it, and nothing happens at all, and I unlock the chain holding you and you walk out of here like you never saw me. But there's only one way to find out, isn't there?"

Fey looked at her, assessing. Could she really trust Alice? The sister who had left them, the sister who had chained her down here? Who had stripped her of her Blade's mark, stripped her of everything she was?

What do you have to lose? Alice's smile seemed to say.

Raising the vial to her in a mocking salute, Fey snapped the wax top open and drank it down.

CHAPTER 46

For the first few seconds, nothing happened. For one brief, blissful moment after drinking it, all Fey felt was a pang of disappointment, a sliver of embarrassment that she'd expected something, anything at all, to have happened. That a part of her had maybe *wanted* something to happen.

And then pain filled her entire body, and Fey felt nothing but searing agony.

I'm dying, she thought as she screamed. Her body arched painfully, and she collapsed, writhing on the ground. *She's poisoned me, and I'm dying, truly dying.*

The golden liquid burned through her veins, and Fey's whole body was on fire with it. She felt it in her blood, pulsing through every part of her, nothing but burning, agonizing pain.

Fey tried to call Water to calm herself, tried to counter this sudden power coursing through her with her own. And her power responded, even stronger than usual, rushing to fill her veins and displace the poison inside her. But this other power, whatever it was, smothered it immediately. The Water she called evaporated into nothing, and the pain surged, stronger than ever.

She was screaming, but through the sounds of her own torture, somewhere far away she could hear Alice.

"You have to embrace it, Fey," she was saying, her voice panicked. "Stop fighting it, you have to let it in. Please, listen to me."

But the pain made the words incomprehensible. Again, Fey called to Water, and again it rushed to answer her like a torrent of raw energy, a world-shattering level of power far beyond what she was capable of. It crashed through her, filling her. And again, that burning in her veins flared in response, smothering every morsel of power she had called, turning it to nothing but vapor.

It was getting worse. She was going to die of this. She was burning alive from the inside, her very bones melting from some invisible heat. This was worse than her fall from the cliff, worse than anything any Witch had ever lived through before. There was no way anyone could survive this.

Something was touching her face, something cool and soft, cradling her cheeks. Hands. Someone was holding her face in their hands, gently. With love.

"Please, Fey." Alice was crying. Her hands were so cold against Fey's skin, like ice. *Why was she so cold? Didn't she feel the heat in this room, couldn't she feel the burning?* "Please don't fight it. Goddess help me, listen to me Fey, you need to embrace it. I can't lose you again, *please.*"

Fey tried to summon Water again, but it felt so distant now, so far from her grasp. Air, then. The world outside her became a whirlwind, her secondary power swirling around her like a protective cocoon, buffeting against Alice as she struggled to hold on to her.

But it did nothing to relieve the pain inside of her, and again Fey screamed, her throat burning from it, like fire was raging up her lungs and out her mouth. The floor roiled beneath her back, moving like it was alive. A living, angry thing, a serpent curled in the ground waiting to strike.

Alice was swearing, but her hands remained steady and cool against Fey's skin.

"Please," she whispered, one last plea. And she sounded so lost, so small, that Fey stopped fighting for a moment. Alice always knew what to do. Alice had never sounded lost, never sounded that scared...

As soon as she stopped fighting, the burning inside of her changed. In that small moment she had stopped calling Air, stopped trying to fight the fire inside of her with Water, the power inside Fey surged and overtook every cell in her body. But it didn't hurt as much, suddenly. The fire licked against her skin from inside her, pulsed inside her.

Let me out, it hummed to her, in a voice that sounded just like her own. *Let me free.*

And with one final scream, Fey did just that.

Fire flowed from her skin. Fire came to her call, answering her call stronger than Air ever had. Almost stronger than Water.

Alice finally let her go, stumbling back and swearing, beating the flames from her clothes, as Fey's eyes opened and she called Fire.

———

THE FLAMES COATED HER SKIN, but they didn't burn. Didn't hurt, not anymore, not now that she controlled it. It didn't even singe her clothing.

Fey watched in wordless fascination as the fire danced around her, covering her. A part of her.

"Fey!" Alice warned. "Fey, pull it back!"

But why? A part of her thought, watching it grow around her like a second skin. *Why would she ever try to stop it when it was so beautiful? So powerful? How could she ever stop something that felt so good?*

But another, more rational part of her understood the danger. If she kept this up the building would catch fire. The bedroll she had been sitting on was already nothing but ash. She could inadvertently kill everyone in the factory above them, everyone here... including herself.

Including Alice.

Reluctantly, Fey pulled the Fire back, closer to her skin, and it hummed happily in response to her demand. She reigned the power in until the flames were nothing but a single blaze, a dancing ball of white-hot power that fit in the palm of her hand.

"I was right," Alice said in amazement, her eyes wide as saucers. "It works."

With effort, Fey pulled her eyes from the flame in her hand to look at her.

The flames may not have hurt Fey, but Alice hadn't been so lucky. She held her hands palms up, in her lap, the hands that had held Fey and brought her back into her own body. They were blistered and burned, the skin inflamed and already starting to swell.

The fire in Fey's palm died immediately.

"Alice," she whispered, horrified. "Your hands."

Alice shook her head, with a reassuring smile. "I'm fine, really. Perks of being a Fire Witch, myself—it never hurts me as much as it should. We have healers here, upstairs, anyway—Demons that can draw the burn out, and I'll be as good as new. Honest."

Fey stared down at her own hands. They looked the same, even when she turned them over to look at the backs. Exactly the same. Shouldn't she look different? It seemed impossible that she could be the same Witch on the outside, not with this *power* roiling inside her.

"Try to call Earth," Alice suggested.

Fey looked over at her like she was crazy, but Alice just smiled. "Just try it, Fey. Trust me. I felt you shift the ground earlier."

So had she. Taking a deep breath, Fey reached inside herself and tried to call Earth.

It was harder. Harder than calling Air, and infinitely harder than calling Water. And it felt... different. Where Fire had been a pulse, and Water a torrential flow, Earth was drum.

But she felt it, felt it in her body just as clearly as she had felt the others. And when she called it, the floor around her shifted, turning liquid and flowing like water for a moment before stilling and returning to its solid state.

"I thought you might have all four," Alice admitted, but she still sounded shocked. "But seeing it? That's something else. That's... wow."

"But...I don't understand," Fey said, staring down at her hands in amazement. "How can I control all four elements? Am I... am I a royal?"

"No," Alice answered instantly, shaking her head. "No, you're not from the royal family. At least, I don't think you are. You've been lied to, Fey. We've *all* been lied to. The royal family aren't the only ones who can command all four elements," she explained. And she pulled another vial from her pocket—this one silver grey. Fey recognized it instantly, her stomach twisting in horror as she looked at it. She'd been dreaming about that elixir for years, after all. Dreaming about when she drank it during her Awakening.

"They've been poisoning us, Fey." Alice continued. "The Queen's White Priestesses have been poisoning young Witches for generations, making sure no one was ever powerful enough to challenge the throne. What I just gave you? It wasn't Allium.

"It was the antidote."

CHAPTER 47

With her new powers, Fey felt her hunger return with a vengeance. Alice left to get more food and have her hands tended to, and while she was gone Fey couldn't help but call her powers again.

Water came even easier than before. Stronger, too. It filled her not like a rushing river, but like an ocean. An endless sea roiling inside her, so deep she thought she might never touch the bottom.

Air felt just the same as before, though. A soft, gentle power that she called and dismissed.

Earth was difficult, and though the element responded to her, it felt distant, harder. Like a language she had to concentrate to understand.

And Fire?

Calling Fire was as easy as breathing.

How have I lived without this, Fey wondered, watching flames dance from fingertip to fingertip at her command.

No wonder she couldn't heal, couldn't use her primary power the way it was intended, she realized. Was *this* her real power? Her whole life she'd felt out of place, just as Alice had said. She had been forced to reshape Water to be a weapon... was it all because of *this*? Because of something that had been taken from her? A power that was made just for her, that had been stolen away before she ever knew that she had it?

Fey heard Alice's footsteps on the stairs and advance across the basement, and she dismissed her power, letting the flames disappear into nothing.

"Don't stop on my account," Alice said, appearing with a grin. Her arms were loaded with food, and Fey's stomach growled loudly at the sight of it all.

"You need to eat," Alice warned. "That power has to come from somewhere, and if you're not careful you'll lose all those muscles you've worked so hard to get in training."

Fey nodded, thinking about the Med Witch who had said something similar, and took a plate from her sister. Alice set the rest down around them and grabbed an orange for herself, peeling it slowly, removing the skin carefully in one long strip.

I forgot she did that, Fey realized, and remembering it made her smile. Alice, eating oranges in the kitchen, Merle swatting at the peel from the floor as it grew longer and longer.

"So," Alice began. "How much Allium did the White Priestesses give you during your Awakening?"

"That was Allium?" Fey asked.

Alice popped an orange fragment in her mouth. "The silver elixir they gave you to drink? Yeah. That was Allium, all right."

Her nightmares reared in the back of her mind, and Fey shook them away. Maybe they weren't nightmares, after all, she realized. Maybe a warning, from something. From the Goddess herself, even.

"Do you remember how much the Priestess gave you?"

"Yeah," Fey answered. The food was delicious, but she barely tasted it, she was eating so fast. She swallowed. "She filled two goblets and made me drink it all."

Alice whistled through her teeth. "Two *full* goblets? Fuck the Goddess, you might be even stronger than I'd hoped, Fey. They must have been *terrified* of you." She chuckled.

"Why did they do it?" Fey asked, her voice small. Hurt.

Alice shrugged. "Control, is my bet. The royal family is only in power because they were blessed by the Goddess with control over all four elements, right? But what if, over time, the Goddess's blessings outside of the royal line became even more powerful? What if Witches all around the realm were becoming stronger, not weaker, over the years?"

Alice motioned toward Fey with an orange slice before popping it into her mouth. "You're a walking threat to the throne. Not because you could kill the Queen, though you obviously could, if what you did earlier is any indication. But your real threat, Fey, is what you *represent*. A stronger Witch, Goddess blessed with all four elements, and not of the royal family line. Your very existence is a direct challenge to the Queen's legitimacy."

Fey's stomach sank.

"How many Witches like me are out there?" she asked.

Again, Alice shrugged. "Who knows? Could be ten. Could be a hundred. Or it could just be you." She chewed her orange thoughtfully and said, "You're the first we've given the antidote to, though. The first one who received Allium during their Awakening. Most Witches weren't strong enough to be given any. Maybe one in twenty, as best as we can tell."

"Were you?" Fey asked.

Alice shook her head. "No," she admitted. "No, and I was one of the first to take the antidote, just as a test, but it didn't do anything to me. The Witches who were given Allium weren't picked at random, either. The Priestesses are looking for something. All those rituals, all the cards and bones, they're assessing our power, somehow."

Fey remembered the old Priestess, the way she had scrutinized her, tested her. Spent seemingly far longer with her than the other Witches who had been there that day.

"When they find someone that they deem too strong? They use the Allium to dull their powers, cutting off their connection to certain elements. And they've been doing it for generations. Taking our young girls and ripping their birthrights from them, just to maintain the Crown. Just to convince us all that the Goddess chose their line to rule over everyone."

Fey felt sick. Thousands of girls throughout the realm, every year, were sent to the Goddess Temples. How many of them were neutered like she was? Made lesser, more insignificant, all to maintain the status quo?

"How did you find out about this?" Fey asked, stunned. "How did you uncover any of this?"

Alice stared at her for a long moment, assessing.

"You," she said, finally. "Or, you were the first piece to the puzzle, I guess." She set her orange aside. "It was something you mentioned when you were inducted into the Blades, years ago. I brought you a healing elixir for your sigils, do you remember?"

Fey nodded.

"Dameon must have assumed you would make one for yourself, being a Water Witch, but I saw you the next day and you weren't healing fast enough, and you clearly hadn't taken anything for it."

Fey remembered.

"So, I brought you one, from our own stock in the training gym. And you know what you told me? You told me it tasted awful." Alice laughed.

"It did," Fey said. "Like garbage water. It was foul."

"Yeah, so you said… But do you remember what you told me next?"

Fey shook her head.

"'It tastes like garbage water,'" Alice quoted. "'But it's not half as bad as the shit they give you during your Awakening.'"

Alice stared at her, unblinking. "That stuck with me, Fey. Not just what you said, but the way you said it. It was such an offhand comment, like you were talking about some universal experience that everyone goes through. But they *never* gave me anything to drink at my Awakening, Fey. And I'd never heard any other Witch mention it before.

"So, I started asking around, just out of curiosity, at first. And everyone I spoke to had the same experience as me. They had never been made to drink anything. But then I mentioned it to Joy."

Fey's heart skipped a beat. *No. Not Joy. They couldn't…*

"Joy drank the elixir at her Awakening, too, Fey. Said it was the worst thing she'd ever tasted."

Joy. Joy who could command Air better than any Witch in history. Joy had her power taken from her. Reduced. Anger burned bright and hot in Fey's stomach at the thought that someone could have done that to her sister, could have taken something so special that was meant to be hers.

"I asked more people, and over time I found more Witches. Witches who'd been given something to drink at their Awakening, or who'd known someone who had. No one knew what it was, though, and no one knew why it was only given to some of them."

"I thought it was to unlock my primary," Fey whispered.

"So did a lot of them," Alice replied, her tone gentle. "I even went to the head of the Water Coven to ask her about it. I know, I know," Alice laughed when Fey immediately made a face. "You don't like her. And I don't blame you, believe me. Sana can be an uptight twat, and no one is denying that. But I figured if anyone would know what the elixir these Witches were given was, it would be her, right?"

Fey agreed, but Alice shook her head back and forth. "Except she had no idea what I was even talking about. She said that the Awakening ceremonies were handled entirely by the White Priestesses, and she'd never made a single elixir for them over the years. Not one. And she couldn't identify it for me based on my description, either.

"But... she said something as I was leaving. I don't even think she thought about it, not really. But it was about the color. She said she'd never even heard of a silver elixir... So, I started to think... what if it's not an elixir at all?

"And that's what I found when I broke into a Temple and stole some."

Fey choked. "You broke into a Temple of the Goddess?"

Alice shrugged the comment off as though it was nothing. "It wasn't the last time, either. Not the one in the city, obviously. Too many people, too much risk. I went to one in the second octant, miles from here. And inside I found the 'elixir' they'd given to you. Given Joy. And I took a few bottles."

Something clicked inside Fey. "And you gave them to a chemist... Someone who would recognize it if it wasn't an elixir, someone who was an expert in poisons. You gave it to Phillip Danvers."

Alice's smile was genuine and a little proud. "Well done, babe. Yeah. That's exactly what I did."

"That's what he told you, when you met him at the club, wasn't it? He told you it wasn't an elixir; it was a poison."

Alice nodded. "A poison he already knew, could already identify just by sight—one they used to use to cut Witches off from their power when they were sentenced by the Crown. One that used to be used on Blood Witches."

Fey felt like she might be sick.

"But they stopped that practice years ago, Fey. And do you want to know why?"

"Because someone made an antidote," Fey answered, her voice sounding far away. Willow had told them that, hadn't she? She'd read it in one of Lilith's books on poisons.

"Yeah...because someone made an antidote," Alice said. "A gold-colored antidote that cleared all the Allium from your system, almost instantly."

"Phillip told you all of this?"

Alice nodded. "He did. And he even gave me instructions for making it. That's what I've been doing here, Fey. That's what all of this space is for. I've been trying to make enough antidote for every affected Witch in the realm, enough that Phillip says will guarantee they'll all be cured."

Fey swallowed, struggling with how to break the news. "He's dead, Alice," she said, softly. "Phillip Danvers was killed a few weeks ago."

Alice swallowed. "I... I figured he might be. We lost contact with him, but we'd hoped...Was it you?"

Fey shook her head. "No. But it was one of us. Dameon gave the order."

Alice nodded, understanding. "I don't think Phillip understood the danger of what he was getting involved with. Of any of it. Neither did I, not really, until that night when he gave me his findings, and I realized what was happening. Realized what it meant."

"The night you faked your death?"

"I had to," Alice insisted. "Fey... there's no way the Queen doesn't know about this, no way she didn't sanction this. Her own *twin* is the head of the White Coven. They are purposefully cutting Witches off from their gifts. All to keep themselves in power. And if Dameon sent a

Blade to kill Phillip, if he sent you to burn down my warehouse, they must know that someone is on to them, someone is trying to fight them. They know it's only a matter of time, and they'll get more desperate and more dangerous to keep this from getting out."

Fire roared in Fey's veins, as though in response to the challenge Dameon and the Queen posed. She could have gone her whole life without knowing this part of herself, Fey realized. Gone her entire life missing such a vital part of her, a gift entrusted to her by the Goddess herself.

"So... what now?" Fey asked, giving in to the rage that flared inside her.

"Now you know the truth. And I can unlock your shackle and let you go if you still want to. But if not? If you want to help?" Alice's smile was full of menace. "Then we're going to make them pay for what they've done."

Fey considered it. Considered what they'd taken from her. From Joy.

"Unlock me," she told Alice. "And I'll help you however I can."

Alice's smile widened. "You and I are going to take down an empire, babe, and with you by my side, there's nothing any of them can do to stop us."

CHAPTER 48

Fey had managed to melt a few segments of the chain that held her shackled to the floor during her second Awakening, freeing herself to walk around. Still, it was a profound relief when Alice unlocked the manacle at her wrist and it dropped free.

"That was an incredibly fucked up thing to do, Alice," Fey said, rubbing at the skin where the metal had chaffed her wrist.

"I know," Alice answered, and to her credit she managed to look appropriately ashamed. "I know, babe. Look, I'm sorry, but... you have no idea how much we've sacrificed to get to this point, and if there was a chance—even just a tiny, insignificant chance—that you could have stopped us, then all of that would have been for nothing."

"Fuck you," Fey told her, but there was no heat behind it anymore, no venom. "You could have come to us about this. We would have helped you."

"Really, Fey?" Alice asked, holding her stare like a challenge. "No, I need you to really think about it and put yourself in my position. Our entire job is protecting the Realm. You're telling me, without any doubt, that you would have jumped up to help me take down the very institution you trained your whole life to protect?"

"I..." Fey stuttered and paused.

And that was it. She didn't know, did she? If she hadn't seen Dameon slit her sister's throat, if she hadn't had reason to doubt the forces behind the throne, would she have believed Alice? Would she have offered her help?

Or would she have turned against her, choosing her identity as a Queen's Blade over her own sister?

Alice chuckled at her silence. "See?" she said. "I would have been asking you to turn your back on everything you knew and trusting that you wouldn't just kill me outright. It was a risk, Fey, and one I couldn't take."

"And Joy?" Fey asked, unable to hide the bite in her voice. "You couldn't even trust Joy? With everything she meant to you?"

She flinched and looked away, unable to hold Fey's gaze any longer. "Even Joy," Alice whispered in a small voice. "Fey... what do you know about our sisters from before they joined the Blades?"

Fey opened her mouth, then closed it quickly. Nothing, she realized, and that was the point. She knew nothing about their lives from before they were her sisters.

"You told me a little about your time in the army, a little about your family and who you were," Alice was saying. "But Joy? Lilith? I know so little about their old lives. About where their loyalties really lie. How could I trust them, with so little information?"

"Lilith always said it didn't matter," Fey insisted. "That who we were before died the moment we became Blades."

"And you'd be willing to bet your life on whether or not she was lying? Not even your life, Fey—would you be willing to bet the lives of everyone in this building? On this block?" Alice gestured around them. "Because they're *all* in on this. Thousands of us, working together for months, some of them *years*, to bring an end to the Crown's oppression. Would you be willing to bet every single life here on that?"

No, Fey realized. She wouldn't.

"Not telling Joy... *Leaving* Joy... Fey, it was the hardest thing I've ever done, believe me. Even if we both survive this, what do you think are the odds she'll forgive me? I *lied* to her. Hell, I made her think I was *dead*." A single tear slipped from Alice's eye and rolled down the dark skin of her cheek. "I had to sacrifice that, *all of that*, to be here. I had to throw it all away like it was nothing, when it... it was the best thing that ever happened to me. *She* was the best thing that ever happened to me, Fey."

Fey glanced away, giving her sister the privacy of her own emotions as Alice's careful veneer of strength began to crack.

"But this is bigger than me. Bigger than Joy. For years, the Queen has let them steal our powers, the power the Goddess herself gave to us. And she has to pay for that. She has to pay for the starvation in this city, for the Fallen who have been forgotten and who fell through the cracks all because she never cared about anything but her *own* Faction."

"Is that why you're working with Prey for the Crown?"

Alice almost laughed. "Yes," she said with a smile. "Goddess bless them Fey, they were in shambles when Phillip put me in contact with them. They're children trying to play in the big leagues. The biggest move against the Crown they'd ever made was to stage a sit in at one of the Temples."

Fey chuckled.

"And now? Now I have them staging a *coup* alongside Demons, of all things. It wasn't hard to find people dissatisfied with the Queen, you know. Things are... bad here, for most citizens. It hurts to think I never saw it, before, that I never noticed ..."

They were silent for a few minutes, each taking a moment to struggle with their own emotions. It's easy to be blinded to suffering. But once you see it, once you open your eyes to the less fortunate around you, there's no turning back.

After a while, Alice stood, shrugging off their conversation and motioning for Fey to follow her.

"Come on, it's time you met everyone."

EVERYONE, it turned out, was only three people.

"Fey, this is Karla, Sam, and Rex," Alice said, pointing to them each in turn. "Everyone, this is Fey."

Alice had walked her from the nook where Fey had been held

captive, back through the huge basement laboratory and up to an office on the second floor of the factory. Sunlight poured in through the factory windows, and the assembly line floor was now filled with workers. However long she'd been held down there, at least it seemed like the world hadn't stopped spinning in her absence. There was a strange comfort in that.

"Is she the one who killed David?" The big, heavy-set Shifter—Rex—asked Alice, ignoring Fey entirely.

"The Shifter boy who was in the warehouse," Alice explained, all four of them watching Fey for her reaction.

Staring back at the Shifter who had asked, Fey shook her head slowly. "No," she said, honestly. "But I was there when he was killed. We had no idea who he was, or why he was there, and he pulled a knife on us."

Rex snorted, crossing his arms, and looking away. A Bull Shifter, maybe, Fey guessed. His face certainly had a distinct bovine look to it, with that long drawn-out face and small deep-set, wet eyes.

The smaller Shifter at Rex's side sighed. "That does sound like David," he said, in a light delicate voice, edged in pain. "He always wanted to play the hero." He gave Fey a small but inviting smile. "I'm Sam. I'd welcome you to my building, but Alice tells me you've actually been with us for a few days now."

Chained in the basement, Fey thought sourly, shooting Alice a glare. She just shrugged.

"I had to be sure she was safe," Alice explained.

"And?" Rex asked gruffly.

"And she's anything *but* safe, but she's on our side, at least."

"Is it true?" the Demon, Karla, asked, leaning forward over the table to get a closer look at Fey. She had delicate, curved horns that circled her ears. "That the antidote worked, I mean? And you have control over all four elements?"

Fey glanced at Alice, waiting for her nod before she spoke. "Yeah," Fey said. "I do."

Karla whistled, impressed, leaning back in her chair.

"Well, we're really glad you're here, Fey," Sam said. His eyes were just a fraction too large for his face, the color like molten chocolate.

Hare Shifter. "We have been giving Alice all the help we can, but... we aren't warriors, you see. I have helped by providing this space, my equipment, and whatever she has needed to make that, that potion of hers, but when the fighting comes..." Sam looked uncomfortable. "I can't, in good conscience, send my brothers and sisters to die for our cause. I can't put them in harm's way."

"I could," Karla said quickly. "But it's a fifty-fifty chance they'd turn right around and kill you first if the fighting turned against us."

Rex just snorted.

"You've done plenty," Alice assured Sam. "Thanks to you we have more than enough antidote to go around. And thanks to Fey, we now know that it works. I won't need to ask any of you to sacrifice anymore of your friends and loved ones." She turned to Fey and gave her a wide smile. "Not if Fey agrees to help me, at least."

Fey shook her head. "No. Not until you tell me exactly what it is you're planning, Alice. No more secrets, no more surprises. Tell me the plan. Then we'll see if I agree to do what you ask."

And, with a huge smile, Alice told her.

FOR YEARS, Fey had said that Joy was the most brilliant Witch she'd ever known. She would stand by that, even decades later. But today, listening to Alice's plan, Fey couldn't help but think that even Joy couldn't have come up with something so clever.

"When?" was all Fey asked her, after Alice had finished explaining everything. Sam and Rex had kept quiet throughout most of her explanation, only jumping in a few times to clarify some of the finer aspects of the plan. Karla had been sent from the room, with even she herself admitting that it was best not to let her know too many details just in case she decided to turn them in for some sort of reward.

"Three days from now," Alice told her. "We get this one chance, Fey. And if we don't get it exactly right, this could be a bloodbath."

Fey nodded. One chance.

"I won't tell you not to warn them," Alice said, softly. And Fey knew without asking which two Witches Alice meant. "But you have to promise me you won't do so until after your part of the plan is over. We can't risk it, Fey. Even if you trust them to help, I need you to wait until your part is over."

"I understand," Fey answered. She rolled her shoulders back. Her body itched for the kind of relief only a few hours punishing herself in the training gym would provide.

"And you," Alice said, looking from Sam to Rex. "You need to work with Karla to make sure you keep your Factions off the streets that night. We need to keep civilian casualties to a minimum, and I am relying on you three to keep the peace. We can't have anyone taking advantage of the distraction to wreak havoc in the city. Or, even worse, having them caught up in the slaughter."

"You'll have no trouble with us," Sam insisted.

"What about the predators?" Fey asked, and Sam blinked at her with his large, liquid eyes.

"My dear lady, I speak for *all* of us, not just the prey," he insisted. "We are not as... separated, I think, as you have been led to believe. I have been working with a representative from the Wolves and the Lions of the city, and they have assured me that whatever date we tell them, we can expect nothing but quiet from them and their kind."

Fey nodded. "And the Vampires?"

Alice visibly winced. "That is our only problem," she sighed. "I only met Sam through Phillip—he put me in touch with all the other Shifters, and with Karla. But no one, and I mean *no one*, has any reliable connections to deSanguine or any of the other Vamp families. And every message I've tried to get to them has been ignored."

"I can help with that one," Fey admitted with a sigh.

Alice shot her a surprised look. "Don't tell me you've been associating with Vamps in my absence, little sister."

Fey only smirked in reply. "Trust me," she said. "I can get the word out, and you won't have to worry about the Vampires. You don't need me until the big night, right?"

Alice shook her head. "No. You know what you have to do. And you know where to find me if something changes."

"Good," Fey said. "Can you help me get a message out to someone?"

"That depends," Alice answered, cautiously. "On exactly who it is you are trying to contact."

"Not any of the Blades," Fey clarified.

"Then probably, yeah. Who did you have in mind?"

Fey smiled. "The Prince of the Vampires."

CHAPTER 49

It took a few hours before Alice managed to find her an untraceable phone, and she warned her that any messages Fey sent could still be intercepted and recovered, if Alastair were being monitored. It would be best, she advised, to couch the message in some sort of code.

In the end, Fey decided not to text Alastair directly at all, just in case. Instead, she pulled the wrinkled business card from the pocket of her fighting leathers and sent the message to Jasper.

Goddess Park. Midnight.

Fey stared at the message after it was sent, frowning. She needed a way to let him know who the message was from, to give him a clue that it was her, and who it was meant for. When she realized how, she smiled, and sent one last message:

Love, Shirley Temple.

Then she handed the phone back to Alice, who promptly popped it open, removed the sim card inside, and snapped it in two.

"You can never be too careful," she insisted, calling Fire to burn the slivers of plastic away to nothing.

———

ALASTAIR WAS WAITING for her when she arrived, just before midnight, and Fey couldn't help but wonder if he'd been standing there at the foot of the Goddess Statue since sundown. She wouldn't put it past him.

The park was empty, aside from the two of them. Only Vamps and party kids were typically out in the city this late on a weeknight, and neither of those groups spent much time in this district. Overhead, the moon hung high and bright in the dark, night sky, casting a white glow over the world. It illuminated Alastair's messy black hair as she approached him.

"Hey," Fey called softly, and his head jerked up at the sound.

Before she knew it, he had her wrapped in his arms, crushing her against him.

"They said you were dead," he whispered gruffly against her cheek. "I didn't want to believe it, but... *fuck*, it's good to see you, Witchling."

"Yeah, well, I'm not dead," Fey laughed, but as his words sank in, she leaned back, tilting her head up to look at him, her smile slipping. "Wait, what do you mean? Who said I was dead?"

Alastair blinked down at her.

"The Queen announced it," he told her slowly. "Wait, you didn't know? Fey, where have you been? Haven't you heard any of the announcements?"

Fey was shaking her head. "No, no, you must be mistaken. They don't announce it when a Blade falls. They've *never* announced it when a Blade falls, Alastair."

"Witchling," he said softly. "They named you."

Her heart sank in her chest like a stone.

"They named you as a traitor to the Crown. They're saying you went rogue and killed two of your sisters. Fey... there was a bounty on your head until... Fuck. They think you're dead, and we should keep it that way. We need to get you off the street. Come—I'm taking you back to my place. The entire realm knows who you are right now, and it's not safe for you to be out here."

I*T MADE SENSE*, Fey thought through the numb haze of too many emotions. Dameon had to pin the blame on someone. But to reveal a Blade's name, to show her likeness... that had never been done before. It was a slap in the face to everything she'd done for them. Everything she'd sacrificed.

What were her sisters thinking, she wondered. Did Lilith and Joy believe what was being said about her? Whatever lies Dameon had concocted? Did they think even for one second that she could have been responsible for what happened to Willow?

She couldn't think about it—*wouldn't* think about it. She had to trust them, trust that they knew her well enough to know that she could never have hurt Willow.

Her fingertips trailed over the wound on her arm, the one that had severed her connection to her sisters. She ached to feel them again, to know what they were feeling, to know that they were safe...

Alastair brought her to an elegant townhouse in the Shifter District, not too far from his club. It was unmistakably *male* inside, and though the furniture and decorations were expensive, the place felt hollow, like he'd never put much thought into making it a home.

"There's a shower through there," Alastair told her as he welcomed her inside. The living room was bigger than the massive common room she had shared with her sisters at the palace, and the long L-shaped couch in the center of it looked big enough to sleep at least two people. He motioned toward a closed door. "Just through the bedroom. You can't miss it."

"Is that your way of telling me I smell?" Fey asked.

Alastair smirked, but he didn't look up at her as he pulled his phone from his pocket and began to message someone. "I just assumed you'd want to clean up, after all you've been through," he said, shrugging. "I'd never be stupid enough to suggest you smell. Even if you do," he added with a pointed look.

"Good," Fey said. "Smart Vampire."

She headed through the door he indicated, ignoring the weight of his eyes following her as she walked out of the room.

Goddess bless me.

His bedroom was stunning. Twice as big as her bedroom back at the palace, the bed was big enough to sleep five people comfortably, and all she wanted to do was climb between those sheets and sleep for a few days...

Shower first, Fey promised herself, turning away from the bed with difficulty and heading into the most beautiful bathroom she'd ever seen in her life.

THE SHOWER WAS WONDERFULLY, blessedly *hot*. Standing under the falling water, Fey practically purred with pleasure as the water fell all around her. How long had it been since she'd been able to wash herself?

Way too long. She sighed, letting her body relax under the steady rain of water.

It wasn't just the pleasure of finally being clean, after—at least—three days with no shower. It wasn't just that Alastair's shower alone was the size of a small room, and had not one, not two, but *three* shower heads, one of which came down from the Goddess-blessed *ceiling*.

No, it was so much more than that. Because for the first time in her life, Fey could feel the heat surrounding her on an entirely different level.

Fire.

The steam filling the room danced with the power of Air, Water, and *Fire*. Even Earth, she realized, feeling a soft beat of that drum inside her—microscopic elements of iron, copper, and salts hiding within the droplets. It was incredible, unbelievable that she couldn't feel it before. Her body hummed in response to all that power, hummed with the unseen energy it carried.

What am I?

Fey tilted her head back, letting the water wash over her body, washing away the grime and suffering of the last few days.

The world around her felt brighter, fuller, somehow so much *more* than it once had been. She could feel it all, every element humming with energy in the world around her, in every*thing* around her. It was like having another sense entirely. Like she could see a new world layered on top of the one she already knew.

What am I?

When she'd shied away from healing magic, when she'd chosen instead to embrace her power in a darker, more violent way, a part of Fey had always thought she should have been born a Fire Witch. Felt she was more suited to the rage and violence that was associated with the Fire Coven. And now that power, that energy danced inside of her, raw and powerful.

But it wasn't her. Wasn't *fully* her, anyway.

Each of the four elements was a pulse inside her now, flowing through her like her own blood. But one sang louder than the others, one called to her on a deeper level, beat in time with the same pulse as her heart.

Standing in the heat of the shower, feeling the air and water and fire and earth all around her, Fey knew with absolute certainty that she was a Water Witch after all.

It was strange to acknowledge it. She'd always rejected it, always thought the Goddess had chosen wrong when she had gifted her the power over Water. She didn't use it the right way, hadn't even once used it to heal, or help—not knowingly, anyway. But Water didn't just heal. It could drown you, freeze you, boil you. It was death just as much as it was life. And now that she could feel the Goddess's touch in everything around her, she knew she wasn't using her power wrong at all. Had never been using it wrong.

What am I? she asked herself. And this time she knew the answer.

She was Fey. She was a Water Witch. Always had been. This was the power the Goddess had chosen for her, knowing how she would use it. It wasn't blasphemy, what she did with it. It was... right.

She felt complete. For the first time in her life, alone and fractured from her sisters, Fey finally felt complete. Sure, the resurgence of Fire and Earth in her body had helped, but it was the surge of Water that had filled her that completed her.

Fey reached for a bottle of soap and began to wash herself, knowing that no matter what happened in the coming days, at least she had this.

At least she finally knew who she was.

CHAPTER 50

ALASTAIR

"Thanks for this," Alastair said, taking the pizza boxes from Jasper. "Really, I owe you. Now get the fuck out of my home."

Jasper chuckled, leaning back against the door behind him. "You're the boss," he said, but instead of leaving, instead of turning his ass around and walking right back out the door, he tipped his head to the side, as though listening.

"Is that her?" he asked. "In the shower?"

"I hear a lot of talking, and not a lot of 'getting the fuck out of my home,' Jasper."

Jasper's smile only grew, a predatory glint in his eyes. "You mind if I join her in there? I haven't had a chance to shower yet, and it sounds like she's had a stressful time lately, you know? I bet she could use some relaxation, and if there's one thing dogs are great at, it's licking—"

"Jasper, if you finish that sentence, I will fucking kill you. If you think about getting into that shower again, I will fucking kill you. If you look at her, if you glance in her direction, I will fucking kill you."

"Yes, boss."

"Get the fuck out of my house, Jasper. Be a good doggy and get your ass to work before we have a problem."

Jasper's laughter followed him out and onto the street as he left, but even still Alastair stayed in the doorway a little longer than necessary, to make sure he'd gone.

Smart ass fucking Wolf, he thought. Alastair had never been the jealous type, not really. But after spending the last few days thinking Fey had been found and killed, he couldn't stand the idea of another male being around her right now. Some protective, fucked up instinct was rearing its ugly head and was taking full control of him.

Satisfied Jasper had, in fact, gone to work like a good puppy, Alastair closed the heavy door and engaged the lock. Faintly, he heard the shower turning off, so he carried the pizzas into the kitchen and began to assemble everything he would need to make sure his Witch was well fed.

"Is that pizza I smell?" he heard her call from his bedroom. The eagerness in her voice made him smile.

"Pepperoni and meat lovers," he called back, and when she groaned in response, his cock twitched.

Fuck. He'd been hard since the moment she'd left to shower. Since the moment he started picturing her wet and naked and perfect, and it had taken all of his *very* limited self-control not to break the door down and join her. But food, first. Sleep after. She must be exhausted—wherever she'd been these last few days, whatever she'd been doing, she looked raw and hurt. His cock could wait.

As if on cue, it twitched again, as though to say *no I fucking can't. Not with her.*

Alastair growled.

He heard her footsteps on the wooden floor of his living room and quickly piled a few slices of pizza on a plate for her.

"Did you want something to drink?" he asked, poking his head out of the kitchen to address her. "I have wine, or—" Alastair stopped midsentence. Stopped and stared.

"Do you mind?" Fey asked, smiling, holding her arms out to her sides. She was wearing one of his white dress shirts, and though it was long enough to reach her mid-thigh and baggy enough to leave *everything* to the imagination, she'd only bothered to button two of the buttons, at her stomach. The crisp line of the shirt front only seemed to accentuate how little fabric separated her body from his view. "My clothes need to be washed, and I didn't have anything else to wear, so I raided your closet."

Mind? No, he didn't fucking *mind*. He never wanted her to wear anything else again, not with how mouthwateringly good she looked in his shirt. And something about knowing it was his, knowing that she was wearing his clothing...

"Alastair," Fey purred in that luscious voice of hers. "You're dropping my dinner."

The plate he was holding tipped dangerously in his grip, and he hadn't noticed the slice of pizza slide off and drop onto the floor.

"Fuck," snapped Alastair, looking down. He snatched the slice from the ground and retreated into the kitchen to grab fresh pizza for her and something to clean up the mess.

When he emerged again, a plate full of four new slices in hand, Fey was curled up in the corner of the couch, her legs tucked underneath her.

She looked divine, sitting there. Alastair wanted nothing more than to drop the food he was carrying and pin those long legs open, wanted nothing more than to hear her say his name as he used his tongue and fingers to make her forget everything but him.

Instead, he clenched his teeth together, ignoring his throbbing cock. He could wait. Goddess grant him the strength to wait.

"Did you really leave to get us pizza?" she asked as she took the plate of food he offered her. He hadn't grabbed any pizza for himself—just a glass of wine.

Alastair shook his head, settling himself on the couch. He wanted to sit next to her, wanted to touch her, feel that perfect skin under his fingers, but he gave her a few feet of space. "No. I messaged Jasper to pick it up for us and bring it over. I didn't want to leave you here, alone."

Fey rolled her eyes. "You didn't want to leave me here, all alone and defenseless, huh? My savior," she said sarcastically. "So...you messaged your *bartender* to bring us pizza?"

She was already on her second slice, and Alastair couldn't help but smile at her while she devoured it.

"He's more like..." He waved his hand, searching for the word.

"More like a friend, I guess. Though, fucks me how that happened. He's like that with everyone, sneaks into your heart somehow."

"Do you trust him?" Fey asked, nibbling a piece of crust.

Alastair laughed in response. "Trust him? I trust him not to tell anyone you're here, if that's what you're asking. But otherwise?" He snorted. "No, I don't fucking trust him. That fucker had the gall to ask me if I'd mind if he joined you in the shower."

Fey laughed, taking another bite.

"Oh? And why didn't you let him in?" she teased, wriggling in her seat. "Maybe I would have liked the company?"

Alastair's teeth clenched together, and he took a deep swallow from his glass to keep his jealousy in check. "He's lucky I didn't kill him for even suggesting it, the weaselly fucking bastard."

"Weasel, huh?" Fey laughed. "I thought he was a Wolf."

"He is. Massive fucking thing, too. Bigger than Ferus, if you'd believe it."

"Mmm," she purred. "Maybe you should have sent him in to join me then."

"Why? Are you feeling lonely, Witchling?"

She shrugged, taking another bit of pizza and moaning at the taste. Alastair licked his lips, watching her, his eyes traveling up her bare legs.

"I could call him back if you are," Alastair said. "If Wolf is your taste."

"And where would you go?" she goaded him.

"Who says I would go anywhere? My bed is more than big enough for three." His eyes glittered dangerously as they moved from her body to capture her stare. If she could play this game, well, so could he. "Would you like that, Witchling?" he asked her, huskily, shifting closer to her. "Would you like to have two males worshipping you?"

Her breath hitched, and he smiled. She was so fucking beautiful when she blushed. So beautiful when she wasn't in charge.

"Is that... something you've done before?" she asked. So casual, too casual. The pink in her cheeks and the jump in her heart rate was giving her away, though. *Naughty girl.*

"Oh yes," he answered honestly, trying not to smile at her look of shock. "Two men, two women. I've been around a long time, Witchling; you might be surprised at the things I've done."

Moving his wine glass to his other hand, he reached over, running a finger up her thigh and toying with the hem of the dress shirt she wore.

"But you didn't answer the question, Witchling. Is that something you would want?"

She swallowed, audibly, and every signal coming from her body was a resounding yes.

Interesting, Alastair thought with a smirk. But...

"Relax, Witchling," Alastair said, leaning back to give her space once again. It was hard, so fucking hard when all he wanted to do was touch her.

He cleared his throat, trying to diffuse the tension pulsing between them. "You're welcome to stay here," he said, finally. "For as long as you need. The sheets on the bed are clean. I can sleep on the couch, or if you want your own space, I can sleep at the club. I have a room with a bed there, and you can stay here, free of charge."

Fey cocked an eyebrow at him. "You'd leave me here, all alone, in that giant bed? Hell, Alastair, maybe you should call Jasper to come back here."

His eyes were serious when he looked at her. "You called me for help, Fey, and I answered. There are no strings attached. The apartment is yours until you no longer need it." His eyes darkened. "But if I stay, if I share that bed with you, I won't be able to keep my hands off you. It's taking every ounce of my willpower not to rip that shirt off you right now, Fey. And I think you know that."

She smiled at him, taking another bite of pizza. And slowly she parted her legs, just a few inches, but enough for him to see she was nude beneath his shirt.

Alastair growled deep in his throat.

"I don't want to sleep in that bed alone, Alastair," Fey told him.

Feeling something loosen in his chest, he smiled. "Then come here, Witchling," he said, patting his lap. Fey set her now empty plate on the table, crawling over the couch until she was straddling him, one knee on either side of his body.

Her hair was still damp from the shower, and he brushed it over her shoulders, tucking it behind her ears gently. "Do you want to talk about what happened?" he asked, his voice soft.

Fey stilled and slowly shook her head.

"No," she said. "Not tonight. Tomorrow maybe, but... tonight I need a distraction. Tonight, I don't want to think about any of it."

Alastair smiled. "I don't mind being a distraction," he assured her, his free hand traveling down the front of her shirt, toying with the buttons. *Fuck* how did she look so good in it? He took a deep drink from his wine glass.

"You're not eating?" Fey asked, looking at the glass in his hand.

"No," he told her, taking another sip of wine. "No, I already ate."

She eyed the wine glass suspiciously.

"Is that...?" She raised an eyebrow at him.

Alastair stared into the wineglass, swirling the dark liquid inside. "If you're asking if this is, indeed, a full-bodied and quite delicious merlot, then yes, Fey, it is. And there's a full bottle in the kitchen if you would like some." He took a sip, watching the color rise in her face. "But if you're asking if I am drinking *blood*..."

She shrugged a single well-toned shoulder. "Maybe," she said, settling back against his thighs. The slight shift brought his shirt higher up her thigh, and Alastair took advantage of her closeness to slide his fingers lightly up the skin there, feeling her shiver under his touch.

He chuckled, gently caressing her exposed skin. "I'm young, Fey. I only need to drink blood a few times a year, and I don't do it from a wine glass with a beautiful woman on my lap."

Fey put her hands on his chest and closed her eyes, relaxing under his touch. Alastair's fingers trailing over her knees, the soft inside of her upper leg, inching higher and higher.

"Who do you feed from, anyway?" she asked. He smiled at the huskiness in her voice, the way she twitched every time his fingers moved further up her leg.

"Why?" he asked. "Are you jealous, Witchling?"

She didn't answer, just groaned so softly he could almost have believed he imagined it.

"Other Vampires," he answered finally. "I feed from other Vampires."

"Women?"

Alastair barked a laugh. "You are. You're fucking jealous."

Fey opened her eyes and scowled at him, but she inched further up his lap, her legs opening a little wider.

Fuck, she was intoxicating. His hand moved higher up her leg, reaching up under the dress shirt and caressing her hips. She was nude, under his shirt, and knowing that nothing stood between her and his hard cock except his own clothing made him suck in a sharp breath.

Fey's hands moved down his chest, touching him through his shirt. He groaned encouragingly, then clutched her tight to him so he could lean over and set his glass of wine on the table. He wanted both hands free, needed to have both hands on her.

"Could you feed from me?" she asked in a whisper.

"No," Alastair answered quickly. Too quickly, as he settled back on the couch. Her touch stilled and withdrew.

"Why not?" Fey asked. The soft arousal in her voice replaced with a cold chill. "Is there something wrong with drinking from Witches?"

He liked this, Alastair realized, trying not to smile. This small jealousy from her, this misunderstanding of what he meant. Ignoring the anger now simmering behind her eyes, Alastair took her hand, gently kissing her fingertips.

"We only feed on the weak," he answered, trying to explain it as best he could. "Or, we only feed on those weaker than we are. I'm the second strongest Vampire alive—not a brag," he added. "Just a fact. In a few years, I might eclipse my father's power, and eventually I think my brother will eclipse me. In fact, I *know* he'll eclipse me, and I'll be glad of it. But being this powerful means I have plenty of others to pick from when I need to feed." He nipped her fingertips lightly.

"And you won't drink from me, because?"

"It's... disrespectful, to drink from someone more powerful than you are. It's almost like saying they're beneath you." He sighed. "Look, it's hard to explain, but letting me drink from you would be like... it would be like asking me to say you were beneath me. Nothing, to me."

She considered this.

"You're saying I'm more powerful than you?" Fey asked, watching him carefully.

He considered how to answer this, his hands continuing to explore her body, moving higher, over her hips to her waist, pushing the fabric of his shirt up as he did so.

"Before? Maybe not. It would have been close, too close to tell. But now?" He pulled her closer, kissing her cheek, the soft skin of her neck. Breathing in that delicious scent of hers. "Something changed while you were gone, Fey. If you're not ready to talk about it yet, that's fine. Goddess knows you don't owe me an explanation. But now—" He kissed the delicate spot on her neck where her pulse was strong. Powerful. "You smell like raw power. Energy." His tongue snaked out to taste her skin, and she trembled. "It's overpowering. Yes, Witchling, you're more powerful than I am. And it would be distasteful for me to drink from someone so much higher than me on the food chain."

"Maybe I should drink from you," she teased. The anger was gone from her voice, he noticed with relief.

"Maybe you should," he purred. "I can get you a glass and a knife from the kitchen if you'd like?"

She laughed, and he pulled her even closer on his lap, pressing her as close to his body as he could, until he knew she could feel how hard he was for her. Knew when she felt him, from her sharp intake of breath.

He snaked his fingers over her back, gently cupping her ass. She quivered against him.

"What does it feel like? To have someone feed from you?"

"I wouldn't know," he answered her, truthfully. "No one has ever fed from me. But," he continued, "the women I have fed from—and, yes Witchling, it has always been women—tell me it is... a pleasant experience."

That was putting it mildly. Based on the languid state of the women after he'd fed from them and the satisfied smiles on their faces, he believed it might have been a bit more than a "pleasant experience" for them.

"Why so interested in how I feed, Witchling?" he asked, his voice a whisper against her skin. He brought his hand from behind her, slipping it between them so he could tease between her hips, and he smiled at the way she wriggled in his grasp, trying to get him to touch her properly. "Did you really want me to feed from you?"

"I don't know," she admitted, her hips jerking under his touch. "Maybe, it wouldn't be disrespectful if I agreed to it? If I asked you to do it? Maybe I want to—"

She arched against him and gasped in shock as he bit into her neck, both fangs puncturing the area right above her pulse.

He held her there, impaled on his bite, but didn't feed. Didn't draw any of her blood from her body. He wasn't sure if he could, anyway; the idea of making her submit in that way was too sordid, even for him. And she needed all the strength she had for whatever it was she was dealing with. But this? A simple bite, he could do. Just to give her a taste.

To give *him* a taste.

Fey rolled her hips against him, trembling in his hold.

"Alastair," she whimpered, and he groaned in response. He could feel her pulse under his mouth, and it would feel so good to take a pull of that power, to truly taste her.

It felt so perfect holding her here like this, even without feeding. It felt *right*.

"Please," she pleaded, legs and hips shaking as his fingers continued to tease around her, never quite touching her where she wanted, where she needed to be touched. She groaned, clearly enjoying the feel of his bite, of his touch.

He couldn't answer her, not with his fangs buried in her neck, and when he continued to tease her, brushing his fingers over her but not *quite* touching, she let out a frustrated growl and grabbed his hand, pushing it against her, grinding against him, until—

Fey shuddered and gave a small gasp. She came, a soft, mild orgasm rolling through her, his hand pressed against her clit.

Alastair released her, pulling his fangs from her neck and leaning back against the couch, eyes wide.

"Holy shit," he whispered. Something inside him roared, begged for him to sink his fangs back into her. He was *hungry*, he realized. *Starving.* But right now, in this moment, he just wanted to watch her come again. "Do that again."

Fey was panting, eyes unfocused. "Do...?"

Alastair grabbed her hips, grinding her pussy down onto him, pushing her against his cock and into the palm of his hand. "Use me like that, again, Fey. Take what you need from me."

It was too soon after her orgasm, too much stimulation too soon, but still Fey gasped when he pushed against her, gasped and arched, murmuring his name as another small wave rushed through her.

Fuck, Alastair thought, watching her shudder in his grip. He felt untethered and raw, intense need crashing through him.

"Bed," he demanded in a snarl, wrapping his arms around her and under her legs, and lifting her from the couch. "This time I'm fucking you on a real bed."

CHAPTER 51

Head still spinning, Fey let herself be carried to the bedroom. She hadn't expected to enjoy his bite that much, hadn't expected to lose control of herself like that. But something about the jolt of pain, something about the way he was holding her, completely immobilized against him... she shivered, just thinking about it.

She wanted more.

The moment they were in the room, Alastair tossed her onto the bed, and Fey squealed. He pulled his own shirt off and was on her in a second, hands ripping open the shirt she was wearing hard enough she was sure he was tearing off the buttons.

"Alastair!" she gasped. "Your shirt!"

"Fuck it," he snarled. He pulled the fabric open, revealing her breasts, her bare body. Leaning over her, he licked a path down her skin, between her breasts and down her stomach. "I'll buy another," he said, into her skin, and she arched under him. "Fuck, I'll buy a thousand of them, just to rip them off you again."

He bit her again, hard, on the inner thigh just below her hipbone, and Fey jerked underneath him.

"Alastair," she hissed, half in shock, half in pain.

He pulled back immediately, licking his lips. "Sorry," he whispered, and Fey was startled to see how wild his eyes were, how out of control he looked.

Blood lust could make a Vampire unpredictable, dangerous. And based on the crazed look in Alastair's eyes, she might have brought him a little too close to that edge.

"Come here," Fey demanded, holding out her arms for him, and he came to her immediately, letting her kiss him and pull him down toward her. Letting her roll him over, until he was under her, her legs straddling him.

She pinned him underneath her and sat up on his hips to look down at him.

"Calm down," she said, and he took a deep shuddering breath. "Maybe, you should just lay back and let me play with you for a while?"

"If you want me to calm down, Witchling, that's the exact wrong thing to say," he told her, but the wild animal that had appeared in his eyes was starting to fade.

Fey smiled, seeing more of Alastair returning, his dilated pupils constricting again. She kissed him, swatting his hands away when he reached for her. Kissed him deeply, fully, letting her tongue touch against the sharp tips of his teeth. He groaned, and she moved to the edges of his lips, kissing down his jawline, his neck.

"*Fuck*, Fey." He hissed, arching up as she kissed down his chest. His cock twitched underneath her, through his pants. She wanted to touch him, feel his hard length in her hand, in her mouth.

When she reached his waist, and began to unbuckle his belt, Alastair reached for her again, trying to pull her back up to him.

"I need to touch you, Witchling," he hissed. But she swatted his hands away, smirking up at him as she unfastened his pants and slowly pulled his zipper down.

He wasn't wearing anything underneath, and Fey felt him jerk under her touch as his cock sprang free. Eyes still locked with his, holding his gaze, she trailed her hand up the length of him.

There is a different sort of power here, Fey thought with a smirk. Alastair watched her, eyes wide and desperate, as she touched him. His hands clutched the sheets, and he swore softly as her hands explored.

She held him in the palm of her hand, literally and metaphorically, and it felt divine to have such power over another person.

When she took him in her mouth, swirling her tongue over the tip of him, Alastair's eyes never left hers. But they widened, and he swore, hips bucking off the mattress. She took her time with him, enjoying the feel of him in her mouth.

"Fey," he moaned. "*Fuck,* that feels good."

She smiled, her lips curving up around him, taking him deep into her throat, and back out again. Then repeating it, her eyes never leaving his.

That did it. Unable to hold back anymore, Alastair's hands came out to grasp her hair. He pushed himself deeper into her, as deep as he could go, and Fey fought against her gag reflex as the tip of his cock hit against the back of her throat.

"*Fuck the Goddess,* Witchling, that's incredible," Alastair hissed, holding her head as he fucked her mouth, thrusting up to meet her.

It was, Fey thought, moaning around him. He was thick enough to fill her mouth entirely, thick enough it was difficult to catch her breath around him. And then he was releasing her, letting go of her head and sitting up enough to grab her by the ribs and pull her back up to him.

He kissed her roughly, one hand tangling in her hair, and the other positioning her on his lap, maneuvering her legs to either side of him. Fey let him take over, falling into the kiss, taking his face in her hands. She let him lift her thighs, let him position himself at her entrance.

Fey arched her back and moaned as Alastair entered her. His hands on her hips, he pushed her down to sit on him, forcing every inch of himself inside her.

Alastair wrapped his arms around her, forcing her hard against him and capturing her mouth again with his kiss. She rode him, moving up and down in his lap, and he met her movements with his own, thrusting his hips up to meet hers and burying himself deep inside her.

Fey could feel herself approaching her peak, and she broke their kiss, sitting up and arching as she climbed further and further up to bliss.

With a snarl, Alastair rolled them both, pinning her beneath him. Fey gasped, in shock, but it immediately became a moan as he moved inside her, fucking her hard against the bed.

Alastair buried his face in her neck, and his fingers found the space between them, rolling nimbly over her sensitive clit. Fey screamed, tightening her legs around him.

"Fey," he whispered against her skin. "Fey if you don't come soon, I'm going to lose it, I—"

Fey's entire body arched as her orgasm ripped through her, taking the breath from her lungs. She couldn't even make a sound, could only dig her fingernails into Alastair's back as she shuddered, cresting over and over again.

Alastair groaned and followed her, pounding into her once, twice, three more times before his body shuddered and his fingers dug into her leg where he held her.

"Alastair," Fey gasped. They were both breathing heavily. "That was—"

He kissed her, stealing the words from her. A gentle, sweet kiss. Kissed her, as her body came back to the world, as her breathing calmed and her pulse slowed back to normal.

Languid and satisfied, she pulled away to look him in the eyes.

"I'm so glad you came back to me, Witchling," Alastair said. And Fey realized she was glad, too.

CHAPTER 52

Fey had never knowingly slept next to another person, and it was a slight shock to wake up several hours later and realize she wasn't alone.

A shock, but not altogether unpleasant.

Fey stretched, pointing her toes, and relished the sheer amount of room she had all to herself in Alastair's massive bed. Then, rolling over and propping herself up on her elbow, she looked down at Alastair as he slept.

He was on his back, still as death. And he was...

Beautiful, Fey thought to herself. He was beautiful, lying there, all sharp angles and soft skin. She reached up, unable to stop herself, and touched an errant lock of his dark hair. It was like silk between her fingers.

He didn't move. Didn't seem to be breathing. Panic built in her chest. He *did* look dead, lying there, so pale, eyes closed... But he couldn't be, right? Couldn't have...

"Alastair?" Fey asked, leaning close enough that her breath moved his hair slightly. He didn't move, and her heartbeat was even faster. "Alastair, is—"

His finger pressed against her lips, his face fixed and cold as marble, as she blinked.

"Coffee," he whispered, his mouth barely moving as he spoke.

Beneath his finger, Fey's mouth quirked up into a smile. She moved away from him, but he reached out for her, eyes still closed. His hands found her hips, and he lifted her effortlessly, laying her on top of him and wrapping his arms around her waist.

He made another noise, almost words, and Fey smiled, relaxing against him.

"What was that?" she asked.

"Coffee," he grunted. His face buried in her neck, his hands holding her in place, he mumbled sleepily. "I need coffee."

"Make Jasper bring it."

He chuckled, and she could feel the sound reverberate through her body. Then he lifted her again, depositing her next to him, and placed a gentle kiss on her lips.

"You stay here," he told her softly. "I'll be back."

FEY DID NO SUCH THING, of course. After a few minutes alone in bed, she grew bored and restless, unable to fall back asleep. Tossing the sheets aside, she grabbed another of Alastair's shirts from his closet and put it on, venturing out to find him.

The house was full of delicious smells, she noticed immediately. Coffee, yes, but also something sweet and mouthwatering. Something she wanted, immediately.

"You were supposed to stay in bed," came a growling voice from the kitchen. She entered to find him in a pair of sweatpants and nothing else, his cell phone pressed to his ear.

Fey shrugged, sitting down on a barstool at the kitchen island. "I got bored."

Alastair grumbled but didn't argue more. Instead, he deposited a fresh cup of coffee in front of her.

"I'm making waffles," he said.

Fey couldn't help but smile. "Alastair... it has to be the middle of the day by now."

"I don't care," he told her. "I'm making waffles."

Someone must have picked up on the other end of the phone because Alastair's voice changed immediately, all warmth and teasing leaving as though it had never been there in the first place.

"Ferus," he said in a gruff voice. "Congratulations on your promotion to assistant owner of The Last Drop. Effective immediately. You start tonight, and you're in charge for the next few evenings. I won't be coming in for a while."

Fey looked around at his home, smiling and taking a sip of coffee.

"No, it doesn't come with a fucking pay raise, you greedy little shit." Alastair balanced the phone against his shoulder as he juggled with grabbing a plate and an empty bowl. "Fine, *fuck*, fifteen percent raise. And if you do well enough, twenty percent and I don't break your fucking legs for asking me for more money. Do you have any idea how much I already pay you?"

The coffee was hot and strong. Fey added a little sugar and poured a dollop of cream into it from a small pitcher on the counter.

"Okay, good. Yeah. Ok..." Alastair rolled his eyes. "I'm hanging up now. You deal with that shit. Okay. Don't fucking call me unless it's an emergency. I fucking mean it, Ferus. Good."

He ended the call, tossing his phone on the counter.

"Why do you have windows here, anyway?" Fey asked, looking around at the thick blackout curtains hung over the massive windows all around his apartment. They were the only things protecting him from the painful sunlight outside, and while sun likely couldn't kill a Vampire as powerful as he was, she was sure it would leave a painful burn.

Alastair turned from his cooking to look at her, one eyebrow cocked in amusement.

"I like the view," he said.

"What view?" she gestured at the curtains.

"The city doesn't disappear when the sun goes down, Fey," Alastair explained, a deep amusement in his voice. "I like the view of the city at *night*, Witchling."

"Oh." She felt like an idiot. But a moment later, when he placed a full plate of waffles with whipped cream, and a bowl of fresh strawberries in front of her, she forgot all about it.

"Eat," he said, walking around behind her, and leaning over to plant a kiss on her neck. She shivered.

"Aren't you going to have any?" she asked, her voice teasing.

Alastair reached over her, plucking a strawberry from the bowl and dipping it in her whipped cream. He popped it into his mouth and chewed.

"There," he said. "Now, *you* eat."

Fey rolled her eyes. Still, she picked up her fork and cut herself a piece of waffle with plenty of whipped cream and syrup.

When she took a bite, it was hard not to moan at the taste. It was perfect—buttery and soft, with just the right amount of crisp to the dough. Alastair chuckled, behind her, as though he could tell how much she enjoyed it, and he trailed his fingers down her arms and leaned close enough to bury his face against her neck.

"So," he whispered, lips brushing against her hair, fingers giving her goosebumps where they delicately brushed against her. "Are you going to tell me what's going on, now?"

Fey stilled, swallowing a mouthful of waffles.

"It's... complicated," she said. She poked at a strawberry with her fork, chasing it across her plate.

He made a small noise behind her, his fingers never pausing as they trailed lightly over her skin. "I can do complicated. Try me."

Fey sighed. She set her fork down.

"Something... something is going on," she started, trying to think how to explain it all to him. "With the Crown."

"Hm, very vague and unhelpful, thank you, Witchling."

Fey couldn't help it. She smiled.

"I can't tell you everything," she explained. "I promised I wouldn't tell anyone. That makes it a little more difficult."

"Okay, why don't you start with just *one* thing?" he asked. He shifted back slightly, granting her a little more space, a little more room to breathe. Still, with his hands on her shoulders, his body looming over hers, she couldn't help but feel comforted by his presence. Protected by him.

Fey sighed. "Okay," she said. "You said I feel stronger to you, right?"
He nodded.

"I am," Fey told him. "Much, much stronger."

With no effort at all, she held her hand above the table and called Fire, letting it dance across her fingertips. Then Water, pulling it from the glass next to her plate, and bringing it to dance among the flames. Salt next, calling Earth to join the dance. And finally, a ball of Air, sounding them all, pulling them all together like a globe of energy.

Behind her, Alastair hissed through clenched teeth.

"You can control all four elements?" he asked, awe in his voice.

Fey nodded, not trusting herself to speak. She let her power slip, vanishing the fire and air and letting the water return to her glass, sprinkling the salt into a pile on her plate.

"The Crown took this away from me," she explained, flicking a few errant salt crystals from her fingertips. "They've been... hobbling us. Reducing our powers, so the Queen can stay on the throne, unchallenged. My sister, Alice, found out, and now she needs my help."

"Your *murdered* sister?" Alastair asked, surprise and disbelief in his voice.

"Well... yes," Fey admitted. "But she's not as dead as we thought, it turns out... and she needs your help. *We* need your help."

Fey remembered the last time she'd come to him for help. Two minutes, he'd promised her. And even then, he'd only helped her to keep his own club clean.

Would he extend that same level of help again?

"Anything," Alastair said, leaning forward to plant a kiss on her hair. "Whatever you need, Fey."

"I need you to get a message to your father," she told him.

Alastair froze, his lips still pressed against her.

"Anything but *that*," he said, moving away, but when Fey twisted in her seat to look at him, he sighed, irritated. "Fine, don't give me that look, fuck... What's the message you need me to give him?"

"Tomorrow night, we need every Vampire off the streets. This is important, Alastair. Something big is going down, and we need everyone to keep their heads down and keep away from the palace. Keep away from everywhere but their own homes if they can. We can't guarantee the streets will be safe, not for anyone."

Alastair shifted uncomfortably behind her. "The other Factions…"

"The other Factions have already agreed to this. We need a truce for one night. To keep everyone safe."

He sighed, then nodded. "Consider it done," he said. "I'll reach out to him tomorrow and set up a meeting. He can get the word out quickly."

"And if he doesn't listen?" Fey prompted.

Alastair laughed. "He'll listen. Don't worry about that. My father… well, he's a shit father, I can tell you that. And there are things I can never forgive him for. But he's not a bad leader, Fey. He'll listen. And he'll do what I ask."

Fey nodded, relief washing through her. That was all she could do for now. All she could do until the time came for Alice's plan to trigger.

Fey pushed her plate away, suddenly not hungry. Alastair brushed her hair off her shoulder, peppering the skin there with kisses, and she let herself relax back against him.

"So," he whispered into her neck. "Tomorrow night, huh?"

"Yeah," she answered.

"I'm guessing it will be dangerous, what you're doing?"

She swallowed. "Yeah," she repeated.

"And do you need to do anything until then?"

Fey shook her head, and her pulse quickened as he licked the tender spot where he'd bitten her neck. He groaned into her skin as he closed his mouth over that spot and sucked gently.

"Well, in that case—" he said, nipping at the mark he'd left there. "Why don't we go back to bed, Witchling? Give me until tomorrow night to try and convince you that you should come back and find me when this is all over. Let me convince you why you should survive whatever it is you have planned."

Laughing, Fey agreed and let him drag her back to bed.

In the end, he was very convincing.

CHAPTER 53
SANA

There was a Blood Moon the night that the Eternal City fell. It's a rare occurrence, where a full moon coincides with a lunar eclipse. Years later when historians recorded the events of that night, many would say it was a sign from the Goddess herself of what would come. They would say it was destined to happen that night, of all nights, and that the two events could not have been a coincidence.

They were right. It was no coincidence, but it wasn't the Goddess or fate or the alignment of stars who planned it that way.

It was Alice.

The rarity of a Blood Moon ensured the Temples would be packed with Witches, ensured that a sizable minority, if not an outright majority, of Witches from the Eternal City would be gathered in one place. And that was necessary if this was going to work. Tonight, the moon itself would be awash in a blood-red haze. Witches of all elements, of all alignments, would spend the evening at their temple, giving homage to the Goddess as she toyed with the celestial powers at her command.

Sana, of course, knew none of Alice's plans, knew nothing of what was to come. But she did know one thing: She was, woefully, behind schedule.

The Water Temple was, historically, the temple most closely associated with the lunar cycle. Water Witches are by their very nature as in tune with the moon's ebb and flow as the oceans themselves. Tonight, her Temple would be packed, every seat filled, and it was Sana's job to prepare the sermon, to prep the candles and offerings for her members. Her speech tonight—on forgiveness, on new beginnings and understanding—was only partially written, and there was still so much to do.

Sana's mind was full of things that still needed to be done, boxes that still needed to be checked off on her mental to-do list. She was understandably distracted, her mind elsewhere as she gathered herbs and oil for tonight's events. So distracted she didn't even notice the figure lurking in the dark shadows of her workshop until Fey spoke.

"Did you know?" Fey asked, her voice dangerous and low.

Sana dropped the scrying bowl she was cleansing with a startled cry, spinning around in shock.

Fey sat on the edge of the old wooden table in the center of her workshop, the table she often ate her meals at, reluctant to be far from her work here in the temples. She was wearing her Blade leathers, but no mask. No cowl. The air around her seemed to spark with energy.

"Fey?" Sana gasped. Tears stung her eyes as she looked at the Witch before her. The Witch the Queen had assured them all was *dead*. "Oh! Thank the Goddess you're okay, I thought—"

Fey tossed something at her, and Sana caught it. It was a glass vial, full of some sort of silvery liquid. She frowned at it.

"Did you know?" Fey asked again. And something in that energy that swirled around her changed, becoming dangerous.

Sana's heart skipped a beat in her chest, and she swallowed. She wasn't a weak woman. She had endured her share of loss and pain and come through it all a stronger Witch than before. But Fey? Fey scared her. Had always scared her, in truth, though she tried to hide it.

With the anger that flashed in Fey's eyes now, though, and the energy that seemed to spark from her very skin, Sana found herself more frightened than ever.

Still, Fey was a Water Witch, like herself. And she owed her understanding, not fear. Sana swallowed her terror, wrapping it tightly in a box deep inside herself and pushing it down. She looked hard at the vial in her hands.

"Your sister asked me about this once," she whispered. "The short-haired one—Alice."

"Do you know what it is?" Fey asked.

Sana rolled the vial in her fingers, watching it catch the light. "No," she said finally. "No, I'm sorry, but I don't. And I told Alice the same thing when she came to me about it. It's no elixir I recognize."

Sana looked up, staring deep into Fey's eyes. "Fey, what is this about? The Crown has been looking for you, child—the things they're saying, they're—" She swallowed again and steeled herself. When a line is drawn in the sand, you must pick which side you stand on. And Sana chose hers. "Whether what they are saying is true or not does not matter. I can help you, Fey. There are temples in the outer octants where you could hide, where you would be safe until whatever this is dies down."

Fey hopped down from the table, not listening. She kept her eyes on Sana.

And the table at her back burst into flames.

Sana screamed. Not in terror, not in horror, but in simple shock. Her hand clutched her chest, squeezing the blue shawl she wore. A mark of her Coven.

Her eyes flickered from Fey to the table and back in quick succession.

"How... how did you...?"

"It's poison. Allium," Fey whispered. She nodded to the vial still in Sana's hands, and Sana flung it from herself reflexively. It clattered against the floor and rolled somewhere beneath one of her cabinets full of herbs. "They've been poisoning us, Sana. The White Priestesses have been poisoning us."

"No," Sana shook her head, from side to side, not wanting to believe it. "No, they wouldn't do something so... something so monstrous. No one would do something so monstrous... It would be blasphemy, the worst blasphemy imaginable against the Goddess's will..."

"I can burn something else, if you'd like more proof, Sana," Fey threatened. The table continued to burn behind her, the flames rearing up as though in response to her words. "Or I can call Earth, instead. I

319

could bury this whole Temple, and everyone in it. Would that be enough proof for you?"

"You... you hold all four powers?" Sana asked, shocked.

Fey nodded, watching her carefully. "I do. And other Witches might as well. Can you see what they've taken away from us, Sana? What they've stolen from us all?"

She could. And the thought that anyone would do such a horrific thing... it sickened her, to her core. She called on Water, from deep inside herself, letting it ease her. It moved inside her like the gentle lap of the tide against the shore and gave her the chance to breathe.

Finally, Sana managed to get her breathing under control, letting the Water under her power guide her back to a place of safety, to a place where she could think clearly.

"Please put that out," she said, finally, pleased to hear her voice was steady. "I *liked* that table, Fey, and I don't want to lose any other furniture in here."

Fey smirked, and behind her the flames dancing over the wood of the table pulled back and died. Sana was pleased to see the damage was minimal—the wood burned, but not ruined. If Fey had done so on purpose, held back her power to such a fine degree, it must have taken a remarkable level of control.

"I need you to do something for me, Sana," Fey said. "To help make this right."

Sana nodded. "Anything," she said. "Whatever you need. You have my full support."

Fey told her, explained exactly what she needed—what Alice needed —from her and the other High Priestesses. And Sana listened. Understood.

"And you?" she asked when Fey was finished. "What will you be doing, Fey?"

The smile Fey gave her was sharp and deadly as a knife. "Me? I'll be doing what the Crown trained me to do."

Fey turned away, then, and began to move toward the backdoor of Sana's workshop.

"Wait!" Sana called, and Fey paused, looking back at her.

There are many types of strength. It takes strength to be a fighter. It takes strength to be a leader. And it takes strength to be honest—with yourself, and with others.

"I never hated you, Fey," Sana told her, hoping she could hear the truth in her words. "I know we've never seen eye to eye, I know you've kept your distance from me, and I don't blame you, I swear to the Goddess herself I don't. But I need you to know—I never hated you. I never judged you for how you used your power. If anything, I envied you.

"I've dedicated my entire life to the Goddess's gift of Water," Sana continued. "And you? You found a new, remarkable way to use it. I envied you for that. Envied the connection you share with the Goddess that I don't... but I never judged you for it, no matter what you think."

Fey stared at her long and hard. Then she nodded.

"I suppose I was wrong all this time, though," Sana said with a half-smile. "It seems like you weren't really a Water Witch at all. I hope... I hope that you find Fire suits you. I hope if you join Leandra's coven, you do so with an open heart and find peace there."

Fey looked away, shaking her head.

"No, Sana," she told her, with a sad sort of laugh. "You were right all along. I *am* a Water Witch. And when this is done, if... if I survive the night... I hope your invitation to join the Temple still stands."

Sana thought her heart might burst. "Oh, my child," she murmured, coming forward and opening her arms to wrap Fey in a hug. "Of course it does, and I would be honored to—"

"Nope!" Fey danced out of her reach. "Nope, none of that. Fuck the Goddess, Sana, pull it together, and don't *ever* call me child again. We're nearly the same age, for fuck's sake."

Still, even as Fey turned and left, slamming the door behind her, Sana's grin was wide, and her heart was full of the Goddess's love and pride for a child of her temple.

CHAPTER 54

Enlisting the Temple High Priestess had taken longer than she would have liked, and by the time Fey had finished delivering Alice's package to Sana and explaining what she needed from her, the moon was high in the night sky overhead.

She was running out of time, and her next mission would be infinitely harder.

Fey still wasn't sure they could trust Sana, still wasn't sure the Priestess hadn't known, but it was a chance they had to take. There wasn't room for failure, wasn't room for doubt. If this were to work tonight, they needed to trust one another.

Alice had given up on trust, but Fey hadn't. Not yet.

And tonight, staring at the full moon, heavy and ripe in the night sky, Fey prayed to the Goddess her trust wouldn't be misplaced.

She'd asked Alice for just one favor before she'd left. A mask, just like the one she'd left at the palace the night of Willow's murder. Alice hadn't questioned it, hadn't put up any argument. The mask she'd given Fey had been her own once—one she'd kept, all these months, with her old Blade's uniform.

For the last time, Fey attached her mask and donned her cowl. Anonymity was her best disguise for tonight. If this were the night she was destined to die, she would die as she had lived. A Queen's Blade.

Sparing a glance at the full moon hanging lazily over the city, Fey steeled herself and made her way to the palace.

———————

SHE COULD HAVE BEEN any Blade in her uniform with her mask on, and none of the guards she passed stopped her when she approached.

Her first stop was the empty wing in Solare. Her old home.

Fey stood in her old room, looking around at it with a heavy heart. When she called Fire to her fingertips, and set the bedding ablaze, she did it reluctantly. The loss of this place felt like a physical pain in her chest.

It was a shame, really, that so much of the building had been abandoned. A shame that the soldiers' quarters had been consolidated in one small section near the training grounds.

If they hadn't, maybe someone would have seen her. Would have stopped her. But Solare was empty, abandoned. And it went up in flames like kindling, all the dust and cobwebs that no one bothered to clean adding extra fuel to the fire.

Fey stayed to make sure the flames caught, setting a few more rooms alight on her way out, trailing her fingers over the walls and furniture and feeling that intense pulse of Fire purring inside her as she set them alight. By the time Fey reached the palace, Solare was an inferno at her back.

It hurt to burn the first place she'd thought of as home. But Fey couldn't take any time to mourn the loss, not tonight.

Tonight, she had to find her sisters. She had to save them.

They were the only thing standing between Alice and the Queen, the only thing that might bring them all down.

As she left Solare for the last time, the building ablaze behind her, she could see the faint curl of smoke starting to rise from Lunairea, on the other side of the palace. Alice's doing. It had to be so perfectly timed —with Alice waiting in the shadows for the generals within Lunairea to react to Solare's burning, for them to begin to wake and gather themselves. For them to leave, rushing for the other building to try and salvage what they could.

Only then did Alice set the other building aflame.

Scattered, splitting their forces between both structures to try and keep the fires contained, the army would be distracted. Every available Witch would be pulled from their post and brought to help.

Leaving the palace woefully under protected.

Leaving it vulnerable to their invasion.

THE ALARM BELLS started ringing just after Fey entered the palace, alerting the palace to the fires in the surrounding buildings.

Guards were everywhere, and though Fey tried not to be seen, there was only so much she could do. She held herself straight backed, and walked through the palace with a purpose, with the same haughty air the Queen herself exuded.

"Your Grace!" a guard called after her. "Your Grace, Solare is on fire, get the others! Alert the Blades!"

I intend to, Fey thought, watching him hurrying away.

The palace was waking up around her, people evacuating to the grounds below. Aristocrats and visiting dignitaries from the octants were leaving their plush quarters, arms full of valuables, as they fled outside to safety.

That was good. The fewer people the better.

She prayed to the Goddess that her sisters were still in their quarters. There would be little reason to send the Queen's Blades to fight the fire, especially if they were pulling as many soldiers from the palace as possible. They're job was to protect the Queen, protect the palace. They would remain, the final wall of protection around the Crown. Fey prayed they stayed away from the chaos around her, prayed she could find them before Alice did.

She was near enough to their quarters in the Eastern Wing when the tolling alarm bells faltered and stopped. And a new alarm arose.

Fey cursed under her breath and began to run.

This alarm she knew, had trained for. This was no fire alarm.

This was the invasion alarm. The signal that an enemy had gained access to the palace.

She was too late. Alice and her Shifters had arrived.

She had to find them, had to get her sisters. They had to know what was happening, had to surrender. Alice hadn't told her what would happen if she encountered them, but Fey knew she was singularly focused on her role of getting to the Queen. If anyone tried to stop her —even Lilith. Even Joy...

Fey ran.

Someone was coming down the hallway toward her. Guards.

"Check the rooms. All of them," a voice snapped from the darkness, and Fey skittered to a stop, heart pounding.

Dameon.

Cursing, she ducked into the closest room, just as their footsteps came around the corner, looking frantically around for a place to hide. There was no time to retreat, no time to find a way past him. And he would recognize her, no matter her mask. Dameon would know exactly who she was.

The room was a poor choice for hiding, but beggars couldn't be choosers. It was a nearly bare bedroom, nothing as luxurious as the rooms in the Western Wing, most likely nothing more than a place for the guards to sleep between shifts. There was a bed and an armoire, big enough to hide in, but Fey knew any soldier worth anything would think to search it while sweeping the room. It wouldn't do anything but trap her in here with no escape route.

A noise directly outside in the hallway let Fey know she was out of time and out of options. She flung the armoire door open and ducked inside, closing it behind her, and wincing at the loud *click* the latch made as it shut.

The armoire was completely empty. Nothing to hide behind, no clothing to put between her and whoever searched the room. No way of fading into the shadows. Fey clenched her teeth together in frustration and froze, listening.

Someone was here.

The door to the hallway creaked as it opened, and someone entered. They moved quietly through the room, but Fey could make out some of their movements. A soft swish of the blankets as they searched beneath the bed. The sound of heavy fabric moving as they opened the curtains. And, finally, the sound of footsteps right outside the armoire.

Let them be an idiot, Fey prayed. *Goddess, please, let them be the worst soldier in the history of the Eternal City. Let them leave without checking here.*

But it was no use. She heard the click of the handle turn before the door of the armoire opened.

Opened, and revealed a familiar set of soft blue eyes above the black fabric of a Blade's mask.

Joy's eyes widened in shock at finding Fey. For a moment, Fey worried she would shout, would bring the guards outside running.

But when Joy spoke, her voice was calm, completely unfazed.

"Clear," she said loudly to someone in the hallway. She gave Fey a long look and then shut the door.

"Stay here," Joy whispered through the wood, voice barely audible. "Stay here and stay *quiet*. I'll be back soon, sister."

Fey waited until she heard Joy's footsteps leave. Waited until the guards moved on, down the hallway, before she released the breath she had been holding in one shuddering gasp. Then she settled in to wait.

WHEN JOY RETURNED a few minutes later she was alone. The alarm still blared through the hallways, echoing loudly against the marble of the palace walls.

"Fey?" Joy called softly into the room, but Fey didn't answer. She waited until Joy opened the armoire door again, still not entirely sure if her sister would turn her in or not.

But when Joy opened the door to find Fey still there, her face crumpled, broken by too many emotions.

"Thank the Goddess you're alive," Joy gasped, pulling Fey out of the cramped piece of furniture, and hugging her tightly to her chest.

Fey hugged her back, feeling Joy shudder with barely contained sobs.

"I felt you die," Joy told her. "I felt you *die*, Fey. And I thought... I thought..."

Fey was crying. She wanted to explain it all, wanted to tell her everything. Wanted to tell Joy how much it had hurt to lose her, how much she'd missed her.

But the words that came out of her mouth were, "Joy, Alice is alive. And she's here."

To Joy's credit, she didn't faint. She didn't scream, didn't cry. But when she stepped back and blinked at Fey, her face draining of all color, she looked fragile enough to break.

"Alice? *My* Alice?" Joy asked. "She's alive?"

Fey nodded, laughing through her tears.

"And Willow?" Joy asked, her eyes so full of hope. So full of love.

It broke Fey's heart to take that hope from her. But she had to. Shaking her head, Fey only said, "I'm so sorry."

Joy swallowed and nodded.

"Dameon told us you killed her," she whispered, but when Fey opened her mouth to explain, Joy held up her hand to stop her. That fragility was slowly ebbing away, Joy's strength repairing those cracks in her heart that Fey had seen just moments ago. "I could feel you, Fey. I know. *We* know. You never would have hurt her; you never would have..." She broke off, unable to say the words aloud.

Fey didn't realize how much she'd needed to hear that, how much she'd needed to hear that her sisters hadn't abandoned her. Hadn't thought the worst of her. With a sob, she pulled Joy back into her embrace.

"I have so much to tell you, sister," Fey said, but Joy shook her head, pulling away.

"Not here. The guards will be back. Someone triggered the alarm, but we haven't found anyone in the palace yet, so they'll keep looking and do a few more sweeps before they turn it off. We need to get you back to our rooms before then. We can't let them find you."

CHAPTER 55

Lilith was strapping one of her twin blades to her leg when they entered the common room, her face uncovered, mask hanging limply by one clasp at the side of her face.

Her eyes rose to look at Joy, then snapped to Fey and she froze, her body going stiff as a statue. Shock lit across her face. Disbelief. The knife in her hand slipped and fell, clattering to the floor.

"*Fey*?" she asked, stunned. "I..." Lilith stumbled back a pace, away from her, struggling to catch her breath. She shook her head frantically from side to side. "I don't understand... you were dead. How... how is this possible? How are you here?"

It was strange to see her sister like this, Fey thought. Lilith was always so unflappable. But now? She looked ... terrified. Fragile. It *hurt* to see Lilith this way, and Fey desperately wished she still had her Blade's mark and could still feel what her sisters were feeling. Wished she'd been here when they'd needed her.

"I'd like to understand that, too," said Joy, stepping away from her, and the accusation in her voice, the pain, laced with just a trace of anger, tore into Fey like a knife.

They might not have believed she killed Willow, she realized, but that didn't mean they trusted her.

"There's a lot to explain," Fey began, but stopped as the alarm outside stopped. Joy gave the door behind them that led out of their quarters a thoughtful glance.

"They must have given up," Joy said. "I guess it was a false alarm after all..."

"We don't have a lot of time," Fey told them. "So much has happened, but you both need to know. I never killed Willow. Dameon did it."

Joy sucked in a breath with a hiss, but Lilith just blinked slowly, still in shock.

"Why?" Joy asked, her voice heavy with pain. "Why would he do that?"

"Because they've been lying to us. Dameon, the Queen, all of them. They've been poisoning us, poisoning Witches around the realm."

Lilith was shaking her head. "Fey, don't—"

"Joy," Fey said, turning toward her sister. Joy looked at her with blue eyes, so full of pain, so full of hurt. "Joy... do you remember your Awakening? Do you remember being given something to drink, something silver, like an elixir?"

Joy nodded. "Of course," she whispered. "It was part of the ceremony..."

"No," Fey insisted. "No, it wasn't. That was Allium, joy," she continued, and behind her Lilith swore, covering her face in her hands. She looked ready to faint. So did Joy.

"The White Priestesses have been giving Allium to the Witches they worry might become too powerful, Witches who might stand a chance of resisting the Queen. They've been cutting them off from certain elements, making sure no one is stronger than the royal line."

Joy was shaking her head. "No, no, they only give Allium to Blood Witches, to...to..."

It clicked in her mind, and Joy's face hardened, her eyes darkening.

"They give Allium to Blood Witches to cut them off from their power..." she finished. Her hands clenched at her sides.

"And in the right doses, with the right ingredients," Fey continued. "They can cut any Witch off from any of the four elements."

Joy's eyes flared, shock burning away to anger. The Air in the room moved in fast, deadly spirals, coalescing around her.

"What did they take from me?" she asked Fey, her voice hard. The room was a maelstrom, with Joy at its center.

Fey could only shake her head in reply. "I don't know," she told her. "But we can find out... there's an antidote, Joy. *That's* what we found in the warehouse, that's what Dameon sent us to destroy. They're trying to stop the truth from coming out, trying to keep anyone from finding out what they've been doing and putting a stop to it. And they used us to do it.... Used us to help them cover all of this up, to help them kill anyone who was getting too close to the truth—"

The alarm shrieked back to life, filling the quiet halls with a blast of high-pitched sound.

"What *now?*" Lilith snarled, lifting her head from her hands to glare at the door.

"That," Fey said calmly, "would be Alice."

She had been wrong. Lilith *could* look more shocked. Her jaw dropped open, and her eyes filled with a deeper horror.

"Alice?" she whispered, disbelieving, her face paling even more. "No. No, you can't be telling me that Alice is alive, too. That's... that's not possible."

"She's alive, Lilith," Fey insisted. "And she's here to put a stop to it. She's here to make things right."

Fey didn't say it, not aloud. Couldn't bring herself to say it. But the truth hung in the air between them. Joy and Lilith exchanged a look, realizing what Fey was saying.

She's here to kill the Queen.

That's what it came down to, what this moment was all about.

Joy and Lilith were the Queen's Blades, her personal weapons. They were her justice, her protection. Their entire world revolved around the Crown.

And Alice was here to destroy it. Fey's one chance to keep them safe, to keep all of her sisters safe, was to convince them not to fight for the Queen against their own sister. To convince them to step aside and let Alice do what needed to be done.

Joy looked stunned. She opened her mouth to say something, then closed it.

"Fey..." she whispered, finally, turning those huge loving eyes on her. "I don't... I don't know if ..."

"Stop the alarm," Lilith snapped. Joy's head whipped back up to look at her.

Lilith's face was dark, and there was no confusion, no conflict in her stare. Whatever shock she'd been feeling was gone now, and only grim determination remained. She, at least, had made up her mind. "*Go*, sister. Find a way to stop it. *Make them* turn off the alarm if you have to. But stop it. Before they find her."

Joy blinked at her. Then, with a deep shuddering breath, she nodded.

"Yes," she answered, face hardening, turning resolute. "We need to stop the alarm."

She moved toward the door but stopped. Turning, she pulled Fey into a bone-crushing hug.

"I love you, sister," she said into Fey's neck. "And I'm so happy you're okay."

And then she was gone, racing down the hallway and into the dark of the palace.

Lilith stared at Fey long and hard enough that Fey began to feel uncomfortable under her sister's dark assessing gaze. She was like this, at times, almost cat-like in the way she stared, waiting for the other person to break first.

"When was the last time you ate?" Lilith asked, finally. She knelt to pick up the blade she'd dropped earlier and set it on the kitchen counter.

Fey's stomach rumbled, as though in answer. Hours, she realized. Nodding, as though she had confirmed something, Lilith turned and started rummaging through the kitchen.

"You must be running on fumes," she said. "You need to eat something. You're no good to us if you fall over in the middle of a fight from hunger, and it feels like we've all got a long night ahead of us."

"Thanks," Fey said, smiling slightly. Lilith had never made her anything to eat before, had never particularly liked caring for others in such a domestic way.

Fey pulled up a chair to the kitchen counter, watching Lilith's back as she pulled bread out of a cupboard and began to assemble a meal.

"So, there's an antidote, huh?" Lilith asked as she worked. "Did you take it?"

She glanced at Fey over her shoulder, and in answer Fey called Fire, just enough to produce a ball of flames in the palm of her hand.

Lilith whistled, turning back to her task. "Impressive," she cooed. The butcher's knife in her hand thumped rhythmically against the cutting board and she cut slices from a large red tomato. She fiddled with something in the drawers, and Fey let out a deep sigh.

It was okay. Everything was going to be okay. Her sisters knew, all of them, and Alice was on her way to end it all. Things would be okay, and then, finally, they could all be together again. A family, like they used to be before all of this started. Before Alice left them.

Lilith finally finished and set a plate down in front of her, nudging it toward her. A *very* simple meal, Fey thought, but even still, the sandwich made her smile. Tomato, chicken, and lettuce. It wasn't the sort of gesture she expected from Lilith.

"And Alice?" Lilith asked, tilting her head to watch Fey and she took off her mask, setting it aside and plucking the sandwich from the plate. "Did she take the antidote, too?"

"Yeah," Fey answered. "But she wasn't ever given any Allium at her Awakening, so it didn't do anything... But she's the one who figured all of this out; she's the one who's been making the antidotes. She was behind the warehouse we burned."

Lilith nodded, absently. Then she frowned at the sandwich still in Fey's hand.

"Eat," she pressured. "Go on."

Rolling her eyes, Fey took a bite. Satisfied, Lilith turned back around and began to clean up.

"How many people know?" Lilith asked, stuffing the bread back into its container, and sealing it.

Fey shrugged, taking another bite, chewing thoughtfully. The tomatoes tasted off, bitter. Or maybe it was the lettuce? She made a face, looking at the sandwich in her hands before setting the sandwich back down on her plate, her appetite vanishing.

No wonder Lilith never cooked for any of them, before. She couldn't even make a sandwich right.

"I'm not sure," Fey answered, swallowing the bite she'd taken with no small amount of difficulty. *Yuck.* "Enough that there's no way they can keep it quiet after tonight. And the High Priestesses…"

Her stomach clenched.

Something was wrong.

Lilith put the cutting board in the sink and ran water over it, grabbing the soap and continuing to clean up.

"What about the High Priestesses?" she prompted, but Fey wasn't listening.

Something was very wrong. Her stomach clenched again, more painfully this time.

It took a moment for Fey to understand what was happening, to identify what the powers inside of her were doing. She hadn't called either Earth or Water, but they surged inside her, anyway. There was a hot ball in the pit of her stomach, and her power was coalescing there, swirling around inside her, until the feeling began to lessen and vanish.

Poison, Fey realized, suddenly.

You can't poison a Witch who had control over both Earth and Water. Earth recognized the toxins, pulled them together into one place within the body. And Water, whether commanded or not, healed it. It made the Queen immune to all attempts at poisoning. Made her heirs immune as well.

And now, it did the same for Fey.

But there was no way for Lilith to have known that.

As the poison drained from her system, the painful cramp in her stomach fading, Fey looked long and hard at the sandwich Lilith had made for her.

"Why did you really send Joy away, Lilith?" she asked, her voice low. "Did you figure you had a better chance if you could get me all alone?"

"What are you talking about?" Lilith asked, continuing to wash the dishes in the sink. But her shoulders tensed, almost imperceptibly, and if Fey hadn't known her so well, hadn't spent so many years with her, she might have missed that moment of stiffness.

But she didn't miss it. And seeing Lilith's reaction was all the confirmation she needed. Seeing her reaction was a clue to a mystery Fey hadn't even realized she'd overlooked.

Lilith didn't know she held power over Earth now. Had no reason to suspect poison wouldn't have worked on her.

Lilith had insisted that their pasts didn't matter, that they were Blades first and foremost. Lilith had never shared any stories about her time in the Queen's army... had never even told them she had been in the Queen's army at all, had she?

A memory tugged on Fey's conscious mind, demanding attention. The night that Willow died, the night of the Winter Solstice ball, she remembered what Lilith had said when the Queen's sister had been announced.

She had a daughter, you know.

Fey stared at Lilith's back, at the raven black hair that flowed over her shoulders, at the pale almost bone-white skin. How had she never seen it before? How had they all been so blind?

"Cassandra had a daughter," Fey said, her voice sounding foreign and strange to her own ears. "You told us that, didn't you?"

Lilith froze. Then, slowly and deliberately she set the dish in her hand down in the sink and placed both hands on either side of her on the counter, her head down.

"A daughter the Crown made disappear. A daughter who wasn't Goddess Blessed with all four elements..."

"No," Lilith answered. "She only had one."

And Lilith—the Princess the realm had forgotten—turned and unleashed a wave of Fire.

CHAPTER 56

SANA

The moon in all her celestial glory watched over the Water Temple as Sana took her place at the podium.

The Temple was full. Fuller than Sana had seen in years, and she knew it had more to do with what was happening around the realm than the impending Blood Moon eclipse. People were scared, she knew. When the Crown had named a Queen's Blade, had implied that one of the realm's strongest and deadliest Witches had gone rogue, it had frightened people. And fear often led to devotion, a reliance on the hope that higher forces, like the Goddess herself, were still in control. That no matter how scary the world around them seemed, there was a plan in place that they could rely on. That they could trust.

Sana took a deep breath. They were going to need her strength to get through this. Because there was a plan, after all. One devised to hurt their fellow Witches, not protect them. A plan not of the Goddess's making at all.

And tonight, she would have to reveal it to them.

"We are in troubling times," Sana began, addressing her congregation. Silence rippled through the crowd as they settled back into their seats to hear her speak. Most of them had heard her speeches time and time again, but tonight would be different. As though they sensed it, sensed the strain in her voice, the room seemed to tense, listening to her words with an intensity beyond the norm. "And in times like this, I am thankful. I am thankful for the Goddess, who watches over us and protects us. I am thankful for all of you, for sharing your time with me and our Water Witch sisters.

"But more than anything, I am thankful for our strength as a Faction. I am thankful the Goddess has given us the strength to handle anything.

"Water is the element of healing, my children, but so often do we forget that it is also the element of strength. Persistence. Water can quell the hottest Fire, and even in the roughest storm the ocean remains just as deep and powerful as ever. Even Earth falls before the strength of Water. There is no stone in existence that will not eventually be worn away to nothing under the strength and persistence of a single steady drop of water."

Sana sighed, heavily.

"Tonight, my children, I am asking you to draw on that strength. Because tonight, I am going to reveal something to you that will not be easy to hear. But I ask that you trust me. I ask that you trust the Goddess, who watches over us all."

She held their attention in the palm of her hand, some leaning forward in their seats to hear her speak.

"My children, I am sorry. But we have been deceived."

A ripple ran through them all. Confusion. Fear. Hundreds of eyes focused on her, hundreds of lives about to be changed forever.

"My Priestesses will be handing out vials to all of you. I ask for your trust tonight, and I hope I have earned it."

Around the room, Sana's Priestesses began to disperse amongst the crowd. They carried baskets, filled near to overflowing with glass vials containing the golden antidote Fey had given her.

The other Temples—Earth, Air, and Fire—would be doing the same. Sana hoped their Temples were as full tonight as hers, hoped they had really listened to her when she had gathered all the High Priestesses together to pass on Fey's message. Hoped they had really believed her, as they had seemed to.

"The Queen's White Priestesses have been poisoning us, my children," Sana said sadly, and the murmurs in the crowd grew from a gentle stream and into a torrent. "They have stolen from some of us our most sacred gift—the powers the Goddess herself gave to us."

People were shouting, yelling, demanding answers, but Sana held up her arms to silence them.

"Please, my children, please calm."

They did, but the anger was still there, just below the surface, ready to erupt. Around the room, the Priestesses were finishing their rounds, ensuring every single Witch had a vial. Only then did one of her Priestesses approach her podium, and hand Sana a vial of her own.

Holding it high, so all might see, Sana continued.

"For many of you, the antidote in this vial will do nothing. But, for some, I hope this will restore something that you have lost. Something that has been taken from you."

Sana peeled away the wax top, all eyes of her congregation on her, and drank the antidote down.

CHAPTER 57

Lilith was fast, and the blast of power she released was strong enough to singe the wallpaper as it flooded the room. She was fast. But Fey was faster, and she had been ready. Since the moment the reality of Lilith's past hit her, Fey had been ready for an attack.

Fey flung herself backwards, scrambling over the couch, putting it between her and Lilith mere moments before the wave of Fire struck. Heat roared around her, crackling in the air as it passed above her.

This was bad. Fey had beaten Lilith in combat practice before, but she'd lost far more times than she'd won. Lilith was a better fighter, plain and simple.

But Fey was stronger. And if she had a plan....

"I'm honestly shocked no one figured it out before now," Lilith was saying. She sounded calm, almost bored. "Alice even *met me*; can you believe that? Before they knew I only had the power over Fire, when she was first inducted into the Blades." She laughed a dry, humorless laugh. "Can you imagine? She *met me* and she still didn't put it together when they made me a Blade. Still didn't recognize me."

Fey scrambled to find a way out, looking left and right around the room. Merle's favorite chair had caught fire, and Fey was relieved to find it empty. Wherever the cat was, she hoped he was smart enough to stay there until this was over.

"Come out, Fey," Lilith sighed. She hadn't moved from her spot in the kitchen. "Stop hiding behind the furniture, it's beneath you. Come out and let's end this. Face me like a real Witch."

"We don't have to do this, Lilith," Fey replied, but the words sounded desperate, even to her ears.

Lilith sighed loudly. "Yeah, we do. And you know we do. This isn't a negotiation, Fey. You know what's going to happen, here."

Fey shifted in her crouch, looking around her for options. The couch was burning at her back, and she'd need to make a move soon.

"Did you really think I was going to let you kill our Queen, Fey?" Lilith asked, in a cold jeering voice. "My *aunt*? You took the same oaths I did." She snorted a nasal laugh. "I should have known from the start you couldn't be trusted..."

"What if you do have the power, Lilith?" *Think, Fey, think. You're running out of time.* "You know what they've been doing—we have the antidote, why don't you try—"

A blast of fire hit the couch again, jolting it closer and causing Fey to scramble away with a hiss.

"You don't fucking *get it*," Lilith was shouting over the crackling sounds of the flames as they devoured the fabric and wood frame of the couch. "They *wanted* me to have power, Fey. I could have been *Queen*. They never gave me anything to take my power away. Why would they? My mother would have been thrilled if I could have wielded all four. The realm would have been thrilled if I'd wielded all four. They didn't take anything from me, I was *already broken*."

Fuck. Lilith was moving now, making her way to the couch. Fey was out of time.

"Your fucking antidote won't work on me. This is who I am. *What* I am."

"It's not your fault," Fey heard herself say, but her mind was elsewhere. *Think think think.* "So what if you don't have all four elements? That didn't give them the right to treat you like you don't even exist. To make you a Blade instead of a Princess. That's not fair."

Lilith laughed. "Yeah, well, life's not fair, is it, sister? That's something you never understood. We *all* have to make sacrifices, for the good of the realm, even if they don't feel fair."

"Is that what they told you?" Fey asked, her voice mocking. "That you had to make sacrifices? Is that what they told you when they took everything away from you? Your past, your crown, your *identity*?"

The Fire in the room stilled and pulled back, just a fraction—the only indication that Lilith was preparing to strike. Fey felt it, felt that shift in the balance of Fire in the room, and knew she had to strike first.

Her time was up.

Fey leapt from behind the couch, sending a blast of air at Lilith. Her face registered a look of surprise before the blast hit her, sending her flying back against the wall.

It was the only chance to escape she would get, and Fey took it, rolling to her feet and racing across the room as fast as she could, hurtling toward the door, toward the hallway.

The blast of fire hit her back like a bullet, and Fey twisted and fell hard against the ground.

It wasn't a wave, like Lilith had thrown at her before. It was precise, and practiced, and it knocked the air right out of Fey's body.

"I expected better from you," Lilith spat, walking slowly toward her. Fey tried to move, but only managed to roll to her side on the ground, struggling to draw a proper breath. "But you won't even fight me? You're just going to run, like a fucking coward?"

Lilith crooked her foot back and kicked Fey in the stomach, and Fey groaned, curling around herself.

"Pathetic," Lilith said, more to herself than to Fey. She knelt over Fey, one knee on either side of her, and brought her hands to Fey's throat.

Fey struggled to breathe, one hand scratching ineffectually where Lilith held her. Power surged between them, and Lilith's hand began to burn against Fey's skin as her sister called Fire.

"I'm sorry it came to this," Lilith was saying as Fey struggled. She didn't sound sorry at all as her fingers tightened. "But I told you. I *told you* to let it go, Fey. But you just couldn't, could you? Even after that Shifter nearly killed you, even after I *set you on fucking fire*, you wouldn't stop."

It had been Lilith at the warehouse, Fey realized. Lilith, who had tried to kill her, who had forced her to throw herself off the cliff and into the water below. Lilith, working against them this entire time.

Her fingers were burning through Fey's skin, and flames were licking down the inside of her throat. Lilith was going to burn her alive, from the inside out. It would be painful, incredibly painful. But more importantly, it would be slow.

This was how Lilith killed, if she could. Painfully. Slowly. And it put her exactly where Fey had needed her to be.

With one hand still clawing at where Lilith held her throat, Fey brought her other hand up to Lilith's chest, as though to push her away. But she didn't push, didn't try to move her.

Sometimes, to kill someone, you need to let them get close enough to hurt you.

It had been the first lesson Fey had ever learned about death, the night she had killed her own father. The night she'd finally escaped her family. And it served her well over the years. Being burned from the inside out would be *slow*. An agonizing, slow death.

Water was so much faster.

"I'm sorry," Fey managed to choke out, her voice full of pain and fire and ash. Smoke drifted from her mouth as she spoke.

Fey called Water.

Not in her own body—in Lilith's. Her hand pressed to Lilith's chest she drew every ounce of power she had over the element and gave one single command.

Freeze.

Ice burst like a star from where her palm pressed against Lilith's chest. As Fey watched, their gazes locked together, Lilith's eyes widened in surprise, then in horror. The ice spread almost instantaneously, shooting through Lilith's body, filling every part of her.

Lilith's eyes began to freeze over while Fey watched. Her mouth, open ever so slightly in shock, released a single fogged breath speckled with snow, and then it, too, turned to ice.

It took less than a handful of seconds for Lilith to die, every cell in her body turning to ice at Fey's command.

It took much longer for Fey to peel her sister's hardened, ice-cold fingers away from her own throat. Burned bits of Fey's skin remained stuck to her frozen hands, as though even in death Lilith would not let her go.

When Fey pushed Lilith's body off her, she hit the ground with enough force that her arm shattered, fragmenting like broken glass on the floor.

Fey rolled to her hands and knees, coughing up ash and smoke. Her throat *burned* and every breath was like swallowing sharp bits of metal. But she couldn't stay here. Joy would have felt her final sister die and she'd be on her way back.

Fey had to find Alice.

The faint patter of tiny feet made Fey look up.

"Hey, Merle," she greeted him, coughing. His favorite armchair was still on fire, a causality of Lilith's anger, and Fey sent a silent thanks to the Goddess that Merle hadn't been anywhere near it at the time. Calling her own power, pulling air from the flames until they died out, Fey brought the fires in the room to an end. "Sorry about your chair, buddy."

She held her hand out toward him, and Merle pattered closer, pushing his soft head into her palm and nuzzling against her.

"It's not safe here anymore," she told him, not bothering to question why she was talking to a cat in the first place. He was family, after all. "Go find Joy, okay? You gotta get out of here, bud, just in case."

Merle yawned, stretching and arching his back. Then with one final look at her, he loped away, disappearing in the direction of their quarters. Fey wasn't too worried. He'd found them once, hadn't he?

He'd find them again.

With one last glance at Lilith, her face forever frozen in a look of horror, Fey whispered a quick prayer to the Goddess, got to her feet, and left.

CHAPTER 58

ALICE

Alice scraped the tip of her blade along the wall as she walked through the palace halls. It left a satisfyingly deep mark in its wake, ruining the white stone.

"Edelin," she called down the darkened hallway in a sing-song voice. "Edelin, where are you?"

The fire Fey had started had done its job. The army had flocked to Solare, fighting against an unstoppable inferno to try to salvage the building. Then, in horror, back to Lunairea moments later when Alice had started a fire of her own. Caught trying to quell two massive fires, every available soldier and guard had been called to help. Leaving the palace woefully under manned, if only for a few minutes.

Ripe for the picking.

She'd stayed at Lunairea long enough to keep the flames burning, her power eclipsing that of the other Fire Witches that had come to calm the blaze so much that their attempts to smother the fire barely made a difference.

Let them focus on the fires now, Alice thought. Let them salvage whatever of the buildings they could. It didn't matter, not anymore.

"Come out, come out, wherever you are," Alice called down the long, empty hallway. Nothing answered but her echo.

The few guards who had remained behind were little match for her and the Shifters she had brought. That had been Rex's doing. Sam—sweet gentle Sam—believed wholeheartedly in a bloodless coup. Sam believed they could win this revolution off the strength of their convictions alone.

Sam was an idealist. And, in this, he was wrong.

Alice was no stranger to violence and death, and she knew there was no such thing as a bloodless exchange of power. No. Winning meant wiping out your enemy completely. Winning required death.

If not theirs, then yours.

Rex understood this. But more importantly, the group of Shifters he had sent with her tonight also understood it.

None of the guards left in the palace were a match for her, and they certainly weren't a match for the pack of Lionesses that now prowled the halls on silent, deadly paws. Alice had already found enough partially eaten guards in the hall to know just how effective these particular hunters were.

As she walked the halls, a Lioness stalked towards her, coming from the opposite direction. Four hundred pounds of muscle and death, moving with barely a sound.

"*Throne room*," the Lioness growled as she passed, the words garbled and guttural coming from jaws not made for speech. Alice bowed her head to the Shifter in acknowledgment and thanks, and the cat stalked away, a sand-colored specter of death to any who crossed her path.

Alice should have figured the throne room was where Edelin would head to. It was the heart of the palace—a place the Queen's guard would likely know to congregate in an emergency.

But it was a poor choice, all those entrances making it difficult to defend. Alice smiled as she walked, dragging her knife along the walls as she went.

This might be even easier than she'd hoped.

CHAPTER 59

Fey followed the trail of bodies.

It wasn't difficult. Alice was making no effort to hide her presence in the palace now, and some of the hallways were coated in blood almost deliberately, as though Alice were leaving a macabre trail of breadcrumbs in her wake. Fey had even stumbled upon a Lion Shifter, hunkered over a dead body, ripping chunks from the guard and crunching through bones as though they were nothing.

The Shifter turned as Fey approached, drawing blood-coated lips back in a snarl and baring her teeth.

"I'm a friend," Fey told her, holding her hands up, away from her weapons. *Goddess help me, I hope I'm a friend*, she thought. "Alice sent me."

The Lioness paused, cocking her head to the side, and sniffed the air between them. Then, as though satisfied by whatever she had scented there, she turned back to her meal.

"Thank you," Fey told her. "Uh ... enjoy your snack, I guess."

Fey could have sworn she heard a chuckle from the giant cat behind her as she hurried down the hallway, but it could have just been her imagination.

The dead bodies became more frequent the deeper into the palace Fey ventured. The closer she got to the throne room.

She couldn't find Joy anywhere, but she knew her sister would have felt Lilith's death. And this time, Fey wouldn't be able to tell her that she wasn't at fault, wouldn't be able to look in Joy's trusting blue eyes and lie to her.

This time, she *had* taken Joy's sister from her. Joy's final, remaining sister. And now, she would be alone, truly alone. The last remaining Queen's Blade.

Her heart twisted in her chest, but Fey couldn't stop moving, couldn't give up now. Joy might never forgive her for what happened tonight, but Alice would. Alice would understand that she'd done what needed to be done. And Fey was determined to do whatever she could to make sure her sister succeeded tonight.

It was time to finish what they'd started.

———

SHE HEARD the fighting before she could see it, but by the time Fey arrived it looked like it might already be over.

Ten bodies littered the throne room floor. Some had been burned, nothing but charcoal and bones remaining, and the blackened skulls looked like they were frozen in an endless scream. Others had fallen to Alice's blade, their blood coating the floor, a vibrant red against the white marble.

Alice was fighting three guards when Fey arrived, whirling between them like a storm of blades and death. She wasn't even bothering to draw on her power, not even when one of the guards sent a blast of Fire at her. She simply danced to the side, the burst of flames missing her entirely, and spun back to land a deadly thrust right through the Witch's belly.

The remaining guards fell easily enough.

This was Alice's specialty, after all. She had been the deadliest of them all with her Blades, relying more on her sword work and speed than her power over Fire.

When the final guard dropped, clutching her chest where Alice's blade had dealt a fatal blow, Alice smiled.

Smiled, and raised her blood-coated blade to point at the Queen.

"There you are," Alice said, her smile growing. "Didn't you hear me calling your name?"

Queen Edelin did not run. She did not so much as flinch under Alice's heavy stare. Standing beside her throne, back straight, and head held high, she didn't even look frightened. And that, more than the dead guards at her feet, seemed to give Alice pause.

"Kill her," the Queen commanded, and Dameon, who stood at his Queen's side as her final defender, drew his sword and stepped forward, advancing down the dais.

"Gladly," he said, as he approached, eyes on Alice.

"No," Fey growled. Her throat burned at the words, damaged from her fight with Lilith. Dameon's eyes flicked toward her, and she was glad she'd left her mask in the Blade's quarters, glad for her uncovered hair. She wanted him to know exactly who she was when she killed him.

Fey drew both her blades, readying them at her side. "No, he's mine, sister."

Alice's eyes burned with barely restrained fury, but she nodded, turning her gaze from Dameon to the Queen, now unguarded and alone.

"Let's see what kind of Witch you really are, Edelin," Alice said, striding up to face her Queen.

Whatever shock Dameon had felt when he saw Fey enter, alive and well, was gone in an instant, replaced instead with a hateful sneer.

"Do you know what your problem is, Fey?" he asked, letting her approach, his sword held tight in both hands, the tip angled toward the floor. "You never respected the chain of command. I was your superior, *I* was the one giving you orders, but you were incapable of acknowledging that... You always thought you were better than everyone else, even me."

There was enough anger in his voice to confirm something Fey had always suspected—Dameon didn't like her. Had never liked her. And knowing it brought a smile to her lips.

"Oh Dameon," Fey laughed, circling him. "I am better than you. And I always have been."

He lifted his sword with a snarl and leapt at her.

THERE WAS a truth in what Dameon had said to her. Fey had never really respected his position over the Queen's Blades. After all, despite his orders, despite his training, despite the fact that it was Dameon himself who had taught Fey to wield her twin blades, at the end of the day she had something he never would.

She was a Witch. And that made all the difference.

His sword came down with a speed and strength unmatched by any others in the Queen's army, but he still wasn't fast enough. Fey dodged to the side, easily, knocking his blade aside with her own with a quick flick of her wrist.

She clicked her tongue at him. "You'll have to do better than that, Dameon," Fey mocked. With a roar of rage, he launched himself at her again, bringing his sword down over and over, forcing Fey backward from the strength of his hits.

He was trying to tire her out, Fey realized, parrying the attacks he rained down upon her. Keep her on defense, keep her reacting so she can't act. It's a common tactic when fighting a stronger opponent, and on someone else, it may have worked. But everything Dameon had known about swordplay, he'd taught to her, and Fey had made those tactics part of her life's work.

The next flurry of blows he tried to land hit nothing but Air, as Fey summoned a wall of wind between the two of them, pushing Dameon back and momentarily off balance. But the wall of Air did nothing to stop Fey as she dove right through the shield she'd created, bringing her blade up above her head and slicing the tip down his face at a sharp angle.

Dameon howled in pain, letting go of his sword hilt with one hand, and bringing his hand to his face. He touched the deep wound that now crossed from one side of his face to the other, curving down and angled over his nose. A mirrored match to the scar on the other side of his face.

"There," Fey said. "Finally balanced."

On the dais, Alice and the Queen fought, seemingly oblivious to Fey and Dameon. They fought not with weapons but with power, and the room itself shook with the energy that they threw at one another. Fire and Air rushed back and forth, but Fey knew she couldn't risk glancing at the fight to see how her sister was doing. Not until she finished this.

Glaring at her, blood dripping down his face and over his hand, Dameon took up his sword with both hands again and came at her.

He was no match for her—for any of the Queen's Blades. Even Willow, young and untrained as she had been, would never have fallen to him if he hadn't slit her throat from behind like a coward.

The fight would have been over quickly, and Dameon would have fallen to her blade without any trouble, if Fey hadn't forgotten one thing: they weren't alone. And while Dameon was the Queen's protector, she was also his.

Queen Edelin had never been to war. She had never been trained as a soldier, never been an assassin. Even with her power over all four elements, it had been easy to discount her as a threat.

Easy, yes. But a grave mistake.

As Fey parried the blows from Dameon's sword, as she tempted him ever closer and prepared to finish him off, prepared to finally make him pay for Willow's murder, a gust of Air hit her shoulder, impossibly hard, twisting her off balance and knocking her to the floor.

Stunned, Fey had no time to recover, no time to get up, before Dameon's sword sank into her, through the right side of her abdomen and all the way through to her back. The metal tip clanged like a bell as it exited her back and struck the marble floor beneath her.

With a scream of rage, Fey summoned a blast of Air and Fire that flung Dameon away. He hit the marble wall on the other side of the room and collapsed into a heap on the ground. Alive, for now. On the dais, Alice and the Queen still fought, the very air and marble floors of the throne room becoming weapons in their battle, but Fey couldn't focus on what they were doing.

Dameon's sword remained behind, embedded in Fey's side. She couldn't reach the hilt, and trying to move, trying to shift her body at all, felt like she was being torn apart from the inside.

Struggling to remain calm, her breaths quick and shallow, Fey gripped the sword blade in both hands. Gripped it, and *pulled*, ignoring the pain as the sharpened edge cut into her hands, ignoring the pain as the blade tore again through her body, widening the wound. She whimpered as she pulled at it, hands slick with blood, until finally, painfully, she pulled the sword from her body and let it fall from her hands, where it clattered to the ground next to her.

She was bleeding heavily, and the ground underneath her was wet with it, but Fey could already feel her body responding. Water rolled through her, uncalled, and began to heal what it could.

Shaking and dizzy with blood loss, Fey stumbled to her feet. Dameon was doing the same, across the room from her. Unarmed, still stunned from where she'd thrown him, he rose unsteadily. With a snarl of fury, Fey flung her hand out, wrapping Air around his throat and pinning him to the wall.

She let the Air lift him, until his feet were several inches from the ground, while he struggled and thrashed, his hands pulling at the invisible force that held him in place.

But his hands found no purchase on the Air there. The Air Fey commanded.

"This is for Willow," she said, feeling the breath in his lungs, the life-giving oxygen inside of him, and gathering it together.

"This is for taking her away from us," Fey continued, one hand pressed against the wound in her side as she approached him, blood seeping through her fingers. She gathered all that Air inside him and dragged it out.

Dameon's eyes went wide and bulged. He struggled against the force that held him in place, struggled to draw breath, but he had no power over the Air. She did, and it obeyed her command, refusing to be drawn into him, refusing to fill the vacuum now occupying his lungs.

On the dais, something crashed and broke, and Alice screamed in pain, but Fey wouldn't look away from this. Wouldn't look away as Dameon slowly suffocated to death in front of her.

Another blast of Air hit her, making Fey stumble, but still, she didn't look, still, she didn't lose her focus and drop the power around

Dameon. Instead, she called Fire, wrapping them both in a cocoon of flames, shielding them both from the outside.

"Her name was Willow," Fey said, softly. It hurt, Goddess it hurt to talk. Her throat was so damaged, so inflamed, but she didn't care. She needed to say this, needed to get these words out. "She was our sister, and we loved her. She was so smart, so funny. And she deserved better. She deserved better than to die at the hands of a miserable coward like you."

She was inches away from him now, staring up into his eyes, watching his face turn blue and pale.

"I felt her die," she told him, froth and saliva dripping down his chin as he struggled. His eyes protruded unnaturally in his skull and began to redden as the blood vessels within popped and bled. "And now, I'm going to send you to whatever afterlife exists, so she can have her revenge."

Dameon strained against her hold one more time, releasing a dry gurgle from deep in his throat, and then convulsed violently, before going limp. His eyes were wide and frightened, unfocused, staring at nothing.

Only then did Fey release him, letting his lifeless body crumple to the ground. Only then did Fey recall the Fire that surrounded them, pulling it back inside herself, and turn toward the dais.

To where Alice knelt, stone binding her hands. To where the Queen stood, one hand gripping the back of Alice's head, and the other holding a blade to her throat.

"Stand down," the Queen said, and for the first time, Fey heard emotion in her voice. *Rage*.

"This foolishness is over," the Queen said, her fingers digging into Alice's skin. "I must say, I am *very* disappointed in the two of you."

CHAPTER 60

It wasn't the look of fear in Alice's eyes that broke Fey's heart. It was the resignation.

Alice had fought, fought with all her power and skill. Fought and failed. Now, she knelt there, defeated, and resigned to her inevitable death.

She had given it all and it wasn't enough.

Fey snarled and stepped forward toward the dais. She was still losing blood at an alarming rate, and any minute now she might lose consciousness. But for now, she was standing. For now, she could still fight.

She didn't make it another step. The Queen barely flicked her fingers, loosening her grip on Alice's skull to do so, and Fey went flying backward, struck by a gust of Air, and hit the ground, rolling painfully over and over, until she finally came to a stop.

They had known the Queen was strong. Had known the other Factions feared her.

But this? No wonder they feared her so much. No wonder they'd never tried to overthrow her.

"Run," Alice said. "Leave me, Fey, I knew the risks—*go*."

"You should listen to her," Edelin said, watching Fey come to her feet slowly, painfully.

"No," Fey groaned through gritted teeth.

She made it two steps this time, and the blast of Air that hit her almost blew her out the door and into the hallway.

"What are you hoping to accomplish with this?" the Queen asked loudly, her voice echoing across the long room. She sounded both bored and genuinely curious.

Fey coughed, trying to rise again. It was a wet, horrid cough, and Fey realized with faint surprise, looking down at the red droplets on the ground beneath her, that she was coughing blood. Blood, and specks of ash.

It took her much longer to stand this time.

"Justice," Fey heard herself say, in a voice that didn't quite sound like her own. But, then again, she felt a million miles from her body now. Her legs shook underneath her, but she pushed herself forward, forcing herself closer to the dais step by painful step. Closer to her sister.

"Justice?" the Queen asked, amused. "Where is the justice in killing my consort?" She flicked her gaze over to Dameon's body, grotesquely blue against the pale marble floor. "Where is the justice in getting yourself killed tonight?"

Fey shook her head, trying to clear her thoughts. "He killed my sister. He killed Willow."

She sent a wave of Fire toward the Queen, but it hit a wall of Air she had summoned there and burst into nothing.

"Whatever he did, he did for the good of the realm," the Queen said softly, as though speaking to a child. Unfazed by Fey's approach. "Whatever he did, he did to protect his Queen."

"You're no true Queen," Fey heard herself saying. "You have no right to that throne. Not after what you've taken from us."

Another flick of those powerful fingers, and the ground beneath Fey twisted and bent. She fell forward, onto her hands and knees, and the stone flowed up her arms and legs like water, then solidified, trapping her.

"I have every right to this throne," Queen Edelin snarled, her words filled with fury. "Did you really think you were more powerful than I am? Did you really think two Witches would be enough to take me down? A Witch with command over only Fire?"

Fey called Earth, struggling to free herself, but the Queen's power was too strong, and even with her body healing itself she was growing weaker by the second. The stone crawled further up her arms, up to her shoulders. It reached her neck and wrapped around her throat, pulling her head back so she was forced to look at the Queen where she stood on the dais next to her throne.

Forced to look at her sister Alice, helpless and beaten, where she knelt.

"I hold the very powers of a Goddess in my veins," the Queen continued, and the room seemed to fill with her power as she spoke.

Eyes meeting Fey's, Alice called Fire in one last desperate attempt at freedom. Flames erupted from her hands and coursed up her arms like a snake, heading for the Queen's hands.

They never got there. The Fire died, inches from Edelin's skin, the flames evaporating under the control of someone much stronger.

"Neither of you are strong enough to challenge me," she told them, staring at Fey. "And now you'll learn what happens when you try to kill a god."

In a single motion, the Queen wrenched Alice's head back and raised the knife.

Fey screamed as the blade came down in a flash of silver. Screamed at the spray of blood that followed.

CHAPTER 61

The blade of Air that severed the Queen's hand from her body had been so fast and precise that Fey hadn't even seen it. Hadn't fully understood what had happened, until the knife clattered to the floor, and the Queen's hand fell as a bloody mass beside it.

The Queen shrieked in pain, her remaining hand releasing Alice's head. Alice, suddenly free, didn't move. She sat, frozen, her eyes locked on something behind Fey. On *someone* behind Fey.

The air in the throne room swirled in a maelstrom of fury as Joy entered.

There was no time for the Queen to react, no time to even raise her remaining hand to defend herself.

Joy moved like air itself, each motion precise and exact. Razor-sharp blades of air sliced at the Queen. One by one they severed her sigils, tearing through her nightclothes to destroy each of the markings that granted her extra power. Fey had forgotten them. Forgotten that the only person in the realm granted more sigils than the Queen's Blades was the Queen herself.

While hobbling the Witches of the realm, the Queen had been

granting herself more and more power. Her skin was covered in sigils, and Joy methodically removed each and every one.

When the Queen screamed, bindings made of Air hit her, gagging her and wrapping around her arms like ropes.

"Edelin," Joy said. Her voice was a cold rage, sharp and biting as winter frost, but Fey was surprised to see that her sister was crying. Twin rivers of tears flowed down her cheeks, but Joy's voice was unshaken. She was rage. She was power. She was justice. "In the name of the Goddess, I accuse you of treason against the realm."

The Queen snarled from behind her gag. Blood flowed freely from the stump of her arm, dripping onto the stone below her, and with a single flick of her wrist Joy conjured another rope to bind it, stemming the flow.

"I accuse of you knowingly harming the citizens of the realm. I accuse you of blasphemy against the Goddess herself." With each word the binds holding Edelin tightened, straining against her skin, forcing her body to contort. "And I accuse you of attempted murder of a Queen's Blade. The punishment for these crimes is death. How do you plead?"

There was a noise in the hallway, and Fey was stunned to see people there. Guards... and servants. Civilians. Everyone who had evacuated the palace, everyone who had been called to fight the fires outside, they had come to investigate the noise. Servants, guards, even a few nobles of the Crown. They looked into the blood-soaked room in horror.

Joy loosened the gag of Air that bound Queen Edelin, preventing her from speaking.

"You stupid girl," the Queen hissed the second the gag was loosened. Her voice was strained from pain, but still full of that strength and power that had made her such a formidable ruler. "You have no idea what you are doing."

"How do you plead?" Joy asked again.

"You accuse me of blasphemy? Of treason?" The Queen laughed, a dark awful thing. "You bitch, I am the *Queen*. I am incapable of treason."

A few of the guards looked ready to intervene, to step forward to do something, anything to help their Queen, when Joy spoke again.

"You have knowingly poisoned the citizens of this city," she said, voice loud and clear, carried by Air through the room and out into the halls. The guards stopped, frozen in their tracks. "You have taken the very power the Goddess has given them, and wrenched it away from them, and for what? So you could remain in power? So no one could be stronger than you?"

"I was *protecting them*," the Queen hissed. "If people knew that there were others who could wield all four powers, Witches not from the royal line, what do you think would happen? It would be chaos. It would be war. The other Factions would rise up and challenge us, kill us all. The realm requires stability, it needs a Queen chosen by the Goddess herself." Edelin struggled against her bonds. "You understand that don't you? How many people will die now that this secret is out? How many Witches will kill one another to take the throne? I wasn't poisoning anyone—I was *saving them*."

Joy tilted her head to the side, as though listening.

"It's not too late," the Queen insisted, jumping at Joy's attention. "Let me go, and I'll let you live. Your other sisters here, too; I don't care. Let me go and we can salvage this, we can stop it from getting any further than it needs to. The realm needs stability. The realm needs *me*."

Joy nodded slowly, and for a moment the Queen's eyes filled with triumph. She had won, she had convinced her.

"Guilty it is, then," Joy said, and horror bloomed on the Queen's face as Joy raised her arm to slash the Air.

The blade of wind severed the Queen's neck in a single, precise slice.

Queen Edelin's head tumbled from her body, bringing an end to her reign. Bringing an end to the Witches' rule over the Eternal City.

CHAPTER 62

There were screams from the onlookers as Queen Edelin's head fell from her body, but Fey barely paid any attention to them. The stone that held her in place crumbled, falling away and freeing her.

Her eyes still on the Queen's limp form, Joy fell forward to her knees and threw her head back to scream.

The sound was like nothing Fey had ever heard before. It was full of rage and fury. Full of pain and loss. Full of love, and hate, and everything in between. Every emotion that had been crushing Joy, that had been drowning her. Fey thought they might all break from it, break under the weight of Joy's pain.

Then Alice was there, running down the dais and dropping to kneel at Joy's side. Wrapping her arms around Joy, she held her tight against her chest.

"I'm here," she whispered to Joy. "You're okay, now, love. It's all over, and I'm here and I love you. I love you, Joy."

Joy sobbed in Alice's arms, rocking back and forth as Alice whispered and soothed her.

Fey got shakily to her feet, clutching the wound at her side.

"Go to the Temples and get the High Priestesses," Fey said to the guards who were still standing frozen in the doorway. A few looked up to blink at her, stunned. They were in shock, she realized, too rattled to move.

"*Get the fucking Priestesses!*" Fey snarled at them, moving as though to draw her blades. That did it. Fear replaced shock on their faces, and several guards took off running down the hall. A few servants took off after them, and Fey wondered if they were on their way to the temples as well. Or, if they were just running, as far and as fast as they could to get away.

The remaining nobles and servants were in a very poor state. Someone had been sick, and the throne room was filled with the sour stench of it. A few of them were openly crying.

A noble woman Fey didn't recognize was looking at her.

"What did she mean?" the woman asked her, her face ashen. "About poisoning us? What did the Queen mean by that?"

But Fey only shook her head and didn't answer. She didn't have the strength to go through it again. She was done. She'd given enough tonight.

Sana was the first of the High Priestesses to arrive, flanked by guards, and she paled visibly as she looked around at the carnage in the throne room.

"The Queen," Sana whispered in shock, her eyes locked on Edelin's decapitated head.

"The Queen was found guilty of treason," Fey announced, loud enough for the crowd of people gathered to hear. She was tired. She was so, so tired. And though she was fairly sure she wasn't bleeding to death it would be a very good idea for her to have someone stitch up her side as soon as possible. Just in case.

Sana said nothing. Just stared. Finally, she unfastened the shawl that draped over her shoulders, the crisp blue of the Water Coven, and used it to cover the Queen's fallen form.

It felt too much like reverence, like an act of respect, and Fey heard the snarl escape her lips before she even registered the anger that roared to life inside of her. Sana glanced at her but didn't flinch away or shrink back from her.

"They don't need to see this, Fey," Sana explained, motioning to the hallway. More were coming now, the other High Priestesses but also members of their coven. Others from the palace, too, and the hallway was beginning to fill with faces. Faces full of fear, faces unused to the violence, the horror that this night had brought. "They don't need to see her body."

Fey reined in her anger as best she could and nodded.

The other High Priestesses approached. Someone swore when they saw the body—Leandra, Fey thought.

"What do we do now?" Sana asked, looking at Fey.

Fey laughed, but there was no humor in it. They were looking to her, all four High Priestesses, for guidance.

"That's your problem, now. Not mine. Not anymore," Fey said. Blood was still seeping from her wound and through her fingers, but not as much. That, at least, felt like a good sign. "The city is yours, Sana. Just leave me and my family the fuck out of it."

She turned her back on them. Her sisters needed her, and nothing was going to keep her from their side.

THE NEXT FEW hours were a flurry of activity.

Sana had done what Fey had asked. Immediately when Fey had left the Water Temple earlier that evening, she had called the other High Priestesses to the Water Temple, explaining the situation to them. She gave each of them a portion of the antidotes Alice had left for her.

The antidotes Fey had delivered.

As expected, the temples had been full that night, as hundreds of Witches had flocked to them to celebrate the blood moon. But rather than their usual services, the High Priestesses had instead delivered what Alice had called the most powerful weapon of all.

The truth.

They were the ones to break the news of the Queen's betrayal, and they would be remembered as the city's saviors. Tearfully, after drinking the antidote herself, Sana had explained what Queen Edelin had done to them, what she had made her Temple Priestesses do. She asked her congregation if any of them had been given an elixir during their Awakening, if any had ingested the poison to steal their powers.

They had. More of them than even Alice had expected. Hundreds of them.

It is one thing to hear the truth, to hear of your monarch's betrayal. It is another thing entirely to *see it*. To know the victims of it.

When the first Witch had drunk the antidote, when she had felt her new powers flooding her and burst from her in a raging whirlwind of Air, the temple had erupted in shock. And then in rage.

It had taken everything Sana had to prevent a riot in her Temple. The other Temples were not so lucky.

The Fire temple had reacted the worst, and the rage from the congregation had burned much of their own Temple to the ground. The High Priestess Leandra herself had been given Allium at her Awakening and had taken the antidote in front of her entire congregation. She had dedicated her entire life to her Power over Fire, only to find she could wield Water and Air as well. Her rage had caught amongst her temple members. They shared her fury, her anger, and their power had been too much for them all to hold back.

They reacted with violence, taking to the streets to vent their rage, as their Temple burned.

The news spread like wildfire through the city, through the Witches. And with it, came the anger. They had been betrayed; they had been hobbled in power by the very system in place to protect them.

Had the other Factions not been told to keep inside, not been warned about the violence that might sweep the city, it is safe to say there would have been far more casualties. But the Shifters had listened to their Faction elders and had barricaded themselves in their homes. The Demons had gone to ground, none willing to risk their own lives by getting between the Witches and the object of their rage.

Even the Vampires, receiving word from their King, had stayed hidden that night. Rumor had it his own son had brought him the news of what was to come, setting aside their renowned dislike of one another to ensure the safety of their Faction, together.

And so it was that when the Witches took to the streets, there were few civilians from the other Factions caught in the path of their destruction.

The Goddess Temple in the Eternal City fell at the same time the eclipse apexed. Enraged, Witches had stormed the Temple looking for vengeance, looking for answers. Their fury erupted at what they found there. Allium, just as they'd been told. Shelves and shelves of it.

Some of the White Priestesses fled. Some of them died, casualties of the rage that flowed through the city. A few were apprehended. And of those, enough talked. Enough shared their secrets and crimes, to fuel that rage even more.

Cassandra, the Queen's sister, slit her own throat rather than answer for her crimes. Fey could only hope the Goddess was waiting for her in the afterlife, ready to dole out her own sort of justice.

Sana and the other High Priestesses fought to regain order in the city after the initial violence began to die out. They held open forums that lasted hours, listening to the rage and fear of the people of the Eternal City. They talked until their voices broke, strained from overuse. The rage of the city quelled to a simmer, but it wasn't appeased. And everyone was ready to erupt.

But Fey no longer cared.

Let the city burn, she thought. Let it all burn down.

She helped Joy carry Alice back to a safe house in the city, her body bruised and battered from her battle with the Queen. All three of them were exhausted and filthy. After a quick shower, and after Joy had stitched and bandaged her side, they crawled into bed together and slept.

The realm might fall apart. The Factions might destroy themselves and each other. The Witches might lose the power they held for the last three hundred years.

But Fey found she no longer cared. Two of her sisters had survived the night. And for her that was enough. Let someone else hold the city, let someone else keep the peace.

Fey was tired, and all she wanted to do was rest.

CHAPTER 63

When historians look back on what happened following Queen Edelin's death at the hands of her own Blades, they write about the anger and the riots. They write about the days of violence, how it eventually did bleed over to the other Factions despite everything Alice had done to prevent it, how several innocent people died in the aftermath.

But they forget the uncertainty. They forget that much of that violence came not because of anger at the Queen's actions, but from the fear of what would come. Fear of the unknown, of the collapse of some vital safety net that had once existed and had been taken away forever.

The High Priestesses presented a united front, but there was too much fear, too much uncertainty for them to hold it for long. They held the peace in the city by a single thread, and it was quickly starting to fray.

In the end, the city's savior came from a truly unexpected source.

Three days after the Queen's death Cassiel Salvatore deSanguine, the so-called Fallen King, presented a solution that could save them all. A solution Fey couldn't help but think might have come from one of his sons.

The High Priestesses couldn't hold the city, not on their own. The Queen's army was in shambles—half the generals abandoning their posts during the night of the blood moon, and the others too broken from their leader's betrayal to offer up their lives willingly to any cause. Solare had burned to nothing but ashes, fueled by years of neglect and Fey's endless rage, and though Lunairea still stood, it was damaged nearly beyond repair.

The Witches were in rebellion, and without the other Factions behind them, the High Priestesses would lose the city to chaos. So, Salvatore brought them the other Factions.

The Eternal City they once knew was dead, and the old regime would never rise again. But a new regime could be put in place instead. Not a singular ruler, not the superiority of a single Faction above the others, but an equal counsel of all four.

The High Priestesses were suspicious at first. The Vampires had never truly bent the knee to the First Queen, and this had all the hallmarks of a coup. But there was no regime left to overthrow anymore, was there?

In the end, they acquiesced. There would be no more royalty, but an equal rule of four, representing each of their Factions: Salvatore deSanguine, a Lion Shifter named Kellos, a Demon to be chosen from within the Faction, and the ex-Princess Amalia.

There had been considerable debate among the Priestesses as to what should be done with the Princess. She was, all agreed, innocent in the crimes of her mother, even if she had been aware of what the Queen had been doing—and even in that, there was debate. She was a child, a victim of circumstance. In the end it was decided that she would lead the next generation, under the guidance of the High Priestesses themselves.

And so Princess Amalia became Counsellor Amalia, the representative of the Witch Faction.

It wasn't perfect, by any means, but it worked. It held the peace. Witches, furious over the betrayal by their Queen, were even more furious at the news that they would no longer hold sole rule over the city. Now they found themselves on equal footing with the other Factions, brought to the same level as the Fallen.

But the other Factions rejoiced. For the first time in three hundred years, they had a say in their rule. Their hope, their optimism, helped hold the city together.

Joy had brought the Eternal City to an end. But hope kept the realm alive.

CHAPTER 64

The council summoned them a week after the Queen's death.

In politics, you can tell a lot about your enemy based on who they send to negotiate. If your enemy wants war, they'll send a general. If they want peace, they'll send a diplomat.

The council sent Sana.

"Did you know the front door to your building is broken?" Were Sana's first words when Fey opened the apartment door. "And the windows are all shattered?"

Fey knew. Alice had fit the window frames with wood planks, to keep out the elements, but the lobby and door were just as broken as they had been the night Alastair had come to find her. The night he had discovered what they were.

"I know," Fey answered. Her voice sounded scratchy. It still hurt to speak with the damage in her throat.

Sana licked her lips, looking concerned. "Is it safe for you to be here, with the door like that? Anyone could come in, Fey."

"Like you?" Fey asked, raising an eyebrow at her.

Sana's answering frown was the closest to a scowl Fey had ever seen her make. It was almost endearing.

Almost.

"We're fine," Fey insisted with a smile. "Do you really think anyone would be stupid enough to break into this place? With the most powerful Witch in the realm living here?"

She'd meant it as a joke, but there was enough truth in it to make Fey immediately regret saying it aloud. Though the antidote continued to be dispensed to Witches in the outer octants, all the reports coming in were the same. Most Witches who had been given Allium had been cut off from a single element, and a handful had been found with three full powers. Joy fell into that category. With her antidote, her gift of Air had become even stronger, and now she could call on both Fire and Water.

But, as far as anyone could tell, Fey remained the only Witch aside from Princess Amalia who could control all four.

Merle made a break for the open door, trying to dash between Fey's legs and into the hallway. Fey sighed as she leaned down to grab him, hoisting him into her arms. Two days after they'd left the palace he had shown up, inexplicably, outside of their apartment door. When they'd heard scratching on the door and opened it to investigate, Merle had walked in like he'd been here a thousand times before. Like he belonged here.

Joy had been thrilled. And Alice was thrilled with anything that made Joy happy.

"Come in," Fey said to Sana, as Merle wriggled in her arms, struggling to get down. "Before you let this little monster out."

As soon as the door closed behind Sana, Merle lost all interest in leaving. Fey set him on the ground, stroking him twice. He arched his back against her hand and purred, all ideas of escape vanishing from his fuzzy little mind.

"Have a seat." Fey motioned toward the couch. "Did you want something to drink? Tea?"

"Tea would be lovely," Sana said, sitting on the couch, and folding her hands in her lap.

Fey set the kettle to boil and busied herself pulling two mugs from the cupboards, wincing at how the wound in her side stretched as she reached to grab them.

"How are you healing?" Sana asked.

Of course she'd noticed. Fey sighed.

"Fine," she said, simply. The wound from where Dameon had stabbed her had almost entirely healed now, but the area was still tender. And her voice had yet to recover from the damage Lilith had managed to do to her throat.

"I could have a look if you—" Sana began, but stopped, mid-sentence, her mouth hanging open. A moan came from the nearest bedroom. Unmistakably sexual.

The kettle whistled, and Fey hid her grin by turning away from Sana as she prepared the tea.

That had been Alice. She and Joy had been spending a great deal of time together in that room since they'd been reunited. After their first night back, when all three of them had fallen asleep basking in the comfort of being together, Fey had moved into her own bedroom to give them space. Privacy. She barely noticed the noises anymore.

Joy had forgiven Alice after all. Had forgiven all of them—Fey, for killing her last sister, and Lilith for her betrayal. Love came so easily to Joy, and Fey... Fey was starting to find it was coming easier to her, as well.

"You were saying?" Fey prompted, setting the mug down on the coffee table in front of Sana and taking a seat on the other end of the couch to watch her. She held her own mug with both hands, her face the picture of innocence as Alice moaned again, louder this time, from the bedroom. Joy's voice was too low to hear, but whatever she'd said made Alice moan even louder.

"I... I can't recall." Sana stumbled. Her face was beet red.

Embarrassed, yes, but something else was there as well. Priestesses were forbidden to take lovers, forbidden to indulge in the carnal arts, but Fey had always assumed it was a rule none of them really bothered to follow. For the first time Fey wondered if Sana were, in fact, completely naive to sex.

The look on Sana's face when she glanced at the closed door to Joy's bedroom wasn't judgmental, or disgusted. It was full of yearning. Envy.

"Why are you here, Sana?" Fey asked.

Sana fought to compose herself, picking her tea up from the table and sipping it.

"The council would like to see you," she said. "To see all of you."

Fey set her own tea down, fighting the flicker of anger in her chest that threatened to grow to an inferno. They'd expected this. Or, at least, Alice had. There had to be consequences to killing the Queen, she had said. Someday, probably soon, the council would demand someone be held accountable.

And the three of them would have to be ready to respond.

"And if we refuse?" Fey asked, her voice low and dangerous.

Sana shook her head, sadly. "This is not a demand, Fey, it is a request. From all of us. We want to put this behind us and move forward. For the security of the realm. They only want to talk to you, understand how everything happened."

"You *know* how everything happened," Fey challenged.

"Please don't fight us on this, Fey. The council doesn't want to be your enemy."

But we could be, was the unsaid warning behind those words. The threat that Sana, sweet gentle Sana, would never say out loud.

Merle rubbed against her leg, and Fey stroked him absently.

"When?" she asked.

"Tomorrow," said Sana. "Midday, if possible."

Fey nodded. "Okay," she acquiesced. Sana didn't need to know that they'd anticipated this. That they'd already agreed to be interviewed by the council if asked. "We'll be there."

The sounds from the bedroom were increasing in volume and pace. Fey continued to act as though nothing was amiss, as though there was nothing unusual about it.

And, from her point of view, there wasn't.

"Would you care to stay for lunch?" Fey asked with a wide smile, raising her voice slightly to be heard over the crescendo of Alice's orgasm. Merle hopped up to the couch, yawning, looking for a place to curl up and lay down. "I think my sisters are finishing up, if you'd care to see them as well?"

"No," Sana said, too quickly, standing so fast she startled Merle from the couch. He lopped away grumpily, shooting her an irritated look and swishing his tail at her as he left. "Thank you, but no. I must be going I think."

Fey watched her escape, Sana's face beet red, and smiled even wider.

CHAPTER 65

They didn't wear their uniforms when they came to the palace to stand before the council. There were no more Queen's Blades. And now that there would be no more Queens, there never would be another group of Queen's Blades again.

Instead, the three of them had dressed like civilians. Fey supposed that's what they were, now.

The council had set up in the palace throne room, though they had made some changes. The blood and bodies had been removed, and the walls were so clean you might be tempted to believe all the violence and bloodshed had been nothing but a bad dream.

The dais and the thrones that sat atop it at the far wall of the room had all been removed. In their place, a large wooden table had been added, and though the chairs that lined one side of the table were ornate and well-made, no one would be tempted to call them thrones.

They arrived at the palace early—Alice leading them, Joy and Fey at her back. Early enough that the council itself hadn't yet convened.

Sana rushed forward to greet them when they entered the throne room. Only she and the other three High Priestesses of the remaining covens were present. They stood on the other side of that wide wooden table, and Fey couldn't help but meet their eyes one by one. Leandra,

371

embracing her new powers, had added a stripe of blue representing the Water Coven and a stripe of yellow for the Air Coven to her red Fire shawl. She gave Fey a small nod when their eyes met.

Claudia, High Priestess of the Earth coven, looked as though she'd aged thirty years since the last time Fey had seen her. The tragedy of the Queen's betrayal had taken years off her life, and when she met Fey's eyes she looked as though she may cry.

It was Linh, High Priestess of the Air Coven, who gave Fey pause. Ancient and wrinkled, she looked no different than before. But the sneering smile she gave Fey was all venom.

One Priestess, at least, had no interest in making this a pleasant experience for them.

"Thank you for coming," Sana said as she approached, taking Alice's hands in her own and smiling at the three of them.

Fey had argued against their coming, even after they'd agreed to it. There was nothing they could tell the council that they didn't already know. And this—all of this—felt far too much like a *trial* for her liking.

But Alice had insisted, and Joy had readily agreed with her. A new government had risen, she said. And if they wanted the citizens of the city to respect this new council, respect the laws that they would enforce, they had to show that same respect and deference themselves. They had to set an example for the realm. Especially now that the realm knew who they were.

At least they had one trick up their sleeves, if necessary. Fey hoped it wouldn't come to that, but something in Linh's face made her reconsider.

"Of course," Alice said to Sana, mirroring her smile in answer.

"The others will be convening in just a moment," Sana explained. "And each council member will be allowed to ask whatever questions they believe relevant. Just tell the truth, as it happened, and everything will be fine."

Fey did not find her nervousness terribly reassuring, but before she could argue, before she could raise the idea of leaving with Alice again, the herald spoke.

"Introducing the representative of the Shifter Faction, Kellos, of the Lion Order," she said, her voice crisp and carried by Air to fill the entire room. Fey recognized her as the same herald that Queen Edelin had used and was pleased to see she hadn't suddenly found herself unemployed in the new regime.

Or killed, during the violence of the Blood Moon.

Behind the wooden table, where the thrones had once stood, a door opened and Kellos entered.

Fey had expected that the Shifters would elect a representative from amongst their strongest, their most powerful, and found herself a little surprised at the male they'd chosen instead.

Kellos was older than she expected, well into his sixties, and well past his prime fighting age. He wore his hair long, and it grew in heavy, golden white curls, around his face, like a mane. His face was heavy with lines, but above his thick beard his eyes were sharp. When he looked at the three of them, meeting their gaze one by one, Fey saw a deep wisdom in those eyes. A calm, intelligent leader.

So, the Shifters had gone for wisdom and experience over strength. Something about the choice gave her a small semblance of comfort. It was a smart choice. Maybe she'd underestimated them.

Salvatore deSanguine was announced next.

Now that she knew their relationship, the resemblance between him and his son was unmistakable. It was a wonder Fey had never seen it before. The same strong face, the same angry eyes, the same almost painful masculine beauty.

Like Kellos, deSanguine met each of their eyes in turn. Not in anger, or in challenge, Fey was surprised to find, but in respect. When he met her gaze, he inclined his head ever so slightly to Fey.

"Introducing the representative of the Witch Faction, the former Princess and heir to the Crown, Amalia Goddess Blessed."

Fey swallowed hard when Amalia entered, her head bowed low. She had been hidden by her handmaids that night when the fighting started, kept safe and far from harm, and Fey had been glad of it. Had she been in this room, with her mother and father that night, Fey wasn't sure she would have left that room alive.

But she had been kept safe. Safe, but not wholly protected from it all, Fey knew. Afterall, they couldn't protect her from the fallout of that night. No. Her parents, her title, her very identity, were ripped away from her on the Blood Moon.

Ripped away by the very Witches who stood before her today.

Amalia did not look at any of them as she entered. Still dressed in the same frilly dresses her mother had always styled her in, Amalia looked down at the ground the entire walk to her chair and took her seat without raising her eyes to anyone.

Linh put a comforting hand on hers when she sat.

Several minutes passed as the council awaited their final member. Enough time for an oppressive awkwardness to settle over the room. Fey shifted from foot to foot, and even Alice began to fidget. The High Priestesses glanced at one another uncertainly.

"Oh, for God's sake," deSanguine snapped, finally. "If the Demons still haven't deigned to elect a leader, then I see no reason why we should be forced to wait. Perhaps we should just get started—"

A shadow fell across the room.

No, Fey thought, glancing around. Not a shadow. It was as if the very light itself was being pulled away, being smothered by something else. Something more powerful.

Run.

The command came from her. Some ancient instinct, something deep and primal inside her.

Run.

Fey looked around at the others, trying to see if they felt it as well. Kellos was only looking around in confusion, taking in the change in the lighting around them with slow, deliberate blinks. A predator unused to threats. The High Priestesses seemed unfazed, and had begun to chatter amongst themselves, whispering about what to do in the event a council member did not show. Arguing about who had sent assurances that the Demons had chosen a representative.

But at Fey's side, Joy shivered.

"There's something here," she whispered. "Something strong."

"Karla told me there were Demons in the eighth octant who were like nothing we'd ever seen before," Alice said in a low voice. "Things more powerful than we could ever dream of..."

Amalia's eyes rose from the table before her, and she glanced quickly at Fey. She could feel it too, Fey realized. Amalia's eyes were wide. Scared.

RUN. That instinct screamed.

"Introducing the representative of the Demon Faction, from the eighth octant, Kallista of the Undying."

The woman who entered was the most beautiful creature Fey had ever seen. Her thin stiletto heels clicked rhythmically as she walked to her seat, and the black tailored dress she wore clung to every curve of her body when she moved. She wore her straight, white-blonde hair down, where it cascaded over her shoulders. She wore no crown, but she held herself with the regal air of a Queen.

Her chair moved on its own, without a single identifiable flick of power from her, and Kallista sat, her ice blue eyes traveling over each of them in turn.

RUN, that voice inside Fey's head screamed, as the Demon turned that cold stare on her and held her gaze. Held her gaze and smiled, revealing a row of perfect, white teeth.

In the Eternal City, Demons are as common as cockroaches and just as powerless. They are a nuisance, if anything. Fey had fought more Demons than she could count. But this? This creature in front of her now was nothing like anything she'd ever encountered before. If this was the sort of Demon who occupied the eighth octant, if the horror stories about creatures out there who were stronger than Witches in every way possible, were actually true?

Then they were all completely fucked.

"I apologize for my lateness," Kallista said, and even her voice sent shivers down Fey's spine. "It is difficult for me to travel in the way I am accustomed at this time of day."

Shadows appeared and danced over her fingers, spinning around her long black matte nails, and coalescing to form a pen. Completely solid. She held it delicately in her fingers, as though prepared to take notes.

"Shall we begin?" she asked.

At her side, deSanguine chuckled. "Kallista, my dear," he said, looking her up and down. "What a pleasant surprise to see you here." He smiled, showing sharp fangs. "I had heard you were dead."

She turned those cold eyes on him and smiled back. "Hello, Cassiel," she said. "I do hate to disappoint. But I'm certainly not surprised to see you here, begging at the Witch's table for scraps, as always. Some things never change, do they?"

The Vampire king bared his fangs at her and snarled. Behind him, Kellos hissed, lips curled back to reveal his own sharp teeth, unnerved by the anger in the room.

"That's enough," Sana snapped. She stood at Amalia's side, straight backed and proud, and only the slight shake in her hands as she clasped them before her gave away the nervousness she was feeling. "If we are going to be working together then we gain nothing by treating one another with disrespect. I ask that the members of this council present themselves with the decorum these positions require."

Kallista considered her carefully.

"Tell me, Priestess," she said. "Why does this council have five representatives for the Witch Faction, when the rest of us have only one? I was led to believe this was a council of equals, and this," she gestured toward the four High Priestesses. "This feels less than equal to me."

Sana's face reddened. "We are not representatives," she explained. "The other High Priestesses and I are here to advise our representative, Princess Amalia, and nothing more. We are here to offer her advice until she comes of age. The Witch Faction can cast a single vote, the same as all other Factions."

"Princess Amalia," the Demon said, rolling the title in her mouth as though tasting it. Her eyes moved to regard the Princess. "But, not a Princess, is she? Not anymore."

Amalia glanced up at her.

"Do you wish to be called by this title?" Kallista asked. Her voice was not mocking, nor cruel. Curious. "Do you wish to still be called Princess?"

Amalia swallowed, hard. Then looked away.

"Yes," she said in a voice with more steel in it than Fey expected. "Yes, I do."

Kallista only nodded. "And you wish to keep these advisors?" she asked. Shadows seemed to circle the Priestess as she spoke, like snakes.

"Yes."

"Then they can stay," Kallista conceded with a smile, and those circling shadows vanished. "Until you decide you no longer wish to keep them."

There was a threat to those words, Fey noticed. She wondered, absently, what would happen to those four Witches if Amalia told Kallista she no longer wished for their service.

"Good," said Sana, her hands obviously shaking now. "Good. Then let us get started.

"The council welcomes Alice, Fey, and Joy, of the Eternal City," Sana said. "I hope that we will not take up much of your time, but we have brought you here to clear up any questions the council may have about your... involvement in the Queen's death. I will open the floor to questions."

Kellos spoke immediately.

"The Shifter Faction has no questions for the Witches before the council," he said in a deep voice, and Fey glanced at him in surprise. At her side, Alice just smiled. She, at least, was not shocked by the support.

"I have spoken with the Lionesses who were present that night," Kellos continued. "As well as several respected members of our Faction. And I am satisfied with the justice that was delivered. The Shifters offer their thanks to these Witches for their protection of the realm."

He inclined his head to them, blinking his wise eyes at them in a way that was unmistakably feline.

"The Vampire Faction has no questions for the Witches before the council," deSanguine said, waving his fingers at them with a smirk. Linh and Leandra were speaking together in low, urgent voices. "We, also, offer our thanks to the three Witches," he continued, and looking right at Fey, he smiled.

"On a personal note," he said, sitting up straighter in his chair. "It seems one Witch in particular deserves special recognition." His smile spread, and while it wasn't cruel, Fey couldn't bring herself to entirely believe it was kind. "It takes a very special creature to capture one of my son's hearts," he said, softly. "I hope you are worthy of it."

Joy coughed, loudly, to cover her laugh, and Fey shot her a scowl.

Kallista said nothing, though she watched the proceedings with obvious, growing amusement.

This was, clearly, not the reaction that some of the High Priestesses had expected. Certainly, not the reaction that Linh had hoped for.

Sana, Fey was pleased to see, had relaxed considerably. She gave Fey a comforting smile, her eyes warm and friendly.

But when Leandra spoke, her voice was anything but.

"Regardless of the feelings of the Vampires and Shifters," she said, shooting deSanguine and Kellos a dismissive glance. "*We* do have questions."

"Then, by all means," Kallista said, turning in her chair to watch her. "Let your representative ask them."

Leandra opened her mouth, then shut it. She glanced down at Amalia, who still stared at the table before her, as though in a trance.

"Amalia, dear," Linh prompted.

Princess Amalia looked up.

"Don't you have questions for these Witches?" Linh asked, pointedly.

"I do have a question," she said, so softly her voice was barely audible.

When she looked at them all, Fey recognized the emotion in her eyes.

Hatred.

"Which of you did it?" Amalia asked, softly. "Which one of you killed my mother? Which of you dishonored your vows and killed the Queen you were sworn to protect?"

"I did," said Joy in a pain-laced voice at the same time Fey stepped forward and said, loudly, "That was me."

Amalia blinked, looking between the two of them and frowning.

Leaning on her hand, elbow propped on the table, Kallista's smile widened. "Interesting," she cooed softly. Shadows danced in her eyes as she looked at Fey.

"I killed the Queen," Fey insisted.

"Fey, don't," Joy hissed, but Fey ignored her.

The council brought them here for this, no matter what Sana had assured them. They didn't want to know what happened. They didn't need any questions answered. Someone had committed the ultimate treason and murdered their Faction's ruler. Someone needed to pay for it.

And so long as she was standing, Fey wasn't going to let it be Joy

"I killed her," Fey insisted. "Don't listen to my sister. She's only trying to protect me."

Joy opened her mouth to argue, but Alice reached out and placed a hand on her arm, shaking her head. She knew what Fey was doing. And if the choice was losing Fey or losing Joy, she would choose to save Joy. Fey couldn't blame her. They deserved their happiness.

Even if they would get it over her dead body.

Linh was shaking her head. "There were witnesses, you forget. Servants, and guards, and friends of the Crown, all of whom have testi-fied to us that they saw *that* Witch"—she pointed at Joy, and Fey bris-tled at the thought that she might not even know her name—"behead our Queen."

"No," Fey argued. "What they saw was a blade of Air behead the Queen."

"Yes," Linh insisted. "And before us stands a Wind Witch who—"

Wind whipped through the room, cutting her off.

Fey let it dance around them all, let it touch each and every council member, let it hit against Linh, jostling her, before calling it back to herself, where it swirled around her.

"No one present that night could tell you who killed the Queen," Fey insisted, letting them see the air around her dance and spin, catching dust motes in its wake. "Only that someone used Air to do it. Joy and I were the only Air Witches there that night, but the blade came from me. I am responsible for the Queen's death."

"Then the Witch Faction asks the council to sentence this Witch for her crimes," Linh said with a snarl. "The Witch Faction calls for her death."

Sana spun around, "*What?*" she gasped. Leandra paled, putting a hand on Linh's shoulder, and hissing in a low whisper, "Sister, this is not what we discussed…".

"You heard it from her own mouth," Linh snapped. She straight-ened her back to stand as tall as she could, though age had taken much of the height from her. "She *murdered* our Queen. That is treason. And treason is punishable by death."

"It *was* punishable by death," Kellos said in a soft, amused voice. "When there was a Queen. But if there is no Queen, how can there be a rule against killing one?"

Linh and the other High Priestesses were arguing, ignoring him entirely.

"How can you do this?" Sana hissed. "You promised me they would be safe here, they *saved us,* Linh!"

"They have doomed us," Linh hissed back.

Amidst their arguing, Amalia stood.

"I am the representative of the Witches," she said, enough of her mother's strength in her voice that Sana and Linh stopped to listen. "And the vote is mine, and mine alone to cast."

She looked across the room at Fey.

"My mother was not a kind woman," she said. "She was not a loving woman. And she made choices that she thought were right, even if they weren't. Choices she thought were for the good of the realm. I believe she made those choices thinking they were for the greater good.

"You also made choices you thought were right. You chose to kill my mother, your Queen, the woman you swore your life to protect. You chose to kill her, rather than arrest her, rather than try to bring her to justice through nonviolent means," Amalia's voice broke, but no tears fell from her eyes.

She's stronger than any of us gave her credit for, Fey thought. *It'll be a shame if she makes me kill her.*

"And so, I must make my choice," Amalia continued. "I must choose what I think is right. And I cast my vote for death. And I beg the other Factions present to do the same, for the good of the realm."

She sat down then, not glancing at the High Priestesses, stunned and silent at her shoulders. Not glancing at the other representatives. Just staring at Fey, her eyes full of anger.

Fey nodded at her. It was what she'd expected, after all.

"How?" Fey asked Amalia. And when she didn't answer, Fey continued, looking instead at Linh. "How do you plan to kill me?"

"We can discuss details of execution after the vote," Linh said with a sneer.

Fey shook her head. "No, you misunderstand me," she said. And she smiled at them all, then, letting them see the danger in it. Letting them see the monster she'd kept behind the mask. They had wanted the Queen's Broken Blade brought before them. And she would give it to them. "I don't mean 'by what method' you plan to kill me. I ask the council *how* you plan to take me down. I want to know which of you thinks you are strong enough to risk your own lives to try and take me into custody."

She let the threat hang in the air for a moment, let the blood drain from Linh's face, before continuing. "I am a Queen's Blade. I am a murderer. I was built to kill, built to be the most dangerous Witch in the realm. Were you?" Linh looked away, and Fey turned her eyes instead to Amalia. "Were you?" she asked in a whisper.

The Princess only stared at her. She had but a shadow of her mother's powers, and she knew it.

"Do any of you believe there is anyone in our city strong enough to take me down?" Fey asked. "Because, if not, you will want to think very seriously about how you want to cast your vote. I make a dangerous enemy."

This was their secret weapon. If the council voted to send her to death, Fey was ready. Ready to face anyone they sent to kill her.

Ready to fight.

While the High Priestesses paled, while they considered the implications of what Fey was saying, considered the very real possibility that Fey would kill them all if they sent anyone after her, deSanguine spoke up.

"I think it goes without saying that the Vampire Faction votes *against* death," deSanguine said, with an irritated sigh. "This Witch did you all a favor, whether you're too blind to see it or not. She saved this city. And it's not only insulting to request she be punished for it, but clearly suicidal. We vote no."

"The Shifter Faction votes against death," said Kellos in a low growl. "And it is... distasteful that it be suggested in this forum."

Only one vote remained. Fey had no idea what would happen in the event of a tie between all four Factions, but she feared they were about to find out.

The Vampire king and the Shifters had their reasons for backing Fey, for owing her thanks. But the Demons?

Fey had no idea what to expect from them.

Kallista regarded her curiously. The pen in her hand dissolved back into shadows and disappeared.

"Explain something to me," she said, her voice soft but dark with power. "I am naïve to the laws of your Faction. But didn't the royal line follow power? Wasn't the sole reason Edelin was Queen because she was the only Witch in the realm, with the exception of her daughter here of course, who could wield all four elements?"

She addressed the question to Fey, but Sana was the one who answered.

"You are right," she said. "The First Queen was the first Witch to be blessed with all four powers, equally, and since then only her daughters that were similarly blessed were judged worthy enough to inherit the throne."

"Then, as the representative of the Demon Faction, I do have a question for the Witch before I vote." The room dimmed slightly as Kallista spoke, shadows licking up the walls. "Why, after you killed Queen Edelin, did you not crown *yourself* Queen?"

A shocked silence followed the words, and Sana paled. The other Priestesses, however, looked bemused.

Sana never told them, Fey realized. She never told the other high Priestesses what she was, that she and she alone held the power over all four elements. It showed a loyalty from her that Fey hadn't expected.

"Ah, I see your confusion," Leandra said, in a condescending tone. "Only Witches with all four powers may ascend the throne, and Fey here—"

"Oh, I don't think I am the one who is confused," Kallista said, never taking her eyes from Fey. "The Witch you've brought before us, the Witch who claims to have killed your Queen, she holds power over all four elements in her veins. Don't you?"

The council had gone very still. Linh paled at Amalia's side, suddenly realizing the power of the Witch she had just threatened. A sound not unlike purring arose from Kellos, and at his side, deSanguine leaned forward in his chair, his movements so quick it was as though he'd jumped. His eyes sparkled.

All eyes on her, Fey slowly nodded.

"So, I ask again," Kallista continued. "Why did you not crown yourself Queen? Do you not have that right?"

"I don't want it," Fey said simply. It wasn't the truth, but it was close enough. The truth was it hadn't occurred to her at the time. Even if it had, though—her answer would have been the same.

"You don't wish to be Queen?" Kallista pressed.

"No," Fey insisted. It took all her strength, but she held the Demon's stare as she said it. "I have no desire to rule. I don't want to be Queen. I don't want power. I just want to be left alone."

Kallista smiled, and it was both a beautiful and terrifying thing to witness.

"In that case," she said. "The Demon Faction votes no to death. And we would also like to thank these upstanding Witches for their time, and for their role in bringing the Queen's crimes to our attention. We hope this council will have no further reason to bother them in the future."

AMALIA LEFT the moment Kallista had voted no, not acknowledging Linh or any of the High Priestesses. She had simply stood, turned her back on them, and left the council room without another word.

"You should go," Kallista advised Fey, with a smirk, nodding toward the door. Leandra and Sana were arguing, close to shouting, and Kellos looked wildly uncomfortable with their public display. DeSanguine was laughing, more to himself than anyone in particular.

They didn't need to be told twice.

"Come on," Alice hissed, pulling them out the door.

Someone had removed much of the art and crimson curtains that Fey associated with the palace interior, she noticed as they snaked through the hallway and toward the open doors leading out of the palace.

"You go ahead," Fey told them when they reached the palace entrance. "I'll meet you back at the apartment later tonight, okay?"

"Are you sure, Fey?" Alice asked, a hint of concern in her voice.

"Yeah. I have a few things I need to do." Fey insisted.

Joy pulled her into a tight hug.

"I should kill you for what you did back there," she whispered, and Fey chuckled when she instead squeezed her tighter. "But I know you did it out of love."

"I did," Fey admitted.

Joy gave her a wide grin, and then, clasping Alice's hand, they descended the palace steps together. Fey watched them go, smiling after them, knowing that whatever happened next at least they had this—this love, between Alice and Joy. If nothing else good came from the Queen's death, this was enough.

Fey watched them until they faded from her sight, and then she settled in to wait.

CHAPTER 66
KALLISTA

They bickered like children, these mortals.

Such sad, short lives they had, and they chose to waste it arguing about such trivial matters. It was exhausting.

Kallista tasted their shadows while they argued amongst themselves. The Witch in Yellow, far older than the others, tasted of anger and fear — two scents intrinsically linked in Kallista's experience. Fear made people angry, made them rash. She would be a problem in the council's future, Kallista thought, but a small one. Easily solvable.

The Blue and Brown Witches tasted of sadness, one so deep it would break her. And soon. A pity. The Red Witch was strong, but not as strong as she thought. Another pity.

The Cat's shadow tasted old and sinewy, like wild mutton. It wasn't a bad taste, all things considered. Now he, Kallista found intriguing. The Mother of Shifters had been more Wolf than anything. Did he know that? Did they remember her, all these hundreds of years later?

She began to taste the Vampire's shadow, but Cassiel's eyes shifted to her immediately, flaring in anger. She smiled and gave him an apologetic shrug.

Can't blame a girl for trying, can you?

The council spent another two hours finalizing rules and expectations for future meetings, and each minute spent in that room—surrounded by the scent of fresh death and too much light—felt like an eternity.

Kellos, the tasty Lion, had grown irritated by the end, growling and snapping at the others, before one of the remaining Witches, the soft faced youth in Blue, had declared them finished for the day, and organized the date for their next meeting.

On Kallista and Cassiel's insistence, they agreed to change the meetings to after sundown.

The entire building reeked of death, Kallista noticed as she left. They wouldn't be able to sense it—the Shifters or the Witches. Cassiel Salvatore, maybe. But to her? It was strong enough to burn her nostrils. Omnipresent and overpowering.

Taking great care to breathe through her nose as little as possible, Kallista navigated her way through the palace and to the exit.

The scent of death was strong here, too, but at least it was bearable in the open air of the outdoors. The afternoon sun burned bright and hot in the sky, and though she lacked Cassiel's vulnerability to it, she certainly didn't find it *pleasant*. Calling the shadows toward her, Kallista spun them together, forming a parasol of deep, impenetrable black. She rested it on her shoulder, letting it block the sunlight, and began to descend the palace steps.

Kallista sensed the Witch immediately but waited until she descended the steps behind her before she stopped and spoke.

"It's rude to sneak up on someone," Kallista said, tilting her parasol just far enough to regard Fey. The Witch stopped, frozen under her stare.

Now this one? Even with just a sliver of shadow available for her to taste, the sun stealing all but a fraction of it, this one tasted like raw power. Kallista breathed it in, savoring the taste like a fine wine.

"How did you know?" the Witch asked, and Kallista couldn't help but smile at her. She was strong, this one. Very, very strong. And brave enough to look her in the eyes, even with all that strength warning her away.

"How did I know about your powers?" Kallista asked and laughed. She turned away, continuing her descent down the steps. "The real question should be how they *didn't*, with all that power coming off you in there. A blind man could have seen it."

"No," Fey insisted, hurrying down the steps after her. "How did you know I wasn't the one who killed the Queen?"

Ah. That.

Kallista stopped, letting the Witch catch up to her again.

"I saw it in your eyes," Fey continued. "You knew I didn't kill Queen Edelin, the moment I claimed it. *How?*"

"Your guilt gave you away."

Fey's eyes flashed. "I don't have any guilt over what happened," she hissed.

"I know," Kallista said. "But your friend did. Two Witches, each claiming to have killed their monarch, but only *one* felt any sort of guilt. That's what gave you away—you didn't feel anything at all over it."

The Witch finally looked away from her, glancing down at the steps instead.

"Why didn't you say anything, then?" she asked, finally. "Why did you let me protect her?"

Kallista shrugged. "Why should I say anything? What loyalty do I owe to the old regime? To the old Queen? I saw that you were willing to die to save your friend, and I decided to reward that. Don't expect me to make a habit of it."

The Witch still looked unsure.

"You can thank me, you know," Kallista smirked and was rewarded by a furious glare from her.

"I don't like to be in anyone's debt," Fey explained. "Especially someone I don't know. And I don't have any idea who, or what, you are."

"Consider it payment to someone else, then," Kallista told her. "I owe a debt to a Witch I knew a long, long time ago. I never rewarded her loyalty, so instead I'll reward yours, in her honor. You owe me nothing for it, and there is no debt between us."

Still, the Witch didn't leave, and Kallista sighed.

"What else did you want, Fey? I have things I need to do today, and I want to get far away from the smell of this place."

"It's just... you seem so unfazed by all of this," Fey stated. "Everyone is either panicked or rejoicing over all of this and you seem... so calm."

"I've lived through regime changes before, many, many times, this is nothing new to me. I survived the rise and fall of humans, after all."

"What's a human?" the Witch asked, confused.

Kallista couldn't help but laugh. *That would have stuck in their craw, to know how they'd been forgotten.* "Oh, horrible things, really. Distant ancestors of yours, I'm sorry to tell you. Though, you have them to thank for this." She waved a hand at the city around them. "Electricity. Internet. They loved to make new things, loved trying to bend the world and its rules to their own desires, even when it fought them every inch of the way."

"What happened to them?"

"Gone. Dead, most of them. Others changed. Adapted. Some developed magic," Kallista smiled at Fey. "Some learned to change their shapes. But most of them died and were replaced. And now they're relics of a forgotten age."

Shifting the parasol against her shoulder, Kallista turned to leave.

"Take care of yourself, Fey," she called over her shoulder. "I hope, for your sake, that we never meet again."

CHAPTER 67

The howling began before she was even halfway down the block.

It started with a single Wolf, but it was quickly picked up by another, and then another. Fey tried not to smile, as the evening around her erupted with Wolf song.

The bouncer hadn't even spoken to her—just opened the door, wide-eyed—and gestured her inside. The Last Drop wasn't open for the night, not yet. The sun had just disappeared over the horizon, and the red and yellow fingers of sunset still stretched across the skyline.

"Hello Jasper," Fey said as she approached. Her voice was a strangled, dry thing even now. It would recover with time, Joy had assured her. And the marks on her neck, a perfect imprinted burn from Lilith's hand, would fade.

Jasper's face split into a wolfish grin at the sight of her.

"Welcome back," he told her, green eyes sparkling as he looked her up and down. And then, as though remembering something, he snapped his fingers. "I have something for you."

"Oh?" She laughed, and she realized she was genuinely happy to see him. Genuinely happy to share in his company. To be in this seedy, ridiculous club, surrounded by Wolves.

He mixed the drink with the speed that only comes from years of practice behind the bar and passed it over to her. The red, bubbly drink topped with a cherry instantly made her laugh.

"A Shirley Temple. What a surprise," she said, taking a sip. The drink was blissfully cold and soothed her throat as she drank, but there was something new in this one. She moaned. Sweet, and delicious, and very alcoholic.

"Not quite," Jasper told her, eyes sparkling. "It's my twist on a Shirley Temple, in your honor. I call it a Witch's Temple."

"Oh, Jasper," Fey gasped. "I could just kiss you; this is incredible."

His smile widened. "I wouldn't stop you," he said, leaning forward over the bar. But his eyes shifted from her to something over her shoulder, and that flirtatious grin fell to a smirk.

"Hello, Witchling," Alastair said from behind her, and Fey's heart skipped a beat at the sound of his voice. His fingers teased the skin of her neck. "I've missed you."

"Hello Alastair," Fey said, smiling. She leaned back into him, savoring the rich smell of his skin. "I guess you managed to convince me after all."

EPILOGUE

"Vee, are you even listening?"

Vee blinked slowly, pulling herself back to reality.

"Sorry," she answered, absently toying with the ends of her hair. "I was a million miles away."

Jayce rolled his eyes, but he smiled at her to take the sting out of it. "Yeah, Vee. We could all tell."

She sighed, tilting her head back to stare up at the night sky. The stars sparkled like diamonds. Maybe that's what they were. A whole universe, full of diamonds, too far away to touch. Too far away to steal. "Are you sure about this, Jayce? You're *sure* this is a good idea?"

"Promise. Cross my heart and hope to die. This is the best time to go through with it. Everyone is caught up in what's happening with the Queen or whatever—we're never going to get another chance at a big score like this, and no one is paying attention to what's being sold on the underground. It's no risk."

The other boys agreed, nodding eagerly along with Jayce. But boys were like that, weren't they? They couldn't tell a good idea from a bad one half the time, and sometimes it felt like they somehow got dumber when there were more of them in one place. Like the collective intelligence of the group dropped every time another boy was added.

"Fine," she said, finally. The group practically cheered in response. "I'm in."

"Great!" said Jayce. "He should be gone all night, so the place will be empty. You'll love this score, Vee. This guy has been buying off Witches for years, his place is *full* of crap we can sell. *Good* crap."

Vee pulled a face. Yeah, they definitely got dumber in groups. *Good crap*? They didn't need *crap*. They needed things they could flip—the faster the better, and preferably before anyone even noticed the things were missing.

"I said I'm in, Jayce. You can stop trying to convince me," Vee said. "So... when is it all going down?"

Jayce gave her a wicked grin. "How about now?"

JAYCE PICKED two other boys to go with them, to keep watch. Vee hadn't bothered to learn their names, yet. That's how it was with strays like them, sometimes. Kids came and went, some finally getting out and finding something better, and some... well, some just disappearing. The city fed on kids like them—chewed them up and swallowed some of them whole.

Most people in the city were smart enough to lock their doors, but you'd be shocked at how many of them never bothered with their windows. Sure, most didn't open far enough to warrant locking, but that was why the gang brought Vee in the first place.

Well, one of the reasons, at least.

The window only opened a few inches, but Vee managed to slip in without much difficulty with Jayce giving her a boost. Vee was built like a blade of grass—all straight lines, made to bend under the slightest pressure. Squeezing into the house through the window was a cinch for her.

Inside the room was pitch black, and Vee flicked the heavy blackout curtains open so she could see around her. Jayce's smiling face greeted her on the other side of the window.

"Vamp?" she asked, giving the curtain a shake to open them a little wider. No one but a Vamp needed this sort of protection from the sun.

"Yeah," Jayce answered. "Some wanna-be big-shot, too. But he's a heavy buyer, and he's loaded. All my sources say he's the guy all the rich, snooty Witches sell their shit to. He should have all sorts of stuff in there —devil dust, jewelry, gold marks, you name it. You just gotta find it."

"And you're sure he's not here?"

"Positive," Jayce insisted. "He's at some fancy, hoity toity Vamp thing tonight. The place is empty."

Accepting his answer, Vee went off to find the goods.

It wasn't hard. A quick trip around the place gave Vee a good idea of where a guy like this would store his valuables. She pocketed a few rings and necklaces she found around the place, and a stack of gold and silver that was near the door, before focusing her attention on the bedroom where she'd entered.

Jackpot.

A well-carved, ornate wooden chest in the closet was the clear winner. It hadn't even been hidden.

"You need the lockpick?" Jayce asked from the window.

Vee examined the chest, feeling around the seam.

"Nah, doesn't look like I'll need it. It's just a latch." If Jayce were right, this would be one of their easiest jobs in months.

But then again... when was Jayce *ever* right?

The alarm sounded the moment she opened the chest and, panicked, Vee immediately slammed the lid shut as though she could undo it. The alarm didn't stop, though, and if the Vamp had a sensor on him, he'd know immediately that someone was in his house, going through his stuff.

"*Shit,*" Vee hissed. A heavy thud on the wall alerted her to the window slamming shut. The alarm on the chest was enchanted to close and lock all avenues of escape.

Vee began filling her pockets and bag with fistfuls of whatever she could grab from the chest. She wasn't leaving without her loot.

"*Leave it, Vee,*" Jayce hissed from the other side of the window. His voice was barely audible through the thick glass, but even muffled as it was, she could hear the panic there. "*Come on, you need to get out of there before—*"

The front door slammed open, hitting against the wall hard enough the sound echoed through the bedroom.

On the other side of the glass, Jayce winced.

"Sorry, Vee," he said with a shrug and a smile that said, *That's just business*. "You're on your own."

"Don't you *dare* leave me, asshole!" Vee hissed at the window, looking around for something to grab to break it. Normally she didn't like to swear, but if any situation warranted it, it was this one. But it was too late. Jayce was already gone, his two little nameless cronies following him.

Fucking prick! Vee thought. She pushed against the window, trying to get it to open, but it was stuck, held tight with magic. She looked around the room frantically for another way out. There had been a window in the bathroom, hadn't there? Maybe that one wouldn't have locked, maybe...

The thought vanished the moment she saw the Vamp enter the bedroom. He was a scrawny thing, but Vee was even scrawnier, and even with the stupid pendant hanging around his neck and his ridiculous outfit, he looked like someone she should be scared of.

"*Thief*," the Vamp snarled at her. "Stupid little girl. You think I'd keep my shit unguarded?"

Vee made to run past him, hoping to get to the front door, but the Vamp grabbed her and tossed her against the wall. She hit hard, crying out in pain as she crumpled to the floor.

"Do you have any idea who I work for? Who my uncle is?"

Vee tried to get up, but the Vamp kicked her hard in the ribs, and she fell back again, whimpering. She held her hand up, palm toward him, as though to fend off another kick.

"No one steals from me and gets away with it," the Vamp was saying, and Vee knew he was readying to kick her again. "You stu—"

Vee clenched her fist together, silencing the Vampire mid-sentence. With a groan, she managed to sit up slightly, shifting back on her heels. She wiped tears from her face, scowling.

"That hurt," she snapped at the Vamp. She *hated* crying in front of people. It made her feel like a little kid. Gingerly poking her ribcage, Vee whimpered when she touched the spot his foot had hit. Not broken, she didn't think, but *damn. Ouch.*

The Vamp just watched her, mouth still open mid-insult, completely still above her, caught in the middle of drawing his foot back for another kick as though frozen in time. His weaselly face had been contorted with anger before, but now his eyes were wide with fear. No, not fear. Terror.

Vee scrubbed at her face with her sleeve, wiping away the tears still there. Then she flicked her fingers, and the Vampire crumpled to the ground in a grotesque position that resembled kneeling.

Vampire blood felt different from the other Factions, Vee thought, feeling the way it beat through his body. His heartbeat was much slower than the animals she'd been practicing on.

Not that it mattered. Blood was blood, that's what she'd figured out over the last couple of years. And so long as it *had* blood, she could control it.

Leaving him there kneeling on the ground, Vee got to her feet and walked back to the chest to resume scooping out the treasures inside and filling her pockets with them. She was going to *kill* Jayce for leaving her like this. It didn't matter that he knew she could handle herself. If that Vamp *had* managed to break one of her ribs, you better believe Jayce would pay for the Med Witch.

"*Please*," the Vamp managed to whisper. Impressive. Maybe Vamps were more resistant to Blood Magic? Most things couldn't make a single peep under her control. Vee flicked her fingers again, and he screamed as his body twisted, bones snapping as she willed his body to bend in ways it was never meant to bend.

"'*Please*'," she mocked. Her heart did a flip when she pulled a necklace from his chest with a ruby the size of a quail's egg. *Holy crap*, they were going to make so much money off this score. "Tell me—why should you get all of this? Why should you get to make so much money buying and selling these things for rich aristocrats, while some of us can't afford to *eat*?"

He wasn't listening, though, but Vee could never stop herself once she got on a good rant. "You're just a parasite, you know? A *leech*. Living off the backs of Witches, taking their money and giving *nothing* to the people who need it."

When she'd finally cleared him out, her pockets and bag bulging with stuff to sell, Vee stood. She'd stopped crying, even though her side still really hurt, and she was feeling pretty proud of that.

"I guess it doesn't matter now," she told the Vamp, bent and broken at her feet. "But that shirt? It looks *really* ugly on you." She waved her fingers at him one last time before heading to the door to leave, twisting his head around and snapping his neck.

Jayce should be thankful she was the forgiving type, or he'd be spending the rest of the night finding out exactly what a Blood Witch was capable of.

THE END

WANT MORE?

Fey's story will continue in The Blood Witch, The Broken Blade
book two

For release announcements, sneak peeks, and bonus content visit our
website at evelyn-ward.com and follow us on social media:

instagram.com/evelynwardbooks

tiktok.com/@evelyn.ward.books

amazon.com/stores/Evelyn-Ward/author/B0D932HHG9

goodreads.com/Evelyn_Ward

facebook.com/328082750395931

ABOUT THE AUTHOR (...S)

We're so sorry to tell you, dear reader, that Evelyn Ward does not exist.

The real authors of this book are two best friends we'll call M and K. Sorry for lying to you, but the anonymity makes certain things (job interviews, dating, maintaining eye contact with relatives over Thanksgiving dinner) much easier.

K is a resident of New York City where she lives with her cat. She enjoys scary movies, reading, soccer, and crushing the patriarchy. She is a polyglot, an appreciator of good wine, and an all-around Badass Bitch.

M is a resident of Seattle, where she lives with *three* cats and her spouse. She enjoys scary movies, hockey, and pretending she isn't just three raccoons in a trench coat. She has a PhD in something scientific and boring and spends most of her days in a lab dreaming up horrors to write.